PATH
OF THE
ECLIPSE

PATH OF THE ECLIPSE

Chelsea Quinn Yarbro

a historical horror novel

Fourth in the
Count de Saint-Germain Series

St. Martin's Press
New York

Copyright © 1981 by Chelsea Quinn Yarbro
For information, write: St. Martin's Press,
175 Fifth Avenue, New York, N.Y. 10010
Manufactured in the United States of America

Library of Congress Cataloging in Publication Data

Yarbro, Chelsea Quinn, 1942-
    Path of the eclipse.

    I.   Title.
PS3575.A7P37   813′.54   80-53085
ISBN 0-312-59802-5

for
Joan Hitzig,
who, four books ago,
took a chance
on an honourable vampire

This is a work of fiction, albeit one concerned with actual historical events. No character should be construed as representing or intended to represent any actual person or persons living or dead.

In thirteenth-century China there were no less than one hundred six different almanacs in common use, and for that reason assigning dates to events has been difficult. I have arbitrarily used the current Chinese dating system and cycled it back to the time of the narrative. India was no less complicated, for though there was a standard calendar in occasional use, regional systems were prevalent. Reliable records for conditions in Tibet are few, but I have made use of translations of contemporary reports wherever possible.

Although there were female warlords in Tang Dynasty China in the seventh and eighth centuries of the Christian calendar, the tradition had, in fact, died out by the time of this story. The writer hopes that the reader will not be too disturbed by this anachronism, or any others that may have inadvertently crept into the text.

In A.D. 1211 the Mongolian chief known as Temujin invaded China, and three years later captured the Northern Capital, Pei-King. He proclaimed himself Khan (Lord), taking the added name Jenghiz. His grandson became Emperor of China, founded the Yuan Dynasty and is known to history as Kublai Khan.

This story begins in the spring of 1216, in the old Tang Dynasty capital of Lo-Yang. At that time, Lo-Yang was the administrative center of northern China, but K'ai-Feng was the Imperial capital, which essentially divided the bureaucracy, a strategic error that contributed significantly to the poor resistance to the invasion by the Chinese army.

Though China was in the throes of the Mongol invasion and conquest for more than twenty-five years, and the Mongol Empire by 1218 extended from China to Persia, the west, and Europe in particular, was in a much more chaotic state. In

England King John died leaving England still in debt to France and the Pope. Spain was Moorish in the south and Christian Visigoth in the north. In 1215 the Dominican Friars were founded in Spain, beginning the six-hundred-year rule of the Spanish Inquisition. Other major religious orders founded at about this time include the Franciscans and the Carmelites. In Brussels, Rheims, Amiens and Salisbury, cathedrals were being erected. Fully a third of the armed forces of Europe were in the Near East on Crusade against the sultanate of Egypt, which senseless effort ended in failure. In France, persecution of the Catherists or Albigensian heretics had been going on for almost a century and had at last become a matter of state policy as the Catholic Church struggled to gain absolute ascendancy over the Christian communities of Europe.

The revolutionary three-field system of planting was spreading through Europe, and the Romanesque society was slowly being replaced by the Medieval society. Though the Black Death had not yet arrived in Europe, smallpox, cholera, typhus and malnutrition claimed thousands of lives annually. For the average peasant or artisan, life expectancy was about 32–35 years, for the military nobility, assuming one did not die in battle, the average life expectancy was roughly ten years longer. Most women, if they did not enter the church, were married by age 13 and produced an average of eight children before dying of childbirth or related causes at age 27. Childbirth was by far the most common cause of death for women in Europe, and there is little difference between the survival rates for upper- and lower-class women.

By contrast, China at that time had attained an average life expectancy of 41–44 for peasants and artisans, 55 for the martial nobility and 62 for the academic and bureaucratic classes. Though childbirth and its complications claimed a fair number of women, the average life span was somewhat longer —about 38 years, and upper-class women had life expectancies about equal to that of their husbands.

In India, the Delhi Sultanate had been founded, bringing the still-unresolved conflict between Hindu and Moslem to that subcontinent. Most of India was divided into a number of minor principalities, of which Natha Suryarathas is a fictional example, though there were a few large and fairly strong states in the thirteenth century. China, Tibet and India each possessed its own version of Buddhism, though only in Tibet did it become the state religion, where, in the fifteenth

viii

century, the institution of the Dalai Lama replaced the monarchy. There were also a few small communities of Nestorian and Thomist Christians throughout Asia, though they had little or no contact with the Western branches of their faith, and in time died out.

The hard-pressed Byzantine Empire had been eclipsed by the Holy Roman Empire in Europe, though it still commanded a degree of lip service from the west, more for military than cultural reasons, since the Greek-speaking Byzantines, though they thought of themselves as Romans, were essentially an Asian society.

In the west such cities as Pei-King and Moscow were generally thought to be legendary, though some slight communication between east and west had been maintained since the second century B.C., and commerce between China and Europe did exist.

Though this story takes place before the travels of Marco Polo, many of his observations are extremely useful to any student of this period, for though the Chinese court was Mongol instead of Tartar by the time Polo arrived there, most of the culture was as it had been fifty years before. What is particularly revealing about Polo's records is his own attitude —the reaction of a Western Christian from the important maritime Venetian Republic to the vast and ancient civilization of China. For Indian sources, works of certain Persian scholars and travelers of the period are highly informative, and the journey of the alchemist Ch'ang-Ch'un from China to India gives a reverse perspective and has the advantage of occurring at the same time as the events in this novel.

Acknowledgments

The writer would like to thank those people who gave generously of their time and expertise in the preparation of this book, in particular:

Barton Whaley, for his inexhaustible scholarship, in several languages, specifically his information on the rise of the Mongols;

David Nee, researcher extraordinaire;

Jo Feldman, for providing access to Chinese vampire lore; and

Charles Smith, for knowing where to find the unfindable.

Any errors in fact or misconceptions are certainly not the fault of any of these good people.

PART I

T'en Chih-Yü

Text of a letter from the literary candidate Feng Kuo-Ma to the Magisterial Tribunal of Lo-Yang.

On the day of the Dragon Boat Festival in the Year of the Rat, the Thirteenth Year of the Sixty-fifth Cycle, to the August Magistrates:

The inquiry of the August Magistrates regarding the foreigner known as Shih Ghieh-Man has been given to this humble person in order that he may render a full account to the Tribunal and the Imperial Court at K'ai-Feng of what he has observed as a student of this foreigner.

While it is true that Shih Ghieh-Man is a wholly appropriate name for this man, and he informs me that it is not dissimilar to the name he was given as a child, he also has been known by the barbarous name Ra-Go-Shkee, which syllables not only come most inelegantly to the tongue, but imply nothing of his nature. As Shih suggests, he is something of a magician, and may be possessed of various magical secrets, though this humble person wishes to assure the August Magistrates that he has said nothing of this directly. As Ghieh implies, he is a man of courage, and though his beauty is that of the West, yet it is a fine beauty, so that Man is not unsuitable. The August Magistrates have undoubtedly been informed that this Shih Ghieh-Man prefers to dress in black, which he relieves with red and silver, making him a most striking person as well as honoring our laws. Though this Shih Ghieh-Man has mastered many alchemical arts, he has never offered the effrontery of wearing yellow or gold, which would be singularly offensive. Shih Ghieh-Man has told this humble person that it has long been his custom to wear black, red and silver, and all of his students have honored him for his tact in this matter.

3

However, in regard to the question of the origin of this Shih Ghieh-Man, Candidate Feng is desolated to be unable to provide the requested information. The foreigner Shih Ghieh-Man has often indicated that his native land is in the West, though he has revealed little more. He has the appearance of the West in the shape of his eyes and the shade of his skin, and though his hair is dark, it curls. His accent, while quite good for one not born to the language, is similar to that of the Western Black Robes who came here in the Year of the Horse.

In regard to the question of his possible affiliation to that demonic rabble that follows the despicable criminal Temujin, whose forces now occupy Pei-King, Shih Ghieh-Man has often said that he has been in the desolate city of Karokorum, the capital of the Mongol forces, though he indicates that it was some time ago, and from the description he has offered, it would appear it has been many years since he was last in that place. He has never professed to admire Temujin or the rapacious war that has been waged against us by the malignant northerners.

Candidate Feng respectfully reminds the August Magistrates that he has had the privilege of studying with this Shih Ghieh-Man for little more than four years, and there has been a proper reserve in the relationship. Some of that reserve may be due to his foreignness, but this humble person has often thought that the loneliness he has perceived in Shih Ghieh-Man goes far beyond that of a foreigner. Apparently Shih Ghieh-Man is content to endure this, for he has never approached this person or any of his other students with offers of friendship beyond the respect of master and pupil.

In regard to the natures of the studies of Shih Ghieh-Man, the Candidate Feng is not yet sufficiently qualified to speak with any authority, but he begs the August Magistrates to consider his unworthy and uneducated opinions, bearing their value in mind. Shih Ghieh-Man has shown himself to be most skilled in all the alchemical arts, far more than any other such from the West has been, though his techniques are often unorthodox. This may be due to his Western training, but this humble person has had no opportunity to discover whether or not such is the case. These considerations aside. Shih Ghieh-Man excels. His is the intellect of discernment and discrimination. He has not engaged much in the production of dangerous substances, preferring to create jewels and gold from the application of his skills rather than to tamper with burning powders. He has also, when respectfully requested to do so by the garrison captains, provided alloys for their armor and weapons which the distinguished captain Lao Gan-Ti has commended as being capable of piercing the hides of elephants and crocodiles. The captain has spoken to the foreigner Shih Ghieh-Man of late, and though this humble person is not privy to their discussions, he had made a number of assumptions that he will reveal to the August Magistrates. This humble person believes that the captain Lao Gan-Ti is interested in a new method of laminating bows for greater force and resilience. The foreigner Shih Ghieh-Man has said that he knows of an ancient method that would indeed produce the required characteristics, but he has yet to demonstrate an example of this material.

In regard to the questions of the personal habits of the foreigner Shih Ghieh-Man, the Candidate Feng must plead much ignorance. It is not fitting that he should intrude on the privacy of his master. However, there are certain things which this humble person knows and will divulge to the August Magistrates. The foreigner lives in a large enclosed compound to the west of the old walls of the city, near the Temple of the Taoists. He has one servant who accompanied him from the West, Ro-Ger, whose family name is unknown to this person. Shih Ghieh-Man has a large staff of servants, all of whom appear to be well-treated. He has three concubines who live in their own wing of the compound and are said to be beautiful, though this humble person has often observed that all concubines are rumored to be beautiful. The foreigner Shih Ghieh-Man, as the August Magistrates must know, often entertains in a tasteful and lavish manner. His guests are among the most distinguished officials and scholars of this city. It is said of him that some of his personal habits are unusual, but this humble person has observed that the personal habits of all foreigners are unusual. While it has been remarked that Shih Ghieh-Man does not dine with his guests, there is nothing to suggest to the candidate Feng that this is in any way significant.

It has been bandied about by certain irresponsible persons, doubtless known to the August Magistrates, that Shih Ghieh-Man is actually a Taoist monk who has, through their sorcery, transformed himself with the intent of embarrassing the university and the teachers. While it is true that Shih Ghieh-Man is most interested in the alchemical studies that are the main thrust of the reprehensible Taoists, he is also firmly committed to the principles of Kung Fu-Tzu and has said within this humble person's hearing that though he is a foreigner, he understands the benefits of the correct life and personal integrity, and that he himself reveres the ties of blood.

In regard to the question of the foreigner Shih Ghieh-Man's honor, therefore, this humble person, though not truly qualified to speak of the matter, believes that there is no one he would wish more to have beside him in battle than this foreigner, and no one who is more determined to excel in scholarship. The worst that can be said of this dedication is that he is often driven to tasteless studies of all manner of crude things; rather blame his zeal for knowledge than any Taoist perversity.

Written by the Candidate Feng's own hand and submitted in person to the Municipal Tribunal in accordance with the instructions of the August Magistrates, with the hope they will excuse the lack of elegance in this report.

1

CUSTOM DICTATED that she address the official from her knees, though she was of the martial nobility and the official was little more than a glorified clerk.

"And the nature of your request, General T'en?" the bland man said as he smoothed his beard.

"Is for troops!" she declared. "And I fear the Elevated One has suffered a lapse of memory. It was my worthy father who was a General. I, being a mere woman, by law, can only be a Warlord." Her tone of address was offensive and T'en

Chih-Yü knew it, yet she refused to abase herself further to this expressionless, long-nailed old fool.

"Your worthy father, in the celestial realms where he receives the judgment of his forebearers must surely be distressed to realize that his daughter has conducted herself in such an inappropriate manner," the clerk said severely, eyes narrowing. "It is not seemly that those who have petitions should be so uncivil in their address."

T'en Chih-Yü touched her forehead to the floor with such elaborate courtesy that it was more insulting than she had been before. "This most insignificant person begs and beseeches the Elevated One to overlook her lamentable boorishness, since it is born from her fear that her district is in danger of being overrun by Mongols!"

The official sighed. He had received eight petitions that morning, all of them demanding the full attention of the Emperor. "He who wears the Imperial Yellow," he began to this irate young woman, "has all of the people of his country in his thoughts at all times. It is impertinent of you to suggest that he is not aware of the difficulties we have on our borders, and disrespectful to imply that he would make any decisions that would be to the disadvantage of his subjects."

"Of course. How could this insignificant person have forgotten?" T'en Chih-Yü asked, feeling helpless. "When our villages are burned and the dead are hacked to pieces, and the screams of the wounded are loud, then this insignificant person is apt to assume—obviously most incorrectly—that the court and the army and the governing bodies have temporarily turned their attention to other things."

"General Wei is even now on the march to drive the Mongols from Pei-King."

"Doubtless that is necessary. The Northern Capital is of great strategic importance. The Elevated One must forgive this insignificant person for reminding him that her stronghold, such as it is, is in the west." Her voice had risen and her slender hands were clenched on her knees. "Is there an army on the march for Hsing-ch'ing? That would be of some use to us."

The clerk's face had grown colder. He had not wanted to receive this unfeminine woman, he remembered. He had remarked to his scribe that she would be unreasonable and demanding, and would bring him nothing but ingratitude. He tapped one of his long nails on the lacquered wood of his tall desk. "Your request shall be examined for merit, and, if it is appropriate, an investigation will be made."

"Investigation? Examination?" she repeated, starting to rise. Her empty scabbard scraped on the painted tiles of the floor. "Did you hear nothing of what I said? Fully a third of the villages around my district have been razed and their people slaughtered. I have only two hundred militiamen at my command, and that is not enough. I have ordered patrols, but half the time the riders are caught and killed before we can be warned. I need soldiers, and weapons and supplies and horses and spies. By the time you send some doddering old philosopher to assess our danger, there will be nothing left but skeletons and burned buildings!" Her linked-segment tunic jingled as she strode forward. "We must have help now!" She knew she was only making it worse, but the disappointment of her ten days in Lo-Yang made her reckless now.

"That is quite enough, Warlord T'en. Your unseemly conduct will be reported." He stepped back and removed the official cap from his head, indicating that the interview was over and that T'en Chih-Yü was dismissed. He refused to look at her, but said to his scribe, "Yao, I will walk in my garden to restore my peace of mind. And should that terrible young woman who fancies herself as one of authority—though it is everywhere acknowledged that it is the duty of the father, not the mother, to carry the onerous burdens of authority—present another petition to this officer, you are to deny her access to me and all of those officials within this ministry." As the scribe bowed, the official left the room.

During her days in Lo-Yang, T'en Chih-Yü had been rebuffed, but never so comprehensively rejected. Though she was aware she had overstepped the bounds of propriety, she was not prepared for the treatment this official had given her. She slapped her hand down on the tall desk and swore by the excrement of turtles.

Yao, the scribe, looked offended at this obscenity, but hesitated as he turned to gather up his writing equipment. He put the ink cake and brushes aside and turned to the young woman. "This humble person, though unqualified to make recommendations to the Warlord T'en, nevertheless takes it upon himself to offer a suggestion, if the Warlord will hear him out."

"Warlord T'en," she responded in surprise, "is grateful for

any aid the scribe is willing to give her. It is the first help she has received since coming to this city."

"It is often so," Yao agreed with a somber nod. "What this official said was extreme, but it is true that we rarely see women, particularly unmarried women, presenting petitions to officials. It is not remarkable that he should receive you so ... severely. Surely you have relatives here, with more immediate recognition in the world, than you have who, for the sake of the honor of the family, would be willing to present your requests at a higher level of government." Yao spoke with great delicacy, but there was no flattering aversion of his eyes, and no false sympathy to his comments.

"If you mean a well-placed male relative, it is unfortunate, but my only living kin in this city is my father's aunt, who, though the widow of a distinguished man, the great scholar Fei S'un-tsin, lives retired and has not been to Court for more than ten years. My nearest male relatives are in Hang-Chow and do not have the leisure to travel here. Not that they would be heard." She folded her arms and the scale tunic rang softly. "Scribe Yao, I did not exaggerate when I described the conditions in the west. They must be worse in the north. I have seen severed heads piled into pyramids for carrion birds to feast upon. There was a raid not more than fifty li from my stronghold. We could see the farms burning and there was a stench on the wind for days afterward that made all of us retch. Without soldiers and equipment, the same thing will happen to us."

Yao studied her, and was pleased with what he saw. She was distressingly masculine, but he supposed that those were the required qualities in this situation. "Have you told others of this?"

"They have been like Lun Shui-Lun," she sighed, able now to use the departed official's name since the man himself was no longer present. "They have told me all things I must have are impossible, and have refused to tell me where I might find aid."

"That is most unfortunate." The response was only what good manners required, but the scribe was sincere. "You have come a long way to meet with such great disappointment."

Chih-Yü could not bring herself to answer. She clasped the top of her empty scabbard, then paced the length of the chamber with a long, mannish stride.

"Is there no one else you might call upon to assist you?

There must be someone who knows you and will address members of the Court on your behalf." He knew that the relationships of blood were complex and intricate, but he was well aware that this young woman, warlord or not, could not gain her ends by the simple presentation of petitions.

"My not-to-be-spoken-of brother was in this city for a time and he made himself odious to all of those whom I might have been able to call upon. It is profoundly disquieting to realize that a person of rank who does not have well-placed friends cannot bring petitions before the officials and have them attended to at once. The danger I have spoken of does not affect my stronghold alone, but all of this country. We have lost Pei-King. Must we lost Lo-Yang as well before the officials will decide that there is real danger in those Mongol warriors?" She stopped before the scribe and stared at him, as if hoping he could give her an answer.

"It is true that there are unwarranted difficulties in approaching the highly placed ones," Yao said with careful circumspection. "That was why I suggested that you have a high-ranking kinsman present your requests, but that is not possible, it would seem." He sighed. There were often such knotty matters as this to be decided, and he always felt the helplessness of his station when he listened to the pleas of those who needed aid and would, in all likelihood, not get it.

"What am I to do?" Chih-Yü demanded of the air. "If my brother were still here, I might have a way to reach someone in authority through his friends. Oh, he was debauched," she said bitterly to Yao. "He was debauched, but only with those of the highest rank. If he had not discovered two poison attempts and fled, he might still know well-placed persons."

Yao pursed his lips. "Is there a way you might be able to speak to your brother's friends?"

Chih-Yü laughed unpleasantly. "A woman would have to be a great fool to present herself to such men. They would not assist me. My brother had some hold on them, but I do not." She put her hands on her hips. "I killed a highwayman who tried to assault me. I would do the same to a Prince."

"Of course." Yao once again took up the writing implements from his low table. "I am sorry that there is nothing more I can suggest, except . . ." He paused, considering T'en Chih-Yü carefully. "If you do not mind going among soldiers, you might want to visit the temple of the God of War. Soldiers, though rough fellows and well below your rank, still are more apt to listen to your plight with understanding. Officials like Lun"—he nodded toward the closed door which Lun Shui-Lun had used a little while before—"are ignorant of the reality of your struggles. Soldiers might not be."

The Warlord inclined her head. "I thank you, Scribe Yao, for your wise and sympathetic words. I am desolated to inform you, however, that the priests at the temple of the God of War have more requests for audience than even men like your Lun Shui-Lun." She turned and started from the audience room.

"Forgive this further impertinence, then," Yao said quickly, stopping her before she could leave.

"What is it?"

He studied the brushes clutched in his left hand. "Have you considered going to the university?"

"The university?" Chih-Yü looked at the scribe, her dark eyes alive with impatience. "No, I have not. What good are students to me?" She felt what little hope she had left desert her. There had been too many disappointments these last ten days.

"No, the Warlord misunderstands me," Yao said with a placating smile. "I was not implying that the Warlord would find support among the students—though that is a possibility—but rather, I meant that the Warlord T'en would find others. There are men of great learning at the university, and where you cannot find help from those with power and arms, you may find another strength, that of well-honed and patriotic minds. Men who are trained to observe and remember are often fine spies as well as good professors. Those who can make elixirs to save lives can help your soldiers and poison your enemies. Those who can smelt metal compounds may use them for arms as well as for ornaments. The man who can translate a book can act as interpreter for a captured foeman." There was almost no expression in his lowered eyes, but his hands were so tense that they shook.

Chih-Yü listened attentively, and when Yao fell silent, she had new respect for the scribe. "I must confess that your comments are new to me. I came here so determined to find troops that I have not given any other possibility my consideration. Now that I have talked with you, I will reassess my position. You have done me good service, Scribe Yao. I will remember it when I make my reports." Her expression had lightened, and as she left the audience chamber, her step was lighter than it had been before.

The guards at the entrance to the building raised their thick brows at the sight of a woman in military gear, but did not detain her as she started down the wide street. A moment later, one of them heard her speak to him.

"I am not familiar with Lo-Yang," Chih-Yü said to the guard on the southern side of the steps. "Will you be kind enough to inform me of the most direct route to the university?"

The two guards exchanged tolerant smiles of the sort always reserved for ignoramuses from the country.

"Looking for a student, are you, my girl?" the guard she had addressed asked her, winking at his companion.

"No," Chih-Yü answered in a voice well-known to her militia. "I am on official business for the stronghold Mao-T'ou. I have inquiries to make of the scholars there. Now, tell me at once where the university is."

Neither guard had ever been spoken to in such a manner by a woman. The farther one straightened and flushed, but the nearer one attempted to bluster. "Now see here, my girl, it's all very well to go running about dressed up like a fighter, but—"

Chih-Yü cut him short, her anger for all the frustrations she had encountered in Lo-Yang welling up in her. "This person is of the family T'en," she announced loudly enough for passersby to hear her. "My distinguished father was General T'en. Perhaps you have heard of him?" she asked sarcastically, knowing that her late father was one of the most revered tacticians of the kingdom. "This person, being his rightful heir, is properly addressed as Warlord T'en, not 'my girl.' Now, where is the university, fellow?"

The nearer soldier cleared his throat and came to attention. "The Warlord T'en, if she will give herself the trouble, will find the university near the old city walls, two li from here, two streets to the west of this one." He had directed his eyes toward the roofs of the three official buildings across the square from the one he guarded. "The Warlord may avail herself of a guide, which this humble guardsman would be honored to summon for her."

"That will not be necessary, soldier, unless your instructions are faulty." She gave him a challenging look and waited for his denial, and tapped her booted foot on the raised paving stones.

"This humble guardsman assures the Warlord T'en that he has provided instructions to the best of his poor ability." He was still looking at the rooftops, but his voice had hardened.

"Then there should be no difficulty, should there?" She stepped back and found that there was a large number of people gathered to listen to her upbraid the guard. Chih-Yü understood why the guardsman was so resentful, so she added, "The Warlord T'en appreciates the assistance given her, guardsman, and will so inform the official Lun." She turned away smartly and shouldered through the crowd. She wished she had applied for the right to carry her sword inside the city walls instead of the scabbard alone. Somehow, that empty scabbard made a mockery of her rank. Walking more quickly, she made her way through the bustling crowds down the long avenue toward the crenellated outline of the old city walls.

———◆———

Text of a dispatch from the scribe Wen S'ung to the Ministry of the Imperial Army in Lo-Yang. The messenger was ambushed by raiders and the message never delivered.

In the fortnight of Great Heat in the Year of the Rat, the Thirteenth Year of the Sixty-fifth Cycle, to the Ministry of the Imperial Army, at the behest of the General Kuei I-Ta.

To the Ministers of War and the Protectors of the Imperial Presence, greetings:

The General Kuei I-Ta finds himself and his men in desperate straits. The perfidious Mongols have once again breached the defenses we established near the village of Nan-Pi on the northern side of the Sha-Ming Pass of the Tsin-ling Mountains. The casualty toll of men now stands at 347 dead, 861 wounded, with another 212 ill from various diseases. This latest offensive

on the part of the men of Temujin has effectively cut
our supply lines, and if the Mongols are allowed to keep
their hold on this pass through the winter, this garrison
will not survive to oppose them.

It has come to my attention that two companies of
Imperial bowmen are stationed no more than eighty li
from this place, in the Ma-Mei valley. Half of this force,
speedily sent, would be of great assistance to us here,
and would make it possible for us to rout the despicable
Mongols.

It is my sad duty to inform the Ministers and the officers of the Secretariat that the stronghold of Pei-Yo
has fallen and all the men, women, children and chattel
of the place hacked to pieces. We of this company tried
to penetrate the Mongol forces to save those valiant defenders, but without archers and sufficient cavalry, we
were helpless against their superior numbers. Six sallies
were attempted, but all failed. The Mongols, since the
taking of Pei-King, believe themselves to be invulnerable
and mandated by Heaven to conquer all of our country.
We have learned a dreadful lesson from these terrible
fighters, and we dare not ignore it.

Two days ago, Junior Officer S'a Gan led one hundred
men toward Pei-Yo under cover of darkness with the
hope of rescuing those few defenders who remained
alive. This morning, the heads of this company adorned
spikes around the Mongol camp and their horsemen
have been throwing the flayed skins of our comrades
over the barricades we have erected. Pei-Yo is less than
twenty li away from us, and it will not be long before
the Mongols turn their attention to us once more. Con-
trolling Pei-Yo, as they do now, will make their work
easier, for they will not have to fall back very far and
will fight on fresh horses.

General Kuei I-Ta respectfully requests that the most
prompt assistance be rendered him and his men. If relief
is not authorized quickly, it will come too late. Those of
us defending the Sha-Ming Pass will gladly remain until
the last of us is slain, but we ask that our deaths purchase a victory for our country. It is honorable to fall in
battle, and we do not shrink from our duty. It is for
those who come after us to hold our sacrifice at high
cost.

Our courier will leave two hours before dawn and it is hoped that he will be at the camp of the Imperial bowmen in the Ma-Mei valley by nightfall. If this report is sent promptly, marching orders should be delivered to the garrison by the fortnight of the White Dews, and may well be in time to avenge us without endangering the Ma-Mei valley by the action.

General Kuei I-Ta prays that his words be regarded as those of a dying man, and given that devotion and respect incumbent upon such messages.

By the hand of the scribe Wen S'ung in the second hour after sunset, near the village of Nan-Pi.

2

A BROOK had been diverted through the garden to splash over a course of smooth stones in plaintive, endless melody. Night-dappled, it gleamed where the nodding trees let the starlight through. There was a tang in the autumn wind as it fingered the leaves, loosening them one by one from the branches, dropping the first few in token of the winter to come. Low in the west a waning moon vied with the coming dawn, casting long, soft shadows across the compound and garden, touching the elaborately carved eaves and the open door, stretching along the silken carpet of Saint-Germain's private chamber, reaching at last the brocaded coverlet of the wide bed where Ch'uan-T'ing lay alone.

Saint-Germain sat in a chair of carved rosewood on the far side of the room, where the night was the deepest. He held a volume of the works of Li Po in one hand, his finger marking the page he had abandoned earlier, while he looked contemplatively at the young woman sleeping. His black silken sheng lei rustled no more loudly than the wind as he rose, setting the book aside. He crossed the room in five swift steps, and stood for some little time at the foot of the bed, his dark eyes resting on Ch'uan-T'ing's still face.

Softly he dropped to his knees on the bed, moving with utmost care so that she would not be disturbed. Unhurriedly he stretched out beside her, away from the moonlight so that he could see her face without shadow. He braced himself on his elbow and gave himself to the perusal of her face.

Her features were tranquil in sleep, her lashes on her cheeks like tiny dark crescents, her brow untroubled and unlined, her hair haloing her head. Ch'uan-T'ing sighed in her sleep, her lovely, arched lips opening slightly. At this subtle movement the coverlet slid back, revealing her small, high breasts and the gentle rise of her ribs. The moonlight bleached the color from her skin so that she appeared made of the finest rice paper painted by the brush of a master.

With fingers gentle as the wind, but more lingering and warmer, he traced the curve of the shadows on her face, her throat, her breast. Drifting petals or fresh snow was no softer than the passage of his hands over her. Had Ch'uan-T'ing been made of the rarest, most fragile porcelain, he could not have been more delicate. His caresses skimmed over her shoulder, along the curve of her arm where her scented flesh was most tender. He did nothing in haste, nothing abruptly, nothing forcefully, yet he kindled a desire in her that she would never have dared acknowledge when awake. Seeing the alteration in her features, he smiled enigmatically in the shadows.

Ch'uan-T'ing turned toward Saint-Germain, sleep lending this movement a strange grace, as if she were under water. Half her face was obscured now, though the line of her cheek shone like the petal of the most pale blossom. Her head was back at an angle, and she drew in her breath quickly as a tremor passed over her.

Though he was tempted, Saint-Germain did not press her response. He had made that mistake once, bringing her out of her sleep. He recalled that night, three years before, with chagrin. Ch'uan-T'ing, schooled to place her lord's needs foremost, had been appalled at her own arousal, and was overcome with shame. Saint-Germain had tried in vain to assure her that it was only through her fulfillment that he could achieve his own: she was repelled by her passion. Now he approached her only when she slept, rousing her as a dream might.

She began to breathe more deeply, languor spreading through her with her emerging need. Saint-Germain kissed her, barely touching her skin with his mouth, yet evoking new pleasures in the sleeping woman. His hands moved under the coverlet, seeking the source of her ecstasy. She trembled, sighed, still sleeping. Surely, sadly, he found the source of her unacknowledged desire. How much he wished that she would waken and accept her joy with pride, reveling in the shared gratification. He could not bring himself to test her again, recalling what desolation he had felt at her reaction, and how carefully she had avoided him for some time afterward.

She moaned as her first spasm shook her, and lay back, rapturously vulnerable. His touch, still maddeningly light, continued to enhance her response, drawing out her release to add to his own contentment. She whispered a few incoherent words as Saint-Germain's lips drew away from her and his hands at last were still.

The sky was edged with light in the east as Ch'uan-T'ing sank back in slumber and Saint-Germain at last rose swiftly and silently from her side. He slipped the coverlet up over her shoulder, then went to the open doorway to close it, for the morning was chill.

The chamber adjoining the one where Ch'uan-T'ing lay was startling in its simplicity, given the grandeur of the rest of the extensive house and grounds. There was only a narrow hard bed atop a large chest, a chair and writing table, and a small chest of antique Roman design. Paper screens blocked the light from two tall, narrow windows, giving the room a perpetual dusk. Saint-Germain went to the chest and stood before it, alone. The new day was bleak to him. He chided himself inwardly for his loneliness, but could not banish it.

He untied the sash of his sheng lei, dropped it, then shrugged himself out of the loose silken robe, letting it fall around his feet. For a few moments he stood naked; then he turned away from the chest, crossed the room and drew back a panel, revealing three drawers of carefully folded garments.

Imperial decree forbade all foreigners to dress in completely Chinese clothing. Ostensibly this was an aesthetic regulation, so that the full diversity of the Chinese world would be more easily appreciated; in fact, the regulation allowed the officers of the various tribunals to identify aliens on sight and simplified their occasional mass arrests of foreigners. Saint-Germain was not deceived by the Imperial decree, but had no desire to oppose it. Over the years he had been in Lo-Yang, he had evolved his own style, an amalgam of Occidental and Oriental fashions that was all his own.

When he emerged from his private quarters, not long after sunrise, he wore a black brocade Byzantine dalmatica over a kneelength red sheng go. His black trousers were of Persian cut, but tucked into high, ornate Chinese boots. A belt of chased-silver links was around his waist and the silver pectoral was ornamented with his device—a black disk with wide, raised wings, the symbol of the eclipse. He was comfortable in this hodgepodge of styles and cultures; he was also aware that it was complimentary to him in a way that a more homogeneous fashion would not be.

His servants were busy already, the day's tasks beginning before dawn and continuing until well after sunset. He addressed them when he came upon them, giving a word of praise to one, inquiring after the health of the father of another, as he made his way to his extensive library on the north side of the compound.

His mind was not truly on his reading, and it was some time before he selected a volume in Greek and pulled it from the shelves. It was an effort to concentrate on Aristotle's meticulously dry phrases, but eventually he let himself get caught up in the words.

Rogerio found him at his reading an hour later. "Pardon, my master," he said in Latin, "but you have a visitor."

Saint-Germain looked up from the pages spread before him and answered in the same language. "A visitor, you say? Remarkable. I would not have thought . . ." He did not continue. Decisively he shut the old leather-bound parchment book. "A visitor. Who is it? Do you know?"

"Master Kuan Sun-Sze has called," Rogerio told him, picking up the book and returning it to its place on the shelves.

"Master Kuan?" The somberness that had marked Saint-Germain's features now faded. "Why didn't you say so at once?" He rose from the table.

"He is in the larger reception room," Rogerio informed his master as he stood aside to let Saint-Germain pass into the hall.

"How long have you kept him waiting?" There was no criticism implied in the question, for he knew he was often hard to locate.

"Not very long. When I discovered you weren't in your chambers, I tried the library." The manservant had switched from Latin to awkward Chinese.

"We'll talk in the withdrawing room upstairs by the terrace. See that tea and cakes are brought to the room, if you please." He felt the despondency that had gripped him give way to curiosity and gratitude. As he approached the door to the larger reception room, he motioned Rogerio away, saying,

"Never mind, my friend. I can announce myself," as he reached to open the door.

Rogerio bowed slightly and said, "I will see that the tea and cakes are delivered. I'll bring them personally.

"Thank you," Saint-Germain said quietly, then stepped into the reception room.

The chamber was designed to be impressive, though it was not as formidable as many such rooms in Lo-Yang. Rich hangings covered the walls, there were silken carpets on the floor, and the chairs were of rose and cherry wood, carved by master artisans and cushioned with brocaded pillows. A moon door opened onto the garden and the sound of the brook was faintly audible. Brass and porcelain vases were filled with fresh flowers, as they were every day from early spring through the end of autumn. Amid these Oriental things there were occasional foreign touches: on one wall a tempera portrait of a Roman lady hung beside a Tang Dynasty scroll. Near the door there was a tall iron candlestick made by the craftsmen of Toledo. Beside the moon door was a tall chest of intricately inlaid wood from Luxor.

Kuan Sun-Sze looked up as Saint-Germain closed the door behind himself, and a smile stole over his severe features. "Shih Ghieh-Man," he said, nodding a casual greeting.

"Master Kuan," Saint-German responded, coming toward the distinguished scholar. "You do me great honor."

"What's this?" Kuan Sun-Sze marveled, too dignified to express surprise. "Master Kuan? Honor?"

Saint-Germain took a seat opposite his guest. "My friend," he said in less formal accents, "you are the first master who has deigned to come to my house since the Tribunal excused me from teaching at the university. I was afraid that perhaps the rest of you feared contamination." His sarcasm was startling even to himself. "I'm sorry," he went on in a more chastened tone. "I had thought I was not truly bitter, but I discover that I am."

"With good reason," Kuan Sun-Sze allowed. "It was an arbitrary decision the Tribunal made. I have sent them a formal complaint, telling them that your studies in the West have been of great aid to us, for they show us new approaches and methods we can use."

"Did you?" Saint-Germain smiled faintly. "That was kind, considering how much you have taught me." He regarded Master Kuan Sun-Sze evenly. "And my students?"

"All but two of them are well. The two, I regret having to tell you, are Feng Kuo-Ma and Li Djieh-Wo." Kuan Sun-Sze laced his soft fingers together.

"Feng and Li argued in my favor to the Magistrates, didn't they?" Saint-Germain asked without needing the answer. "What will become of them?"

Kuan Sun-Sze did not speak at once. His eyes traveled about the appointments of the room, and he sat back in his chair. Saint-Germain remained silent while the great scholar considered. "The Li family," he said at last, as if giving a lecture, "is an old and meritorious house and has given many excellent officials to the service of he who wields the Vermilion Brush. Doubtless there are Masters of Literature who would welcome a member of the house of Li as a student, particularly one of so quick a mind as Li Djieh-Wo. Feng, sadly, is another matter. The District Magistrate Feng was implicated in a great scandal not nine years ago, and for that reason there are few who are willing to extend themselves to those belonging to the family. Feng Kuo-Ma has been offered a post by an uncle, I have heard, that will take him away from this city, and though his career may be less brilliant than what had been hoped, still, he will find himself in an excellent position to be of service to the Empire and his family, and in times such as these, it is possible that unsettled events may yet bring him to the awareness of those in high places who may avail themselves of his skills."

"I see," Saint-Germain said heavily. "The boy is banished because he spoke out on my behalf." He stared blindly toward the moon door, but saw nothing of it or the garden beyond. "If I had known this might occur, I would have tried to dissuade him."

"No, no," Kuan Sun-Sze said at once. "You must not feel so. It is proper to one of his nature to behave as he has, and I believe that it will go well for him, when his pride has recovered. He himself has been aware that his family is not in a favorable position at court, so trying his wings in the provinces may be what is required for him to advance to the limit of his abilities rather than the limits of his cousin's folly." He leaned forward, bracing his elbows on his knees. "All things happen as they should, Shih Ghieh-Man."

"Do they?" Saint-Germain's smile was wintry. "That's curiously Taoist of one so much a part of the traditions of Kung Fu-Tzu."

Kuan Sun-Sze gave a tilt to his head. This was an old game between them. "We all know that the Taoists are misled men who are so blind that they will devote their studies to anything and do not care if it has to do with the proper conduct of human society or not."

"Lamentable," Saint-Germain agreed, and only the corners of his mouth twitched.

"Oh, very," Kuan Sun-Sze said with perfect gravity. "Though it is not always easy to discern how the behavior of wild crickets, which I have been known to study, will be mirrored in human society."

Saint-Germain got to his feet. "My good and treasured friend, I would be delighted if you would accompany me to the withdrawing room on the floor above. My kitchen will provide some trifling refreshment for you, and we may continue our conversation in more congenial surroundings."

"It is always a pleasure to spend an hour in the company of well-spoken men," Kuan Sun-Sze said as he followed Saint-Germain to the door. "And since I rose unusually early, I broke my fast some time ago and light refreshment would be welcome." He walked at Saint-Germain's side down the wide hall to the beautiful staircase leading to the next floor. A large brass lantern hung from the ceiling, two stories above, and shone in the pinkish light that filtered through the tall, narrow windows that flanked the door. "There is no other house like this in Lo-Yang," he remarked to his host.

"I'm not surprised," Saint-Germain said as he started up the stairs.

"What possessed you to design your windows thus?" the scholar asked, gesturing over his shoulder toward the main door.

Saint-Germain shrugged. "I have seen such windows before, in lands far to the west, and I learned to like them. It seemed foolish to ignore them here, when they provide precisely the light and privacy I require."

"And your lantern?" Kuan Sun-Sze was aware that his manners were atrocious this morning, but was enjoying himself too much to apologize for his impertinent questions.

"My own design from various influences: a little Greek, a little Frankish, a little Moorish and a touch of Khemic." He said it lightly enough, wanting to dismiss the matter, but his memories flooded in on him. There had been that long debate one afternoon in Athens; how many years ago? It was about the time Alcabiades had been banished for breaking the phalluses off the Herms. There had been an evening when he stood in a small, drafty castle in Aix-la-Chapelle, listening to monks chant while an illiterate man in threadbare purple upbraided a motly crew of unwashed and cynical knights. That was more recent, but the years between distressed him in a way they had not done before. The Moorish influences had come from Spain not so long ago. He recalled an uneasy morning with a Mohammedan prince. What had been the trouble? The prince had been angry—after a moment it came to him: they had begun with a discussion of mathematics and astronomy and ended with an argument about the relationship of learning to religion. The Khemic was the most distant of all, remote, though he could still see in his mind the long-vanished majesty of the temple of Thoth in the first blue moments of dusk standing above the bend of the Nile. The sacred poems of the priests of Imhotep resounded within him . . .

"Shih Ghieh-Man?" Kuan Sun-Sze said as his host continued to wait on the stair, gazing at the large brass lantern.

"Ah?" He turned quickly to look at the scholar beside him. "Forgive me. When one is far from home, reminiscences are overwhelming at times. Your question, I fear, brought back much I had not thought of recently."

Sun-Sze nodded sympathetically and quoted one of Li Po's most famous poems as he climbed the rest of the stairs beside Saint-Germain.

The withdrawing room was small, cozy without being cramped or too cluttered. The door panels were drawn back and the terrace over the garden stood ready for them, the sound of the brook rising softly through the whisper of the leaves. Lacquered tables and deeply upholstered chairs were attractively arranged for easy conversation and a lack of formality. On the walls were three large mosaics Saint-Germain had commissioned some years before in Constantinople. They were out of place in the room, but neither man minded.

Saint-Germain chose a chair away from the light so that his guest would have the easier and more inviting view. He propped his heels on the central table and leaned back against the cushions, inviting Kuan Sun-Sze with a gesture to do the same.

"A very pleasant room," the scholar said, giving this familiar courtesy real feeling. "Being in your house is like traveling the length of the Old Silk Road without going one li from the city." He, too, sank back against the cushions. "It was folly to move the government to K'ai-Feng. In time the ministries will regret it. Lo-Yang has been the center of the Empire for several hundred years. It is absurd to think that K'ai-Feng is as suitable." His sentiments were common ones in Lo-Yang, for though the government had moved more than a generation before, much of the literary and artistic traditions were in this Tang Dynasty city and the resentment was still strong.

Saint-Germain realized that Kuan Sun-Sze would not discuss what was really on his mind until after cakes and tea had been served, so he remarked, "But capitals have often moved, my friend. Rome moved with Constantine, though, I think, Rome will have revenge for that one day."

"These are Western cities, are they not?" the scholar inquired politely.

"They are. Rome is still there and flourishing after her fashion. I have a . . . an old friend there who sends me letters periodically. A second seat of government—or third or fourth or fifth, depending on how you count—has risen there. It could go the same way here, if the battles with the Mongols do not disrupt your world too much." He said it honestly, having seen it before.

"Mongols!" Kuan Sun-Sze scoffed. "Oh, they've had their victories against militia and farmers, but the army has accounted for them quite handily." He paused again. "It is treasonous for Generals to take independent command of their troops, but it has happened of late. Shi Pai-Kung took his archers and cavalry without orders. He said he could not bear to stand by while his countrymen were cut to pieces by those northern barbarians. They had to execute him for it, but his intervention saved the day."

There was a discreet scratching at the door, then Rogerio came into the room with refreshments. He set them down and said, "Tea, cakes, a paste of almond and honey, fruit wedges." He bowed respectfully to Saint-Germain's guest.

Kuan Sun-Sze was clearly pleased. "Wonderful, wonderful." He waved Rogerio away, but the man lingered until Saint-Germain signaled him to depart. "Will you join me?"

Saint-Germain shook his head. "I've taken nourishment not long ago. Thank you." He reached to pour the tea for Sun-

Sze, then settled back again. "What is on your mind then, my scholarly friend?"

"A great many things," Sun-Sze said, refusing to be rushed. He was willing to make limited concessions to Saint-Germain's foreign ways, but his sense of good manners forbade him to plunge into his discussion. "You have an excellent kitchen staff."

"So I have been told," Saint-Germain agreed with a sigh. Though he respected the traditions of this country, he occasionally found them infuriating. "I will see that your praise is repeated."

"Fine." He popped one of the honey-and-almond confections into his mouth and smiled. "When I was a child," he said a moment later, "I thought that honey was the most delicious food on earth. My father showed me how to find a honey tree, but did not tell me how to deal with the bees. I learned a great deal from that."

"And you still like honey," Saint-Germain added.

"Oh, most certainly." He was busy with the refreshments a little longer; then he moved the tray to one side and established himself more carefully in his chair. "This business with Feng Kuo-Ma is symptomatic of more serious issues. When you were forbidden to continue teaching at the university, we all felt it was an arbitrary and overly cautious move, but I am no longer certain this was the case. The news from the north is grave, and the south is unwilling to accept the extent of the danger." China's division into two separate kingdoms was irritating to both the northern and southern rulers, but the north, dealing with the ravening horsemen of Temujin, was starting to negotiate for an alliance with the south.

"Why should they? They have experienced almost no attacks. They probably think that if they wait, they will be able to take control of the north again, when the Mongols have made you more willing to compromise." He had seen such plans laid before, but knew that success was far from assured.

"There has been an embassy dispatched to the south in the hope that they will listen to reason." He sighed, smoothing his robes with his soft hands. "These are most unsettled times."

"Yes." Saint-Germain waited, knowing that Kuan Sun-Sze had nearly reached the reason for his visit.

"There was a Warlord at the university a few days ago, one of a distinguished military family. She is the heir to a great general—"

Saint-Germain interrupted. "She? A Warlord?"

"It is most unusual," Sun-Sze conceded. "Yet it has happened before, and General T'en was not an easy man to refuse. One of his sons suffers from a crippling disease and the other is debauched. He had only his daughter, and she has proven herself worthy of his trust." He said this quickly, as if to excuse the woman. "She is much in need of aid. She commands her father's stronghold, in the west. The nearest city is Lan-Chou, though her outpost is many li distant. There is not time for her to appeal her requests for troops to the High Court in K'ai-Feng, and those in the ministries here are too much burdened to be able to assist her. The Secretariat of Armies and Supplies has sent her word that they will not be able to respond to her petition until after the end of winter. She has said that she cannot be gone from her stronghold for so long."

"That's wise of her," Saint-Germain said, feeling sympathy for this female Warlord who had tried to breach the walls of custom and protocol that protected the ministries and secretariats in the old capital.

"She has come to the university three times now. She says that she needs one skilled in the sciences of war. T'en Chih-Yü has indicated that she needs more and better weapons, machines of defense and a plan for the best uses of her resources, which are not extensive." He looked up at the carved beams of the ceiling. "There have not been many who were interested in her problems, for most of our scholars are not in any way desirous of participating in battle. A few of the students were excited at the prospect, but they had little to offer Warlord T'en, and she expressed her regrets that she could not avail herself of their assistance."

So this was what the older scholar had come to tell him. Saint-Germain nodded slowly to himself. "And does the Warlord T'en," he began in a slightly formalized style, "insist that her aid come from one of her own countrymen?"

Kuan Sun-Sze's sigh was audible. "I have taken the liberty of mentioning you to her, and she has said that if you are willing to speak to her, she would wish to discuss matters further with you." He cleared his throat. "It would require some time to aid her and in the days you are gone. I am confident that much of the dislike of foreigners will abate. Also, when the ministries and the Magisterial Tribunal learn that you have gone to assist the arming of a Warlord, many of their doubts must be quieted forever." He looked at Saint-Germain, hoping for a response, but the foreigner was silent. "It is hardly fair that one who has been of such great assistance to us should have to prove his good intent, but though there is much talk of virtues in this world, few are often found. There is much wisdom in extending yourself on T'en Chih-Yü's behalf."

"I am aware of that," Saint-Germain said slowly. "There is no one else who can help her?"

"No one in the court here can approach the high councils, and the Dragon Throne, well . . ." He sat forward, making a steeple of his fingertips. "There are those who say that one of the reasons that the army has not been sent into the west is that the military tribunals believe that those lands are lost already, and they are saving the men and equipment to defend the capital."

"And what do you think, Sun-Sze?" Saint-Germain inquired.

"I think that T'en Chih-Yü needs your help. I think that if she stays here, no matter how high her petition is presented, she will ultimately be disappointed." He had said this quite precisely, looking at his touching fingers instead of Saint-Germain. "It would be a sensible move for you to make, my friend. It would be a realistic solution to your predicament."

Saint-Germain felt a forgotten ache return within him. "It would also benefit the university and my students if I were to . . . disappear for a time, too."

Kuan Sun-Sze had the grace to be embarrassed. "Yes, that is true. It was not my primary consideration in asking you to aid Warlord T'en, but it did occur to me."

"Thank you for your honesty." He got up and walked to the terrace. "What if the Mongols make an all-out assault on the west? Is there any way Warlord T'en's stronghold could resist?" Though he did not expect an answer, he was disappointed in Kuan Sun-Sze's silence. "Under such circumstances, my presence would make little difference to the Warlord T'en."

"But there may not be a full assault. Now that they have taken the Northern Capital, and Temujin is calling himself

Jenghiz Khan, it may be enough." He was repeating specula-
tion he had heard, but he reiterated it without conviction.

"You don't believe that any more than I do," Saint-Germain reprimanded him gently. He had braced one forearm
against the doorframe and was staring out into his garden,
thinking how beautiful it was, and how much he would miss
it.

Kuan Sun-Sze turned slowly and studied his host, whom he
had known for fifteen years and who was still so much a
stranger to him. "I was thinking that once you are into the
west, it would be no great difficulty to continue back toward
the lands of your people." He knew that he should not have
put it so blatantly, but the words were out now.

"When I left Europe," Saint-Germain said as he continued
to look at the trees of his garden, "four of my blood had
been most barbarously killed by hysterical townspeople in
Lyon. They confined my . . . kinsmen to a barn, and then
set it afire. Between this crusading fever and the fear of heretics, there are few places for those of us who . . ." He could
not go on. As he pressed his forehead against his raised arm,
he said wearily, "Mongols or monks, what difference? Tell
your female Warlord that I will speak to her."

A moment before, Kuan Sun-Sze had been convinced that
Saint-Germain would insist on staying in Lo-Yang, and he
had been prepared to honor that decision. He was so startled
to hear Saint-Germain agree to meet with T'en Chih-Yü that
he blurted out, "You relieve me."

The breeze was soft off the fields, and the garden was filled
with the clear morning light. Saint-Germain could see the
closed door behind which Ch'uan-T'ing still lay asleep. He
chided himself for the fondness he felt for this place, his
friends, his students. Surely, he told himself, after all this
time, he must have learned how futile it was to care for
houses and friends and students. Yet the pain of loss tore at
him, and he had no cure for it.

"When will you see her?" Kuan Sun-Sze asked, and
brought Saint-Germain out of his profitless introspection.

"Today. This morning. As soon as possible." He stood up
and turned his back on the terrace and the garden beyond.

Text of a safe-conduct from the Ministry of Warfare in K'ai-Feng.

On the Festival of the Descent of the Nine Kings of the North Star in the Year of the Rat, from the Secretary of Co-Ordination of the Regional Militias:

The bearer of this document is a foreigner known as Shih Ghieh-Man. He has long been a resident of Lo-Yang and for a time was an instructor at the university. He travels with one bodyservant, also a foreigner known as Ro-Ger, and six hired riders. He carries three wagons of goods which have been inspected and authorized by the Magisterial Tribunal of this city. His destination is the Mao-T'ou stronghold, where he is to work for the Warlord T'en Chih-Yü.

All reasonable assistance is to be rendered to the foreigner Shih Ghieh-Man if it is not inconvenient to do so. In disputed areas, proper escort must be provided in order that he may successfully carry out his duties at the Mao-T'ou stronghold. Shih Ghieh-Man has agreed to pay for his lodgings and the lodging of those who accompany him, but in areas where such is not conveniently available, the commander of the nearest garrison or the Magistrate of the nearest city is requested to house him and his party, though compensation may be asked at the discretion of the commander or the Magistrate in question.

Reports of the passage of the foreigner Shih Ghieh-Man and his party are requested at the Ministry of Warfare.

At the order of Secretary S'a Tieh-Pao, by the hand of the scribe Ma Cha, written at the Offices of the Ministry of War in the Street of the Yoked Oxen in the city of K'ai-Feng.

3

ABOUT NOON it started to rain, the water wind-sharpened so that it drove like minute darts against the party on the road that was quickly becoming a swath of mud between rapidly filling ditches.

Saint-Germain brought his horse back close to the wagons and kept a wary watch over them, fearing that the wheels might become mired in the deep ruts. He had pulled his long woolen cloak tightly about him, but knew that he would be thoroughly soaked by the time he reached the city of Tuan-Lien, no more than five li distant. Squinting through the rain, he could make out the walls and the Buddhist temple outside the southern gate.

One of his riders cursed as his mount slipped and floundered in the mud. The others watched him apprehensively until he had the horse under control and heading down the road once more.

"Master!" Rogerio shouted as he brought his mare up close to Saint-Germain's big gelding.

"What?" He could hardly hear his own voice, let alone any other but the wind's; he held his gray steady and tried to listen to what Rogerio had to tell him.

"The third cart! The back wheels are sliding! It may be trouble with the axle! Or . . ." The middle-aged manservant looked up from under his soggy straw hat and shook his head in bewilderment.

"Or it could be the rain. These aren't the best vehicles I've ever seen." He knew that Rogerio had not heard all he had said, but that was just as well. He forced himself to answer loudly and carefully, "Watch the wheels! If there is any trouble, let me know at once!"

Rogerio nodded to show that he understood, and dropped back beside the faltering wagon.

It was more than an hour later that Saint-Germain and his traveling company drew up at the gates of Tuan-Lien. There were no guards to greet them, and the massive wooden doors were bolted closed from within.

Saint-Germain gave a fatigued and exasperated sigh, then dismounted to look for the entrance gong to summon the guard. He moved slowly as he made his way along the wall. The ground underfoot was slippery and every step splashed yellow mud over his boots and leather Byzantine-style trousers. He turned the corner of the walls of Tuan-Lien and saw the outline of the Buddhist temple again. With a little more briskness in his step, he made his way toward the temple.

An old priest came to the door in response to Saint-Germain's prolonged pounding, slid the door open a handbreadth and peered out into the night.

"Where is the bell?" Saint-Germain shouted, hoping that the old man was not hard of hearing.

"The bell?" was the answer. The old man's voice was high as a boy's, as if in age he had returned to the innocence of youth.

"To get in!" Saint-Germain said loudly. "We're travelers! We need shelter!"

"Oh, but the gates are locked," the priest said mildly, and moved as if to close his temple door as well.

"I know that," Saint-Germain said, raising his hand to stop the old man. "Tell me where the bell is and I won't trouble you any longer."

The old priest tilted his head to one side. "The Magistrate won't like it." He seemed about to close the door, then stopped. "You may tie your horse to the front railing. The bell is on the north side of the walls, but there is an entrance to the city from this temple."

Saint-Germain closed his eyes with relief. "There are others with me. May I bring them here?"

"I suppose so. How many are there?" His face grew guarded and his hand tightened on the door.

"There are eight of us. I have six riders, my manservant and myself. If that is not too many . . ." Saint-Germain could tell that the priest was openly pleased to hear this and he resolved to find out more when he had brought the others to the Buddhist temple. "I will return shortly. I would very much appreciate it if there might be hot wine for my riders."

"And for yourself?" he inquired cynically. "What do you require?"

"Nothing," Saint-Germain said, knowing it was not quite the truth. Later, he promised himself, he would seek out a sing-song girl on one of the streets where the widows of poor men lived. "You are kind to ask."

The priest stared at him, shrugged and closed the door with the assurance that he would be ready to admit the travelers shortly.

After leading his horse around the temple and tying it to the rail the priest had mentioned, Saint-Germain made his way back to the eastern approach where Rogerio and the riders waited with the carts. The rain was heavier, less stinging and more battering. His sodden cloak was little protection now, and he wanted to be rid of it.

"Master?" Rogerio called out as he saw Saint-Germain come into view. The wind had made tatters of the brim of his straw hat and he looked like nothing so much as a mounted scarecrow with rags flapping around his lean frame.

"The priest at the temple will take us in!" he shouted back over the storm. "The west gate!"

Rogerio nodded vigorously to show that he understood, and tugged at his drooping mount's reins to pass the word to the other six. He turned once and saw Saint-Germain trudging back toward the south wall. Slowly the little party followed him.

"If you will come this way," the priest said as he opened the door to Saint-Germain, "you will find a room there on your left. The baths are there. No doubt you will want to use them."

Saint-Germain put one hand to his brow. "Indeed. You are most courteous to a foreign traveler, and I most humbly thank you for the kindness you do me and those accompanying me." He exchanged polite half-bows with the priest, and trod off in the direction the old man had indicated.

He was sitting in a darkened, steam-filled room when he heard the others arrive, announcing themselves with tramping feet and exhausted curses. He poured a last bucket of hot water over himself and rose, leaving the bath free for the others of his party.

In the private dressing room he had been allocated, he looked about for his clothes, and was vexed to find them gone. Even if the priest had intended to have them dried, he found the kindness awkward, for he did not relish spending the evening in a borrowed robe. He was looking for his boots, in the hope that they had been left behind, when he heard the door behind him open.

"This is the foreigner?" asked a voice Saint-Germain had not heard before.

"It is he, Elevated One," was the priest's answer as he hovered in the doorway.

Saint-Germain had turned and found himself confronting a harried middle-aged man with a pursed little mouth and restless, narrow eyes. He was clad in the sheng liao of a high official, and his cap of stiffened silk indicated that he was the local Magistrate. "August One," Saint-Germain said, concealing his annoyance as he made a formal bow. He felt ludicrous in his wide towel, but he knew that denying this acknowledgment was unforgivably rude; he tied the end of the towel high under his right arm as he straightened up.

"En Jen," said the Magistrate with a nod toward the old priest, "has very correctly informed me of your arrival."

"I am grateful he did," Saint-Germain said, and knew that the Magistrate was offended to be addressed as an equal. "I had planned to present myself and my credentials to you as soon as I was appropriately attired, and I hope you will forgive me for my lack of clothing."

"You had planned to present yourself?" the Magistrate echoed nastily. "Had you really? I have only your word for that, foreigner."

Saint-Germain felt a quiver of alarm but kept it in check. "If I could locate my clothing, I would be honored to present you my safe-conduct from the Secretary of Co-Ordination of the Regional Militias in K'ai-Feng." He hoped that this simple declaration would be enough to still the suspicions that were obviously possessing the Magistrate.

"Fine words, but what has a foreigner to do with the Secretary?"

It was, Saint-Germain realized, likely to be a difficult interview. He forced himself to respond with an affability he did not feel, "I have little to do with the Secretary: I have never had the honor of meeting S'a Tieh-Pao. I am going to the Mao-T'ou stronghold to work for the Warlord T'en Chih-Yü."

"And the Warlord, does he expect you?" Behind the unconvincing blandness there lurked a dangerous smugness. The Magistrate seated himself on one of the two benches in the room.

"The Worthy Magistrate is misinformed," Saint-Germain said smoothly. "The Warlord T'en, who pays me the compliment of hiring me, is a woman. Quite a young woman, in fact. I would estimate her age at no more than twenty-two or

-three." He could see that the Magistrate was surprised and he decided to press his advantage. "I have, until recently, lectured at the university of Lo-Yang under the sponsorship of Kuan Sun-Sze. You may address me as Shih Ghieh-Man—"

"A foreign name!" the Magistrate scoffed.

"And, as you have so correctly pointed out, I am a foreigner." He heard the sound of boots in the hall, louder than the gibbering rain, and he feared for Rogerio and his outriders.

The Magistrate folded his arms and tucked his hands into his voluminous sleeves. "You come here with wagons and armed men—"

"Three wagons and six outriders," Saint-Germain interjected.

"You will not speak until I give you leave to do so!" the Magistrate burst out, his face flushing. "You will stand in a respectful attitude and you will keep silent." He glared at Saint-Germain until the other inclined his head slightly. "Very well. You have come here with wagons and armed men. We are a country at war, though the imbeciles in K'ai-Feng and Lo-Yang seem unaware of that fact. Glib foreigners are not given the same freedoms here." His expression soured as he spoke. "My illustrious uncle, Hao Chen-Nai, has received many foreigners in his home and entertained them as he would the Emperor himself!"

Saint-Germain nodded inwardly, recognizing the rancor of a member of a junior branch of an illustrious family. This Magistrate was close enough to real power to be tantalized and embittered by it. "I have not met your uncle," he said to the Magistrate, though it was a lie—he had met the sagacious Hao Chen-Nai nine years ago, shortly after he had finished his house in Lo-Yang. He had not seen the cultured old man since. "You are fortunate in your distinguished name and your highly regarded ancestors."

"Thank you," the Magistrate Hao said curtly. Then he added, since he was grudgingly well-mannered, "My personal name is Sai-Chu. I have been District Magistrate here for four years."

And, thought Saint-Germain, in another few years he would be transferred, as the law required, to another equally unimportant post in some provincial city, never allowed to reach any higher position than what he had already achieved. He felt sympathy for Hao Sai-Chu even as he admitted that the man's frustration made him dangerous. "It is a pleasure to renew my acquaintance with your family. The dedication of the Haos to the Empire is legendary."

"Dedication," Magistrate Hao repeated sullenly. "Yes."

En Jen, the Buddhist priest, stepped in from the hallway. "August Magistrate," he said quietly, "the guards have asked to have your instructions for the others."

Hao Sai-Chu glared at the old man, half-rising as he listened. He shot a swift look at Saint-Germain and resumed his place on the bench. "Hold them for the time being. I will send word when I am through here and will tell them then what is to be done." He watched Saint-Germain covertly to see how this pronouncement affected him.

Saint-Germain looked up at the beams of the dressing room and fixed his thoughts on the sound of the rain on the roof tiles. It would not benefit him or the men accompanying him if he let himself be harried by this contumelious official. Idly he wondered what had happened to his safe-conduct and his clothes. Surely, he told himself, he would not be made to appear in the tribunal wrapped in a towel? He could not entirely convince himself of that.

"Your men . . ." Magistrate Hao was saying. "Where did you hire them?"

"The outriders were hired in Lo-Yang through the good offices of the Ministry of Roads and Transport. These men were recommended because of their long experience and knowledge. They have been most useful, as this part of your country is largely unknown to me." He kept a level tone and easy manner, though it was becoming an effort.

"And the seventh man?" Hao Sai-Chu leaned forward. "What of him?"

"Rogerio comes from the city of Gades. He has been my servant for many years. I have traveled a great deal, Magistrate, and this man has been with me much of the time." He doubted that Magistrate Hao had ever heard of that Roman city in Spain, and he decided to press this advantage. "Instruct your guards to speak to my servant. He will tell them the same thing."

"No doubt," was the sarcastic answer. "Do not think that because I am in a remote city that I am unaware of the subtleties of you crafty foreigners. I am not one to be deceived by convincing lies."

"It is not my intention to lie to you, Worthy Magistrate

Hao. Why should I, when I am on legitimate business?" He lowered his voice as he spoke but did not look at the Magistrate, knowing that such men do not like their authority challenged.

"I have only your word on that, foreigner." Hao Sai-Chu gave Saint-Germain a thorough and appraising scrutiny. "You are very strong. I think you are stronger than you look."

Saint-Germain did not answer this, though he realized with ironic self-appreciation that half his lifetime ago he would have confirmed the Magistrate's evaluation by putting his fist through the wall. Such fruitless demonstrations were behind him now, but the memory of those events still had the capacity to sting him.

"You say nothing," the Magistrate snapped.

"I was thinking on the follies of my youth," Saint-Germain answered with a wry smile.

"Youth is an abuse of men unless it is eternal." His face showed he would brook no opposition. "They say that the Taoist charlatans have a skill in such matters. It is said that they know the secret of the Elixir of Life."

"So I have heard." A sizable portion of the alchemical studies done by Taoist scholars was devoted to that very question.

"You would know nothing of that, of course." Hao's restless eyes grew fervid.

"Taoist alchemy is transmitted from master to student by word of mouth, Worthy Magistrate. What master would accept a student of my age, and a foreigner to boot?" He hoped that Hao Sai-Chu would be sufficiently gratified by this response to overlook the fact that Saint-Germain had not answered his question.

Magistrate Hao nodded ponderously. Then he turned to the door as a small man in scribe's garb bustled into the room. "What is it?"

The scribe hesitated. "The inventory . . ."

"Let me have it at once." He held out his hand in a peremptory way and waited until the small scroll had been placed in it. "You may leave us," he informed the scribe as soon as his fingers had closed around the paper. The scribe bowed and departed, though neither Magistrate Hao nor Saint-Germain paid him any attention. "Three wagons," Hao said to the foreigner after a moment.

"That is correct." His senses were sharpened again, and he made himself seem disinterested.

"One of the wagons is filled with containers of earths and liquids." Hao said, reading from the scroll.

"It is part of my work, Worthy Magistrate. They will be required by Warlord T'en when I arrive at Mao-T'ou stronghold." The rain was heavier, though the wind had slackened. He could feel the drafts decrease.

"One of the wagons has personal items of clothing, beddings, saddles, and other such materials." He sounded vaguely disappointed. Then his face brightened. "I see here that there are also two large wooden panels with pictures in colored stones in that wagon."

Now that it was too late, Saint-Germain regretted bringing the Byzantine mosaics with him. "I have had them for some time," he remarked, waiting for the Magistrate to comment further.

"I have seen such pictures. There are very few of them in this kingdom. A man who possesses one might be counted extraordinarily fortunate."

Saint-Germain closed his eyes once, swiftly, and then said what he knew he must say. "If the Worthy Magistrate Hao finds my poor mosaics so much to his taste, I would be deeply gratified—far above the paltry value of the pictures themselves—if he would be willing to accept them as gifts." He loved those mosaics. They had been made when Justinian ruled, and Saint-Germain had been able to keep them with him on most of his travels in the intervening centuries. To have to part with them now felt like a betrayal of friends. He did not want them to go into the hands of this jealous man.

"You flatter me, Shih Ghieh-Man. The gift is a handsome one, and I will do my poor best to be sure they are correctly appreciated. There is nothing that would delight me more than to have these stone pictures hang in my private quarters where I may take the time to contemplate their foreignness." Hao made no attempt to apologize for the gloating success he felt. He gave Saint-Germain an ingenuous smile.

"I hope they will bring you joy." It was a legitimate wish, he knew. For otherwise the Byzantine mosaics would be shut away in some neglected storeroom, and would eventually fall to ruin.

"Very gracious of you," the Magistrate said, getting to his

feet at last. "Well. You will want to put on some clothes, I think. It is really quite cold in here.".

"And my men?" Saint-Germain asked, not quite able to disguise his contempt.

"Ah, yes. Your men. I fear that we are very shorthanded here, and the militia can use every man it can get. For that reason, I think I must insist that three of your outriders remain here in the service of our Marshal of Defense. Being honorable men, they could have no objection to aiding us. We have much need of skilled fighters, as the Mongols have been raiding just two valleys away." He tapped the little scroll with his long nails. "I think it is possible to spare three for you."

"And Warlord T'en also has need of skilled armed men," Saint-Germain reminded the Magistrate with angry civility.

"Why, of course she does. But she does not have a city to contend with. Her militia will be of a different sort." There was such consummate arrogance in Hao Sai-Chu's voice, such deprecation in the curl of his lip, that Saint-Germain was appalled that this man was allowed even the modicum of power he wielded here in this isolated district.

"I will do my best to explain your actions to her," Saint-Germain said in a carefully neutral tone.

"There is nothing to explain," Magistrate Hao said lightly, gesturing with the closed scroll to indicate of how little importance the matter was. "She knows how things are here. No doubt she will be more than satisfied with the three outriders. I am certain that three are more than she requires." He was at the door, but did not open it. "I have already had the fourth meal. I have always made a habit of taking my fifth meal in private. Perhaps tomorrow . . ."

"Thank you, I will fend for myself," Saint-Germain responded, more brusquely than he had intended.

"Excellent. I will have someone send you word." He tugged the door open rather abruptly and found En Jen hovering less than a step away. "If you say one word of this, priest, I will order you sent to the Ai-Ming monastery."

En Jen blanched, and Saint-Germain was taken aback. The Ai-Ming monastery was reserved for those monks and priests who had dishonored their calling. The place, built halfway down a canyon on the edge of the desert, was named for the emotion it evoked—despair.

"I heard nothing," the old priest declared staunchly, though his hands trembled.

"Good. Remember my words if I should ever learn otherwise." He started into the hall, then turned back. "Is there anything you require? If you are truly on your way to the Mao-T'ou stronghold, I suppose I must offer you what poor assistance I can."

Saint-Germain wanted to demand the return of his outriders, but said calmly, "If I may have access to a forge, I would appreciate it. One of my wagons has a damaged wheel and the axle is worn. I would like to rim the wheels with iron and put in heavier axle pins."

Magistrate Hao shook his head sadly. "If I had a smith to spare, I would be pleased to do this, but—"

"I will do the labor. All I require is a forge. I have my own iron and tools." He was standing very straight and there was a light in his eyes that glittered unpleasantly.

"Oh, very well," the Magistrate grumbled. "Your clothes will be brought to you presently. I cannot imagine why it has taken so long for them to be delivered."

"Can't you." Saint-Germain folded his arms and regarded Hao Sai-Chu sardonically. "How grateful I am for all you have done."

"You should be," the Magistrate agreed, and there was a threat under his words. "A foreigner in this part of the country . . . well, no one would blame me had I decided to question you more . . . shall we say rigorously?" He met Saint-Germain's eyes for a moment, then stared down at the scroll he held once more.

"I imagine we understand each other, Worthy Magistrate," Saint-Germain said, his voice cold.

"Yes." Hao was about to close the door when Saint-Germain spoke once again.

"I am aware that your minions might be somewhat lax in the performance of their duty. When one is hurried, many courtesies are forgotten. I would count it as a token of your goodwill and the efficiency of your servants if I found my safe-conduct in the innermost pocket of my sheng go where I left it." He watched Magistrate Hao until he saw the man duck his head in acceptance. "Very gracious of you, Worthy Magistrate. And very wise."

Hao Sai-Chu could not resist planting a final barb. "I intend to make a full report to the Secretary for the Co-Ordi-

nation of the Regional Militias. If it turns out that you have
in any way misrepresented yourself—"

"The Secretary may send soldiers to the Mao-T'ou stronghold," Saint-Germain finished for the Magistrate. "I am certain that Warlord T'en will welcome them."

A sudden gust of wind curvetted through the dressing
room, and a few muffled voices were heard. Steps approached, and a moment later a man in the official dress of a
tribunal scribe entered the hallway and gave Hao Sai-Chu
formal greeting. The Magistrate scowled, but stepped back to
hear the whispered words of the scribe. Saint-German did not
move; he watched the two men through the half-open door.

At last Magistrate Hao turned to him with a penetrating
look. "Your clothes are being brought," he said shortly.

"And my safe-conduct?" Saint-Germain inquired politely.

"It is in order!" With this irritated announcement, Magistrate Hao swung away from the door and stamped off down
the hallway.

Some little time later, Rogerio opened the dressing-room
door and stepped inside. He carried a stack of carefully
folded garments. He himself was already dressed in his usual
somber manner.

"Did they trouble you?" Saint-Germain asked as his manservant held out the black sheng go.

"A few questions and a great many threats," he answered
calmly.

"Were you harmed?"

Rogerio paused an instant. "No."

Saint-Germain knew the man too well to accept this.
"What happened?"

"You know that we are losing three of the outriders?" He
did not wait for Saint-Germain to answer. "They've also intimated they might confiscate the wagons."

"When?" Saint-Germain had picked up the quilted woolen
dalmatica, but paused in the act of pulling it over his head.

"When did they intimate that? When they had us in the
dressing rooms." Distaste tightened Rogerio's mouth.

"Then you need not worry yourself," Saint-Germain told
him sadly. "That has been resolved."

"Resolved." Though Rogerio did not inquire further,
Saint-Germain relented.

"It appears that the Worthy Magistrate has a taste for
Western art. He has permitted me to give him my Byzantine

mosaics." Now he did not conceal the bitterness he felt, and he saw an answering ire in Rogerio's features. "So you see." He opened one hand fatalistically.

Silently Rogerio handed Saint-Germain his Persian-style leggings.

As Saint-Germain bent forward he felt oiled paper press against his chest. He straightened up and reached into the unfastened collar of his sheng go. "Ah." He pulled out a tightly folded packet. "The safe-conduct, I assume."

Rogerio offered Saint-Germain a pair of thick-soled slippers. "I watched the scribe read it and seal it, and I myself replaced it."

Some of the reserve faded from Saint-Germain's dark eyes. "That was well done of you."

"I also took time to be certain that nothing was added to the documents," Rogerio added after a short silence.

Saint-Germain stepped into his slippers. "This is much better," he said abstractedly. "Yes," he went on as he secured his wide belt, "you've been very wise. Hao Sai-Chu has cost me too much already. I have sacrificed my mosaics to his greed. It would be unpardonable to become victims of his stupidity. I assume that there was another document?"

"The scribe told me it was an accident and that the two papers had stuck together," Rogerio said quietly.

"And the second letter was an order for imprisonment or execution." His compelling gaze rested on his servant's face. "Execution," he said softly. "I will work the forge tonight. Tell the other three that we leave at first light." He went to the door of the dressing room. "The rain is stopping. That's in our favor."

Rogerio bent quickly, and when he stood again he had a thin Egyptian dagger in his hand. "You may have need of this, I think," he said as he offered it to Saint-Germain.

Saint-Germain's small hand closed on the hilt. "So I might," he said lightly, and tucked the weapon into his sleeve before stepping into the hall.

———————◄●►———————

Text of a letter from the Pope of the Nestorian Christian Church of Saint Thomas in Lan-Chow to the Nestorian community in K'ai-Feng.

In the twelfth month of the Year of the Rat, the Thirteenth Year of the Sixty-fifth Cycle, the one thousand two hundred seventeeth Year of Our Lord, to the Pope and congregation in K'ai-Feng.

Greetings from Lan-Chow:

We are certain that you have heard of the latest Mongol incursions here, and we wish to reassure you that we are, by the Grace of God, unharmed. There have been many battles to the northeast but they have not penetrated this far, and we are confident that the reinforcements promised to the garrison here will be sufficient to keep the barbarian invaders from reaching our walls.

A fortnight ago, during the first real storm of winter, one of the local customs inspectors discovered that an innkeeper has been passing messages to the Mongol spies. This despicable act was related in the Tribunal and the man has been sentenced to death by exposure, both for the sake of expediency and as a warning to any others who may seek to enrich themselves by such treason. We have said a Mass for the repose of the wretch's soul, as Our Lord has admonished us to do, but I must add that most of us believe that the criminal is far from redemption.

The last news we heard of the outer world came some little while ago from a foreigner passing through Lan-Chow to the Mao-T'ou stronghold. He informed our District Magistrate that he had seen evidence of Mongol raids at two locations along the road here, and had lost one of his three outriders in a skirmish with a band of outlaws, though he could not say whether they were

Mongols or highwaymen. From him we have been led to understand that the Paulist Church in the West is filled with tribulation, just as Cha Ts'ai prophesied so long ago. It comes from departing from the words of the master and listening instead to the disciple. We will pray that they may be guided out of the darkness of the soul they have made for themselves, and remember at last that the Way of God is found through the brotherhood of creatures, and the dedication to those principles for which Our Lord died. In this, certainly, we are in agreement with our Taoist brothers.

We have agreed to provide this Shih Ghieh-Man with more information as we get it from the other churches in the Empire, and he has said that he will send word to us if he learns anything of importance.

The signs are for a long, wet winter here, which will bring more snow into the mountains, and will block the passes until late in spring. Already travelers are being warned of the danger of venturing too far into T'u-Bo-T'e, as the Land of Snows is treacherous at the best of times. The farmers in the district have been saying that they are apprehensive about their winter crops because of the heavy rains, and it is true that onions and cabbages are not as plentiful as they were at this time last year. Many valleys to the north of us were visited with blight, and as a result there is little grain for them to store away. If the Mongols have suffered equally, they will return with the ferocity of hunger when the rains stop. It has been suggested that all farmers establish a system of sentries so that they will not be taken unaware if Temujin's horsemen should decide to come into the western mountains again, which seems all too likely.

We have agreed to send three of our congregation into Tien-Du and K'i-Shi-Mi-Rh to discover if any of our churches still endure there. If our future is as bleak as some of the army captains have warned us it might be, we all may be forced to leave this place and seek elsewhere for our homes. Mei Sa-Fong will head the group, for he is the most knowledgeable of the congregation, and has traveled farther than any of the rest of us, and knows the cities to the east and south. He takes with him Chung La and his sister Mei Hsu-No. The three will travel by water most of the way. Rivers and canals will carry them to the sea, and it has been arranged that they will go by sea around the end of Tien-Du. Mei Sa-Fong has been instructed that if he does not find Christians there, he is to continue westward. We have provided him with routes to Mi-Sz'i-Rh and Ki-Sz'i-Da-Ni, where Shih Ghieh-Man tells us that the Church rules everywhere since the time of an Emperor for whom the city is named. I have always believed that such a place was more legend than fact, but he assures me that the rumor, if anything, underestimates the city. A few of the elders have said that we are not wise to put our faith in so few of our number, but no one else in the congregation is as competent. Should this party visit you, I ask that you will receive them in the name of the master and give unstintingly of your aid. What they may discover will be of use to you as well as to us.

Mei Sa-Fong and Mei Hsu-No spoke at length with this Shih Ghieh-Man and said that he was most helpful to them, though he has not been in Mi-Sz'i-Rh or Ki-Sz'i-Da-Ni for a very long time. He said that since the Muz-Lum followers have taken much territory, it is not as easy for Christians to move through their countries as it once was. Mei Sa-Fong informs me that if he can face Mongols, he can deal with any Muz-Lum he encounters.

My congregation and I pray that our Christian brothers and all our countrymen come safely through the ordeal that is ahead. Even as Our Lord was tested, so are we, and we must show ourselves worthy of His struggle. We have been taught that those who rule the earth are the self-disciplined, which we must keep in mind through the coming years.

With my blessing to you and your congregation, this by my own hand.

Nai Yung-Ya
Pope of the Nestorian congregation of Lan-Chow

4

MAO-T'OU STRONGHOLD sat at the end of a ridge of hills above a winding road between two narrow valleys, very much like the spearhead for which it was named. The keep itself was of thick, ancient timbers but the outer fortifications were of split logs standing in foundations of mortared stone.

"As you see," T'en Chih-Yü was explaining to Saint-Germain as they rode up the approach through a powder of light snow, "the north flank is our strongest, but if assault came down the crest of the hill, we would not have a chance against any large force. Thirty, forty men we could withstand, but no more than that."

Saint-Germain nodded grimly, holding his gray to the pace of the Warlord's feisty sorrel. "You will need to build up most of the walls. An outer retaining wall might be helpful." The approach was steeper here, and a few pines grew in this fold of the hill, though higher up they had been cleared off, both to provide lumber for the stronghold and to provide attackers little opportunity for concealment.

Chih-Yü's scale armor jingled as she urged her horse up the incline. It was necessary here to ride single file, and as she took the lead, she called back over her shoulder, "We're short of labor, so it might be difficult to undertake more building. I was hoping there was a way to strengthen the walls as they stand."

"There is," Saint-Germain assured her, "and it is better than nothing. Do you have manpower enough to dig a ditch—a deep one—around the stronghold?"

"A ditch?" Her voice rose in surprise.

"Mongols fight on horseback. A ditch would deter them for a while. It would certainly slow them down. You'd have to contend with the archers, but you have your own bowmen." His horse, unfamiliar with the ground, stumbled, and Saint-Germain strove to bring the gray's head up. The hooves scrambled on the frost-hard ground, and though he did not fall, the gray was favoring his off-front hoof as he resumed the upward climb.

"What happened?" Chih-Yü asked, drawing in her sorrel some little way up the track.

"He cast a shoe, I think." Reluctantly Saint-Germain swung out of the light Persian saddle he favored, and drew the reins over the gray's head. Speaking softly, he stepped to the horse's head and bent to lift the leg. "Yes. If you'll give me permission to use your forge, I'll replace it this afternoon." He began to walk up the hill, leading his horse.

"You may do what is necessary, but my own smith can attend to it." She had brought her sorrel back toward him.

"Undoubtedly, but as I prepare my own alloys, I prefer to work them myself." He looked up at Chih-Yü, and his expression became enigmatic.

"About this ditch. Do you think it would make a difference?" There was intelligence and determination in her face, which, though not pretty, had a strength of character that made her attractive.

"It might very well. The Mongols do not use heavy armor, so it will not be as much to their disadvantage as it would be to a troop of Frankish knights, but their horses will not want to gallop through it, and if we put gravel on our side of the ditch, they will fall if they jump. It might keep them from mounting a full assault on the stronghold."

She gave this her consideration and accepted it for the moment. "I'm not in a position to overlook any advantage we might find. I will give orders in the valleys that we need workmen. The winter has been mild so far. Usually there is a foot of snow here when the new year comes. The holding damns on the streams have kept the rain from causing much flooding, though two shepherds lost some sheep during the last storm. I will issue orders that each family is to send one man for two days in every fortnight to make this ditch, and to strengthen the walls of the stronghold."

"Will they obey?" Saint-Germain could not help asking. He had seen how many of the farmers were unwilling to assist the militia, choosing flight instead of confrontation with the Mongol horsemen.

"They will," she said with confidence. "I will give the same order to my soldiers, and the farmers will see that no one is being treated preferentially." She rode well, with an economy of movement and capable hands. "I will work on the ditch as well."

Saint-Germain's fine brows lifted. "You?"

"I am Warlord here," she reminded him sharply. "If I give orders, it is only fitting that I follow them myself. That way, my men will go into battle knowing that I will not desert them." She glanced at the scabbard on her left hip and smiled. "I have my father's sword, and it is revered."

"Isn't it unusual for you to have your father's sword? I am aware that there is no reason you should not, but I understand you have brothers. Under the circumstances . . ." He had been curious about this for some time, but had never felt at liberty to ask her about her family. Now, as they went slowly toward the rough walls of the stronghold, he thought she might be willing to speak to him.

"My older brother," she said slowly, "had no liking for this life. He left Mao-T'ou stronghold as soon as he was allowed to, and has not come back. When last I heard of him, he was living in the southern Empire with three sing-song girls. He went through his inheritance and I was forbidden to provide him with any funds except for his honorable burial." Her eyes were flinty, fixed on the pass below them. "My other brother was born with a malformed foot. He is a good and gentle man, living now with our mother's uncle, who retired from diplomatic service three years ago. He was pleased to have my brother with him, and the way of life is less strenuous in Pei-Mi." At the mention of her younger brother, her features softened. "My father found that I was capable of martial skills, and trained me to continue his work."

"And you have encountered no opposition?" Saint-Germain could not believe this was the case.

Chih-Yü laughed, and the sound was crisp on the cold wind. "I have encountered nothing but opposition. My mother said that she could not allow this for it would ruin my chances to marry, which is probably true enough. My uncles tried every ruse thinkable, and a few unthinkable, to foist one of their sons on my father. He was adamant. So, here I am. As for opposition now, well, luckily, I thrive on it."

Listening to her, Saint-Germain recalled his conversation with Kuan Sun-Sze, three months before, who had suggested that he offer his services to the Warlord of Mao-T'ou stronghold. "I doubt you would be here if that were not the case."

She gave him a quick, appraising look, then raised her hand in signal to the guards of Mao-T'ou stronghold to open the gates.

As they passed through the narrow archway shortly afterward, Chih-Yü called out to her captain, "Jui Ah! I must see you at once. There are preparations to be made." She turned back to Saint-Germain for a moment. "Ghieh-Man," she said quietly, using his personal name alone for the first time, "when you have finished with your horse, I would be pleased if you would come to my quarters to discuss the ditch with me further."

"I will be happy to," he said at once, and watched her with some curiosity as she dismounted and gave her sorrel into the hands of a groom before striding into the old wooden building that was the heart of the Mao-T'ou stronghold. He led his gray into the stable and encountered the cool looks of the grooms. "I must replace a shoe," he said, and encountered blank stares. The dialect here was so unlike any of the other Chinese dialects Saint-Germain spoke that he could find no way to talk with the farmers and servants here. He had heard enough of their particular tongue to realize that they had far more than four inflections in their speech, but he had not yet succeeded in identifying them. He gestured to his horse's hoof and indicated that it had lost a shoe. One of the grooms nodded his understanding and went back to his task, raking out the stalls and laying clean straw down for the horses.

Saint-Germain found the forge at the other end of the stable, and was pleased to see it was well-equipped. In so remote a place, there was no room for shoddiness. He glanced around to familiarize himself with the arrangements, then tied his gray to a handy post while he went to get the metal he required.

When he had finished with his horse, he led him back to his stall and put him inside with a dish of oats and a pail of water. He took his saddle and bridle to the tack room and noticed, as always, the grooms refused to touch the alien things. He rolled down the sleeves of his sheng go and walked across the cobbled courtyard to the central building.

Most of the servants no longer stared at him, though a few were pointedly ignoring him. Saint-Germain had experienced that often enough in his long life that it no longer rankled with him. He made his way up the wide, shallow stairs to the second floor, where Chih Yü's personal quarters were.

Chih-Yü heard the click of Saint-Germain's thick-heeled boots before he knocked on the door, and she was relieved. Jui Ah, her Captain, was still bending over her back, ostensibly to look at the drawing of the Mao-T'ou stronghold, but actually to try to stroke her neck. She would have to rebuke him openly, but at the moment she was too much in need of his assistance to risk offending him.

The knock, when it came, sounded in the room like distant thunder. Jui Ah jumped back, and in so doing revealed his cupidity. Chih-Yü gave the Captain a hard look and called out, "Who is here?"

"Shih Ghieh-Man," he answered, puzzled that she would ask after requesting that he join her.

"You may enter," she said, and rose as Saint-Germain came into the room.

This unusual courtesy was not lost on him, nor was the quickly concealed disgust in Jui Ah's eyes. Saint-Germain bowed in the Frankish manner to Chih-Yü. "Warlord T'en," he said most politely. "You have favored this person with the opportunity to serve you."

She did not quite smile, but there was a flicker at the tails of her eyes that showed her appreciation of his conduct. "Earlier today you suggested that we might dig a ditch around the stronghold. You indicated that your experience has shown you that such a ditch is one method of defending against cavalry attack. Since we are all three of us aware that we stand in considerable danger of just such an attack, I would appreciate it if you would enlarge on your comments."

Jui Ah braced one hand on his belt, every line of him showing derision. "A ditch is a waste of time. I've told you that before. We must double the thickness of the walls and make them higher."

"Oh, yes," Saint-Germain agreed. "That is also desirable. But it is also sensible to take certain precautions, wouldn't you agree? If the Mongols do not reach the walls, it is easier to pick them off, isn't it?" He waited for Jui Ah to speak, and when the captain remained stubbornly silent, he went on. "A ditch, dug completely around the stronghold, will make it more difficult for the mounted soldiers to approach, and may throw them into some disorder. All of that is advantageous to us. The ditch should be fairly deep—certainly as deep as a tall man, and more if possible. It should be wider than a horse can comfortably jump. There should be loose rocks and gravel on the inner wall of the ditch so that once the horses are in, they cannot easily get out. Sharpened stakes planted at the top of the inner rim of the ditch are also useful, for then, should a rider get his horse up the inner wall, he will not be able to approach the stronghold. All this won't take the place of the men of this stronghold, and it will be their skill that will save us, but these things will delay them and that will get us the time that the stronghold militia must have to defeat the attackers." He hoped that he had given sufficient praise for Jui Ah's vanity.

Chih-Yü was seated once more and she spread out a map of the stronghold and the pass. "Tell me, Shih Ghieh-Man, where would you dig this ditch, if you were the one to give the order.",

Though Saint-Germain had long since decided where such a ditch must be dug, he made a show of considering the map and pondering the terrain, even going to the window and staring out for a moment. Finally he went to the table where the map was spread. "I would begin it here, where the ridge dips before rising to the stronghold. I would keep it fairly far from the walls here, where the hill is steep, but would bring it in closer here, where the ground is flatter. We do not want to give them much area in which to gather once inside the limits of the ditch. If there is too much room, they can mount a charge and the whole purpose of the ditch will be lost."

Chih-Yü studied the map where Saint-Germain had run his finger. "There is a stream that runs here in spring," she remarked. "It would cut through the walls of your ditch."

"Then dig the ditch inside the path of the stream. In fact, you may want to build a retaining wall between the ditch and the stream so that the ditch may be flooded." He thought to himself that he had now persuaded them to accept a moat. How best to describe a drawbridge? He had seen many of them over rivers and canals, but only one fortress he knew of had used a drawbridge as part of its defense, and that fortress was far to the east, near the coast.

"First you want us to dig a ditch for you, and now you're telling us to divert a stream," Jui Ah said with arrogant spite. "Is this part of your foreign knowledge, or are you trusting to our simplicity? We are not fools because we choose to live away from the cities, and you cannot deceive us with your plans."

Saint-Germain looked at the captain with steady eyes. "I am not trying to deceive you. I am trying to help prevent complete destruction here."

Jui Ah put one foot on an upholstered bench and clapped his hands sharply once. "You have heard all these tales of Mongols, and you believe them. Yet I know that every time they have battled our armies, they have been totally defeated. They have some skill with horses, we all know that, but against well-trained men, they are as ineffective as children."

"I hate to bring it to your attention, Captain," Saint-Germain said, at his most affable, "but there is no army unit garrisoned nearby, and it does not seem likely, with Temujin in Pei-King, there will be many units to spare for the borderlands. It is the intention of K'ai-Feng and Lo-Yang to reclaim the capital before summer"—privately he thought the task would be impossible, but he did not voice this opinion—"and for that reason, any request for army assistance will be given reduced priority. I don't disparage your abilities, or the talents of your men. But I have seen a great many battles in my life, and I have learned that it is wise to take every advantage you can."

"Fine words, fine words," Jui Ah muttered. "It is a sad thing when we are reduced to dealing with foreigners, I can tell you that." This last was directed at T'en Chih-Yü, and she set her teeth before she was able to answer.

"I am willing to use any help that there is, whether it comes from the Emperor himself or from the lowest slave in Sa-Ma-Rh-Han. The Mongols will not care who gives us aid. Their concern will be to take this stronghold and destroy it. I cannot allow that to happen." She had not risen, but it had taken all her will to remain seated.

"And you think that ditches and stakes will help you?" Jui Ah demanded. "We need more men! I have told you that for more than a year. You went to Lo-Yang for troops, not for fancy foreigners who talk like waitingwomen and—"

"That is enough!" Chih-Yü said, and though the words were softly spoken, there was such force in them that Jui Ah obeyed her. "I have told you that there were no troops. I will not do so again. I have said that it was fortunate that a great scholar told me of this man. I will not do so again. Rather than grieve for what I cannot have, I intend to accomplish as much as I can with what is available to me. That means," she went on briskly, "that I will order a ditch dug. I will implant stakes. I will divert streams. I will scatter caltrops on the road. I will give pikes to the farmers. I will put watchtowers on every hill around the valleys. Anything that may save one man, one house, one field, one hour, I will do."

Saint-Germain listened with increasing respect to the young woman. He looked toward Jui Ah and said, "Though I may be a foreigner, that will not weigh with the Mongols. Should we be attacked, I stand in the same danger you do." That was not quite the case, he thought with a degree of self-mockery, but he had learned enough about the Mongol soldiers to know they had many ways to kill him—fire, decapitation, crushing beneath stones—all of them would be truly fatal to him.

"But would you be here, foreigner, that's my question. Would you not leave under cover of night and let us wait behind our ditch, thinking we were safe?" Jui Ah's eyes were like black pebbles, flat and hard in his face.

"Where would I go, Captain?" Saint-Germain inquired. "Your distrust of foreigners is nothing compared to what the Mongols feel."

"This does nothing but breed acrimony," Chih-Yü interrupted, and gave each man a quick, impartial glance. "I must see to my fortifications, and if neither of you is willing to discuss it with me . . ."

"I am at your disposal," Saint-Germain said, grateful for the diversion she had created. He watched Jui Ah closely, thinking that the Captain might consider this a further challenge.

"It is useless to talk to you," he yelled, and stormed to the door. "You may do as you wish, Warlord T'en, but I will take my men and drill them."

"Fine," Chih-Yü answered evenly. "Just be certain that each man spends two days a fortnight digging the ditch." She winced as the door slid shut with a crash.

Saint-Germain waited in the sudden silence. He did not move. He could see that Chih-Yü's shoulders were hunched and the muscle in her jaw stood out against her umpampered skin.

When she spoke again, it was of inconsequent things. "Your quarters are to your satisfaction?"

"They are," Saint-Germain said honestly. He had lived in hovels and palaces, in great forests and in the sewers of ancient cities. "The rooms are good-sized and I can set up my supplies quite satisfactorily. The view is pleasant."

"I understand that you have a compound in Lo-Yang. I was told it is very beautiful." Her voice had grown smaller but there was no meekness in it, only resignation.

"Yes, it is beautiful." He came a few steps toward her. "Warlord, when you asked for my assistance, I told you I was willing to come here. That was true then and is true now. Yes, my home in Lo-Yang was more sumptuous than this, and there were things I love in it. Would you, given the choice, not prefer to live among beautiful things? But in Lo-Yang I was under suspicion. My studies were curtailed, and those who had previously been pleased by my company no longer wished to know me." He smiled, and his dark eyes brightened. "I do not regret coming here, T'en Chih-Yü, though I deplore the reasons that compelled me to make the decision."

The lacquer on the walls was old, and the grain of the wood showed through. With the windows open to the air, Chih-Yü's quarters were frigid. She looked up at Saint-Germain and turned up one hand, indicating this. "You say that here?"

"Yes." He sat in the chair opposite her. "I do not deceive you. Believe that."

Her shoulders were less rigid now, and the tightness was fading from her face. "Why?" she asked.

He met her eyes. "Suspicion poisons everything it touches."

"And Jui Ah?" she said quickly. "His suspicions?"

"That's for you to say. One man's blustering is a nuisance only, but if you doubt me, tell me now."

"You will return to Lo-Yang."

"No."

She blinked, though whether from surprise or sudden tears, neither of them knew. "I do not doubt you, Shih Ghieh-Man, but I cannot promise that my men will not side with Jui Ah."

He took a deep breath that was not quite a sigh. "If you wish me to leave, you have only to tell me and I will go."

One of her fingers rubbed at the corner of the map. "Is Hsing to your liking?" she inquired in another voice.

"She's very beautiful and most acquiescent," he said. "I thank you for sending her to me."

"I have heard that you do not trouble her much."

"It is not my way," he explained obliquely. He had thought the prettiest servant girl, which Hsing undoubtedly was, was an obvious but malleable spy. He had only to treat her as he had Ch'uan-T'ing, coming to her in her sleep, and her reports to Chih-Yü would continue to be unremarkable. For an instant he wished that he had that greater intimacy, and the image of Olivia in distant Rome came to his mind, and Ranegunde in her bleak stone fortress.

Chih-Yü looked puzzled. "What is the matter?" she asked when his eyes were on her once more.

"Nothing. I was remembering those of my blood." He did not want to admit to Chih-Yü how profoundly his loneliness had shaken him.

"Ah," she said with understanding. Her finger was still on the map. "Perhaps, Shih Ghieh-Man, you will show me again where you would dig this ditch, and then later this evening, after the last meal, I will tell my soldiers what is required of them. Tomorrow morning, we will send word to the valleys so that work may begin at once."

Saint-Germain held her gaze with his. "I am grateful, T'en Chih-Yü." He managed to speak more lightly. "The ground is hard now, and digging in it will be arduous."

"That is true enough," she allowed, "but if we wait until the ground is softer, we may not be finished in time, and the Mongols may arrive before we are ready for them." She took a brush and began to draw the line of the ditch.

"Show me where the stream goes," Saint-Germain said, giving his attention to the map. "There should be a way to rig a spillway that we can regulate from inside the walls."

Her features sharpened. "Excellent." She pushed a stray tendril of hair off her face and began to make notations on the map as she and Saint-Germain went over the plans again.

An order from the District Magistrate Wu Sing-I to all the militias in his region, including T'en Chih-Yü's.

On the Feast of the Lanterns in the first fortnight of the Year of the Ox, the Fourteenth Year of the Sixty-fifth Cycle, to all the Militia Commanders within the Shu-Rh District.

Your Magistrate does not doubt that any of you are unaware of the grave dangers that confront us as the winter comes to an end. Though many of us have re-joiced that the crop losses of last autumn were not com-pounded by deep snows and empty hearths, yet the rain has been as unrelenting as the snows, and where frost did not claim lives, hunger did. Surely none of you make light of these problems. However, this spring we must prepare not only for the tasks that always renew themselves with the year, we must be ready to confront a deadly and terrible foe.

Each of you has heard by now of the devastation

wrought by the horsemen of Temujin in areas to the east and north of here. It is criminally blind to deny the possibility that we will come under similar attack. For that reason, the district is ordered to prepare for the contingency of war. Let no one regard this as an exercise. It is essential that all be willing to do every task carefully and thoroughly. Remember that if you fail now, you will be at the mercy of your own failure as much as the rapacity of the Mongols.

Word has been sent from K'ai-Feng and Lo-Yang that ministers from the Secretariat of Armies and Militias will visit this district during the summer on an inspection tour. Their report will determine how much aid and armed protection we will receive from the capitals. We must not let ourselves rely on the judgment of these men, for it may be that there will be others who demand more. We are an outlying district, and will not be at the highest place on their schedule of priorities.

Each fortress and stronghold should provision itself to withstand two months of summer siege. You must not assume that crops planted in spring will be harvested. Provision for livestock should be considered, and an adequate plan of evacuation of villages be drawn up. No stronghold or fortress should guarantee protection to more farmers than they can house and feed for two months. If the facilities of your stronghold or fortress are not adequate to this demand, hidden camps should be established in the mountains. If you have shepherds in your area, deal with them, and with foresters. Leave nothing to chance. Be certain that every man is aware of what he must do should the Mongols attack.

Set your smiths to your forges making pikes and spears and arrows and quarrels. Every weapon will be needed. If you command militia, take time to drill them so that they know what they must do. If you have only guardsmen, see that they are prepared for every contingency. A lax guardsman could be the ruin of a stronghold or fortress.

Those whose strongholds and fortresses guard roadways, make certain that the road is under constant guard. Unless it is impossible, find ways to make traps along the road. String wires across the road at important places, and be certain that there is someone on guard who can raise the wire to trip the horses.

Fields, too, may be given extra protection by the judicious building of traps. Concealed pits may be put around a field. That way, nothing will stop the farmers from tending their crops and livestock, but the hazard will be there for the incautious Mongol who charges the farmer. Hods may be filled with stones and placed on roofs or hillsides, and tipped over on those below.

Turn your own ingenuity to these problems, good Commanders. All of you are aware that we stand in grave peril. It is your wit and determination that will be the greatest defense we possess.

I charge each of you to send fortnightly reports to my Tribunal so that preparations and knowledge may be shared. Do not use militia or guardsmen as messengers, but select a groom or other servant who can be sent without decreasing your preparedness. If the reports are not indicative of sufficient activity, the judgment of the Tribunal will go against you, and your name and rank singled out for disgrace, here and in the capitals.

From the hand of the Scribe Keh at the order of the District Magistrate, Wu Sing-I, chief administrator of the Shu-Rh District, affixed with his chop.

5

NONE OF THE farmers looked up from their planting as T'en Chih-Yü rode by the newly turned field. The air was filled with the ripe smell of the earth, and the cool spring breeze scampered over the land like a puppy.

Saint-Germain rode beside her, his eyes moving quickly over the field and farmhouse. "They have not yet built up their fences nor finished the stockade around their houses and barns," he said to her.

"I am aware of that. I talked to Mrs. Zhie. She is the oldest member of the family. She claims that it is because they do not have sufficient wood." Her mouth set. "I will see to it that more wood is provided, and if she has another excuse, it will be necessary to order her children out of the fields until the work is done. I don't wish to do that."

"Mrs. Zhie," Saint-Germain repeated. "The names here are not like those in other regions."

Chih-Yü chuckled. "You mean that they are impossible. I agree. Do you know that the farmers in Oa-Du"—she nodded toward the road that led through the low pass to the other, smaller valley—"speak differently than they do here in So-Dui?"

"I thought it might be the case." He pulled his gray into a walk as they neared a freshened stream. "The words I have picked up confused me until I learned about the two dialects."

She was riding her bay this morning, and she reined him in by the stream, letting him lower his head to drink. "Yes, and the scholars in the capitals look down upon us because the language is so distorted. They are not willing to learn . . ." She twisted in the saddle to look at Saint-Germain. "There was a scholar here some years ago. He came to visit my father, and to make a report on the Shu-Rh District. Though he stayed at Mao-T'ou fortress for more than a year, he never bothered to learn more than a dozen words of the local dialects, and then, when he returned to Lo-Yang, he informed his superiors that the people here were unintelligent clods who were little better than cattle."

Saint-Germain said nothing, for he had heard the scholars at the university in Lo-Yang discuss their countrymen most unflatteringly. Even Kuan Sun-Sze, for all his erudition, thought of farmers, shepherds and foresters as intolerably dull, hardly more capable than the beasts and fields they tended.

"What will happen, is that the inspectors will come, very thorough and grave, most certainly, and they will listen to my reports and the reports of the other commanders in the district, and they will look at my stronghold and see nothing but the old buildings and the rough-hewn stockade, and will listen to Jui Ah, hearing only his accent and not his words. Then, having made their inspection, they will return to Lo-Yang and they will submit their report, along with fifty others, and these will be reviewed by the undersecretaries, who will add their own comments and pass them to their superiors. Eventually the secretaries themselves will read a representative selection of reports, and they will advise the Emperor and the Commanders of the Armies and the Council of Generals. And some time after that, orders will be sent out from K'ai-Feng and Lo-Yang to the garrisons, authorizing them to act in certain ways in certain areas." She had grown increasingly caustic as she spoke and her eyes traveled over the So-Dui valley with restless concern. "By that time, the Mongols may well have come and gone, and there will be nothing left here but bones and ashes."

"And you cannot form an alliance with the other Militia Commanders in the area, can you?" He could read her distress and shared it more than he wished to admit.

"Why, certainly not," she said with a bright, artificial smile. "Those who take command of armed men without the authorization of the Emperor or his duly appointed Ministers and Secretaries is considered a traitor to his country and is condemned to public dishonor and execution by the Death of a Thousand Cuts. You have to be very courageous or very desperate to risk that." She nodded toward the ridge of hills. "Two valleys away, the Mongols struck. They executed every person living on a farm and put most of the crops to the torch. Their Warlord was away and the militia had no leadership. That didn't matter, because the Mongols destroyed the fortress as well as the town."

"What would you have done?" Saint-Germain asked as he brought his gray's head up from the stream. "General She went against Imperial edict and saved most of his district . . ."

"And they killed him for it," she finished. "His integrity is most unusual, no matter what you hear about the correctness of men in high office. You know that's true."

"What would you have done?" he repeated.

"With the Mongols? What I did do, which was little. We took half of the militia to escort those few who escaped, and kept spies on the crest of the hills in order to make a full, accurate and complete report on the extent of the devastation." She turned away from the road between farms and started up the track toward the high meadows. "I have two shepherds and a forester's family to see yet before returning to Mao-T'ou stronghold. Do you mind coming with me?" Her tone, the angle of her head, the way she sat her horse showed that she was more tense than she wanted to admit. "It is peaceful here, just now, but it could all be gone in a night unless we prepare."

He favored her with a quick, sympathetic smile for her unexpected candor. "It would please me to accompany you, Warlord T'en."

She answered his smile tentatively with one of her own, then pressed her bay to a canter, sliding back in the tall saddle to force her mount to stretch as he ran. For almost two li she raced ahead of Saint-Germain, but as the path grew more narrow, she reined in, feeling the cleansing exhilaration of the speed linger with her.

The hillsides were newly green, littered with wildflowers and soft grass. It was pleasant to take the winding trail to the high meadows where the shepherds lived for the warm months. As the way diverged from the stream, it broadened out, allowing the riders to go abreast. Twice, as they reached forks in the path, Chih-Yü pointed out the correct way as they rode in companionable silence. Once, as they rounded a bend, they saw a deer standing in the way. The horses faltered and the deer, after one liquid glance, sprang noisily away through the brush.

Chih-Yü pointed toward the disappearing buck. "A good sign!" she called out to Saint-Germain, who waved to let her know he heard.

Three li farther on, they came to a clearing in which squatted a collection of twigs and wattle, like an enormous inverted bird's nest. A rickety enclosure occupied perhaps one-quarter of the meadow, and within its confines the close-cropped grass gave silent testimony that this was a sheepfold and the odd, flimsy building must be the shepherd's hut.

"He will be on the hillside at this time of day," Chih-Yü said as she drew in her bay. "He won't return until sunset. I suppose we must search for him."

Privately, Saint-Germain thought that was a fool's errand, but he said, "Where would he be, do you think? There's a great deal of hillside."

"We must try the falls first. There is a still pool beside it where the sheep will drink. Fan often takes them there." She pulled her horse up close to the hut and bent to look through the cloth-covered opening that served as a door. "He has gone for the day."

Saint-Germain shook his head, reflecting that it was less than flattering to realize that his kind shared an aversion to running water with sheep. "Then we must try the drinking pool, I suppose," he said aloud.

"Yes." Apparently she was familiar with the way, for she

headed her horse into the straggling pines, motioning Saint-Germain to follow her.

By midafternoon they had found three of the shepherds and had given them instructions. Fan and his cousin Djo took the orders well, but the old shepherd, No-ei, heard T'en Chih-Yü out grudgingly, remarking when his Warlord had finished, "It is not fitting that you should be saying such things to me. You are a woman and young; I am a man of advanced years and great experience. It is I who should lead and you who should follow."

Leaning forward in his saddle, Saint-Germain addressed the old man gently. "Shepherd No-ei, Warlord T'en is responsible for your safety, and the safety of this district, as was her father before her. Are you refusing to cooperate in her defense plans?" He was aware that he spoke the local dialect badly, but it was plain that No-ei understood him nevertheless. He scowled angrily.

"A woman and a foreigner!" the shepherd jeered. "Better Mongols than this state of affairs." He trod across T'en Chih-Yü's shadow and glared defiantly at her.

Chih-Yü reacted quickly to this insult. She reached for her scabbard, and swung it so that it caught the shepherd a sharp blow on the shoulders. "Speak such things where anyone else can hear you and I promise you, you will be flogged." She pulled her horse around. "I release the ignominious person No-ei from his obligations to the Mao-T'ou stronghold, and give him official warning now that the forces of the Mao-T'ou stronghold will not be used for his protection. Should the despicable No-ei seek refuge there, it will be denied him. Should he ask for militiamen to guard his flocks or his life, they will not be given. Should he require escort, such will not be extended to him from the Mao-T'ou stronghold. Should he be starving, injured, cold, thirsty or ill, he will not be allowed to avail himself of the assistance offered in such emergencies by the Mao-T'ou stronghold." When she had finished this formal sentencing, she turned her horse away abruptly, clapped her heels to the bay's flanks and rushed off down the hillside.

"I've rarely heard so succinct a civil excommunication," Saint-Germain said dryly in Latin to the old shepherd. He felt a touch of pity that he knew, even as he saw the horror in No-ei's squinted eyes, he could not afford. He wheeled his gray and hurried after Chih-Yü.

Fury still clouded her face when he caught up with her, and she refused to look at him. "That unconscionable old fool!" she muttered to the space between her horse's ears. "He thinks women are good for nothing but bearing children, keeping accounts and serving their husbands and sons. He should have heard my father on the subject of husbands and sons."

Saint-Germain said nothing, but he slowly pulled his gray to a trot, and Chih-Yü did the same.

"Only a reckless person lets a horse plunge down a slope the way I did," she said, chagrined, as she turned to Saint-Germain. "I should not have let that old man distress me so. He said nothing I have not heard before."

"Perhaps," Saint-Germain suggested as he watched the rutted trail winding ahead of them, "it was because you wish to defend your region, and he would not do his part, that you lashed out at him. Oh, yes," he went on quickly, "you certainly did that. He has paid dearly for his recalcitrance."

"Better that now than betrayal later." The words were harsh but her tone was colored by doubt.

"Yes," Saint-Germain agreed at once. "It isn't pleasant to condemn pigheaded old men, but you cannot expose all the others in your district to the hazard he has become. His rancor has fester too long and you can no longer change it." This was, he sensed, the only comfort she would accept from him, and he told himself that it was honest, since nothing he said distorted the truth. Yet he felt a surprising compassion for the Warlord T'en. He could hear in his thoughts the way Rogerio would upbraid him if he knew of Saint-Germain's interest in this woman, and he chuckled.

"You are amused?" Chih-Yü demanded, her ire still warm enough to give her words heat.

"By myself, T'en Chih-Yü," he said, continuing in another voice, "You wanted to speak to the forester and his family, didn't you?"

Chih-Yü glanced up at the sky. "It is getting late. I doubt we could find them before sunset. Tomorrow I will send Jui Ah to the forester."

Saint-Germain realized that was not her only reason, that she feared another encounter like the one with No-ei. Instructions from Jui Ah would be more acceptable. He looked at the branches and shadows overhead: the sun was well over his left shoulder, dropping into the western mountains.

"We've come quite a distance into the hills," he allowed, "and it is most unwise to be abroad at dusk."

"It is," she said gratefully, and gave her attention to picking a way down the slope.

They were in a rocky, shallow gully where a freshet tore at the muddy banks, when there was an unexpected sound—sharp, like a tree limb cracking, but more metallic.

Chih-Yü looked around quickly. "Where was that?"

Saint-Germain shook his head, listening. Was that a footfall? he asked himself. "Mongol scouts?" he inquired casually in the dialect of Lo-Yang.

She answered in the same. "More likely highwaymen. Scouts usually keep to the crests and ridges in order to observe as much as possible."

There was another, soft sound nearby, and Saint-Germain put his hand to his sword hilt. "I think it would be wise to take a few precautions."

"We could spur out of here," Chih-Yü suggested.

"But what's ahead? They may want us to do that, so they may drop nets over us, or trip our mounts with ropes, or ambush us from that turn in the trail." Even as he said this, he saw that the same cautions had occurred to her.

"How many do you think there are?" she went on conversationally, still speaking the dialect of the old capital.

"Four at the least," he answered, listening to the subtle signals that were hardly sounds at all. "Two on the right, two on the left. There are probably more up ahead." The tone of his voice suggested that he was discussing the weather.

"Undoubtedly," she answered, loosening her sword in its scabbard. "How soon?"

"They may be waiting for us to move." He bent in the saddle and felt for the dagger tucked into his boot.

"Then we will oblige them. I would prefer better ground than this gully if we're going to fight." The indecision had left her. It was with an effort that she kept her words sounding casual. "We will get out of this gully, and try for that glade over there. It is good footing, and it is off the trail, so that any other men will have to come through the brambles. Will your horse mind the thorns?"

Saint-Germain looked at the berry-vine thicket and raised his brows. Chih-Yü had hit upon the best delaying tactic available. Certainly men on foot would have trouble getting through that prickering, scratching wall to the glade beyond. "He won't like them, but he'll go where I tell him to."

"Excellent." There was a flush of excitement in her face and she sat straighter in the saddle. "I think the four are nearer."

"Keeping to the shadows, but nearer," Saint-Germain concurred, his penetrating eyes seeking out the forms of three of the men in the underbrush. "One of them is trying to get behind us."

"Ah?" She pulled up her reins. "Are you ready?"

"Whenever you say, Warlord." Some of her exhilaration was communicating itself to him. He gathered the reins and set his boots more firmly in the stirrups.

She gave one nod. *"Now!"* she cried, setting her bay sprinting up the bank of the gully. Mud and stones flew from the horse's feet as he gathered himself for the last surge upward. Then he bounded forward, crashing through the underbrush toward the thicket of berry vines as Chih-Yü drew her sword and gave an incoherent yell of challenge.

Saint-Germain was not far behind her. His gray, a deep-chested, long-legged mixture of Turkish and Russian breeds, had been carefully taught and responded quickly to the pressure of his master's knees. Branches whipped around them, and as they raced after Chih-Yü the thorns gouged them, but the pace did not slacken.

Behind them, the four men burst from their cover with baffled, enraged cries, and one of them ran up the track, shouting orders in a guttural tone. Now that the men were in the open, it was seen that they were highwaymen, probably former soldiers or militiamen who had deserted their companies and had taken to banditry. Two of the men had long, well-cared-for swords and a third had a pike with the handle broken off short for close combat.

"Turn!" Chih-Yü shouted as she burst through the berry vines into the glade. She had already tugged her bay around, and he was crouching low on his hind legs, his forelegs pawing the air with the strain of this sudden reversal.

The gray whinnied in dismay as Saint-Germain dragged on the rein. The horse reared, almost overbalanced, then came to stand as he had been trained to do. There was a darkening of his withers, but he had great stamina and did not pant too deeply.

"They're coming," Chih-Yü said as she brought her sword up. "When they break through the vines, charge them."

Saint-Germain nodded and drew his short sword from the scabbard on his saddle, cursing mentally the law that prohibited foreigners carrying long weapons. He touched his dagger again, to be sure he could reach it quickly.

There were cries and thrashings and the thicket of berry vines whipped in its private gale. There were loud protestations, and in a moment, legs were visible.

"Ready." Chih-Yü did not look at Saint-Germain as she gave the order: her attention was completely on the men in the berry vines.

Though it was hazardous, Saint-Germain glanced away to assure himself that the other highwaymen were not coming up on their flank, and was disquieted to see a number of crouched figures running forward.

The men broke through the berry vines and rushed forward with a shout. Chih-Yü answered this with one of her own as she dug in her heels and set her horse for the men.

Beside her, Saint-Germain did the same, raising up his sword to strike at the man carrying the long-handled pike. The curved blade sliced the air and Saint-Germain brought his sword down behind it, and had the momentary satisfaction of feeling the wooden handle crack under his blade.

Chih-Yü rode down the nearer of the highwaymen, ignoring his scream as her horse's hooves crushed his hips. She swung her sword low, taking a long swipe at the second man.

He ducked, but did not entirely avoid the cut. A red smear appeared on his shoulder and he howled with the pain of it. He could not bring his weapon up again, and knew in that instant before Chih-Yü's sword bit into his neck that he was lost.

Saint-Germain caught this exchange out of the corner of his eye and felt an odd touch of pride. Warlord T'en deserved her title, he thought as he brought his gray onto his hind legs so that he could hack down the fourth man, who had just freed himself from the thorns. He was pulling his sword out of the highwayman's shoulder when he heard another shout—a loud, harsh sound—and saw that there were more men running in from the trees.

"There!" Chih-Yü cried out, pointing with her blade. "I make it seven men."

"Seven," he agreed, wheeling the gray. He assessed the

weapons quickly, and was more concerned for the two long-handled spiked clubs, not unlike Crusader's mauls, than for the swords. A well-aimed blow from those clubs would smash bones as easily as a mallet crushed eggs. With this grim thought to spur him on, he rode toward the nearest man armed with a club.

Chih-Yü brought her arm down as she rushed two of the men, and her sword descended with inexorable deadliness. One man fell, blood fountaining from an enormous wound; the second tripped and was given a painful but relatively harmless nick on the ribs.

"Kill them! Kill them!" one of the oldest highwaymen shrieked. "Bring them down!"

One of the highwaymen, much younger than the rest, made a rush at Saint-Germain, his long cavalry sword raised over his head. Saint-Germain swung his horse away from the blow, and kicked out sharply as the youth started to turn. His booted foot caught the highwayman on the chin and snapped his head back with a crunch. The young man fell, legs splaying, and was still.

One of the highwaymen had caught hold of Chih-Yü's mount's reins and was trying to drag the horse down. Chih-Yü hacked at him, once on the face and once at the thigh, and the man collapsed, but not before his companion with a club had broken her horse's hind leg. The bay screamed and tottered.

Saint-Germain had cut down another highwayman when he heard the agonized sound of Chih-Yü's horse. He turned to see the man with the club strike again at the bay's other hind leg just as the oldest of the outlaws reached to pull Chih-Yü from the saddle. He reached into his boot scabbard and in one quick, fluid motion sent the dagger sailing to lodge high in the old man's back.

The highwayman did not even scream. His arms lifted higher; then he toppled backward just as Chih-Yü's horse fell.

Though pinned to the ground by her bay, Chih-Yü still fought. Her sword laid open the nearest man's belly while she struggled to get free of the weight of her feebly thrashing mount.

One of the highwaymen broke and fled, and at that, the others faltered. Knowing that the skirmish was almost won, Saint-Germain singled out the man with the club and rode at him. This time he did not use his sword, but in a feat of amazing strength carried the man from the ground as he passed and flung him bodily into the berry vines.

Chih-Yü had just worked her way free of her fallen horse when Saint-Germain reached her side and came out of the saddle. She gave him a long, appraising look. "Who cut you?"

Until she spoke, Saint-Germain was unaware that there was a wound on his forehead that was oozing blood. "I don't know," he said honestly as he blotted the wound with his sleeve. "It isn't serious."

"Apparently," she said, then looked down at her horse. "It's a pity," she said, before she brought her blade down to end the animal's suffering. She stood staring down at the bay as she wiped her weapon and fitted it into the scabbard.

"And you?" Saint-Germain asked when the distant look was gone from her eyes.

She shrugged. "It's senseless. There are Mongols coming to destroy us, and we must lose a good war horse to highwaymen." She glanced toward the man in the thicket, who was moaning low in his throat. "Impressive."

Saint-Germain said nothing. Her suspicion now could be fatal to him. Instead he wiped his sword on the lining of his dalmatica, then slid it into the scabbard before bending to turn the oldest highwayman over and pull the dagger from his back.

"You've fought before," Chih-Yü said when she realized he would not speak to her.

"I have." Unbidden, the memories came. He felt the futility of it, as he so often did now.

"In the West."

"Yes." He had put the dagger back in its boot sheath. "Will you ride behind me?" he asked.

"I haven't much choice," she said wearily; then her expression changed. "I did not expect something like this to happen. I would have brought armed militiamen with me if I thought we were likely to be attacked."

"Perhaps it was not quite as simple as it seems," Saint-Germain suggested gently as he brought the gray up to her.

Her eyes held his, each with their dark brightness. "You mean No-ei may have sent them word? . . ."

"It is one possibility. There are apt to be Mongol scouts in the area as well." He offered her his joined hands, and tossed her up onto the gray's back behind the saddle.

Once again she studied him. "You are stronger than I thought," she said to him as he mounted.

He nodded, replying carefully, "Those of my blood are noted for strength."

After a moment of hesitation, she put her arms around his waist as the gray set out through the whispering forest. She was silent until the track to the Mao-T'ou stronghold was reached, and then she spoke softly to him. "When I hired you in Lo-Yang, I thought you were a very poor bargain, but I knew I had to return with someone, or everyone here would lose heart. I was, I think, more fortunate than I knew when you agreed to come here."

Saint-Germain could not quite smile. "You honor me, Warlord T'en."

"I wonder," she said, then lapsed into silence again as they made their way toward her stronghold.

———◆———

A letter from Kuan Sun-Sze in Lo-Yang to Saint-Germain at Mao-T'ou stronghold.

In the fortnight of a Thousand Blossoms, in the Year of the Ox, the Fourteenth Year of the Sixty-fifth Cycle, to the learned foreigner Shih Ghieh-Man at the Mao-T'ou stronghold in the Shu-Rh District:

Though it is always a pleasure to remember the affection of those we respect, yet on this occasion I would wish that my reasons for sending this message were only those of friendship, but sadly, this is not so.

I have been thinking back with pleasure to the many hours I have spent in your company, of the long and erudite conversations we have shared and of your courtesy and distinction. Therefore it is doubly hard for me to write to you now and inform you of what transpired here eight days ago.

The temper of the city has been uncertain, for there are disturbing reports and even more disturbing rumors circulating regarding the Mongol forces. It has been said that Temujin's men have conquered far more territory than the Ministry of War will admit. If this is so, then we are most surely lost, for what we have heard is bad enough. I am telling you this so that you will understand how events have come about here, and realize that it was not you but your foreignness that provoked the students and soldiers.

As I read this, I see I am trying to postpone the moment of telling you, and that is a disservice to you and the friendship we have shared to do so. Very well, then: eight days ago, a mob numbering several hundred, mostly students and soldiers from the local garrison, maddened by the latest report of heavy losses in the north, went rampaging through Lo-Yang, destroying all that was foreign. It gives me great pain to inform you that your compound suffered greatly at the hands of these distraught men. Your gates were torn open and many of your belongings were ruined. Those that were not, I am sending to you with two university messengers to guard them and a formal decree that exempts them from seizure. Most of what survived are Chinese works of art. There are two jade lions, one large silk hanging, which is a little singed in one corner, a number of ceramic pieces, all but one of your collection of musical instruments—I fear that your bowed lyre did not survive the wrath of the students. There are also your supplies from your laboratory. The walls there were very stout and the students and soldiers did not trouble themselves to destroy that side wing of the house. That lantern in the main hall, the one I have admired so often—that was pounded out of shape and given to the metal workers in Street of the Blind Poet.

The officers of the Tribunal did not arrive in time to save the central part of the house, but contained the fires before they spread. The August Magistrates have issued a formal statement of condemnation for the barbarity of the acts of the students and soldiers, and will in time, they assure me, present you with a proper apology and restitution for the damage done.

Most of the supplies in your laboratory will be held here for you, but I have arranged to have the four metal chests sent with your belongings, as well as the two foreign chests of compounds and such supplies. I took the liberty of examining the metal chests to be certain they had not been rifled, as a number of your chests and cases were, and found that they contained earth. I recall that you explained to me once that you have long been convinced that earth has certain properties that are not fully understood and appreciated. I thought at the time you might be involved in experimentation with those properties of earth, but we did not pursue the matter. I trust now that you will forgive me if I ask to be kept abreast of your experiments so that I may apply what you discover to my own study. As you may recall, I told you that since many insects live underground, I have often thought that the earth in some unknown way nurtures them.

There, you must forgive me. I have had the audacity to make a request of you at the very moment I am telling you of your own great loss. I would understand if you chose not to reply to this letter, or to communicate with me again, for though I have long admired you and taken pride in the honor of your friendship, yet, when it was put to the test, I failed you. Will you, of your compassion, pardon me for this? Your generosity would lighten the burden I carry on my conscience, but there is no reason you should extend it to me. Do as you think best, Shih Ghieh-Man, and I will accept your decision as just.

Written by my own hand, and delivered by the officers of the Lo-Yang tribunal, to the foreigner Shih Ghieh-Man at the Mao-T'ou stronghold of the Warlord T'en Chih-Yü in the Shu-Rh District.

Kuan Sun-Sze
Master, University of Lo-Yang

6

SMOKE HUNG over the ridge and the stench of burning filled the air. Saint-Germain stood on the newly constructed ramparts and watched the flat, brassy sky as the smoke trailed across it.

"Any sign?" the gatekeeper called up to him from his post below.

"Not yet," he answered, a frown darkening his face.

"It's early," the gatekeeper said by way of consolation. "Hardly past noon. Jui Ah told us that the troops wouldn't be back until nightfall."

If they're back at all, Saint-Germain thought as he said, "Warlord T'en planned to be off the field by sunset at the latest" to the gatekeeper.

It was a hot day, though not with the thick, drumming heat of high summer. The air was clear, shimmering in the distance, and the gravel in the newly dug trench around the Mao-T'ou stronghold gave back a hard shine where the sun struck them.

"When do you get your relief?" the gatekeeper asked. Saint-Germain had been on the walls of the stronghold since the militia had ridden out shortly after sunrise.

"When the Warlord returns," he answered distantly, watching the smoke smudge the metallic face of the sun. He braced one arm against the hewn logs of the stockade and stared at the distant ridge.

"Now you don't want to fret," the gatekeeper said a little later. He spoke with a soldier's dialect and found it easy to understand the cultured, academic words Saint-Germain used.

It was an effort for Saint-Germain to wrench his attention from the tallest part of the slope to the squat man with white hair and eyes raisin-dark. "I wish I had been allowed to ride with them," he said, knowing that there was also within him a reprehensible sense of relief. "They have said that they will not fight with a foreigner."

"So they have," the gatekeeper agreed. "Don't think too harshly of them. Those militiamen aren't like real soldiers. They see very little of the world. Now, when I was in the army, there was this Tartar fellow, tall, ugly brute and spoke the language worse than a Hang-Chow prostitute, but what a fighter he was! Every man in the company loved him for his bravery and his good sense. But none of the militiamen here would have agreed to go into battle beside him, and that would be their error. You can't let Jui Ah upset you. That's what he's trying to do. It's the Warlord you're here to serve, not that fellow. You ought to remember that." While he spoke, a servant had brought him a bowl of food—a cereal paste with bits of pork and mutton stirred into it. He dipped his fingers into this and glanced up at Saint-Germain again. "It's barley today," he remarked. "Sure you don't want some?"

Half-annoyed and half-relieved by the gatekeeper, Saint-Germain did not answer at once. "Hsing will tend to that later," he said after a silence.

"Now, there's a pleasant thought for a man. That Hsing. What thighs." He paused to gobble more of the barley-and-meat mixture. "Were I a younger man, I'd be jealous of you, but at my age . . ."

Saint-Germain's features were unreadable. "I am not a young man, gatekeeper."

"Oh, not a youth, surely," the gatekeeper said sagely. "But all I have to do is look at you to know that there are fires in you that were extinguished in me years ago." He gave a philosophical gesture and finished his meal.

"I might surprise you," Saint-Germain said lightly, but felt a grim certainty. He stared out at the ridge and saw that there was more smoke. He could smell it on the wind, a charred odor that tainted the clean smells that promised summer. As he watched the spread of gray and brown over the sky, he tried to distract his thoughts with a catalog of Hsing's beauty. She was the most shapely woman he had seen at the Mao-T'ou stronghold, and none of the farmers had any wives or daughters like her. She was, he surmised, the offspring of one of General T'en's concubines. How did Chih-Yü feel about this half-sister? he wondered, but had no answer.

Slowly the smoke obliterated the sun.

Hsing, Saint-Germain reminded himself with an angry desperation as he kept his eyes on the ridge, was oddly complacent, almost bored. She would lie beside him, wholly self-absorbed as he excited her with the full range of his skills. She would close her eyes, going into herself so completely that Saint-Germain was almost certain she did not know when he had taken his pleasure of her. For Hsing, it was not a thing to be shared.

The afternoon was still, and the wind had fallen, but the smoke hung on the air, acrid, poisonous, drifting more slowly now and spreading its blackness over the sky.

Some little time later there was a fluttering movement at the crest of the hill, and Saint-Germain straightened up, his eyes slits as he strove to make out what was approaching. He moved along the narrow catwalk his gaze never leaving the distant ridge. He was alert now, and oddly feral. His black, steel-studded pelisse was Frankish and the black coxalia that clung to his legs were Byzantine; his only concession to Chinese fashion was his thick-soled boots. He had got used to hearing the whispers about his manners and dress and no longer worried when one of the militiamen regarded him with contempt.

"What's happening?" the gatekeeper called up.

"Riders," Saint-Germain said tersely.

"How many?" There was ill-concealed anxiety in the man's voice, for there were only ten militiamen in the stronghold, and if the riders were Mongols, there was not enough time to muster a makeshift defense.

"I can see twenty, perhaps more." He concentrated, damning the smoke that had turned the light ruddy and brought its own shadow to the hills.

"Any indications . . .?"

". . . that they're ours? No." His eyes were stinging, but he continued to search the distant figures in the hope of discovering their identity. "Perhaps you'd better warn the others?" he suggested, and did not look to see whether or not the gatekeeper obeyed him. He gripped the rough timbers of the wooden ramparts, ignoring the splinters that sank into his hands. Who was coming. What had happened. The words sounded in his mind in a dozen languages, and he refused to think of the number of times he had waited to learn what had become of his companions. He wished he had a clarion to signal the approaching men, yet knew that even if he had one, neither Chih-Yü nor her men were familiar with its call.

The few militiamen who had been left behind hurried toward the battlements, one of them pausing to take a stirrup crossbow from its place on the wall.

"I would like to have some artillery," one of the militiamen muttered as he set up his standing quiver where he could reach his arrows without turning away from the walls.

"Get the women into the main buildings," the gatekeeper shouted as he hurried across the courtyard. "Children in the cellars until we know who's coming!"

There was swift, frenzied movement as the people of Mao-T'ou stronghold hastened to carry out his orders.

Saint-Germain was aware of the activity, but he did not allow it to divert his attention. He could see the figures more plainly now, though the distant roiling smoke made everything indistinct. He wiped at his eyes as if to clear the air by this action. "Move, move," he whispered tightly as the mounted figures came over the crest of the hill and the men on the ramparts were readying their weapons. The extent of his relief as he recognized the chestnut roan Chih-Yü had been riding that morning was greater than a sense of good fortune for the Mao-T'ou stronghold.

"Hold!" he shouted to the militiamen, who turned to him in suspicion and surprise. "It's T'en Chih-Yü. That's Jui Ah on the dun. See?" Saint-Germain pointed at the figures, who were now becoming separate from the smoke. They no longer looked like wraiths of darkness, but like what they were—an exhausted militia troop returning with casualties to their base.

"It is the Warlord!" one of the men on the ramparts agreed, shocked, and turned to the man next to him in amazement. "They've made it back."

"Open the gates!" Saint-Germain ordered, and no one thought it strange that he was obeyed at once.

Even as the huge wooden bolt was being lifted, Saint-Germain was climbing to the lookout tower, which had only recently been completed. The last part of it was unfinished, but it gave him a better view of the ridge. He glared toward the smoke, beyond the company T'en Chih-Yü led, fearing to see armed men on squat Mongol ponies racing after them. He watched until he could hear the sound of approaching horses, and was assured. There were no Mongols in pursuit this day. Later it might be otherwise, but for now the militiamen of Mao-T'ou stronghold and their Warlord were out of immediate danger.

The gates groaned open, and shortly afterward, Chih-Yü led her men through them to be greeted by shouts from her guards.

Saint-Germain stayed by the watchtower and looked down into the courtyard.

Chih-Yü's face was darkened with smuts, as were all her men's faces. Her sheng me was torn and her scale armor had several leaf-shaped scales missing. There was blood on her left leg and boot and she had a makeshift bandage around her right hand. As the gatekeeper rushed up to her, she slid out of the saddle.

The gatekeeper looked about in consternation, starting to motion for assistance, but faster than he could act, Saint-Germain vaulted down from his position by the watchtower, landing close enough to her chestnut roan to make the horse whinny and rear.

The militiamen stared at him in awe, and a few made gestures to protect themselves. Jui Ah, who had started toward Chih-Yü cursed and turned to shout orders to the men.

Chih-Yü was already getting to her feet. "What a silly thing to do," she remarked in a shaky voice. "I've been in the saddle too long, I think." She glanced around at the waiting faces—at her troops, who were exhausted, some wounded; at the gatekeeper, who regarded her anxiously; and at Saint-Germain, who stood near her, one hand extended to help her up. "Shih Ghieh-Man," she said, puzzled. "I didn't see you before."

"He jumped from up there . . ." the gatekeeper said, and for the first time seemed aware of the extraordinary thing the foreigner had done.

"Western circus tricks," Saint-Germain said with a shrug of dismissal. He salved his conscience with the admission that it was a circus trick, one he had seen done for the first time in the Circus Maximus when Claudius had ruled in Rome.

"Impressive, nonetheless," Chih-Yü said as she gave him her unbandaged hand and let him pull her up. "I'm famished. My legs feel like lead. My throat is raw from the smoke and the shouting. Have someone prepare my bath and heat up the bathhouse for the rest. We'll need treatment for nine of my men. Two did not come back." This last was said quietly, painfully, and she looked away.

"That's most fortunate," Saint-Germain said quickly, and looked to the others for confirmation. "To lose so few."

"There were men from Shui-Lo fortress there, as well," Jui Ah announced. He swaggered as he got off his horse, parading for the benefit of those who had stayed behind to guard Mao-T'ou stronghold.

"There were more than a hundred of them," Chih-Yü said, silencing her Captain. "They were well-mounted and better armed. Tan Mung-Fa told me he has persuaded his uncle in the Ministry of War to address the Emperor on his behalf, which apparently he did, because at least half his men wore the badge of the Imperial household." She could not quite stop her sigh.

"Then Tan Mung-Fa will have informed the Emperor how it is with us, and your petition will be heard," Jui Ah declared with satisfaction, looking to the other men to give him their support.

One of the injured men screamed as he reached the ground. Until he had dismounted he had not been aware of the severity of his wounds, but the agony hit him at once, and half a dozen of his fellows rushed to his aid.

"Tan Mung-Fa is for later," Chih-Yü said crisply, seeming more herself again. "Get the surgeon out here and tell him to start to work on those who are wounded. When he is through with them, I'd like him to look at my hand."

The others were already moving to carry out her orders as Saint-Germain asked her softly, "Would you like me to examine your hand? I know a little of medicine."

"You do?" She was startled, but just for an instant. "Of course you do. You're an alchemist." With a jerk of her other hand she tore away the bandage. "I got my knuckles grazed," she said, feeling ashamed.

Saint-Germain looked at the caked blood and torn skin. "This must be cleaned first. Afterward I will give you a powder that will take away the sting and will keep the flesh from corruption. If you will allow me."

"Certainly," she said, then turned to the others. "After the evening meal, I will want to speak to all of you in the main hall. We must set our strategy now, or we'll be in as much danger as Bei-Wa was. And all of you saw that fortress burn." The stern set of her face and the clipped words gave emphasis to her orders. Her men would be there in the main hall after their evening meal. "I will also want a complete report on all injuries, no matter how slight. Let no man think he is showing heroism if he makes light of his hurts, for that will make you a danger to all of the rest of us." She looked toward her stablehands. "I will want to know how all the horses are. Be as honest as you can be. If a horse is not fit for riding, tell me so." When she had received an acknowledging wave from the oldest groom, she looked again at Saint-Germain. "Very well. Give me a little time to bathe and I will join you in your quarters."

"Thank you," he responded, making no attempt to conceal his admiration for her.

"And if you indeed have such a powder as you described, make certain that the surgeon has it. I can't afford to have one man sicken." She nodded to Saint-Germain as she turned and strode across the courtyard. Two women stood at the door waiting to assist her and holding a cloak for her.

Saint-Germain made his way through the confusion in the courtyard to the two new buildings that squatted next to the wall on the cliff side of the stronghold. They were incongruous here, looking very much the afterthought they were. The door of the larger building opened as Saint-Germain approached and Rogerio stood aside to let his master enter the alchemical laboratory housed there.

"The troops are back," Saint-Germain said in Latin as he closed the door. "They did not do badly, all things considered." He crossed the room to a locked chest, which he opened as he spoke. "Here. This is the burn dressing, and these"—he gave Rogerio two glass vials of greenish-white powder—"are for the surgeon to treat open wounds. For the love of all the forgotten gods, don't tell him it is made from moldy bread or he won't touch it."

Rogerio held the containers in his hands. "How long will it be, do you think, before they strike here?" He had the appearance of middle age and his sandy hair was streaked with gray. When attending to the laboratory, he wore a Roman tunica of heavy linen, but when among the Chinese, he put a blue quilted cotton coat over his Western garments.

"It's hard to say," Saint-Germain said, only one faint line between his fine brows showing his concern. "Perhaps longer than we know. I would guess that they're trying to get to Lan-Chow, and won't bother too much with little strongholds like this one. If they can cut off these isolated outposts, they will fall more easily at the end of the harvest." He pulled open another drawer in the chest. "Take these, too," he added, handing Rogerio two rolls of linen bandages. "I doubt they have enough in reserve."

"And have we?" Rogerio asked with more concern than condemnation.

"For the moment. A few more skirmishes and most of my medicaments will be low, but that's to be expected." He paused as he reached for one more roll. "Do you remember that battle in Thessaly? Niklos Aulurios almost lost the day. We were pulling our garments to pieces to help the wounded, but it was senseless." There was a haunted look in his face. "Niklos was a fool to battle those Huns. He's a brave man."

"You disapprove of his bravery?" Rogerio asked, started. "You, of all people?"

Saint-Germain laughed sadly. "No. Not of bravery. But the suffering. You'd think the demons of the air would be glutted by now." He closed the case sharply. "Forgive me, old friend. I wish that . . ." A despairing gesture finished his thoughts. "Warlord T'en is coming here when she has bathed. Her hand is hurt and I've offered to dress it for her."

Rogerio stared at Saint-Germain a moment. "Warlord T'en is also a very brave woman," he said at last.

There was real pain in Saint-Germain's face as he said quietly, "I know. I know. And I fear for her."

Wisely, Rogerio said no more, but took the medicaments and bandages Saint-Germain had given him and went in search of the surgeon.

By the time Chih-Yü arrived, Saint-Germain had mastered himself. There was no trace of the bleakness that possessed his soul as he opened the door for her, going on his knee to her in the Frankish manner as she entered his quarters.

Though she was tired, she was able to smile at this courtesy. "I thank you for whatever honor it is you do me," she said as Saint-Germain rose once more. "You look quite . . . splendid."

He had dressed for her in full Byzantine finery, in damasked silk robes with silver embroidery and a wide jeweled collar. His short, loose curls were perfumed with a distillate of roses and jasmine. He took her unhurt hand, bent and kissed it. He was amused to see how his finery puzzled her. "Come," he said as he led her into the reception chamber.

The room was not very big and so it had been carefully furnished. There were two low couches of Persian design, covered in black velvet embroidered with silver, and it was to one of these that Saint-Germain brought T'en Chih-Yü. Between the couches there was a matching table of inlaid rosewood, and against the wall stood a red-painted Roman chest of antique design. It was the chest that Saint-Germain approached, and opened to reveal a number of pigeonholes, some filled with scrolls, some with sealed vials. He took one of the latter and came back toward Chih-Yü.

"I did not know your tastes were so fine," Chih-Yü said, at once nervous and critical.

"When you have traveled as far as I have, Warlord, you learn to love beautiful things wherever you find them." He dropped to his knee again, but this time his purpose was more pragmatic. "Let me see your hand," he said.

She hesitated, then held it out. "It's getting stiff," she told him, as if confessing a moral weakness.

"Small wonder." He examined the torn knuckles and realized that though the tendons were bruised and the skin lacerated, none of the bones were damaged, and the tendons would recover. "How did it happen?"

Chih-Yü raised her chin defiantly and met his dark, compelling eyes. "It was a stupid mistake. If my father were alive and had seen it, he would have boxed my ears for such an error. I tried to block a blow with the hilt of my sword."

"You're lucky, then," he said sincerely, knowing full well what a chance she had taken. "If the blow had been harder, you might have lost your fingers."

"I said it was a stupid mistake." She was defensive now, and her hand stiffened in his.

He had drawn a cloth and a roll of linen bandage from one of the capacious pockets in his robe, and he released her hand to open a little jar that stood on the table. He moistened the cloth with the liquid in the jar. "This will probably sting, but it will clean the scrape. After that, I will apply the powder I mentioned, and then wrap your hand in clean linen." As he said this, he drew the cloth over her hand.

"It does sting," she admitted, her eyes watering. "What is it?"

"A distillate," he answered truthfully and uninformatively. "It's been known to alchemists for several centuries." When he was through, he set the cloth aside and opened the vial he had taken from the chest. "This is the powder."

"My surgeon said that you sent a supply of it to him. I am grateful." The muscle in her jaw stood out and her face had lost color.

"It was your request, Warlord," he murmured, his attention on her hand. He worked swiftly, sprinkling the powder thickly, then wrapping the linen strips skillfully before the powder could be shaken off. When he was through, he was reluctant to relinquish her hand.

Chih-Yü was staring at her hand. "You did that well," she said after a moment.

"I have done it before," he replied with quiet sorrow. He released her hand and rose to his feet.

"Ghieh-Man," Chih-Yü said swiftly, her other hand going out to detain him. "Wait. I would like to talk with you."

He looked down at her, at her strong, exhausted face. "Very well." He took his place on the couch opposite her.

Now that he had consented, she found it difficult to begin. "I wished you to know . . . that it wasn't my choice . . . that you be excluded today. It's my men . . . They won't ride with foreigners. They believe that outlanders bring bad luck. I couldn't overrule them. Not with what we had to do today." She was not precisely pleading with him, but there was a note in her voice that touched him.

"Chih-Yü," he said gently, stopping her, "I'm aware of how your men feel about me. I don't blame you for deciding to respect their . . . superstitions. They are the ones who can defend this stronghold. I must also let you know that I am not anxious to ride into battle again. Too many years of my life have been spent among the slain." It was difficult for him to say the last, but he knew that he owed her his honesty, if nothing else.

"Then you have been in battle before?"

"Many times," he said, his thoughts turning unbidden to his youth, to the last, doomed defense of his homeland, to the Chaldean slave market and the brand that was now little more than a pucker of skin on his arm, to the long, intolerable hours facing the chariots of Sesostris, of the Assyrians, the Mesopotamians, the Medes . . . He blinked, appalled.

"Ghieh-Man, what troubles you?" Chih-Yü's voice was almost shrill as she stared at him.

"Memories," he said sardonically. "They're behind me. Don't concern yourself." He wanted to banish the images that had risen in his mind, so he leaned toward Chih-Yü and touched her undamaged hand across the rosewood table.

"It can be terrible to remember," she said with genuine sympathy. "I do not wish to remember today, but I think it will be long before I am free of it."

His dark eyes filled with compassion as he listened to her; his hand tightened on hers.

"I do not know how it is among foreigners, but it is not appropriate for you to . . ." She looked at her hand in his, though she made no effort to withdraw it, and her protestation had little conviction.

"I am more foreign than you know," he responded, opening his hand so that her fingers lay on his palm. "My ways are not your ways." He had said that so many times before, and every time he felt the full impact of his isolation once again. He got hastily to his feet. "I will not apologize to you, Chih-Yü, for I feel no shame in my desires. But perhaps it would be best if you leave me now." His dark eyes lingered on her face, seeking some clue to her emotions.

"I also feel no shame," she said calmly as she rose. "I feel only gratitude—"

"Gratitude!" he repeated, exasperated.

"—and curiosity. There are many things I must consider before I speak to you privately again." She stood and met his look with frank appraisal. "Hsing reports to me, and I have much to ponder. Surely you will allow this person some little time to examine her heart."

He nodded, and did not wish to remind her that little time was all they had. When he bowed to her this time it was in the Chinese manner, and he spoke with the same formality that Chih-Yü had employed. "This person will welcome anything that the distinguished Warlord T'en grants him, though it be no more than the dust of the road."

Chih-Yü laughed as she left the room.

———— ◆▶ ————

A letter from Mei Sa-Fong to the Nai Yung-Ya in Lan-Chow.

In the fortnight of Evening Heat in the Year of the Ox, the Fourteenth Year of the Sixty-fifth Cycle, the one thousand two hundred seventeenth year of Our Lord, to the Pope Nai Yung-Ya and congregation in Lan-Chow.

Greetings from Mei Sa-Fong:

Our party has reached K'ai-Feng and have been received with poor grace by the congregation here, though we have presented our introductions. The Pope here has explained that with the constant worry about the invading Mongols, there is no time to deal with other Christians. All three of us were disappointed, and my sister took one of the elders of this church aside and told him that she felt he had betrayed the trust put in us by the master. I attempted to rebuke her for this, but I must admit that my feelings were much the same as hers, and I could not be too harsh with her, which may be to my discredit, but for which I cannot apologize.

It is true enough that the Mongols present an increasing danger to the northeastern regions, though some raids have been reported in the west. Some have said that the Mongol triumphs may be laid at the foot of the Dragon Throne, for the Emperor has shown himself reluctant to act at a time when such indecision would be the greatest folly. But it is not for me to judge him, and I must not allow the poor opinion of others to cloud my perceptions.

Tomorrow morning my sister, Chung-La, and I will leave for Hang-Chow in the south, and from there will board a ship bound for Tien-Du. We have been assured that the trading continues at the usual level and that it will not be difficult for us to secure passage. Our funds have been guarded well, and we do not require any additional aid, though it was a disappointment that the Christian community here could not give us more assistance. We will leave a copy of our plans with the congregation here, but I must caution you to guard this letter well, for I doubt that the Christians of K'ai-Feng will go to much trouble to preserve my message.

We will send another message from the coast before we embark for Tien-Du, to provide you with the name of the ship and its captain, as well as the various ports of call expected. That way, should there be any important news to send you, you will already know from where to expect my letters. I feel I should warn you that the time between writing and delivery will grow longer and longer. This should not distress you, but rather be taken as a sign of our success. Think of the delay as a good indication that God favors our venture.

In the name of the Master we ask that you remember us in your hearts and your prayers, that we may have a swift and calm journey, and an uneventful passage home.

By my own hand at midday in the Church of Evange-
lists.

Mei Sa-Fong

7

SHU-RH'S District Tribunal had been moved to the city of
Bei-Wah after Mongols had burned Shu-Rh to the ground
two years before. The new location was more remote and
Bei-Wah less than half the size of Shu-Rh, and the buildings
that housed the tribunal were little more than huts, yet the
District Magistrate Wu Sing-I was dressed with the same
formality he wore at the Imperial Court. He sat at his official
desk with writing tools laid out before him, and gazed at the
five men and one woman before him.

"Magistrate," the oldest man said, "it was you who summoned us. Perhaps you will tell us why." He was in his early
forties, but his seamed and weathered face looked older and
his voice was gruff from the shouting of orders.

Wu Sing-I stared down at his folded hands, and his expression was so somber that the six were silent. "I have had
word from Lo-Yang and K'ai-Feng. It has been decided by
the Secretariat that outlying districts, such as this one, will receive only minimal support from the army so that the bulk of
the strength can be sent to recapture Pei-King." When he finished, he closed his eyes a moment from the shame he felt.

"Recapture Pei-King?" Tan Mung-Fa of the Shui-Lo
fortress stared at the others. He was not yet thirty and his
highly placed relatives at Court had seen to it that he learned
better manners than might be expected of a provincial Warlord.

"That's insane," Shao Ching-Po said, his hand going to the
hilt of his sword. "Pei-King is already lost. We must defend
our own lands if they're not to fall to the Mongols. Hasn't
the Ministry of War made any assessments of the situation?"

"They say they have," Wu Sing-I murmured, looking at
Shao Ching-Po with unnatural calm.

"When? Where? Who decided?" Tan Mung-Fa demanded,
his excellent manners forgotten. "I don't believe that could
happen. I've already got fifty men on loan from the Imperial
army . . ."

"And you are requested to send them back," Wu Sing-I said heavily. "Word came yesterday that the men are expected to join the assault on Temujin's northeastern base this autumn."

Tan Mung-Fa was speechless. He turned to Shao Ching-Po and made a gesture of helplessness.

"They've decided that we're expendable," Shao Ching-Po said quietly and looked toward the oldest of them. "You, Kung. How does it seem to you?"

The old Warlord nodded. "It seems that we are being abandoned for no sensible reason. But it would not appear sensible to us, would it? Considering our position." He put his hands on his hips. "Wu, did you know nothing of this?"

Wu Sing-I put his hands to his eyes. "After Shu-Rh fell, I was certain that we would get help, and so I didn't do everything I might have. I let two army captains make decisions and waited for them to tell the Ministry what was required. I sent a report, of course, but I didn't make the additional effort. It was wrong of me. I should have traveled to Lo-Yang myself and seen to it that all was properly done. I realize that. I have rebuked myself every hour since the message arrived." He fell silent and could not meet the eyes of the warlords.

Hua Djo-Tung, who had been standing somewhat apart, now strode up to the Magistrate's desk. "You are telling us that your stupidity has brought us to this?"

"I? No," Wu began, then stopped. "I must be telling you that. This wholly inferior person begs the Warlords to recognize that he was not in the best position to pursue their interests when it would have been helpful." This lapse into formal speech brought a mutter of protest from the others, though Hua seemed pleased with it.

"Is there no one to whom we can appeal?" the fifth man, Suh Son-Tai asked, though it was obvious from his stance that he had little hope for a positive answer.

"Not in time," Wu Sing-I said flatly. His eyes were lifeless as stones and his face was almost the color of millet. "When I understood what had happened, I tried to contact other officials, but the decisions had already been made, and there was no one who would appeal to the Emperor on our behalf."

Hua Djo-Tung folded his heavy arms and looked at the others. "Do any of the rest of you have access to the Dragon Throne? Tan, do you?"

Tan Mung-Fa looked embarrassed. "I can reach my relatives, but I don't know if they would be able to speak to the Emperor. It isn't easy to do these things, you know," he added petulantly, glaring at Hua. "My Shui-Lo is the easternmost fortress of this district, and for that reason it might be argued that if there are to be soldiers given us, that they come to me, because the Mongols are more likely to strike on the east. If this cannot prevail with the Ministers of War, then I don't know what it would take to convince the Emperor."

Shao Ching-Po snorted. "The Mongols did not burn your valley last month, they burned one of mine. And I am not the easternmost fortress of the district, I am only Warlord of the stronghold on the Tsi-Gai pass, like T'en here." He gave a tentative smile to Chih-Yü. He was the first to speak to her since Wu Sing-I had brought them into the Tribunal. "Your militiamen were a great help," he added.

T'en Chih-Yü's eyes showed her gratitude, but she said in her clipped, unfeminine way, "It wasn't enough to save the valley, however. And if Tan Mung-Fa had not brought his soldiers, I doubt my men and I could have done much for you."

Shao obviously disliked Tan, and could not resist saying, "You made it possible for us to evacuate the farms and to save half the livestock. That is practical help, the sort all of us will need before the end of summer." His family was as old as T'en's, having been part of the martial nobility for more than four hundred years: newcomers like Tan, whose family had been ennobled a mere hundred fifty years before, were not worthy of his consideration and praise.

Tan Mung-Fa smarted under Shao's remarks. He was well aware of his family's status and it infuriated him. With deceptive pleasantness he turned to T'en Chih-Yü. "It was a terrible thing for your father to do, to make you into a soldier, but I know how these old families can be—stuck in the past and unwilling to change. He probably didn't care that no decent man would marry you, or that you would be the laughingstock of the capitals."

It was the wrong thing to say. Chih-Yü fought the urge to draw her sword on this smiling young man, and instead clenched her teeth. "This person was honored by her father, who entrusted his lands and his militiamen to her because he knew she would be able to carry out the trust that has been placed in our family and the Mao-T'ou stronghold for seven-

teen generations. This person bears her rank and her responsibilities with humble pride, and will demonstrate her
devotion on the battlefield alone, if that is required of her."
She was startled to see that though Shao and Hua were
smiling at her, and Kung was nodding approval, both Tan
and Suh were affronted by her manner and her words.

"Warlords," Wu Sing-I interjected somewhat belatedly, "be
more attentive, I ask you. Since there is little reason to hope
for Imperial assistance, it falls to us to find our own defenses."

"And what should we do?" Suh asked contemptuously.

While Wu's folded hands tightened on the desk so that his
knuckles were white, Chih-Yü spoke again. "I have hired an
alchemist . . ." The derision this announcement brought did
not stop her. "He is an excellent man, a foreigner, and not so
caught in tradition that he cannot see ways to improve our
fortifications. There is a deep gravel-lined trench around
Mao-T'ou stronghold, and our outer walls have been greatly
reinforced. Traps have been laid and we have built a sluice
that will allow us to flood the trench on short notice. This alchemist had made caltrops and arrowheads from new alloys,
and is working with my armorer to improve the range of our
bows. All these are little things, I grant you, and less desirable than a garrison of the Imperial army, but I would rather
have this than do nothing, I would rather have my trench and
my arrowheads than to waste the days wondering how to approach the Imperial Court in the hope that the Emperor
might eventually give our district a few moments of his attention."

"Excellent," Shao said quietly. "You put the rest of us to
shame," he added with a meaningful glance at Tan.

"What about your livestock and farmers?" Hua Djo-Tung
put in. "Around my fortress we have nineteen separate farm-
holds, and there is not enough room in the fortress for all of
them. The farmers would resist the idea of traps, for what
would keep their goats and pigs from straying into them? Not
that I fault you at all, Warlord T'en. You have done more
than the rest of us, it would seem. Your stronghold is on a
ridge, is it not? Mine is at the head of a lake. Your methods
are most praiseworthy, but how may I adapt them?"

Chih-Yü knew that Hua Djo-Tung was saying this for her
benefit as much as for any information he might gain. She
smiled slightly at the burly Warlord as she gathered her

thoughts. "You say you are at the head of a lake. Then it would be an easy matter to surround your fortress with water, with one or two bridges leading to your gates. Such defenses are used for Imperial castles, why not for a district fortress? You have seen the raised bridges of those castles. Make them for your own. I will ask my alchemist to send your armorer some of the alloy he has provided, if he has any to spare. It is unfortunate, but it cannot be made quickly or in great quantity."

"Anything is welcome," Hua said eagerly, "but it should be distributed throughout the district. To those who want it," he added with a sidelong glance at Suh and Tan.

Suh was quick to take offense. "You, Kung, are you going to stand for what these men are saying, and this frightful girl?"

The disquiet that had whispered in the back of Chih-Yü's mind now grew loud. She looked at the five men, seeing the canny experience of Kung, the steadfast strength of Shao, the ambition of Tan, the independence of Hua, the hostility of Suh. She could not bring herself to look at Magistrate Wu, for she could feel the gelid despair that engulfed him. There are only six of us, she thought, and Temujin commands thousands. Her face was set as she spoke. "We cannot afford pettiness, Warlords. For our little strengths are nothing in the face of the Mongol armies. Which of us could meet his ancestors and expect their approbation if we fail now, and leave our people and our district open to the predation of Temujin?"

"Fine speeches," Suh scoffed, looking toward Tan for help.

Kung Szei regarded his comrades. "I am appalled that any of you would be willing to reject any help at this time. I hear you bicker and I am covered with shame for you." He fingered his long braided beard. "For as long as I've been entitled to wear a helmet, I've made a point of listening to every opinion offered, and making the most realistic decisions I could. That is why I am forty-three and still alive. I listen to you and I fear for all this district."

At that, Tan's face darkened and he glared at the oldest man. "I assume it is your intention to insult me with these words, Kung?"

"Don't be an idiot," Shao said quietly, attempting to divert the young man. "He's perfectly right, you know. He is the oldest and we should all be giving him our full and respectful attention, in order to benefit from his experience."

From his place at the desk, the Magistrate Wu Sing-I looked up at last. "We need order," he said in a tired voice. "There are things we must plan now. Warlord T'en is right about that."

The six Warlords were surprised to hear the Magistrate speak up. They turned to him as a group and watched as the gaunt man got to his feet and came around his desk.

"I have much to answer for, you need not remind me of that. There are great errors I have made and it is too late to change them. But I do not intend to compound them. The Emperor has entrusted me with the Shu-Rh District, and I will administer it to the best of my capabilities. That means that I will require your assistance and your advice. Each of you is necessary to Shu-Rh, and each of you will be expected to aid the others." He had tucked his hands into the full sleeves of his sheng liao and had assumed a more authoritative attitude. His eyes were still haunted, but their focus was sharp, unafraid.

"What is it you wish of us?" Hua Djo-Tung asked with a lowering of his head in recognition of Wu's position.

Tan Mung-Fa made a coarse sound. "Do you really plan to listen to this old fool? A man who admits that he did not plead your case to the Emperor? How does he deserve your loyalty, Hua?"

"He is District Magistrate," Hua reminded the young man solemnly. "Whatever else he has done, he still has his office, and we are part of his jurisdiction. We are bound by the law to work together through this crisis." He was only repeating what they all knew was so, but Hua spoke with a dignity that gave the words meaning. "If it is necessary, we will die on our own lands, which is fitting."

Tan rolled angry eyes upward. "First we get pious statements from this Magisterial eunuch, and now you start spouting off with all the usual patriotic platitudes. No wonder no one in Lo-Yang or K'ai-Feng would help us." His stance was a challenge now, and he waited for one of the others to answer him.

"You're mistaken—" Kung began, only to be cut off by Tan again.

"You can tell the Ministry of War that if they want their soldiers, they'll have to come and get them. I'm not sending them back, and that is final. I know what can happen, and I'm not going to disarm myself because some self-important clerk in Lo-Yang thinks the soldiers should be elsewhere."

Chih-Yü, remembering the infuriating interview she had had in Lo-Yang with the official Lun Shui-Lun, nodded sympathetically. "I know how you feel, Tan, and I agree with you." She saw the alarm in the men around her. "No," she went on swiftly, "think a moment: he is right. We have been given so little to defend ourselves that we must keep everything we have in order to have any hope at all. If fifty soldiers will make a difference in attacking Temujin in order to recover Pei-King, when there are more than sixty thousand soldiers in the army, then our whole country is in much more desperate straits than any of us know, and we should be sending diplomats to negotiate a peaceful surrender to the Mongols and not be preparing to fight them." She sensed the anger of the men once more, and decided to use it. "And we are asked to help them. We are expected to bow to Imperial will and give up the few soldiers we have, and to stay here, vulnerable to every attack, making only the most meager of defenses so that the army may be wasted in the attempt to win back Pei-King."

"Defiance of the Emperor's order is punishable by dishonor and a lingering death. I am not anxious to endure the Thousand Cuts," Suh growled. "The Magistrate has given his order."

"Has he?" Chih-Yü looked at Wu Sing-I and met his eyes steadily. "Perhaps you were not able to give us the message because it had not been delivered?"

Wu sighed. "My chop and the date are affixed to the copy of the order. They will know that I have seen and read it." He shook his head as he looked from one Warlord to the next. "I have no way to stop this order, good defenders. If there were a way, I would."

Shao stared down at his boots, his lips drawn into a thin line. "I think it may be wisest to offer explanations to the capitals later, when the worst of the conflict has passed. It can always be argued that the danger of attack from the Mongol was so great that we dared not risk the Imperial soldiers on the road where it was known that many attacks had occurred. Which," he added with a grave smile, "is no more than the truth. No one can argue that the danger does not exist."

"They won't believe that," Suh protested. "They will insist that we were in the wrong and we will be killed." His voice had risen and he stepped back from the little group as if wishing to demonstrate that he was not part of them any longer.

"Time to worry about that after we survive the Mongols," was Kung's laconic observation. "If we come through the battles, then we can turn our attention to dealing with those turtles in Lo-Yang."

Wu Sing-I gasped at the insult Kung had so casually offered the Ministry of War, but could not bring himself to contradict the Warlord. Instead he gave Suh a critical look, saying, "We are exposed to greater danger than Imperial wrath, that is certain. We must think of ourselves as isolated, and proceed as best we can." He was aware that he had spoken the most serious sedition and could be given a traitor's death for those words, but he could not retract them. With a lighter heart than he had had for many days, he regarded the Warlords around him. "The Imperial troops will have to remain here because we are not willing to send them into enemy territory: that much is plain. But that alone is not enough. Shu-Rh District is remote enough that it will be difficult for Ministry inspectors to reach us, should any decide to investigate. In a way," he went on sadly, "I wish they would investigate, because then we might get the aid we require. The one promised inspection has been delayed for a year, which probably means forever."

Kung Szei grinned with humorless ferocity. "Then we will make our own plans. So long as they are in the archives, we should be blameless, for the records will be here, if the Mongols don't burn the town."

Chih-Yü closed her eyes. They're talking in circles, she thought. They none of them know what to do now. We're adrift, and no one is willing to give directions. No one. She realized with a touch of bitterness that she did not want to be the one to initiate a plan, and was aghast to hear herself say, "We need a system for getting messages from stronghold and fortress to stronghold and fortress. That way, if an attack comes, there will be ways to give warning and ask for help before the fortress or stronghold is completely cut off. It might be wise to have a regular number of messengers who would ride through the district on stated routes, and that way, if one was late, all would be alerted. That would mean we would have several messengers, but it might be worth-while."

Shao was staring at her, and Suh was already beginning to protest. "A group of messengers, you say, who must be mounted and fed and housed, and are of use only if they are missing? You're demented!"

"Wait," Hua said, motioning for silence. "What sort of messages would they carry?"

"I . . ." Chih-Yü forced herself to think clearly, all the while chiding herself for putting the idea forth. "They would take any messages. Perhaps Tan might know of suspicious travelers and could warn Kung of them, in case they turned up in his area. Or I might have a need for arrow shafts and would be willing to trade them for quarrels. There are many things we should know. If there were"—she stared up at the ceiling—"ten messengers, two from each of us, one going one way and the other the opposite way on the same route, none of us would be more than two days away from news. Hua and Shao are in the most remote locations, and it would take more than a day to reach them, but it might be worth it." Now that she had spoken, she could see all the flaws in her plan, but could not bring herself to utter her doubts as she saw animation come back into Wu Sing-I's face.

"An excellent beginning," Wu said.

"A piece of nonsense!" Tan countered, striding about the room and stopping before the tapestry showing a unicorn. "This beast, I must remind all of you, is the symbol of perspicacity, which not one of you appears to possess." He came back toward the others with long, impatient strides. "All of us admit that we haven't enough men to protect our holdings, and yet you rush to embrace this lunacy that would lose you two men apiece as well as making it possible for all our plans to fall into the hands of the enemy. Have you gone demented with fear, or what? I will tell you this: I will have no part of this madness. Whatever ridiculous solution you reach, do it without me and my Imperial troops." He gathered his wide-sleeved jacket around him and paced out of the hall, refusing to turn when Kung and Wu called after him.

"I'm sorry," Chih-Yü said, her voice faltering. "It wasn't a very sensible plan. I didn't take any time to think it out." She knew she agreed with every point of protest Tan Mung-Fa had expressed.

"No, no," Wu assured her. "It is true that your plan is not

very complete, but it is the only plan any of us has offered.
For that alone it is welcome." The Magistrate adjusted his
stiffened-silk cap and looked at the others. "Well? Do the rest
of you agree with Tan? Do you think each of us should fight
in isolation?" His face was calm but he could not disguise the
worry in his tone. "If any of you feel that you cannot work
in concert with the others, then perhaps it would be best if
you left."

Suh Son-Tai folded his arms again. "I'll listen to what you
have to say, but I make no commitments, none at all."

Wu shrugged unhappily. "I cannot compel you, not as we
are now." He turned to the other men. "Have any of you
more suggestions."

"The messengers might work," Kung Szei grumbled, "but
Tan is right, you know, we can't afford to be shorthanded."

Shao looked up sharply. "What if we do not use fighting
men? We surely know of old farmers who can ride, and
would be willing to take the work on."

"And what happens when they're confronted by Mongols?"
Hua asked with a touch of contempt.

"They will probably be killed. But if a farmer is carrying a
sealed message, he cannot reveal what it says, and most of
the Mongol soldiers cannot read or write. We would lose a
messenger, but our plans would be fairly secure." His brow
drew down as he thought of the matter some more. "Of
course, it would mean that we must choose farmers who understand the risk, and that might not be easily done."

"Appoint someone," Suh said from the corner of the room.

"No. This is not the work for an unwilling man to do."
Shao began to move restlessly about the room. "The messenger system is necessary, I see that, and T'en is right—we
must not use fighting men."

A tentative smile crossed Wu Sing-I's face. "It would make
it possible for us to keep one another apprised of the general
state of each fortress and stronghold. We would be able to
distribute horses and supplies where they are most needed—"

"No!" Kung burst out. "No, none of that. I will not share
either my supplies or my horses with any of the rest of you. I
need them for my people." His face had darkened with his
anger and he turned on the Magistrate. "Wu, you don't have
any idea what this war will be like, and nothing I can say—"

Wu met Kung's furious gaze with more strength than he
had shown before. "I was in Shu-Rh when it was attacked,

Warlord Kung. I saw the people cut down and the buildings put to the torch. I heard the screams, saw the bodies and the blood. And that is precisely why I tell you it is essential that we work together, or all of us will have that carnage to look forward to." His worn face had at last regained its nobility, and he stepped back from Kung without defeat. "Go, if you cannot do this. Go now."

Kung Szei shook his head in disbelief. "Are the rest of you going to accept this condition?" he demanded. "You, Shao? You, Hua? You, Suh?"

It was Shao who answered for them. "It is all that we can think to do, Kung Szei. If you see it otherwise, it may be as well that you leave." He was the tallest of them, and his height added force to his words.

"By the Gods of War and Thunder!" Kung swore, then turned on his heel as he left them.

The tribunal hall was quiet but for the distant sound of Kung's footsteps. The remaining four Warlords regarded each other uneasily.

"I think it would be best if we began with an assessment of our current preparedness," Shao said after a moment, and went to Wu's desk. "Magistrate, do you mind if I use your brush?"

"Of course not," Wu Sing-I said distantly. He listened as Shao Ching-Po began to talk of roads and trails, of passes and bridges and fords. All the while his ears once again resounded with the hideous cries of the dying, the rush and clatter of fire, the relentless beat of the hooves of Mongol ponies which had remained with him since that terrible night when Shu-Rh was razed. He knew it was useless to put his hands to his ears, for the sounds were within him, and, he had begun to fear, would be with him forever.

---•---

Text of an Imperial edict, calligraphed by the Vermilion Brush and distributed throughout the Empire by court messengers.

On the Feast Day of the Descent of Kuan Te in the Year of the Ox, the Fourteenth Year of the Sixty-fifth Cycle, from the Dragon Portals of the Imperial City within K'ai-Feng.

The heat of the summer has begun its embrace of the Empire, and the great activity of the people indicates how much promise they see in all their works. Surely this is in accord with the Will of August Heaven, for it shows that all the people know how wise it is to practice industry and to rely on the gods for their aid and protection. We are well aware that there are dangerous men abroad in our lands who would work to destroy all that which all have striven so mightily to achieve. There are those who declare that the perspicacity of the Elevated Ones is to blame, and that there has not been sufficient provision for the determination of our enemies, but those who are aware of the intent of the laws of the gods know that this is not the Way of Heaven, and that the danger is there not through the will of the Elevated Ones, but because misled and benighted barbarians are unwilling to seek the path of virtue, and instead have determined to subjugate this land to their impious will.

When General Yueh met with the Mongol rabble in the field, he wisely employed the formation of the Frolicking Wolf Cubs, and the men of Temujin were routed. We inform all of you of this so that none may doubt that the enemy is contemptuous and not worthy of the concern of those who live within the borders of the Empire. General Yueh has sent back the horses, batons and heads of the Mongol leaders he vanquished, and these have been displayed to the Court and the city of K'ai-Feng and none may doubt the truth of the report. It is the intent of the Vermilion Brush to inscribe words to the honor of General Yueh upon his arrival in the capital, so that all will know his accomplishments and worth.

Were it only the Mongol warriors we had to oppose, there would be little question of the swift, victorious outcome for the Imperial forces, but it is the most profound source of grief that this is not the case.

There are those of this nation, depraved, dishonored, seduced, who in their error and despicable waywardness have given their aid and abilities to the agents of the

Mongol vermin. Unmindful of the ancient wisdom of Kung Fu-Tzu, departed from the Way of the Taoists, rejecting the Buddha's Threefold Enlightenment, they have blinded their eyes to all but the trophies of pillage. They make themselves lower than the rabid foxes who menace the farmers and their kin alike. They are like the poisoned wells that offer false relief. They are in league with the disruptive spirits in the earth who slumber, and then shake down the world in their petulant wrath. There can be no peace and no haven for such as these. They are lost to themselves and to the vast numbers of the Empire.

Mercy is ever an attribute to him who sits on the Dragon Throne, and it is the greatest good to which the wise man will strive. Yet mercy must be tempered with reason, and justice is that which is merciful to the greatest number. It is no credit to the wise man that he show mercy to the criminal who has determined to slay all his family. That is precisely how the current turmoil has revealed itself, and the wisest course must be taken for the greatest good. For that reason, all nobles, army officers, Warlords, militiamen, Magistrates and Tribunal officers are authorized to seize and hold any person they have reason to believe is acting for the benefit of the Mongol forces. There need be no public endictment, no formal accusation other than that of arrest, and this edict gives discretionary power to all the above-named authorities to try, condemn and execute such persons as are found to be supplying aid to any associates of the Mongols. In order to avoid public scandal and possible riots in outlying regions, the authorities named in this edict are encouraged to proceed clandestinely and to pursue their inquiries with a minimum of public attention. Orders of execution must be preserved for district archives, and copies sent to the Master of Imperial Records, but the full body of evidence and similar documentation, given the turbulence of these inquiries, will not be required with the same stringency as attend on other criminal matters, and the force of the law will not bind the authorities empowered with the usual limitations.

It is sobering to think that this fertile and delightful land could be the object of such perfidy as the Mongols have demonstrated, but it is best to realize how great their desire is, and to determine to oppose it with renewed dedication.

Inscribed with the Vermilion Brush, with the provision that copies be made and distributed to all nobles, army officers, Warlords, militiamen, Magistrates and Tribunal officers, and with provision that copies may be made for district archives.

the Imperial chop

8

EARLIER THAT evening the militiamen had broached two kegs of rice wine, as an aftermath to the midsummer feast. Women from the farmsteads as well as from the stronghold were given free access to all of the little stockade and were quick to take advantage of the opportunities this provided. Farmers sat with their defenders over their earthen cups in the main hall while ribald songs and breathless laughter came in through the open windows from the courtyard.

The evening was hot, with a sultry promise of rain before morning. This in part accounted for the loosened clothing and shiny skin of most of the revelers.

Jui Ah had got hold of a two-stringed lute and was singing the old ballad "Her Garments Fell Like Petals" in a raucous and lascivious manner, urged on by the men around him. As he launched into the third verse, he swaggered to the foot of the stairs that led upward to T'en Chih-Yü's study. The guffaws of his companions both stung his pride and urged him on to more outrageous verses. He knew that Chih-Yü could hear him, that she was sitting alone in that high room, away from the festive gathering. After making a brief appearance at the banquet and giving a pithy and rousing speech, the Warlord had retired to her study so that, she insisted, the others would feel entirely at liberty. But Jui Ah wanted to be with Chi-Yü, isolated in that little room, in the humid night, to watch her flushed with heat, ready to be a woman for him, instead of his Warlord.

In the song he had reached the part that described what the lover saw when his mistress opened her shift and let it drop to the floor. He tried to imbue the words with his will, so that T'en Chih-Yü would appear to him and do the same as the girl in the ballad. The gut strings felt hot under his fingers as he sang.

"Jui," one of the armorers shouted over the general noise, "there's better things to pluck on than strings. F'au makes a prettier melody than the lute," he cried, putting his arm around the shoulder of the woman F'au.

Realistically, Jui Ah knew that even if Chih-Yü wished to invite him to her bed, she would not do it in front of this company, but that did not stop him from desire for just such a public acceptance. He sang the fourth verse in a kind of defiance, though he knew his audience was growing restive.

"Tell me, Jui," F'au called out merrily, "how you would treat me if my robe were open for you." She had a roguish eye and was known to be available to militiamen. Her husband was over fifty and had said that he no longer had a use for women, but still wished for sons, and raised only the most perfunctory objections to her lovers. "I know how to please you," she said in her melting voice, tempting him. "A man should sleep with silken cushions, not swords."

This brought a wave of howling approval from the others in the hall, and one or two obscene suggestions were added to her invitation. These were greeted with high good humor, and Jui Ah himself had to grin at the most incredible of them.

"Jui Ah," F'au murmured as she came up to him, her dark eyes softened by the wine she had drunk and her voluptuous body moving her light cotton sheng pan suggestively.

With a sudden oath, Jui Ah thrust the round-bodied lute away and reached for F'au, clutching at her urgently, his hand slipping into the unfastened opening at her neck. To the sound of whistling and hoots, Jui Ah bore his prize out into the dark courtyard and told himself as he pressed F'au onto her back that this experienced and carnal woman was far preferable to the fiercely remote Warlord in her study, and for a time, as he plundered F'au's flesh for their mutual pleasure, he almost believed it.

The hall was empty but for a few sleeping men sprawled in the corner when Saint-Germain finally crossed the floor and went quietly up the stairs toward that closed door that had so tormented Jui Ah earlier in the evening. He wore a long, loose garment of fluted linen that was wholly unknown in China, the old Egyptian kalasiris. His heeled Byzantine boots were out of place with his clothes, but this did not disturb him unduly. He had chosen the kalasiris because it was cool and because it was in accord with the Imperial edict that required foreigners to wear non-Chinese clothing. When he reached the top of the stairs, he hesitated, asking himself again if it was wise to visit T'en Chih-Yü. Though the question went unanswered, he raised his hand and knocked at the worn, red-lacquered door.

"Who is it?" Chih-Yü demanded sharply. There was no encouragement in the tone of her voice.

"Shih Ghieh-Man," he answered, speaking softly. "You sent word earlier in the evening that you wanted to speak to me."

"That was at dinner," she said after a slight hesitation. "It's very late."

"I have been occupied in my laboratory," he explained, though it was not entirely the truth. It was probably sensible to leave, he told himself, but did not turn to go.

In the hall below him, three militiamen had reeled in from the courtyard, shouting for more wine. The men lying in the hall stirred and one of them yawned and belched as the new arrivals found themselves a corner.

The door behind Saint-Germain opened and Chih-Yü whispered to him. "Hurry in, by heaven. I don't want those sots talking scandal."

Saint-Germain obeyed at once, saying, "Considering their condition, I doubt you have anything to fear. You could probably walk an elephant through the hall and they wouldn't notice."

Chih-Yü put her hand to her head. "I'm glad I posted the sentries before the feast began or we'd be wholly exposed. As it is, I hope that the Mongols don't decide to attack tomorrow morning. We'll be incapable of any action against them." She was wearing a thin silk sheng go and very little else. As she stared at Saint-Germain, she seemed to realize the impropriety of her dress, and drew the long robe more tightly around her.

There was a quiver of lightning that blanched the room and flickered away almost at once.

"I should have come earlier," Saint-Germain said as he looked at Chih-Yü, seeing her fatigue in the darkness under her intelligent eyes.

"And I was about to thank you for being circumspect," she countered lightly as she took her place at the table again.

"I've been reading most of the time, and"—she paused as thunder battered at the hills—"and I have lost track of the time, I fear."

"Your reading must be fascinating." He said it sincerely enough, knowing Chih-Yü to be a well-educated woman.

She indicated the old scroll lying open between two paper-covered lanterns. "Mo Tzu."

"Mo Tzu," he repeated as he watched her, watched how the light from the two lanterns fell on her face and well-defined lips, how her sheng go stuck to her body where it was moist. He forced himself to speak. "Mo Tzu. He was the one who was Kung Fu-Tzu's rival, wasn't he? The man who was opposed to aggressive war and musical entertainments. He wrote a treatise on universal love, didn't he?"

Chih-Yü looked up at him, her face filled with surprise. "You've read the classics."

"Yes, of course, some of them. Is that so unusual?" He had come a few steps nearer and the light from the lanterns fell on his face, too, hiding the full power of his penetrating eyes in shadow, but emphasizing the angles of his features, the ironic curve of his mouth and the slightly aslant line of his nose.

"In a foreigner, yes." She had started to roll up the long, well-worn scroll, but stopped, saying, "I was interested in the part that tells how Mo Tzu went with his disciples to various villages to teach the people there how to defend themselves from large military forces, so that the peasants and farmers would not be at the mercy of the warring Princes. I thought perhaps I would discover a better strategy."

"And did you?" He rested his fingertips on the worn surface of the reading table.

"A few things, of little consequence, though I might put them to use, if only to give the farmers something to do." She sighed once as she finished rolling the scroll. As she wrapped the two silken ribbons around the flaking paper, her eyes strayed to his face. "Tell me, why did you come so late?"

"I told you, I wasn't through until a little while ago." He could not keep from smiling, yet he could find no reason to smile.

When she was satisfied that the scoll was properly secured, she returned it to its appropriate container among the many that stood on the high shelves that flanked the northernmost window. A sudden rush of modesty came over her, such as she had not felt since she was a child. It confused her with its

unexpected intensity that was combined with a new anticipation of pleasure. She clasped her hands, and then, most deliberately, opened them with the assumption of an ease she
could not feel. "Shih Ghieh-Man," she said as she turned to
look at him.

"Yes, Warlord T'en?" There was a sad amusement in his
eyes that intrigued her.

With an effort, she recalled the questions she had wanted
to ask him earlier that evening. "Tell me, is it possible do you
think, for this stronghold to withstand"—she looked away as
lightning spurted through the clouds and was gone—"an attack by Mongols?"

"A real attack?" he asked kindly, wishing he could reach
out and turn her face to him once more. "You mean a fighting force and not a raiding party?"

"Yes." She felt his presence in the room as indisputably as
she heard the drumming thunder.

"The storm is getting closer," Saint-Germain remarked inconsequently. When he spoke again, it was in a different
voice, one that was low, like the melody from deep strings.
"Do I think this fortress could withstand a real onslaught by
Mongols? No, I don't. And neither do you." He saw her lips
tighten against an outburst and he leaned forward across the
table. "You asked me for my thoughts, Chih-Yü, and I have
given them to you. Would you rather I lied?"

"No," she murmured. She was looking down at her hands
now where they lay clasped in her lap. She had learned what
she wished to know, she told herself sternly, and the fact that
Shih Ghieh-Man agreed with her evaluation of their chances
should not amaze her.

With his uncanny understanding, Saint-Germain said,
"Don't condemn yourself, my dear. It takes a great deal of
courage to be willing to face reality and go on in spite of it.
You have done more than many others have been able to."
The others included a few of the most illustrious and notori-
ous names known to men, and he did not know how he could
explain this to her.

"Go on?" She attempted to speak lightly and failed. "Shih
Ghieh-Man, what choice is there? If I order the valleys evacuated and send the farmers into the hills, they will die at the
hands of highwaymen or fall prey to starvation when winter
comes, and it will not matter that they have been saved from
the Mongols. It isn't safe to send large numbers of people into

the towns, for they are not skilled in any way that would give them work to do, and there is no place for them. They would be reduced to beggary . . ." She broke off as a sudden drunken shout came from the courtyard below, only to be quieted by a warning from the men at watch at the gate. There was a trace of a line between her brows that deepened as she continued. "Even in the towns, there is no assurance that they would not fall at the hands of the Mongols if the town is attacked. So what is left to me? As long as my people defend their own lands and their crops and their livestock, they have reason to fight, to resist the invasion and to keep good heart. But if this is lost to them, what is left?"

His face was moon-pale in the sudden jagged light, and then at once indistinct in the muted glow of the lanterns. "Chih-Yü," he asked softly, steadily, "what do you want of me?"

She bit her lower lip, her usually purposeful expression marred by doubt. "I don't know."

"I haven't sufficient cynicism to pretend that you want me to dismiss your anxieties as insignificant." Thunder rang over the hills and rolled down the two small valleys. He waited until it had faded.

Chih-Yü shook her head forlornly. "No, don't pretend. It's bad enough without that." She stared at the nearer lantern as if it were a becon of safety. "I've spent most of my life in the company of soldiers and militiamen. It's what I was born to. But I like the sound of the ch'in when it is played well, and I am truly sad that I can't have a place for beautiful things here. It's foolish to want such things, yet when I saw the exquisite things you have . . ."

Saint-Germain recalled the rapacious Magistrate Hao Sai-Chu, who had claimed the Byzantine mosaics as tribute, and his face hardened. "Yes?"

Though he strove to keep the tension from his voice, she heard it, for she looked up sharply. "I only meant that I wonder if it's wise for you to risk those beautiful things." The lightning was more prolonged, cleaving the length of the sky. "I've never risked keeping such things here. I'm sorry now that I didn't choose one or two things, simple things, to make this room less austere." She made a complicated gesture as she looked up at him once again. "You've been far, and yet you take precious things with you. I saw many of the treasures that came in those cases from Lo-Yang."

"That was all that was left of my house," he said softly. "You say that I take beautiful things with me. It's true enough." He could not tell her how much more he had left behind in his long years. Outside the window he could see the wavering flames of the torches on the walls, one or two of them sputtering in the rising wind.

"Oh," she cried in quick sympathy. "You didn't tell me. I assumed that you requested . . ."

"No."

The thunder provided them both an excuse for silence. Saint-Germain felt his ancient loneliness as he looked at T'en Chih-Yü. He had lost so much more than beautiful things. And he had never been able to accustom himself to the loss. Memories sharp as claws tore at him and he turned away to conceal the pain that filled him.

"Hsing has received an offer of marriage," Chih-Yü announced suddenly, and too loudly, as if she were embarrassed. Why was it so unpleasant a task to tell him this? He had never evinced anything beyond a mild fondness for Hsing. She decided it was his foreignness that perplexed her, though this, she sensed, was not the reason at all.

"Has she?" Saint-Germain asked with polite interest, nothing in his stance or his manner showing that her evaluation of his feelings for the girl was incorrect. He was aware of Chih-Yü's eyes on him and he smiled enigmatically.

"As Warlord, it would be appropriate for me to make other provisions for you," she said, letting the words dangle like a question as the lightning wiggled in the sky.

"Does Hsing like the match?" He could not look away from Chih-Yü.

"Gei's younger brother has made the offer for her. Gei keeps the inn at the far end of So-Dui valley." This was the larger of the two valleys guarded by the Mao-T'ou stronghold. "It is a much better proposal than she has ever hoped for. Considering how her life has been, she is very fortunate." Her throat felt oddly hot, as if she had taken suddenly ill. She welcomed the thunder that boomed and cracked overhead. "I have given my permission to the match if it does not inconvenience you. From what Hsing has told me . . ." She faltered suddenly and looked to him for help.

"It won't inconvenience me," he said.

"I'll be more than willing to assign you other eligible women. There are several who might please you. You have only to indicate your choice." She wished now she had saved this discussion until morning. Here, in the night, with the storm gathering, she could feel a wildness growing in her, and the force of his dark eyes only fostered her abandon.

"Have I." He was still, then bowed slightly, saying with absurd propriety, "Thank you, elder brother."

She blinked, taken off guard, and then laughed. "Elder brother. You're quite right, but . . ." Her mirth faded as lightning scythed down the air, followed almost at once by an avalanche of thunder. Chih-Yü put her hand to her mouth as the open shutters rattled. She forced herself to speak to the stranger on the other side of the table. "Is there a woman you would like?"

"Yes," he said as the white glare of the lightning danced along the far end of the ridge, setting a little fire in the dry grasses. "Chih-Yü," he said as he held out one small, beautiful hand to her, "can you trust me? A little?"

The thunder drowned her answer, but she put her hand into his and rose slowly to her feet. They stood, the table between them, and he spoke to her softly. "When you came to me in Lo-Yang, I was not what you wanted to find. You hoped for many soldiers and in the end were forced to settle for one foreign alchemist. I accepted your offer not because Mao-T'ou stronghold is important to me, but only because I had been warned that it would be wise for me to leave the old capital for a time. Since then, my home there has been destroyed, so doubtless my decision to come here was a sensible one. But now, do you know, I don't regret my choice." His penetrating eyes held hers. "I think my life would be the poorer for not knowing you."

"Shih Ghieh-Man." Her hand lay in his and she thought it odd that it was not shaking, for inwardly she trembled, restless as a flame. "But," she protested rather breathlessly, "you haven't answered my question."

"I have, you know." With his free hand he touched her cheek, so lightly that she was not certain she had felt it. "Offer me any woman here in this stronghold, in this district, in this empire, and I will choose you, T'en Chih-Yü. If you are willing."

Raindrops spattered on the window ledge, and she was grateful for this distraction. She tore away from him and busied herself with closing and latching the shutters. Only when she finished did she realize her mistake, for now she and Saint-Germain were alone in the soft gleam of the lanterns, shut away from the wind and the splendor of the storm. She could hear a few shouts from the courtyard as the rain took the guards and revelers unaware. "But I am Warlord," she said at last.

"Yes," he agreed, coming across the room toward her. His Egyptian finery, though alien in appearance, gave him a majesty that surprised her. She watched him, fascinated, wondering how she could have missed seeing him clearly before.

"Hsing has told me . . ." she began, as if to fend him off, though he stopped a few paces away from her. "Would it be any different with me?"

His dark eyes were sad. "Do you mean would I take you as another man might? No. It isn't in . . . my nature. But it would be different I promise you. If you will trust me. You know that I am not as other men. If you find that repugnant, you must tell me . . .". .

"No," she murmured, "not repugnant."

". . . so that I will not upset you."

"But don't all alchemists keep their seed within them, to lend its strength to their work?" She had heard that maxim of alchemy many times over the years, and knew that some men in an excess of dedication to their art had themselves emasculated in order to perform the work more perfectly.

"It is not a question of alchemy," he said dryly as he stepped back from her.

"If not alchemy, what? Are you like the other Western Black Robes who vow to forgo the pleasures of the flesh?" Outside, the rain was falling more heavily and the thunder crashed along the ridges. The torches in the courtyard were out, as was the fire started on the ridge.

"No." It would be wisest, he thought, to leave and let Chih-Yü select another woman for him, but he could say nothing to her. He touched the open neck of his black kalasiris, trying to remember how it felt to sweat.

"Then what are you?" As she asked the question, she feared he would be so deeply insulted that he would not be able to stay with her. She knew with a start that she very much wanted him to stay with her.

He looked at her gravely. "A vampire."

"A vampire?" she repeated, not able to laugh at him. "A p'o?"

Saint-Germain shook his head, though he knew the legends

well enough. "Not precisely," he said carefully, watching to
see if she was horrified or angry. "Didn't Hsing tell you what
I required of her?"

"You mean the blood?" She saw him nod. "Hsing
described it as very pleasant, better than what other men had
done to her." She had been curious when Hsing had told her
how Saint-Germain used her, and what it was like.

"Does that bother you?" He spoke lightly enough still, but
the pain was in the back of his eyes again.

Chih-Yü considered her answer carefully. "I am a virgin,
Shih Ghieh-Man. It is not through choice. My father was
never able to find a husband for me who was willing to let me
continue here as Warlord, and so I have never been
promised. I'm too old now—twenty-four. I would like to
know pleasure."

"Only pleasure?" He had come nearer, and now reached
out to turn her face to his. "Look at me, Chih-Yü," he commanded her softly. "If it is pleasure you wish for, I will give
it to you within my limitations as often or as rarely as you
want."

The yearning she had felt so many times in the past
possessed her once again. Her body ached to be pliant, to be
molded by passion. She knew, as most women did, what was
expected of her in order to please a husband, but she had not
been able to account for the way her blood stirred at the
thought. "What more is there?"

His face clouded with grief. "There is love."

"I am not a depraved woman," Chih-Yü declared.

Saint-Germain took her face in his hands. "No one has
said that you are," he whispered before he touched her lips
with his. It was indefinably sweet to sense her response
through his mouth and fingers, to feel her spirit waken, vital,
eager. There had been too many complacent, passive women
in the last few years. He did not know how unsatisfactory his
life had become until he drew this woman into his arms and
for the first time in many years felt his desire ignite with an
ardor he had almost forgotten. This was no quiet creature,
unable to meet his need with demands of her own. There was
strength in Chih-Yü, and deep-burning fire.

"Shih Ghieh-Man," she breathed as he drew back from
her. Shamelessly she put her arms around him to prevent
their separation. Her head was pressed against his shoulder,
the fluted linen of his kalasiris creasing her cheek. There had

been many times in her childhood when she had been told tales of amorous courtesans who were foolish enough to love the men who paid for them, and who were overcome by despair when their lovers proved faithless. Listening to these stories and the sensible injunction of her father's two concubines, she had assured herself that she would never be so unwise as to be snared by so useless an emotion as love. Love was for the family and the empire, not for one foreign man. Her whole body trembled as his fingers loosened her belt to open her sheng go. "What will you do?" she asked so quietly that the muffled blast of the storm submerged the question. The legends of the p'o spoke of the malignant wandering spirit who would inhabit abandoned corpses in order to prey on the living. There was nothing of that in Saint-Germain, in his strength, his cradling arms, his dark eyes. "What will you do?"

His senses had warmed to her. "This," he murmured as his hands slowly, persuasively caressed her shoulders and breasts, sliding her sheng go away from her, letting it drop to the floor.

"Shih Ghieh-Man . . ." She knew that her nudity should distress her, but found instead that she was proud of the excitement she felt.

"And this." In one swift, easy move he had lifted her into his arms and held her close as he crossed the room to the low couch where it was her custom to receive official visitors. He lowered her to the silken cushions, pulled the long jade pins from her casually knotted hair and ran his fingers through those ebony tresses, as he knelt beside her.

Her heart was buoyant and the apprehension that had flickered in her as bleak as the lightning was stilled as she felt her need join with his.

"And this." He was aware that Chih-Yü had never experienced fulfillment before, and it was a keen delight to rouse her gently, letting her experience each new sensation thoroughly. He showered kisses that barely touched the skin on her arms, the arch of her ribs. His tongue traced the swell of her breasts, the curve of her hip, the petal-soft interior of her muscular thighs. As he brought her desires to their first tumultuous peak, he touched her throat.

"And this."

Neither Chih-Yü nor Saint Germain ever knew when the storm rolled over them and on into the fastness of the mountains. They were caught up in the joyous discovery of their rapture, and for them the world, that night, was far away.

———◆●◆———

A petition from the District Magistrate Wu Sing-I to the Imperial court.

On the second day of the Fortnight of Great Heat, in the Year of the Ox, the Fourteenth Year of the Sixty-fifth Cycle, from the Tribunal of Shu-Rh District.

To the Most August Wielder of the Vermilion Brush and Glorious Master of the Dragon Throne, with most profoundly reverential respect:

This most unworthy person has been honored with the task of serving as Magistrate of the Shu-Rh District. He was before the Magistrate of the Tai-Lon District and before that the Chief Tribunal Officer of Hsia-Jan. He has been favored by Heaven to be part of a most distinguished family whose members he venerates with every devotion of filial piety.

The Wielder of the Vermilion Brush must wonder, then, why this unworthy person has so far exceeded the sensible limits of society to address the August presence directly instead of proceeding properly through those Ministries and Secretariats most closely allied with the Dragon Throne. This most unworthy person seeks to assure the August and Elevated Son of Heaven that had not the need been overwhelmingly great, he would never have transgressed so far as to send this petition.

The Shu-Rh District has been under attack by Mongol raiders since spring, and there is no sign that this will cease until winter snows make such raids difficult and uncomfortable for the despised men of Temujin. Our district capital, Shu-Rh, was burned some time back, and there are no less than seventy-three communities which have fallen to the Mongol wrath in the last three years. Though in comparison to the larger cities these villages seem little, yet it has been shown that the people there are as loyal to the Imperial Presence as any others, and their suffering is as great as the suffering of the people of Pei-King.

It came to the attention of this most unworthy person that one of the local Warlords had attempted to gain access to those personages who have power to deal with the army. It is most unfortunate that there were few willing to listen to T'en Chih-Yü and there was no aid granted us. That some officials in the capital do not take the time to familiarize themselves with the gravity of the conflict in the west is most lamentable, though with the current state of warfare demanding more forces in the northeast, it is understandable that some officials might, in their zeal to reclaim Pei-King, be unaware that the Mongols are also active in the west. This most unworthy person is not seeking to blame any person in Lo-Yang or in K'ai-Feng. He wishes only to state that only the judgment of the August Occupant of the Dragon Throne is sufficiently attuned to the will of Heaven to make true evaluations possible.

Therefore, this most unworthy person has dared to petition the Wielder of the Vermilion Brush directly, and begs that the Elevated and August Presence will be sufficiently compassionate to overlook the reprehensible lapse of the Magistrate and hear out the plea this paper carries.

This most unworthy person is desperately in need of armed troops. The people of Shu-Rh are subject to the most severe assaults and criminal uses by the troops of Temujin and though the local Warlords have done all that is possible with their militiamen, it is not enough. By numbers alone the Mongols are able to triumph. Where they have been, there are ruined crops and burned buildings and slaughtered families. No matter how much we try to resist, it is not possible for a fortress manned by one hundred militiamen to withstand six hundred mounted Mongols. All the men here have acquitted themselves most valiantly, and those who have lost their lives in the struggle have made good account of that loss. It is not a lack of courage that is the question here, but of numbers and equipment. The Warlord Shao Ching-Po of the stronghold of Tsi-Gai pass has been attacked not once but twice. Thus far he has been adle to resist the onslaughts of the Mongols, but he is low on arrows and quarrels and bows and spears and pikes. Though he has barrels of pitch in reserve, the enemy has not come close enough to allow him to put those barrels to good use. His manpower has been reduced to thirty-two trained militiamen and eight armed villagers. Tan Mung-Fa of Shui-Lo fortress has been asked to lend a few of his fighting men, but has not been able to spare any because of the great danger of attack. T'en Chih-Yü was able to send arrowheads and twelve coats of scale armor, but that is not sufficient. Warlord Shao has said to this most unworthy person that he is aware that his stronghold will fall when next the Mongols attack. He has set many traps within the stronghold so that the Mongols will pay a great price for their prize. Warlord Shao is a man of great courage and integrity and his men are willing to follow him into battle against demons if he asks this of him. Warlord Tan has said that he will make every attempt to send troops to Warlord Shao's aid when the next assault comes, but does not know if he himself will be in battle at that time. Warlord Kung has informed the Tribunal that he has armed his villagers, but does not believe that there are sufficient numbers of them to put up a significant defense should the Mongols attack in earnest. Warlord T'en has made excellent prepartations to resist the Mongols, but her stronghold has only eighty militiamen at this time, and they are not all seasoned fighters. Warlord Hua has sent word to this insignificant person that he has lost more than forty of his men to raiding parties, and he suspects that there may be spies in this region. If we had even half a garrison here, such activities would cease, for it would be possible to enforce the edict that came from the Vermilion Brush regarding such acts. Warlord Suh has sent the Tribunal weekly reports on the stage of his preparedness, and though he has done well, he has depleted his stores, and unless there is aid, he will not be able to feed his militiamen through the winter. There is not time enough to devote more men to the harvest, and the women are not content to work the fields alone and exposed to Mongol raiders, who, as has been reported throughout the Empire, use women most savagely.

This most unworthy person therefore most humbly requests that the August Son of Heaven will be inclined to send troops to alleviate our desperate situation here, and assist us in turning back the soldiers of Temujin. Without such help, we must all prepare ourselves for honorable death at the hands of the most malific of enemies.

From the city of Bei-Wah, temporary capital of the Shu-Rh District, by my own hand with the most profound submission to the will of the Presence of the Dragon Throne.

> The Magistrate of Shu-Rh,
> Family name Wu, personal name Sing-I
> his chop

9

TWO MONGOL scouts had been captured the day before and now hung from trees not far from the Mao-T'ou stronghold. Their skins had been peeled back in strips so that their naked bodies seemed dressed in tattered rags.

"You should not have killed them." Jui Ah glowered at Saint-Germain. "They are the enemies of this land. Killing them was not appropriate."

Saint-Germain regarded the militia Captain narrowly. He could sense other men in the courtyard were listening to their exchange, though he made an effort to speak quietly. "They were past being men when your soldiers finished with them. What is the point in preserving life, if you call a heartbeat life, in broken flesh?" He felt tired as he asked, and hooked his thumbs into the wide leather belt he wore around his Frankish pelisse.

"Of course!" Jui Ah scoffed. "This is not your land, foreigner. These are not your people. You have not heard the screams of your loved ones come from the flames of a burning house—"

"I have," Saint-Germain corrected him grimly. "More than once. But let it pass."

Jui Ah was not going to be put off. "It means nothing to you if the Mongols come. You have only to offer your skills to them and you may leave us to our fate with no more than a single backward glance. Don't tell me you wouldn't do it,"

Jui Ah went on, his tone accusing, "because we all would, if there were any way to do it." He folded his arms, making no effort to conceal the sneer he wore.

"I doubt you or I or anyone else here will have that option." He had asked himself how it would feel to die the true death at last. The Mongols beheaded their captives and burned buildings. Either way, he would be dead at last. He had been thinking of his home, far to the west, and those of his blood who were left behind. Saint-Germain raised his fine brows and regarded Jui Ah.

"How do any of us know what you would do?" The taunt was deliberate, and again the Captain of the militia waited for Saint-Germain to reply.

"You don't," Saint-Germain said dryly, noticing that there were a dozen men watching now, Jui Ah's men.

"Then you must not be offended if we question your loyalty." There was a glint in his eyes as he stared at Saint-Germain. He was clearly hoping to provoke Saint-Germain to action.

"Would my offense make any difference to your opinion?" Saint-Germain inquired before he turned away.

Jui Ah reached out and grasped Saint-Germain by the shoulder. "You haven't accounted for yourself, foreigner."

Saint-Germain stopped. "Remove your hand." His voice was cool and formidably controlled. He did not look at the restraining hand at all.

"Not until you explain yourself." There was a kind of feral glee in Jui Ah's burst of laughter and he jerked at Saint-Germain's shoulder in an effort to turn him around.

"Remove your hand." This time it was a command. Saint-Germain had not responded at all to the force in Jui Ah's arm.

The other man had turned pale with wrath and uncertainty. He knew that Saint-Germain should have stumbled when he pulled at his shoulder, but the foreigner had done nothing. "You're not answering."

"Nor will I until you take your hand away." His dark eyes were intense as live coals, but Jui Ah could not see them and did not read the warning there.

One of the militiamen started forward as if to warn his captain of the sudden danger he saw in the black-clothed foreigner, but Jui Ah was too angry and waved the man away before he could speak. "I won't have any man talk to me that way. I am Captain here. I am the Commander. I'm the one the men will follow in battle, not you. I am the one who will defend the Warlord. You're lower than turtle excrement. You're not suited to feed crows."

"I tell you one last time to release me." Saint-Germain's tone was almost conversational. There was an expression on his mouth that might have been a smile had it the least humor in it. He was poised lightly.

"Release you?" Jui Ah repeated with mockery. "I'll release—" He did not finish, for Saint-Germain had rounded on him, his arms coming up so that they caught Jui Ah low in the chest with a resounding thump. The militia Captain staggered back, gasping for air, his arms swinging wildly.

Without a word, Saint-Germain started away, heedless of the men watching him in amazement. He was almost to the corner of the courtyard when a brick smashed into his back.

Jui Ah could barely speak. His face was contorted and his steps were as unsteady as an infant's, but he glared at Saint-Germain with open ferocity as he lurched toward him. "You!" The word came in a rasp.

Saint-Germain watched as the militia Captain picked up the long curved blade of a pike from where it had lain beside a stack of unfinished shafts. Jui Ah swung the steel blade so that it hissed through the air in lethal promise. "This is madness," he said, knowing that the men would not listen to him. With deep resignation he began to unbuckle his belt.

"You think I don't know about you?" Jui Ah demanded. "You, with your fine foreign airs and your sorcery, you've enchanted Warlord T'en, you've made her your slave." Sparks flew from the courtyard paving stones as the pike blade glanced off them. "You're the one who has convinced her to make that ditch. You're the one who has turned her against us. You've seduced her!" He was less than ten paces away from Saint-Germain now, and the pike blade was held at the ready. It was fine steel, Saint-Germain thought, for he had made it himself.

"Jui Ah," he said as he wrapped the ends of the belt once around each hand, "if you must fight, there is an enemy beyond these walls who will give you more than enough battle. It is foolish to fight here." He sidestepped the first angry thrust of the pike blade.

"Coward! Liar!" The steel descended again, missing Saint-

Germain's foot by less than a handbreadth. Jui Ah was grinning as he took another step closer to Saint-Germain.

It was no use to talk, Saint-Germain knew. The trouble was far beyond that. With unhappy determination he set himself to the fight. The belt was taut between his hands and he moved into a partial crouch. His stance was oddly graceful and as Jui Ah took another swing at him, Saint-Germain dodged swiftly, much faster than the Captain of militia had anticipated.

"Dog's head!" Jui shouted as he recovered for his attack.

This time, as the pike blade cleft the air, Saint-Germain snapped his belt outward, the metal-studded leather snaking toward the steel blade. It wrapped around the tang once, then fell away as Jui Ah cursed in the name of half the demons in China. Saint-Germain caught the end of his belt and wrapped it around his left hand again, then stood, waiting.

Jui Ah held back a moment, assessing the older man's chances. It would not take long, he thought, to wear down that insolent foreigner. A man of his years would not have the stamina for close combat. He smiled and thumbed the pike blade.

More men had come into the courtyard, and one of them had offered to take bets. His comrades had motioned him to be quiet, but a few were already reaching for the wallets looped around their belts. Saint-Germain saw this and was appalled.

"You cannot run from me all afternoon," Jui Ah called, gloating as he approached once more, bringing the pike blade up to strike.

Saint-Germain took the belt into his left hand and began to spin it, making it sing and blur in front of him, like a shield. He started to feint to one side, and was relieved when Jui Ah was misdirected.

Down came the blade, an arm's length from where Saint-Germain stood. The belt continued to whirl.

Jui Ah was puzzled. He knew something of staff-fighting and had been taught classical boxing when he was younger, but he had never encountered this style of defense. He lifted the pike blade and used a number of quick passes, testing the barrier. Once the belt had been arrested, but it wound along the blade, and Saint-Germain had pulled at it sharply, almost dragging the blade from Jui Ah's hands.

From that exchange on, Jui Ah was more circumspect. He

kept his distance and moved in swiftly, darting with the steel blade in the belief that he could bedevil Saint-Germain into exhaustion.

Betting began among the militiamen, and shortly there was a vociferous clammor as the fight progressed. The gatekeeper came away from his post, though he was awaiting the Warlord's return with her daily patrol. This was much more exciting than staring out at the hot afternoon.

"Come closer!" Jui Ah shouted as once again Saint-Germain eluded him. It was infuriating to be unable to rush his opponent. Jui Ah looked about him for a more suitable weapon. It had become a matter of pride with him now to bring this foreigner to his knees with all of the militiamen watching.

For an answer, Saint-Germain stepped nearer, bringing the belt up so that the heavy steel buckle spun by Jui Ah's face. The metal winked in the sunlight, and then was gone as Saint-Germain moved off to the side again, luring Jui Ah after him.

There was a flail sitting out on a barrel, its thick wooden handle ready for rewrapping in leather. The rods were joined to the handle by a stout loop. Each was tipped with a small, spiked ball of iron. It was a dangerous weapon, requiring skill to use. Jui Ah tossed the pike blade aside and grabbed the flail.

This was one weapon that Saint-Germain knew he could not fight with only a belt. He flung it away and retreated before Jui Ah, never taking his eyes from the rods of the flail.

"Coward! Coward!" Jui Ah called out in derision. He began to swing the flail, the long rods clattering. "Not willing to face up to this, are you? Foreign worm!"

Saint-Germain kept his silence, watching for his opportunity. He felt no disgrace in his withdrawal. There was little significance in it, and, he noted with a degree of irritation, Jui Ah was growing cocksure as he came after Saint-Germain.

"Like the taste of iron, foreigner?" He shifted the flail in his hands, taking a wider grip on the haft. "Think how these little balls will kiss you." He squinted as the afternoon sun slanted into his eyes, and was not aware that Saint-Germain had led him into this position.

The stones that paved the courtyard were uneven, and Saint-Germain was wise enough to move cautiously. But now that he had the sun behind him, Saint-Germain began to weave, darting first one way, then another, forcing Jui Ah to rush forward unwarily.

A few of the militiamen shouted a warning to Jui Ah, but he was now too confident of the outcome to heed them. It would end soon, he could feel it. He brought the flail up over his shoulders.

Saint-Germain made one quick, supple motion, seeming to fall toward Jui Ah, but catching the man's chest on his back and lifting him into the air. Without pause, Saint-Germain rose to his feet, reaching around to grab the militia Captain by his arms, tossing the man across the courtyard to land on the stones with a sickening sound of breaking. Saint-Germain turned toward Jui Ah, and found a party of horsemen in the unguarded gateway. He stiffened, and the other men turned toward the sound of hooves.

"Explain this!" T'en Chih-Yü commanded as she brought her sorrel into the center of the courtyard. Her right hand was on her sword hilt, the left on the reins. "Explain."

The gatekeeper rushed forward, reaching up for her bridle. "There was a fight."

"I can see that." Her voice was icy and she refused to look at either Saint-Germain or Jui Ah.

"I was afraid it might become a brawl," the gatekeeper temporized as he went on. "I thought it was best if I—"

"Left your post?" she inquired. "What if there had been a party of Mongol raiders? What then? Who would have stopped them? You? No." She looked around at her militiamen. "And the rest of you. What came over you?" She beckoned to the two men who had patrolled with her. "I want you to take the name of every man here. Every man. And I want those names before sunset." Her face was still with fury.

"Warlord, it was not that way." The gatekeeper clung to her bridle. "There was danger—"

"Be silent." She cut off his protestations. "Ling, what is the condition of the Captain of militiamen?"

The man she had singled out rushed over to the fallen Jui Ah and made a rough inspection of him. Jui Ah groaned and swore as the soldier rolled him onto his back. "His leg is broken, Warlord. The rest is scrapes, cuts, and bruises. "No," he amended. "The collarbone is broken on the right side, too."

"It was that sow's udder of a foreigner!" Jui Ah screamed

up at Chih-Yü, his face contorting now that the pain had hit him.

She sat her horse rigidly, some of her tension communicating itself to her mount, for the sorrel's ears were laid back and he champed at his bit nervously. "Very well. Who began it?"

A babble greeted this question as every man who had watched vied with the others for the chance to give his version of what had happened. Jui Ah had provoked the foreigner, who had attacked him with demonic fury. No, it was Jui Ah who had attacked, but the foreigner had driven him mad. No, Jui Ah had been under the control of the foreigner's sorcery, and had been set to fight so that the foreigner could vanquish him at last: Jui Ah was fortunate to be alive.

"That last is correct," one of the militiamen said calmly. "If you had seen how Jui was cast through the air . . ."

"I did see. I saw a great deal." Chih-Yü dismounted, giving the reins over to one of the grooms, who was grateful to lead the horse away and escape the castigation which all of them surely deserved.

Jui Ah had managed to sit up, but he moaned as he breathed, sucking in air in gasps. His chest was bloody and the ends of his broken collarbone scraped together once, so that he almost lost consciousness. He tried to point at Saint-Germain, who stood alone in the courtyard, his dark eyes fastened on Chih-Yü. "Cur! Vile son of a diseased jackal!" he raged.

Chih-Yü walked over to her Captain of militia and stared down at him, her face quite pale now. "You will say nothing more," she ordered him, her manner dispassionate though she was full of turmoil. She had known for some time that Jui Ah desired her: he had made no secret of it. His lust was inconvenient but she had chosen to ignore it. Now she knew she had been unwise, for he had allowed himself to regard her possessively. She had the right to blame him, but was not quite capable of doing so. "I should send you away," she said at last. "I should order you to depart now, before your hurts are treated. But I cannot afford to do that. We're too short-handed as it is, and no matter how incorrectly you have conducted yourself, I cannot allow myself to do as custom and law require." With that, she started to turn away.

"Whore!" Jui Ah shouted after her.

Chih-Yü swung back and brought her scabbard up, slap-

ping it against his face. "No man in this stronghold may call
me that, no matter what I choose to do, or with whom!"
Now her face was flushed and the masklike composure
stripped away. "I am Warlord here. Remember that, all of
you. If I wish to take a lame camel to my bed, that is my
right, and not one of you is entitled to question it. Is this understood?" She held her scabbard up and her eyes raked over
every man in the courtyard but Saint-Germain.

"That foreigner has bewitched you," Jui Ah muttered
through his split lip.

"No one has bewitched me," she said, quite suddenly calm.
Then she gestured to Ling. "See that he is bound up, and the
bones are set." Her scabbard was returned to her belt as she
left Jui Ah to cross the courtyard to where Saint-Germain
stood.

"I have medicaments, if you wish," he said softly as she
came up to him.

"No, nothing should come from you. It might seem that
you are making reparation, and that would not be wise." Her
eyes met his and there was worry in them. "Are you safe?
Did he hurt you?"

"I am not easily hurt," he said to her kindly. "I'm sorry
only that it came to this." As he glanced around the courtyard, he went on, "Do you think you should be speaking to
me this way? Jui Ah is not the only man here who resents
me."

Audaciously she put her hand on his arm, knowing that
this familiarity would be noted by all the men watching. "It is
not their place to question me." She was a small woman,
coming no higher than his chin, and she wore her strength
with a curious fragility that stirred Saint-Germain deeply.
"They should be aware of what is happening."

He bent his head toward her and whispered, "I thank all
the forgotten gods that you are a Warlord and not some man-
darin's Third Wife, relegated to the women's quarters and
wasting your intelligence and your courage on accounts and
running a household."

Chih-Yü stared at him, astonished. "If that is what must
have become of me if my brothers had been . . . satisfactory,
then I, too, am grateful to your forgotten gods." She glanced
over her shoulder to where three militiamen were struggling
to get Jui Ah onto a plank to carry him to his quarters.
"Dog's tongue," she said contemptuously.

Ling heard this and was so suddenly nervous that he dropped the corner of the plank he carried, and the others, after a few frantic, scrabbling moments, also lost their grip on the rough wood. Jui Ah shrieked as the plank crashed to the flags. Chagrined, Ling made a self-deprecatory gesture and motioned to the others to pick up the plank again.

They had almost raised the board all the way when one of the men caught a glimpse of something lying on the ground just where the plank had been. Ling tried to reach it, nearly stumbled, and pointed to the thing. "It fell out of Jui Ah's wallet," he said apologetically.

"Oh?" Chih-Yü asked, wishing to be rid of the man. "What is it?"

One of the militiamen bent down to retrieve the thing."A string of cash, I think."

Hearing this, Jui Ah cried out in fright. "Not mine!"

"Since when does a militia Captain turn down cash?" Chih-Yü inquired as she reluctantly approached the little group of men around Jui Ah. "A string of cash? How much is it?" She held out her hand to the man with the pierced coins on their leather thong. "Let me see them."

"It's just from gambling," Jui Ah insisted, his voice high.

"But you said they weren't yours," Chih-Yü reminded him as she took the string in her hands and inspected the coins.

Saint-Germain could see from the tightening of her shoulders that Chih-Yü was suddenly very upset. He hastened to her side, putting one small hand on her arm. "What is it?"

Her voice was choked with anger and despair. "Mongol cash."

"I won it!" Jui Ah protested.

"When? Where?" Chih-Yü asked. She signaled the men to set the plank down once more, which they did with horrified slowness.

"I don't remember," he said crazily, licking his lips between each word.

"This much cash and you don't remember?" Chih-Yü said, holding up the leather cord. "Who among you would forget winning this much money. There are brass and copper coins, but most of them are silver." She looked from one militiaman to another, and read the shame in all their faces. She lowered the string of cash, turning the coins over in her hand. "Jui Ah, where did you get these?"

"I won them, I won them," he shouted wildly, retching as his broken collarbone shifted.

"Yet you don't remember when, though the silver is hardly tarnished." The coins jingled in her hands as she shook them again. "What man here would take Mongol cash, no matter where he got it?"

One or two of the men started to boast and were quieted by their comrades. Jui Ah lay back on the plank and set his face.

"Shih Ghieh-Man," Chih-Yü said contemplatively, fingering the coins she held. "What would you do, if the choice were yours?"

"About Jui Ah?" He dreaded this question, for there was nothing he could say that would not alienate him further from these soldiers. He was aware that Chih-Yü was making a point with her men, and he knew that she was relying on his support. "I would search him."

Chih-Yü nodded once. "Search him," she said to Ling, and stood back while two of the militiamen bent to carry out her order.

Jui Ah was cursing softly between ragged breaths as his clothes were systematically and none too gently removed. His color was bad now, and his thoughts were muddied by the relentless, grinding agony of his broken bones.

Ling had drawn off Jui Ah's leggings and was reaching for the boots when he noticed a scrap of paper in the seam of the leggings. His eyes went to Chih-Yü's. "There's something . . ."

"Give it to me." She held out her hand for the paper, glancing at it when it was unfolded. Her whole body felt cold as she examined the drawing, which showed the two protected ways to approach the Mao-T'ou stronghold from the steepest side, and gain entrance to the keep. Convulsively her fingers closed on the paper.

"What is it?" Saint-Germain asked quietly.

Wordlessly she handed the crumpled sheet to him and stood beside him, her face vacant from shock as she realized the immensity of her Captain's treason.

"Is this the only thing you have provided the Mongols?" Saint-Germain did not raise his voice or assume a threatening attitude. He looked down at Jui Ah and deliberately hooked his toe under the Captain's broken leg. "Well? Is it?"

"Desecrator of family graves!" Jui Ah spat, then wailed as Saint-Germain moved his foot.

"Is this the only thing you have provided the Mongols?" he repeated reasonably.

It was some little time before Jui Ah could answer. "Despoiler of—" He did not finish. A shuddering groan passed through him as his leg was lifted by Saint-Germain's toe. "Stop him!" he demanded of Chih-Yü.

She came to stand by his head. "You should be grateful to Shih Ghieh-Man, Jui Ah. If it was left to me to deal with you, I would have your other leg broken as well."

Saint-Germain repeated his question three more times, and each time Jui Ah gave no information. "I don't think it will do any good to try longer," he said to Chih-Yü, hating himself at that moment. "He's bleeding again, and . . ." He turned his palms up to indicate the futility of their efforts.

By now the militiamen were silent, all of them touched by the monstrous act of their Captain. Most of them watched what was being done, a few with wolfish satisfaction in their eyes, some with impassive condemnation. The others stared distantly, refusing to acknowledge the questioning that was taking place.

"Yes," she said. "It will accomplish nothing." She clapped her hands sharply. "Get Ki-Djai."

A sigh passed through the militiamen at this name: Ki-Djai was the executioner.

Before the sun set there was another body hanging from the trees below Mao-T'ou stronghold in silent warning to Mongol scouts and raiders.

Text of a dispatch from the Warlord Tan Mung-Fa of Shui-Lo fortress to the District Magistrate Wu Sing-I in the town of Bei-Wah.

On the fourth day of the Fortnight of the Fire God,

the Year of the Ox, the Fourteenth Year of the Sixty-fifth Cycle, to the Tribunal of the Shu-Rh District.

Word came today from a messenger sent by the Warlord Kung Szei, informing the Warlord Tan Mung-Fa that the holdings of Warlord Kung have been overrun by Mongols, and at the time the dispatch was sent, all buildings in Kung's protectorate were afire and burning or had already been destroyed. Warlord Kung has indicated to Warlord Tan that the loss of life was staggering and that only those who fled into the hills have escaped the Mongol warriors.

Warlord Kung wished to warn all those in the Shu-Rh District that much larger numbers of the enemy have massed and are intent upon occupying all of this District before the autumn rains make battle difficult.

The messenger who brought the report from Warlord Kung has succumbed to his wounds, which were grievous, and for which the Warlord Tan's surgeon could find no remedy. The messenger, before his death, informed Warlord Tan that he had seen the Warlord Kung fall in battle, transfixed by enemy lances and bleeding from numerous wounds.

The Warlord Tan wishes to inform the Tribunal and the Magistrate Wu Sing-I that aside from the messenger, no one has reached the Shui-Lo fortress from any of Warlord Kung's holdings.

It would seem prudent, then, to prepare for a significant increase in Mongol assaults. The Warlord Tan earnestly entreats the Magistrate Wu to submit this dispatch at once to the Military Secretariat for immediate action.

By the hand of the secretary Hso-Yi, verified by the chop of the Warlord Tan Mung-Fa.

10

MAO-T'OU STRONGHOLD was unnaturally silent. Torches that were usually alight had been extinguished and the men who patrolled the walls greeted one another in whispers. No lamps were lit in the hall or the rest of the keep, no conversation came from the militiamen's sleeping quarters.

Chih-Yü paced her study restlessly. All the shutters were

open and what little light there was came from the half-moon
that sailed in the rumpled clouds. She paused at the window,
looking down, and was grateful to see a figure in black waiting below. Though she could not speak, she waved to him, indicating he should come up to her. Until that moment, she
had not realized how intensely she wished for his company. It
was an effort of will for her not to rush to the door and hold it
open, waiting for him.

At last the rap came, quietly, and a voice so low it could
scarcely be heard on the other side of the door said, "Chih-
Yü."

She longed to fling herself into his arms as she drew the
door back cautiously, but held her need in check. There were
other matters, more important now. "Shih Ghieh-Man," she
murmured as she made certain the latch was secure.

He was dressed in his Frankish gear, requiring only a mail
shirt to ride to battle, which she had forbidden him to do.
Though the men of Mao-T'ou stronghold respected him, they
would always regard him as an interloper and would not be
willing to admit him to their ranks.

"I have considered the weapons you have offered me," she
said as she moved away from him. "Tan Mung-Fa has brass
cannon, and has been censored for possessing them. The officials do not like district Warlords to have heavy arms. There
have been too many rebellions that sprouted from just such
seeds as that, and the current Emperor is not a stupid man."

"Isn't he?" Saint-Germain asked, though he knew she
would not agree.

"He is perhaps foolish. That is not the same thing as stupid." She had locked her hands together and stared at her in-
terlaced fingers.

"That's worse," Saint-Germain insisted. "A stupid man
cannot learn, an ignorant man has not had the opportunity to
learn, but a foolish man is able to learn, has the opportunity
and does not do it." He felt exasperated with the man in yellow, whom he had never seen, because he feared for T'en
Chih-Yü. "There's no point to this," he said abruptly, unwilling to argue with her. "What have you decided about the
weapons we've discussed?"

"The long arrows are most acceptable. The men will use
them and trust them. The black powder canisters are illegal,
and the men regard them as ill-omened. The other . . ."—
she drew a slow breath, recalling Saint-Germain's description

of the weapon—"my men have not seen in use, though they have heard of it. Most of them feel that such a weapon comes from demons and will dishonor them." She turned to him, seeking his comfort and understanding. "It may be all that you say, but I must refuse it. If these were army men, it might be different. Militiamen don't like burning weapons."

"Arrows, then; no powder canisters, no Greek fire." He looked down at her, troubled. "The Mongols will not care about whether or not the weapons are demonic."

Chih-Yü did not answer at once, for this was the very issue that had haunted her most of the day. "My men," she said slowly, "would not fight bravely if they believed that their weapons were accursed. They would fear to kill a foeman because his angry spirit might fasten on their souls after death."

"You realize that you are outnumbered?" There was accusation in his words, coming from his worry. "You have seen the Mongols in battle. You and Tan and Kung and Shao have faced them, and you have seen what they do. Isn't there any way to convince your militiamen that these weapons might make it possible for you to stop them, but otherwise they will be fighting against truly impossible odds?"

Her face was still, and she said with remote clarity, "I do not expect you to feel as they do, as I do. You are a foreigner, Shih Ghieh-Man, and our ways are not your ways. I have given my oath, as my father gave his, to defend this stronghold and its lands, and this district. If I suborn my men's integrity, I will violate my oath, and will be deserving of the death that will come to me for abusing their faith." She stood near him now, her palms toward him, entreating him to accept what she told him.

He took Chih-Yü's hands and carried them to his lips. He said nothing.

"Why did you do that?" she asked in a hushed tone.

"It is a mark of homage in the West." His dark eyes rested on her with sadness. "You merit homage."

She made a swift gesture to silence him, pulling one of her hands away, though she stepped nearer to him so she could hear him speak to her. "I haven't been tested," she said, then closed her eyes a moment. "It will be tomorrow, I think."

"And I." He took her into his arms, his hands spread wide on her back as if to provide her with additional armor against her enemies.

"I will give my orders before dawn. We might have the advantage of surprise if we are concealed in place before their scouts arrive." She was not able to imbue her plans with much confidence.

"How many men were in the company seen yesterday morning?" Saint-Germain inquired gently, drawing back so he could look at her face.

Miserably she recalled the horrified face of Ling as he had ridden through the gates of Mao-T'ou stronghold, his horse lathered and sobbing for air, his gear in total disorder. "Ling estimated two hundred, perhaps more."

Two hundred, Saint-Germain repeated inwardly. There were less than half that number of militiamen at Mao-T'ou stronghold now and only fifty-four horses for them to ride. The enormity of the danger went through him like cold steel, and it was with an effort that he restrained himself from shaking Chih-Yü. His hands grew rigid as he held her, and his compact body was taut.

Suddenly and silently she began to weep, and though shocked by these wretched tears, she was powerless to stop them.

"Chih-Yü, valiant Chih-Yü," he said, just above a whisper, as he held her, moving gently, rocking her. "Cry, elder brother." One hand stroked her hair, the other braced her back, lending her his strength so that she could replenish her own. He did not kiss her or caress her—for the moment they were as brothers or fellow-soldiers, and the comfort he offered was uncolored by desire.

A while later she gulped, sniffed and turned in his arms so that she could wipe her eyes on the hem of her sleeve. The anguish that had overwhelmed her was gone, jettisoned in the quiet tempest of her weeping. Her breath caught once in her throat, a last resurgence of her torment. Gradually she became aware of the concern in his whole demeanor, of the steadfast composure that had sustained her. She let herself lean against his chest, feeling serenity touch her for the first time in months. "I didn't mean to be so foolish," she said in an undervoice, and feared for an instant that she would have to endure a second bout of tears.

"You aren't foolish," he promised her as his hand tipped her head back. "A fool would deny the danger and make light of the risk." He recalled what he had said of the Emperor.

"There is great risk, isn't there?" she asked, and did not

need him to answer. "Actually, it isn't a risk at all, but a certainty." Now that she had said those ugly words, she discovered that they had lost much of their power. "Well, I told you there was no choice once, didn't I?" She caught the inside of her lower lip in her teeth, holding it while she mastered herself.

Saint-Germain tightened his hold on her. "You're brave, Chih-Yü. Nothing I say or do will protect you from that bravery."

Her attempt at laughter was a failure, and she pulled out of his arms. It was difficult to speak only in whispers, but she managed to keep her voice soft. "They will go into the valleys, I think. They know we're defended here, and will want to take the valleys first, so they can starve us out. A pile of corpses here and there will be demoralizing. Most of the militiamen come from one valley or the other. They will be distraught by what they see. It will not work to our advantage to let this happen." She had worked out her strategy over the last two days, being as realistic as she could be.

"If the Mongols had information from Jui Ah, they may well know where the traps have been laid around the fields," Saint-Germain warned, unperturbed by her change in attitude.

"I realize that, and I've tried to take it into account while making plans." Her hands closed together, flexed and closed together. "I have assumed that they will come in from the northeast, and cut off the road to Bei-Wah, which will not only prevent us from sending out a messenger to ask for aid, but will give them a strong position to deal with any reinforcements that might arrive. They will have to come through the millet fields, or risk crossing marshy land, which might be dangerous. There are four sets of traps along the boundary paths of those fields, and one or two of them may help. I hope they will, even if the Mongols have been warned of the presence of them."

"Those traps are pitfalls, aren't they?" he asked her.

"Most of them. There are four or five trip-lines, which I think might be more successful." She was frowning now, reviewing in her mind the defenses that had been established throughout the So-Dui valley.

"Do the farmers know what to expect?" He thought fleetingly of the inn at the head of So-Dui valley where Hsing had gone when she married. That lovely girl, he recalled, who had been puzzled but satisfied to be his concubine, now in the path of the most ruthless enemy. Was there a way, he wondered, to get her away before morning?

"They know that it will be deadly fighting and that they can expect no quarter whatever from the Mongols." She looked up, staring out at the wan light of the moon. "We Chinese have a bloody past, but nothing like this. They destroy everything in their path, the Mongols. Houses, farms, men, it is all one to them."

Saint-Germain had no soothing words to contradict her. "They want space to graze their herds, not houses and farms and men around them." It was part of the explanation, but not all of it. He decided to turn her mind from this fruitless reflection. "What about the shepherds and foresters? They've been alerted, haven't they?"

"Yes. I send messengers tonight, immediately after dark, to the farms and the inn to tell them to send the children and old people into the hills. The shepherds will take in a few, they have promised. The others will have to fend for themselves, but it will get them away from the fighting. That way those who remain will not be distracted with worry for them." As she crossed the room the old floor squeaked, and she froze, like a thief in an unfamiliar building.

"No one heard but me," Saint-Germain assured her as he followed her, his light step awakening another such sound. "There. You see how quiet?"

She nodded automatically. "I ordered all of Gei's people into the hills," she said after a moment. "The inn can't be saved, so I have ordered that the building be filled with barrels of pitch. Four men took the barrels down yesterday, and carried Gei and all his family away, concealed under sacking. The barrels were old meat and grain barrels so that if there were men watching, they will have seen nothing remarkable." She studied him shyly. "Hsing is gone."

"Thank you," he said, relieved for the girl, but more moved by Chih-Yü's generosity.

"Then you do care for her," Chih-Yü declared with an unexpected flash of jealousy, which confused her. She told herself sternly that had she married, she would have shared her husband with other women. But a husband would not have stirred her as Saint-Germain did, would not have freed her close-held desire.

"So do you, or you would not have sent her away," was his

kind response. "Naturally I have been fond of her. I cannot treat her as I did and not experience some sort of tie. But you know yourself that her pleasure in me was mild. Of necessity, then, I felt the same mildness for her." He was standing behind her, and he put his small hands on her shoulders, drawing her back against him. "There is nothing mild between us, Chih-Yü," he said in a deeper voice, uncannily echoing her own thoughts. "If you had wanted it, you could have had that from me—a pleasant satisfaction, a dream of easy gratification, nothing more. Hsing never understood what passed between us, either from her sensuality or her fear. Oh, yes, in part she was afraid of me, though I tried every way I know to ameliorate it."

"How could she fear you? How could anyone fear you?" She was astonished at the idea.

His chuckle was oddly sinister. "I am not always . . . courteous," he said dryly, his memories scalding through him.

Chih-Yü recalled the cold skill with which Saint-Germain had fought Jui Ah. Perhaps he could be frightening. "But fear, in this?"

"It has a kind of power. I would rather not use it, but if I must, I will . . ." He stopped, for this would accomplish nothing. "Hsing should not concern you, Chih-Yü. She has nothing to do with what happens between you and me."

"I suppose it is silly. Without doubt you have known others." She was not distressed.

"Many others," he murmured, sensing a new excitement in her.

"And did they all fear you?" She raised her arms and reached behind her head to touch him.

"Not all." His hands moved from her shoulders, under her arms to her breasts. He was not hurried.

"What became of them?"

He hesitated, then said, "Some of them died. Some of them changed."

"Changed?" She felt that strange tightness in her body that marked the beginning of her desire.

"When there is understanding, there is a change, eventually. You know what I am, what my love is, and in time that would change you." Had there been no order for silence, he still would have spoken quietly. His hand cupped her breasts, unmoving.

"How would it change me?" The thoughts of battle were distant now: his voice and his hands were real.

"It would make you what I am, in time."

"A vampire?"

"Yes." He lifted her hair with one hand and bent to kiss the nape of her neck before continuing. "When I am truly known, something of my nature passes from me."

"But a vampire?" The myths haunted her. She heard her nurse's voice telling her of the rapacious p'o seeking endlessly for a body to possess so that it could plunder the living. To her shame, she trembled.

"It need not be terrible," he said, and the ancient loneliness was in his tone. "For those who have changed, death has little hold on them, and they cannot be bound by it, even as I was not."

"But how does it occur?" She felt his hands on her hips, gentle, persistent. Her head went back and her breath came more deeply. As she listened to him, she watched the moon sliding through the clouds, and she let her mind drift with it.

"It . . . evolves. We have been together three times. If you were to let me love you three times more, you have sufficient . . . experience of me. Then, unless your head was struck off, or you were crushed or burned, there would be no death for you." Slowly he opened her sheng go and felt the warmth of her flesh in his hands.

"There are no other ways?" Her body was alive with his touch, eager for him. His small, beautiful hands encountered no resistance as they delved further, reaching to find the source of her pleasure. She sighed languidly, glad to give herself over to this intense moment.

"There is a way," he murmured to her hair as he stroked her intimately. "Those who taste my blood are made like me. If you would wish that . . ." He did not want to offer false hope. "It will not make you invulnerable to steel and flame, but it is some protection." He dared not admit, even to himself, how little defense vampirism would be against the hazards of battle with so implacable a foe as the Mongols.

Her back arched suddenly and she shivered ecstatically. A cry escaped her before she could stop it, but her joy was so profoundly private that the sound was not very loud. She felt flushed, and her feet, which had grown colder, were pulsingly warm in the sweeping delicious frenzy coursing through her. Her fingers were sunk in his dark, loose curls that pressed her cheek as he bent his head against her neck. Though her breath was unsteady, she longed to be able to speak, to tell him that never had she anticipated such complete fulfillment. But words were pallid, tenuous things compared to the immensity of her desire's culmination. Surely, surely there could be no greater satisfaction, yet she was aware that his hands were not idle, and to her amazement she was responding to an evocation of greater joy. Only when she felt as if the very earth moved under her did he begin to calm her, to lead her roiling, glorious senses to inmost peace.

"Chih-Yü," he said out of the soft stillness with such compelling longing that she listened to him with her whole soul, "if there had been time, I would have wanted you with me. You have renewed me."

It was some little time before she was able to appreciate fully what he had said. By then they had drawn apart: the exquisite elation which had possessed her had given way to tranquillity and she was reluctant to surrender that quiet. Finally she met his penetrating eyes. "You speak as if we'll never have the chance to love each other again." Though she had meant to chide him only slightly, the prospect of losing the splendor of their passion tinged her words with bitterness.

He could not reply to her at once, but the pressure of his hands on her own told her how deeply that dart had struck. "Do you think," he said with some difficulty, "truly think, that there will be no more time?"

She looked away. "I don't know."

He touched her face. "Chih-Yü, no pleasant little mendacities. That isn't worthy of you. There is a battle not many hours away, and you know enough of war to know your odds are poor."

"That's why I want to fight in the valleys," she said, sighing as the world closed back in on her. "If we wait here, the valleys will be destroyed, we will be completely disheartened, and in the end, in spite of our defenses, we will go down in flames. There are too many Mongols and far too few militiamen. In the field we might be able to hold them off for a day, or two at the most, and can do enough damage to give these people who live here, who will lose all that they have, a little time to get away." Her voice dropped and she moved to fasten her sheng go.

"You sent a messenger to Tan Mung-Fa yesterday, didn't

you?" He opened his arms to her, holding her as she came to him.

"Yes."

"Do you think he will send soldiers?"

Her eyes were distant a moment; then she said, "No."

"And you will not accept the little protection my blood will give you?" There was anguish in his voice. The moonlight was almost gone as the clouds thickened, and only his extraordinary eyes were able to penetrate the darkness.

This time she actually considered the matter. It struck her then that she knew very little about this foreigner, about his life and the gift that he offered her. She answered him with care. "If I am alive at this time tomorrow, I will welcome your blood." He started to protest but she silenced him. "This is my land, its safety has been entrusted to me. If it is defeated, then I must fall with it. But if it is saved, then I will not refuse your salvation." It was difficult to move back, but she did, staring up at him. "Shih Ghieh-Man, don't try to dissuade me. It would take little to weaken my resolve and that would be . . ."—she frowned, searching for a way to express her feeling—"ultimately disgraceful."

Saint-Germain wished that he could protest, that he could remind her how many other Warlords had left less desperate conflicts than this one and were still regarded as heroes.

She hesitated, then said, "My father followed the teachings of Kung Fu-Tzu, and taught me to revere them. I am acting in his stead, and if I were to fail now, in the face of this tribulation, then I could not face the souls of my ancestors, or bear to have my name entered in the annals of my family."

He heard her out, then said, "I could wish you would prefer life, even my life. Your honor is not at fault. There are fools in Lo-Yang and K'ai-Feng who are too caught up in that ritual of court to know in what danger they all stand. Another ten years of their inept handling and all of this empire will be on her knees. How do such creatures as they deserve your life?"

"I don't know," she said solemnly. "But the people in the valleys have trusted me, and I will fight for them." Her father, she thought, would have wanted her to fight, not for the farmers and their holdings, but for the family reputation. "My brothers are no help to me, and most of my uncles find me an embarrassment. But the farmers here have always respected me, and have provided this fortress with militiamen.

Kung Fu-Tzu believed that those in power should be deserving of it." She turned away from the window and from Saint-Germain. "I should be dressing. My men will muster in another hour. If I fall, see me buried."

"Shall I stay? Would you like my help?" There was so little she would accept from him and it stung him.

"No, I'll see to it myself. The housekeeper set out my things before she retired. My steward will rise shortly to arm me." She looked toward him. "Forgive me. This is difficult for a foreigner to understand. I'm grateful that you have so much regard for me . . ."

"Regard?" he echoed, knowing that she was trying to take the pain out of their separation.

She could not meet his eyes. "More than regard, then." And she looked up, and for one enduring instant their passion flared between them.

"Chih-Yü . . ." he began, but before he could move to reach her, she fled the room, leaving him to stand alone in the darkness.

━━━━━◆▶━━━━━

A letter from Kuan Sun-Sze to Saint-Germain, never delivered.

On the occasion of the Festival of the Harvest Lights in the Year of the Ox, the Fourteenth Year of the Sixty-fifth Cycle, from Lo-Yang:

My excellent foreign friend, I trust that the terrible predations of the followers of the Mongol Temujin have not touched your district. News here is very poor, and so I know very little of what has occurred more than a day's ride from the city gates. In the last few months I have thought of you, and have hoped that the advice I gave you at the time I brought you to the attention of the Warlord T'en Chih-Yü was wise. There has been much change here, and it distresses me greatly to see how different Lo-Yang has become in so little time.

Though there are no armies at the gates, we are like a
city under siege. There are always soldiers in the streets,
and the talk one hears in the taverns is most distressing.
No one has any faith in the Empire. Just the other afternoon I actually heard one of the officials of the Magisterial Tribunal refer to that Mongol butcher as Jenghiz
Khan!

The reason I am telling you this is so that you will
understand when I inform you that you must not return
here. Foreigners are in the most grave danger from the
people. Three days ago, two Korean scholars were
stoned by the women at the vegetable stalls in the Street
of the Bending Willows. You, being so much more obviously foreign, would be the target for greater outrages
than that. Were it possible to travel with any reasonable
margin of safety, I believe that I would accompany this
letter to the Shu-Rh District and ask for a place of my
own at the Warlord T'en's stronghold.

Your acknowledgment of the receipt of those items I
sent you earlier this year was delayed for some time on
the road, but a Captain of Archers brought it to me not
so very long ago. I was pleased to learn that you did not
hold me responsible for the destruction of your house
and compound and that you did not intend to petition
the Magisterial Tribunal for restitution. Ordinarily I
would have insisted that you demand such reparation,
but at times like these, it would be folly to do so.

I understand from a cousin of mine at the Tribunal
that the army expects little difficulty from the Mongols
so far west as you are. The generals believe that the
greatest thrust must be at the heartland and the capitals
in order to paralyze the empire. How fortunate you are!
Here we worry day and night when those frightful barbarians will appear. Where you are, there is protection
from their invasions. Should I learn of any developments
that might prove dangerous to you, I will be certain that
you are notified. Doubtless you will want to be informed
before the Mongols actually come into that district that
they are on the move, not only so that you may warn
Warlord T'en, but so that you may provide passage for
yourself and your servant to more secure areas.

How inelegant my expression has become. I have not
inquired into the progress of your studies, or the delights

of the Shu-Rh District. I suspect that I am too much of a city-dweller, and though I often repair to the country estates of friends, still my heart secretly yearns for the bustle and rush of Lo-Yang. Therefore you must excuse my lack of enthusiasm for your current situation, though I find with the advancing threat of Mongol attack, my taste for the remoter parts of the Empire is growing. Though I write most informally, I know that you will perceive it in the spirit of good fellowship, for to tell the truth, I miss those conversations that we so often enjoyed while you lived here and did me the honor of having me at your house. Also, I find that I am sufficiently prejudiced against country life that I have great difficulty imagining that anyone can work there, and so I have been unpardonably rude in that I have asked nothing about what you have done.

You may be interested to learn that there are new laws against alchemists, particularly the making of gold, for it is reasoned that if the alchemist fails in this endeavor, he will be tempted to steal in order to make up for what he did not produce. The officers of the Tribunal have come to the university once or twice and have spoken most forcefully on the matter, and we all nod and argee and work more circumspectly.

Let me assure you that when this crisis has passed and the Mongols have been driven back into the desert where they belong, it will give me the greatest pleasure to receive you here in Lo-Yang and see that you are restored to your full dignities at the university. For the moment, I would be less than a friend to you if I did not reiterate the need for you to stay away. The danger is most grave, and will continue to be so until the Imperial army has cut this menace down to proper size. In a few years, we will laugh about this, most certainly, and think back to these perilous days as one remembers an incident in childhood.

The Magisterial Tribunal has ordered your name removed from the university roles, but I have taken the liberty of placing all your records in the archives so that when you return, you will have your notes and other papers available to you. The Provost does not know of this, at least not officially, but he has tacitly sanctioned such actions before, and I have assumed he will extend such approval to my decision, if it is required.

When you are able, send me word of your activities there, and I will attempt to keep you informed of the movements of the Mongols and the successes of the Imperial army, so that you will be prepared. You must surely know by my lamentable lack of literary style that this comes by my own hand to you, and that it bears my sincerest greetings as well as my continuing friendship. I have made no copy, and request that you do not keep this.

Kuan Sun-Sze
University of Lo-Yang
his chop

11

FROM HIS vantage point on the ramparts of the Mao-T'ou stronghold, Saint-Germain watched the battle below. The air, which in the morning had been sweet with the harvest scents of early autumn, was now scorched with smoking buildings and charred fields.

T'en Chih-Yü had deployed her men in the Geese Winging Amid the Clouds formation at the point where So-Dui valley narrowed and cut through the gap to the smaller, higher Oa-Du valley. Three farmsteads had provided some cover, disguising their numbers—fifty-four mounted fighters and another thirty-nine men on foot. Many of the farmers had agreed to work with the militiamen, carrying supplies, water, bandages, weapons as they might be needed. Chih-Yü, mounted on her sorrel, had taken up the apex of the long V, with her two most experienced militiamen on either side of her.

It was midmorning before the Mongols came through the low pass into the So-Dui valley. There were more than two hundred of them—rough-looking men with bows, swords and thin lances, wearing light armor and curiously pointed helmets. They were mounted on small, scruffy horses, more like ponies, which proved to be fast, tough and indefatigable. They had begun by setting fire to the inn, as Chih-Yü thought they would, and five or six of them were burned when the barrels of pitch inside the old building exploded.

They were canny men, those Mongol warriors. They had been on a long, destructive campaign. They had been ambushed, booby-trapped and decoyed so often that now this latest outrage neither frightened nor angered them—it was exciting. With eerie, triumphant cries, they had turned their shaggy mounts into the valley and taken up a loose variation of the Propriety of the Six Domestic Animals formation, and rushed in a series of crossing search patterns across the fields. Not quite a dozen of the Mongols were victims of the deadfall traps, and five more were caught by various trip-lines, but their comrades paid such minor misfortunes little heed.

As the Mongols approached, Chih-Yü could see that her militiamen were growing restive with fear. It had been one thing to plan to face these calamitous fighters, but to wait for them, facing them, was another matter entirely. From their concealed positions, they watched Temujin's warriors approach, and terror ran over them with the harvest wind. Chih-Yü bit her lip, her eyes narrowing. The Mongols had not come far enough into her lines for the militiamen to affect the most damage on the invaders, but if she delayed much longer many of her men would bolt, and though each of them knew that to fly from battle brought the most ignominious fame and unredeemable death, the sight of the Mongols would drive this from their minds. Knowing it was disastrous, she raised her lance and signaled the attack.

"No!" Saint-Germain shouted aloud as he watched the militiamen move to close the open ends of their formation. "It's too early!" There was no one to hear him. Twenty women remained at the Mao-T'ou stronghold, along with a half-blind gatekeeper and two ancient grooms. The rest of the servants and slaves had been sent into the hills. Chih-Yü had offered to send Saint-Germain and his servant Rogerio to Bei-Wah or some other town, but he had refused, and when the others had left in the wake of the militiamen, he had hoped that his decision had been wise.

The militiamen spurred forward, their unmounted companions taking up positions with powerful standing bows which were set up horizontally on a tripod, being too long for a tall man to hold and fire. There was a flurry of activity as the remaining farmers rushed forward with the extra arrows for these huge bows, then the loading of the weapons began.

Chih-Yü leaned over her sorrel's neck, holding him firmly so that he would not bolt to join the other horses now racing toward the fierce men rushing down on them. She had to hold the apex or the other men would be endangered by the gap in the line.

One of the Mongol leaders shouted an order and reached for his lance. He was grinning with delight as he spurred straight toward the nearest militiaman, pulling up only when he had to tug his lance from the militiaman's body.

The line of militiamen held for a brief time, then sagged, bent and scattered as the third and fourth ranks of Mongols rode round behind it and attacked the defenders from the rear.

Shouts, groans, cries filled the air as the men of Mao-T'ou stronghold were spitted and hacked by the now-battle-frenzied Mongols. Horses squealed and screamed as they were cut down with their riders.

Saint-Germain could no longer make out the progress of the battle, and for that he was grateful. His hands were white as they gripped the rough planks of the stockade. The fighting was more than a li distant, and he could still smell the carnage on the air.

"Master," said a voice at his shoulder, and he turned to see his servant beside him. "I have taken the liberty of preparing your cases. It might be wise not to remain too long." There was almost no expression in his middle-aged face, but as he looked down, his eyes widened.

"They won't hold out another hour," Saint-Germain said quietly, with dreadful certainty.

"And then?" Rogerio asked.

"Probably the next valley. I don't think they'll take this place until the last. What is there to gain here?" He stood back from the wall, letting his hands drop to his sides. "There are men to be killed in the valleys, and farms to be burned. That's much greater sport than ransacking this place."

Rogerio glanced down to the confusion and slaughter at the foot of the promontory. He blanched, and Saint-Germain saw that his hands were shaking. "How long can that go on?"

"Perhaps an hour, two at the most. And then the Mongols will get into the next valley." He steeled himself to stare down the slope again. The line of militiamen was in complete disorder. There were horses running in panic, men screaming. Two of the Mongols had caught one of the militiamen, had tied him between their horses and were trying to pull him apart.

One small knot of militiamen had gathered at the entrance to the gap to Oa-Du valley and were fending off the invaders with lances and swords. Even as Saint-Germain watched, one of that valiant band went down as a Mongol sword sliced through him and his mount.

"I have a goat cart, Master," Rogerio said thickly. "I will load it at once."

"It might be wise," Saint-Germain said slowly. He felt the uselessness of it, the waste of the land and the lives. The folly of it sickened him, and he turned away.

Rogerio was glad to leave the ramparts. "I don't think I could bear to see much more of that."

"No," Saint-Germain agreed. "But we don't have to. Think of the men down there with Chih-Yü. What a vision to have at the end of life." He put his hand to his forehead, then straightened up. "About this goat cart . . ."

"I had it from the gatekeeper. There is room enough in the cart for three cases of earth and your Roman case. The rest will have to be left behind." He walked beside his master, talking quickly in order to block out the sounds that rode with the stink of burning on the wind.

"Left behind," Saint-Germain repeated dully. "Perhaps I should be grateful to that pirate of a Magistrate who took the Byzantine mosaics. At least they have a chance of surviving this invasion." His acerbity faded as soon as he had spoken. "Yes, I should consider that. Something will be salvaged, though it's only a few pieces of colored stone on wood."

Rogerio said nothing. He opened the door and allowed Saint-Germain to pass into his quarters. Here the noise did not penetrate, and except for the three large cases and the Roman chest in the center of the room, there was little to indicate that the stronghold was in the throes of defeat.

"Where did you put the yellow bottle?" Saint-Germain inquired after he had opened the Roman case and found only the barest equipment.

"It's in the laboratory," Rogerio answered after a pause.

"Get it." He would brook no opposition.

Rogerio started to protest, then caught the lambent glow of Saint-Germain's dark eyes, and wisely fell silent. He went to the laboratory, and with great care removed the large yellow bottle from its protected niche in the biggest cabinet. Gingerly he carried this back to the receiving room and with great care set it on the floor.

"How full is the bottle?" Saint-Germain asked as he tugged off his black dalmatica and rummaged in a lacquered pigskin box for his metal-studded long-sleeved cote of close-fitting black leather.

"I would say three-quarters," Rogerio answered, his tone full of disapproval.

"Have we got a supply of ceramic containers for it?" He flung the silken garments away and pulled the leather over his head.

"There are a dozen or so in the laboratory." Rogerio could not contain himself any longer. "My master, I have never wished to oppose you, but . . ."

Saint-Germain chuckled unpleasantly. ". . . but you are worried about using Greek fire. If it's any consolation, I share your concern." He had kicked off his thick-soled felt boots, and pulled calf-high Byzantine ones from a shelf under his Persian wardrobe. "Have you put earth in the soles and heels recently?" He lifted the boots so that Rogerio could see them.

"Not lately," was the cool response.

"Would you attend to that now, while I finish dressing?" His tone was matter-of-fact, and he tossed the boots to his servant, not looking to see whether he caught them. "Then, when you're through with that, you can help me prepare an amusement for those demons in the valley."

There was a subtle alteration of expression in Rogerio's faded eyes. "What are you going to do?"

Saint-Germain paused in the middle of pulling on leather leggings. "They have killed Chih-Yü." He did not have to explain to Rogerio how he knew this. "They have killed her, and they will be made to pay dearly for that."

"But Greek fire . . ." Involuntarily he glanced at the yellow glass bottle.

"What else can I do?" he asked coolly. "You and I alone cannot stop them. Chih-Yü would not allow me to ride beside her, though she was grateful enough for my horse. At the most, there are thirty Mongols dead down there. How else would you propose we stop them? Would our deaths, our true deaths, avenge her, if the Mongols triumphed in the end?" He stood up and drew on a long belt. "They will triumph, but not now, and not here."

"I'll get proper aprons," Rogerio said with curious distaste.

"How shall we arrange this? Throw the containers down on them, and then flee before the fires can spread?"

"No. I promised Chih-Yü this morning I would see her properly interred." He paid no attention to Rogerio's sudden protest. "I will do that. After Oa-Du valley is burning."

Rogerio started toward the laboratory, distress filling him. He stopped in the door. "And how do you know that she did not fall in Oa-Du valley?"

"I know," Saint-Germain said quietly, and began to arm himself.

By the time he emerged from his quarters, it was nearing sunset. As he stepped into the courtyard, he knew that Mao-T'ou stronghold was deserted. The men and women who had been there when the battle began in the valley below had left. He turned to Rogerio. "The goat cart?"

"I will bring it to the fork in the road near the spring." His face was expressionless. "I will wait until dawn, and then, if you have not come, I will set out toward the west."

A faint smile came into Saint-Germain's eyes. "Thank you, my old friend."

Rogerio made a quick, brusque sound. "Don't thank me. You know I think you are mad to do this. But after so many years . . ." He broke off. "The cart is ready. I loaded it while you were preparing your weapons."

"Excellent. Go carefully. Those highwaymen may be in the woods, hoping to pick off stragglers." He had heard little of the band of robbers in the last few months, but Chih-Yü had assured him that they were known to be in the area still.

"Highwaymen are minor difficulties." He looked up and through the smokey haze the sky was red.

"But you are armed," Saint-Germain said, almost amused.

"Certainly." Rogerio hesitated, then said in a great hurry, "I realize that you will not change your mind, but don't expose yourself to any more than you must." Before he could say anything else, he turned away from his master and stalked across the empty courtyard.

Saint-Germain watched Rogerio go until he entered the stable; then he stepped back inside his quarters and brought out a large, heavily padded box about half the height of a man. There was a crude sort of harness attached to the box, and this Saint-Germain fitted around his shoulders, securing the crossing leather belts on his chest. He pulled the door of his quarters closed for one last time, feeling a moment of the most profound regret. This he deliberately set aside, putting his mind on more pressing matters as he crossed the court-yard for the unguarded gates.

Many of the farmers in Oa-Du valley had been unfortu-nate enough to be taken alive by the Mongols, and were now being used by them for cruel and ghastly amusement. One man, a militiaman, judging by his boots, for the rest of his clothing was in tatters, had been tied around the chest and dragged behind a galloping pony while eight mounted, drunken men chased after him, trying to slice him with their swords when they came near enough to lean out of the saddle. The militiaman was hardly conscious and had stopped screaming some time before.

Another party had taken a dead horse, gutted it and sewed three farmers inside it, and were now roasting the terrible thing over a slow fire. Not far from a smoldering barn, a young man, a farmer's son, was being mutilated by three Mongol warriors. Most of the Mongols stood around a bon-fire, laughing, eating and drinking, and occasionally tossing a severed human limb onto the blaze, commenting on how well this leg or that hand burned and crackled.

Saint-Germain had kept to the edge of the fields, but his night vision made the whole grisly scene unmercifully clear. Rage welled in him as he watched and searched for a vantage point.

He came upon an old barn, fallen into disrepair and quite deserted. With caution he approached the building, and when he had satisfied himself that the rickety place was safe, he crouched low and ran with uncanny swiftness to the barn, huddling there while he loosened the buckles over his chest.

The riders chasing the militiaman came down the field at a disorderly run, their shouts high in the air.

Saint-Germain listened, waiting, as he reached so very slowly into the padded box he carried and drew forth a ceramic cylinder. It was meticulously sealed, but using a small dagger, he peeled away the hard wax from one end, and in the next moment, he had hurled the container directly at the Mongols.

The rush of air ignited the substance in the cylinder, and the container exploded with a muffled sound no louder than the bursting of a pine cone in a fire. Flying bits of eerie, gold-burning material fell in tendrils through the sky, beauti-ful to see. One of the Mongol warriors pulled up his pony to stare at the long, splendid rags of light as they drifted toward him. A scrap of the stuff dropped onto his shoulder, soft and graceful as thistledown, and where it touched, it clung and burned.

Almost at once the others screamed out as the Greek fire wafted among the mounted warriors. Pieces that fell in the grass set it alight, and in a very little time a quarter of the field was in flames.

Satisfied, Saint-Germain took up his padded box and moved back into the shadows of the trees at the edge of the field. No one noticed his swift, silent passage away from the abandoned barn.

The next container was flung not far from where the farmer's boy writhed under the ruthless Mongol knives. Screams and imprecations burst from the three torturers' lips, but before others could rush to their aid, another cylinder burst apart above the bonfire. Now there was so much chaos that none of the Mongols was able to take charge. Men rushed blindly, tearing at the vinelike material that seared garments and flesh equally with scorifying heat that seemed to devour even bone. It was useless to try to dislodge the deadly fibers, for they held fast everything that touched them. Men shrieked in agony as the Greek fire consumed them with a rapacity greater than any they themselves had shown in battle. Horses reared and ran and burned, mouths and flanks foaming. Even the steadfast Mongol ponies were filled with terror and rushed aimlessly through the blazing night until a filament of Greek fire would bring them down.

Saint-Germain did not like killing the horses and ponies. It was only the Mongols he hunted. Yet he threw two more cylinders before he was certain that the invaders would not live to see sunrise. He took little gratification from this, for his hatred was hot as his Greek fire, not calculating and frigid. He knew beyond all doubt that this was an empty gesture, an act of defiance that would go unnoticed in the horror of the invasion. He was also aware that this would not restore Chih-Yü. She was beyond any act of his. Yet, now that his first task had been completed, he turned to the second and more difficult one.

So-Dui valley was an abattoir. Parts of the ground were caked hard with blood. Insects had converged on the loathsome feast: things that scuttled, that crept and flew and buzzed. It had begun with flies in the afternoon, before the last of the battle. Now there were many more varieties going about their scavenging work.

Repugnance threatened to overcome Saint-Germain, but he thought with goading irony that he, of all men, should not be distressed at the sight and scent of blood. He stumbled over a headless trunk, and wondered how many of the militiamen had been beheaded. It was a common Mongol practice to place piles of severed heads near their battlefields. He had hoped that they would wait until the next day, when the killing and feasting were finished, to assemble their hideous trophy.

Because many of the corpses had been decapitated, Saint-Germain went slowly among them, feeling his way. He could see far more than he wanted to, but not enough to distinguish the one female body in this charnel field. Cold, stiffened men were tumbled with their fallen mounts. Bodies and parts of bodies had been tossed into a heap at one place. With all his senses deadened, so that he worked with mechanical efficiency, Saint-Germain picked his way through that abhorrent tangle without finding Chih-Yü.

When at last he found her, it was by the sheerest accident. He had been following a drainage ditch that ran beside one of the fields, and at the edge of a deadfall was what appeared to be a heap of filthy sacking. He almost passed it, when he recognized the brass insignia on a dented piece of armor. Slowly he touched the material, and felt metal under the blood-matted cloth. His chest grew tight and hot as he turned the body over.

He told himself that he was pleased that the Mongols had not cut her head off, but the dire expression that was frozen on her face was harrowing to see. A broken lance was still clutched in her cold right hand and her scabbard was empty. He tried to brush the caked blood from her face and found that half the skin had been sliced away from the side of her head. He was incapable of weeping, for that had been lost to him when his essential nature changed, long ago, and so the sound that tore through him was more like a howl than the beginning of tears. He pressed the dangling skin back into place and held it there. He dared not move his hand for fear the wound would gape once more. With difficulty he used his other hand to get out of the harness that kept the padded box on his back. When that was done, he removed the last of the Greek-fire cylinders, setting the box on the ground.

For some time he worked at putting her into the box, his mind resolutely shut to the grimness of the task. Once, as he pried her fingers from the shaft of the lance, he recalled with overwhelming intensity the way that hand had touched him the night before, and her promise, that if she survived the day, she would share blood with him this night. He staggered away from the box, his hands covering his face until he mastered the despair that transfixed him.

When he was finished, the night was far advanced, but the Warlord T'en Chih-yü lay in a grave that had been dug as a deadfall, Saint-Germain's padded box serving as her coffin. Her name and rank had been carved into the side of the box, and the date and manner of her death. Instead of laudatory verses, Saint-Germain had put the one-character "valor" to recommend her to her ancestors.

Shortly before dawn, Saint-Germain trudged up the path to the fork in the road where Rogerio waited with the goat cart. He was sickened and weary from the appalling night, yet he was grateful that he would have to go far that day, for his fatigue numbed him, and he was grateful for that numbness.

There was the brazen clunk of a bell, and then Rogerio stepped out of the shadows. He said nothing at Saint-Germain pointed up the hill and away.

--- ◆▶ ---

A letter from Wu Sing-I, Shu-Rh District Magistrate, from the town of Bei-Wah, to the Secretariat of Defense at K'ai-Feng.

On the eve of the Festival of the God of Hearths and Furnaces, the Year of the Ox, the Fourteenth Year of the Sixty-fifty Cycle, to the Elevated Officials of the Defense Secretariat in the capital of K'ai-Feng:

This most unfortunate Magistrate must inform the Officers of the Secretariat of the latest disaster which has befallen this most unhappy district. Without doubt some of your number are aware that this most unworthy person has, in the past, beseeched those in high places to see that we in this District were adequately protected from our foemen. At such times as the Elevated Officials deigned to answer this unworthy person's requests, it was to assure him that there was no danger whatever to Shu-Rh District. When this unworthy person took it upon himself to provide information to the contrary, it was ignored or set aside for the more pressing business of reclaiming Pei-King. This most unworthy Magistrate was not accorded the courtesy of aid, and the plans to send a military inspector to this District were set aside when some of your number decided that there was not sufficient reason to do so.

It is my lamentable duty to inform the Elevated Officials that they were tragically mistaken. The Mongol attacks which we have sustained since more than a year ago have not, as certain of your numbers so confidently predicted, decreased, but have grown steadily in frequency and savagery. This most unworthy Magistrate sent you word when the fortress of the Warlord Kung fell to these invaders, and was given no response.

Now there had been another attack. The Mao-T'ou stronghold, with all its militiamen and its Warlord, T'en Chih-Yü, has fallen, and with it the two valleys, So-Dui and Oa-Du. Nothing is left there. The Shui-Lo fortress of the Warlord Tan Mung-Fa has been destroyed, and with it every farmstead and field for six li around. The Tsi-Gai pass stronghold and its Warlord, Shao Ching-Po, has been razed by a force of more than four hundred Mongols. The holdings of the Warlords Hua Djo-Tung and Suh Son-Tai are in Mongol hands even as this most unfortunate person sets his brush to the ink cake. Since the Elevated Officials have shown so little regard for the Shu-Rh District, this unworthy Magistrate seeks to remind them that the forces of these Warlords at this time constituted our entire district defenses. With the fortresses and strongholds gone, we are without the means to resist these foreign devils.

This unworthy person is unable to describe adequately to the Elevated Officials the devastation that has been visited upon this District. Everywhere there are smoldering villages and pyramids of severed heads. The sky is dark from the burning, as though heaven itself wishes to hide its face from the wreckage. The people of the District are without food, without shelter, without aid of any kind, and as such, are filled with horror and apathy, so that they will do nothing now to prevent the Mongols from killing them.

This unworthy Magistrate has a messenger standing by, and as the walls of Bei-Wah are afire, it would not be wise to delay him any longer. The records of this District have been hidden in a dry well on the south side of the walls, and may survive what the people will not.

Since this most wretched person has failed so signally in his tasks, since he has shown himself to be unworthy of the name he bears and his illustrious ancestors, and since he is without hope even of the compassion of Heaven, he will end his life as soon as the messenger has departed. He desires that his name and functions be stricken from the records of the family Wu and that no distinction of any kind mark his passing.

From the brush and hand of the despicable person who was the Magistrate Wu Sing-I, in Bei-Wah.

                                          his chop

PART II

Shih Ghieh-Man

A letter from Mei Sa-Fong to Nai Yung-Ya and the Nestorian Christian congregation of Lan-Chow.

On the Festival of the Wine God, in the Year of the Ox, the Fourteenth Year of the Sixty-fifth Cycle, the one thousand two hundred seventeenth year of Our Lord, to our beloved Pope Nai Yung-Ya and the faithful congregation in Lan-Chow.

This brings the greetings and good wishes of Mei Sa-Fong, his sister Mei Hsu-Mo, and our dear companion Chung La:

We have reached the port of Tu-Ma-Sik, far to the south of our country. The ship we sail on, a merchant vessel, very large and bustling with activity, stopped at Vi-Ja-Ya before coming to this place at the end of a long, narrow peninsula. Here we must transfer to another vessel, for this one has accepted a commission that will not take them toward Tien-Du for several months, and we are anxious to be on with our task. The captain of the ship has introduced us to a man from Pe-Gu, who is returning through the straits here to his home port, and then will cross the sea westward to a city called Dra-Ksa-Ra-Ma, which is near the mouth of a river with the impossible name of Go-Da-Va-Ri. This place is well inside the boundaries of Tien-Du, and there is a city farther up the Go-Da-Va-Ri called Han-Am-Kon-Da, where we are told there are other Christians. We have been warned that there are various warring groups in this region and that there are those who prey upon travelers, offering their demon goddess the lives of those they take.

This is a great delusion, of course, and we will be prudent but not fearful. It is not suitable that those of us who have learned to trust in the Master would turn away from His work because there are men abroad who

147

are most dangerous. We know that there is danger in
Lan-Chow. There is danger in a safe bed at night. If the
Master does not wish to protect His servants, then it is
at our peril that we live at all, let alone travel so far
from the hearths of those we love and who share our
faith. But how timorous a faith that would be!

Chung La has suffered greatly from the wave illness.
Luckily the motion of a ship does not often distress either my sister or myself, though we had one day of tempest when I was certain that every ill in creation had
visited itself upon me. You may imagine my relief when
I learned that half the crew had shared my feelings and
had not been able to handle the ship.

The captain has said that he will take this message
and see that it is delivered to you when he returns to
Hang-Chow. The congregation there has promised to
send any message to you as quickly as may be possible.

All through our travels we have heard rumors about
the Mongols and their impossible feats. One sailor on
this ship was in Pei-King not a year ago, and said that it
will be less than twenty years before K'ai-Feng is in the
hands of Jenghiz Khan, by which he means the man
Temujin.

I must not keep the captain waiting. Be assured that
when we reach this city of Dra-Ksa-Ra-Ma, we will
make every endeavor to get word back to you. I have
been warned that it will take time, but that does not per-
turb me unduly. Certainly if we have come this far, we
will be able to finish the voyage we have undertaken.

From my own hand, to all of you in the congregation,
in the city of Tu-Ma-Sik.

                                        Mei-Sa-Fong

1

IN A LONG, steep river canyon, the village of Huei-Zho
straddled the rushing water in eight places. Of necessity, the
progress of shops and houses strung out for a considerable
distance along the canyon walls. Huei-Zho owed its existence
and its small measure of prosperity to those eight bridges, for
this was the only safe crossing for more than a dozen li in ei-

ther direction. The village boasted a large number of inns and taverns and other hostelries, all catering to the various travelers using the bridges.

It had taken some determined persuading on Saint-Germain's part to be given a room at the Inn of the Stately Pine Trees. The manager, taking one look at the bedraggled men with only four chests on a goat cart, had tried to explain in his unfamiliar dialect that this was not an accommodation for poor men. He also intimated strongly that he did not like catering to foreigners.

Saint-Germain had answered him politely and told him the truth: that he and his servant had fled from Mongol attack—the manager clicked his tongue when he heard this—and that most of their more substantial goods had been left behind. To show his good faith, Saint-Germain produced five strings of cash, two of copper and brass, three of silver, and presented them to the manager with the assurance that these could be applied to his reckoning when he left.

At that the manager had softened visibly and expressed himself very contrite to have discommoded so distinguished a traveler. A quick discussion on the various merits of the rooms of the Inn of the Stately Pine Trees led to Saint-Germain being assigned the room farthest from the river, much to the manager's amazement.

"I am certain the view is magnificent, good man," Saint-Germain had said grandly, "but it is my misfortune to be a light sleeper and I fear that the running water would disturb me."

The manager bowed respectfully and kept his opinions of foreigners to himself as he led the way to the room Saint-Germain had chosen.

A few hours later, Saint-Germain sent Rogerio out with a handful of cash string to learn what he could of traveling conditions. He himself asked for directions to the nearest bathhouse where he could wash away the grime of nine days' walking.

"I talked to a number of traders," Rogerio reported when he returned at dusk. "Their news is grave."

Saint-Germain nodded. "I overheard three men at the bathhouse talking about their travels. I gather that it is true that the Silk Road has been cut?"

"Apparently," Rogerio said quietly. "There is also fighting along the river."

"Naturally," Saint-Germain said dryly. The numbness he had felt at Chih-Yü's death had not left him, and he found it difficult to be annoyed with the information Rogerio brought him. "River travel is not my favorite mode, in any case."

"There may be traders who have dealt with the Mongols who would be willing, for a price, to take us with them." Rogerio did not seriously believe that this was possible. "One man claimed to have been as far as Samarkand. He may—"

"Traders who have dealt with the Mongols are rarely honorable men. I have no desire to find myself in Karakorum with a collar around my neck. My previous years of slavery have given me a distaste of it." He surveyed the room. "It's pleasant enough here. We will wait, if we must." The chests had been brought up from the goat cart and stood in the center of the room. "I'll need one of those to sleep on," he remarked inconsequently.

Rogerio had seen these odd, distant moods come over his master before, and knew that they tokened great suffering. He had learned, in their long years together, not to question him at such times, yet now he felt an urgency. "Do you wish to remain in China?"

Saint-Germain turned away abruptly to look out an open window. "No," he said after a moment. "I have no reason to stay here."

"Then we must find other means of travel." He said it calmly, and though it was obvious, it evoked a gesture of agreement from Saint-Germain. More cautiously, Rogerio went on. "I took the liberties of finding out where the most discreet pleasure houses are."

"Oh, gods," Saint-Germain said miserably, closing his eyes.

"You have lived on the blood of rabbits and dogs for more than a week," Rogerio pointed out. "You need . . . release."

"Rabbits and dogs," Saint-Germain repeated with unpleasant laughter. "Well, it was economical. I had their blood, and you their flesh. A vampire and ghoul. What refugees this Mongol war has spawned." He sank onto one of the large chests. "I could lock myself in this and have it buried. It would be years before I would have to emerge."

"Could you do that?" Rogerio asked sharply.

"I have before," Saint-Germain said quietly. "But not . . . The last time was considerably before you met me." He swung his legs onto the chest and leaned back, so that he lay atop it. "No, Rogerio, I won't do that. I've let myself become too much a part of . . . humanity for that." He rubbed his eyes. "How discreet is this discreet pleasure house?" he asked after a short silence.

"They are used to foreigners, or so they assured me. Even foreigners who are very, very odd." He took a chance, and went on. "You told me once, when we were in the Polish marches in the winter, that living on dogs and rabbits was like living on bread and water. It would keep you alive, but exacted a price. Of course a pleasure house, discreet or otherwise, is not a perfect solution, but given the circumstances, isn't it wiser . . ."

"Oh, this damned appetite of mine!" Saint-Germain murmured. "One day, Rogerio, one day there will be a woman who knows me for what I am, for all that I am, and will accept it without reservation, or condition, not because I am a refuge or an escape or an amusement, but because I am myself, and I am her choice." He sighed. "I feel I'm being faithless. There was a time when this would not have troubled me."

Rogerio drew one of the chairs in the room forward and seated himself. The past days were at once vivid and blurred in his mind. He felt as if he had spent years leading that goat cart, following Saint-Germain through hills increasingly rugged. Saint-Germain had kept a brisk pace, apparently unaware of the grueling effort he was demanding of himself and his servant. Now that it was over, he felt the toll it had taken on him and knew that it would require several days of rest before his strength was renewed. Looking at Saint-Germain's too composed features, he knew that his master was carrying more than exhaustion within him.

"I'm not asleep," Saint-Germain said in a quiet, clear voice.

"Why not?" Rogerio countered.

"I'm thinking over what you told me." There was a slight frown on his brow.

"About the pleasure house?"

"No. About how we should travel. Whatever route we take in the end, we will need a guide. I think it would be wise to begin there," he said, very calm outwardly, but with a tension in him. "A guide is essential." He laced his fingers together at the back of his neck. "It would not be wise to travel eastward. Foreigners are not being well-received in the central part of the country, I have heard. The rivers are not . . .

practical. The Silk Road is too dangerous. I suppose it must be the mountains. T'u-Bo-T'e. I've never been there."

"Then, as you say, we must have a guide." Rogerio leaned forward, bracing his elbows on his knees. "You wish a guide—"

"A circumspect one," Saint-Germain interpolated.

"Yes. Who can take us into T'u-Bo-T'e. Shall I make inquiries for a party of merchants, or would you prefer to have more private arrangements?" Rogerio had realized during the many years he had lived in China that it was considered socially incorrect for a man to negotiate with guides and other such inferior persons if he had a servant to do it.

"It might be wiser to travel with a merchant train, but that would make it necessary that we accommodate the requirements of others. It's true that there is nowhere we have to be, but . . ." He stopped. The pull of his native earth, even through the lid of the chest, had begun to revive him. Slowly he let himself be drawn into the force of it.

Rogerio saw the slight alteration in his master's face, and, as always, it perplexed him. "But?" he prompted.

Saint-Germain's voice was at once stronger and more lethargic. "It might be advisable to find a man who will not mind leading a party of two. Given the times, I think we would do well to be most cautious. As foreigners, in a merchants' train, we might become quite expendable."

"The road to Baghdad!" Rogerio said, remembering the treachery they had encountered there.

"It's not an experience I should care to repeat," Saint-Germain remarked.

"A single guide, then, and we travel alone." He said it with conviction, unable to shut out the recollection of the heat and the rocks and barbarity of their captors. "You did not need to return for me then," Rogerio reminded his master.

Saint-Germain only looked at him, and Rogerio wished he had not spoken. "Be that as it may," Saint-Germain continued, "I hope you will keep that in mind when you search for a guide."

"What shall I offer this guide?" Rogerio asked, glad to be discussing more practical matters.

"Strings of cash, first. Gold and silver coins, not brass and copper. Don't paint too glowing a picture, or we will have every criminal in the district offering to lead us. You have an eye for legitimacy. Exercise your good judgment, as you have so often in the past. But I think it would be wise for us not to linger here any longer than necessary." The restoring influence of the earth in the chest brought back a curious homesickness in Saint-Germain. He could see the long ridge of mountains, so unlike these, curving around the enormous fertile plain. How long ago that had been, and yet it tugged at him with undiminished potency.

Rogerio agreed with this. "Very well, then, I will find a guide. A circumspect man." He rose wearily, prepared to go out again. "And about the pleasure house?" he inquired hopefully as he reached the door.

"Not tonight, I think," Saint-Germain replied as he stared at the ceiling.

Though he was tempted to argue, Rogerio closed the door and went out into the bustling street and made his way to the Tavern of the Excellent Delicacies, where he had been told the most gossip was to be had.

That day, and the next, Rogerio made the rounds of no less than nine taverns, never staying in any one place long enough for it to be noticed that he did not eat or drink. Each day he took the precaution of purchasing a duck or a hare from one of the butcher stalls, so that he always gave the appearance of a man who was getting ready for a meal.

"Which is true," Rogerio observed to Saint-Germain toward the evening of the third day. "I do make a meal of what I've bought."

Saint-Germain turned away from the window. "Yes. And it is of little moment that you, unlike so many others, do not cook it first." He had purchased a calf-length robe of heavy quilted black wool. His Frankish clothing had been somewhat repaired, though the leather garments he had worn on the long march from So-Dui valley were too far gone to be saved. He had pulled on his only remaining pair of Persian leggings and his high boots. Though his eyes were still shadowed and haggard, a degree of his imposing presence had returned.

Rogerio shrugged philosophically. "Luckily, foreigners are thought to be sufficiently peculiar that no one takes any notice of the fact that we do not wish to join the others at table."

"You mean that they have not taken notice yet," Saint-Germain corrected him.

"No," Rogerio said curtly, touched by apprehension.

What Saint-Germain was about to say was halted by a quiet knock at the door.

"Who?" Saint-Germain whispered to his servant.

"I don't know." Rogerio had moved toward the door.

"I have my knife if it is necessary," Saint-Germain said in a low voice as he nodded to Rogerio to open the door.

The figure in the hall was squat and powerful. Stumpy round legs were made more formidable by thick, fur-lined boots that ended just below the knee with heavy, loose leggings. Two layers of long-sleeved tunics lent him some of the aspect of a bear, though his scantily toothed smile was amiable enough. His obsidian eyes, sunk in deep folds, shifted quickly from Rogerio to Saint-Germain and the knife in his hand. The stranger made a gesture that implied approval. "You are the foreigners desiring to enter T'u-Bo-T'e?"

Saint-Germain lowered the knife but did not put it down. "It is possible that we are," he murmured.

"Then it is possible that I am the one you seek." His accent was thick but not incomprehensible. He had some of the manner of an educated man, though none of the refinement.

Rogerio opened the door so that the stranger could enter. He selected the one of the three chairs nearest the window, as if he wished to be assured of an escape route.

"If we are these foreigners," Saint-Germain said, taking the chair opposite the one in which the stranger sat, "why should you think that you more than another would be of use to us?"

The man hawked and spat, looking narrowly at Saint-Germain. "If you are the foreigners, you would want to hire a guide who has made the journey into the Land of Snows by more roads than one, and to more places than one city."

"Why would that be so?" Saint-Germain asked politely.

"Because there are many hazards in the mountains, and many of them walk on two legs. Also, if the snows come, it is necessary to know which passes are traversable and which are not. It is getting late in the year for such a journey, good foreigners, and if you are the ones seeking to go, it would be wise to begin as soon as possible." He had hooked his thumbs into the wide leather belt he wore and he studied Saint-Germain with open curiosity.

"Why do you stare at me?" Saint-Germain inquired, though he was more amused than offended.

"You are a foreigner. Your skin, your eyes, the way you

talk, how you move. I have seen those from Tien-Du and from the wild lands far to the north, but never have I seen a man like you. Your servant, too, with hair the color of ash wood . . . Most unusual." He leaned back and waited.

"Foreigners are often at a disadvantage," Saint-Germain said with a glance at Rogerio. "In their gullibility, they allow clever and villainous men to lead them into the remote mountains, where they are set upon by the companions of the unprincipled guide."

The stranger nodded. "Often it has happened thus, and those who are honest decry it, for we are painted in the same dishonored colors."

The man was, Saint-Germain decided, a runaway Buddhist priest. His language and attitude, though roughened with his occupation, had enough of the monastery flavoring that it was still detectable after what Saint-Germain guessed to be the passage of several years. He bowed very slightly. "I am known here as Shih Ghieh-Man, which is not unlike my name in my own tongue. My servant is a native of Gades, a distant city on a great sea. We desire to go into T'u-Bo-T'e at once. I am prepared to pay well for a trustworthy man to guide us."

"It is an honor to meet so distinguished a foreigner," the stranger said with the remnant of trained courtesy. "This humble person has the family name of Tzoa and the personal name of Lem. It has been his livelihood for many years to guide merchants and teachers through the mountains. If you question this, Shih Ghieh-Man, you may send your servant to ask, at whatever place he wishes, of the truth of this."

Rogerio interrupted. "How are we to know that the tavern-keepers are not in your pay, willing to tell us whatever will be advantageous to you?"

"The servant is keen-minded," Tzoa Lem remarked to Saint-Germain. "It could happen thus. Do not confine yourself to the taverns and inns. Ask at the stables and the temples. You will learn that it is as I say."

"He's engaging, whatever else he may be," Saint-Germain said to Rogerio in Greek.

"That does not necessarily accrue to his benefit," Rogerio responded in the same language. "I will ask at the places he suggests, and in other places as well."

"What tongue is that?" Tzoa Lem demanded. "I think I have never heard it before."

Saint-Germain continued in Chinese. "It is a language of the West, old by their standards, somewhat younger by yours." He paused before saying, "Tzoa Lem is not . . , usual. The sounds are not of the Four Tones, and the syllables are not familiar."

"The Four Tones!" Tzoa Lem scoffed. "That is for those caviling swine in the capital. Here we keep to the true old words, not these flowery, impossible phrases."

"Of course," Saint-Germain soothed. "You will forgive my ignorance. Those who come from distant lands do not always have the opportunity to study as comprehensively as might be wise."

Tzoa Lem was somewhat mollified. "Well, there are more than enough men of this country who haven't your excuse and still keep to the Four Tones." He looked up at Saint-Germain. "I don't wish to force you to a hasty decision," he said carefully, "but perhaps I should tell you that in five days I will go into the mountains, whether you or anyone else accompanies me."

"I see. Five days." Saint-Germain tapped the knife on the palm of his hands. "What would such a journey require in preparation?"

"Oh, that varies, depending on your needs. Food we must have, and animals to take your belongings over the passes. Oxen do well enough on the plains, but are useless in the mountains. Ponies, if they are bred for the work, can go quite a distance in the mountains. There are those who prefer dogs and goats, and each animal has its virtue." He put his hands flat on the arms of the chair. "Animals must be fed, which you will have to consider when you make your purchases."

"Since you are the one who has traveled the way," Saint-Germain said respectfully, "you would be the most knowledgeable, and I hope that you would advise me. If you had to outfit this journey, what would you do?"

"For three men?" He shrugged. "Food, shelter, clothing, whatever goods you are carrying, fodder for the animals, strings of cash, weapons; all would be needed."

This lackadaisical manner affronted Rogerio, but Saint-Germain persisted. "And what beasts would you purchase?"

"It would depend on how much you had to carry." Tzoa Lem gave the chests a calculating stare and looked pointedly back at Saint-Germain.

"Yes, these chests are a part of it. There are four of them.

The fourth"—he indicated the Roman chest—"is somewhat smaller but not significantly lighter. They are all fairly heavy and bulky, but that cannot be helped."

Tzoa Lem pulled at the scrawny mustache that blurred his upper lip. "They will be a problem. You will have to allow for them in calculating the climb and daily progress. Such burdens will slow us down, but if there is no alternative, then . . ." He lifted his shoulders to show his resignation.

"How much of a difference could such a burden make?" Saint-Germain asked.

"It would depend. If there is rain, it is an inconvenience, but if there is snow, that's another matter. At a guess, I would say that such burdens might well turn three days into four. It will depend on the sort of animals you choose to carry them." His black eyes twinkled. "There are some Spiti ponies that can be bought at a reasonable price. They are your best choice, but they are not cheap, and they must be fed. They are slow at lower altitudes, but once we reach the first crest, they will be brisker." He gave Saint-Germain another one of his measuring looks. "They eat coarse barley gruel made with lamb broth. They're used to having a little meat with their food and do not do well without it."

Saint-Germain had heard rumors of such ponies, but had not been certain he believed the reports until this moment. "I assume we will be able to hunt as we go." It would be necessary for Rogerio to hunt, of that he was certain.

"If that is your wish," Tzoa Lem said after a slight hesitation. "Many travelers do not like to take such a chance."

"And prefer sickness from rancid meat to one day of poor hunting? An odd economy, I should have thought." Saint-Germain tucked his knife into the wide belt he wore. "How many of these ponies will we need?"

"One for each of us to ride. That is essential, believe me. One for each of the trunks. One for relief. One for other baggage. That means nine."

"What will nine Spiti ponies cost?" Saint-Germain inquired as if the matter were of little interest to him.

"That depends upon who buys them. If you buy them, perhaps ten strings of silver cash, but that will include the pack saddles and the rest of their tack. If I buy them, perhaps six or seven strings of silver cash, including not only tack but part of their feed."

Which, Saint-Germain assumed, meant that Tzoa Lem

would reserve one of the strings of cash for himself. However, even allowing for this, it was undoubtedly cheaper and would gain him the respect of the guide. "You are the one who has experience in these things, and since I am as a beginning student, I entrust myself to you. By all means, purchase the ponies. I should warn you that I have some knowledge of horses and ponies. Don't think to fob broken-down animals off on me."

"I'd have to be a fool to do that," Tzoa Lem said. "Since I'm going with you, I'd risk as much as you."

"There is that," Saint-Germain agreed urbanely, knowing that a man leading others into a trap might give himself away with inferior animals, obviously never intended to finish the journey.

"You may inspect them before I pay the final fees," the guide added. "It might be wise if you did, if, as you say, you know something of horses and ponies." He paused, staring reflectively at the far side of the room. "My fee to guide you to Lhasa, which is the main city of T'u-Bo-T'e, will be four strings of cash in gold. I will not haggle about the sum. You will find no other guide as capable as I am, and none more honest. Consider that." He lumbered to his feet. "I will expect to have the first two strings before we leave, the last two when we arrive. Expenses at inns along the way—although I warn you now that they are few—will be paid by you. Do you agree?"

"If those are your conditions, I accept them." Saint-Germain bowed very slightly. He stood aside to allow Tzoa Lem the opportunity to reach the door.

"Tomorrow I will ask you to inspect the ponies," Tzoa Lem announced, then went on somewhat more petulantly. "You will have to inform me what quality and quantity of food you wish me to purchase."

"You may safely leave that to me," Saint-Germain said with a singular expression that was not quite a smile and yet showed his small, even teeth.

"That's up to you." The guide bowed as deeply as his heavy clothing permitted, then let himself out of the room.

Saint-Germain held up one hand to silence Rogerio's objections until the heavy tread of the guide faded on the stairs, and then he said softly, "Follow him. Don't let him see you."

Rogerio nodded. "He will not lose me."

"By tomorrow, we should know with whom we are dealing," Saint-Germain observed to Rogerio as the servant slipped, unnoticed by any other guest, into the hall.

——————◆————————

Text of a letter from Kuan Sun-Sze in Lo-Yang to Saint-Germain at the Mao-T'ou stronghold. The letter was impounded by officers of the Magisterial Tribunal of Lo-Yang as evidence in their investigation.

On the eleventh day of the Fortnight of the Autumnal Fogs, in the Year of the Ox, the Fourteenth Year of the Sixty-fifth Cycle, to the learned foreigner Shih Ghieh-Man, now in the Shu-Rh District in the employ of the Warlord T'en Chih-Yü at Mao-T'ou stronghold.

This respectful person must perform a most disgraceful duty: with this letter, he must, most regretfully, sever all relations with the stranger Shih Ghieh-Man. He cannot tell in any words how much he wishes it were otherwise. He has struggled with the August Voices of Authority and earned himself the censure and general odium of his colleagues. Consensus would not be enough to sway the personal loyalty of Kuan Sun-Sze—he beseeches the foreigner Shih Ghieh-Man to believe this, though there is little to support this assertion. Sadly, it is the decision of the Magisterial Tribunal of Lo-Yang that requires such action of this person, and he must bow his head to their urgings. Indeed, he must bow his head in more than one way.

Perhaps the foreigner Shih Ghieh-Man recalls a reckless and ill-considered act that this person perpetrated not so many months ago. The act alluded to here was the foolhardy act of placing the various records of the foreigner Shih Ghieh-Man in the archives without obtaining the approval of the various officials of the university. At the time, it seemed to this person that he was serving the interests of learning, but he now realizes that he was acting in an improper and dangerous way, and that it was contrary to the benefits of the Empire that he should do this thing, and he is most heartily sorry for his rash and inexcusable act.

The foreigner Shih Ghieh-Man will understand that though this person does not diminish the worth of their former association, he is aware that it is not appropriate for the association to continue. Not only is this Empire under threat of attack from the Mongol Jenghiz Khan, but there are personal obligations that each man has to the sanctity of his family. In putting a foreigner's friendship before the good of his sons and brothers, this person has shown himself to be beneath reproach and guilty of the most reprehensible conduct. If the dictates of filial piety teach us nothing else, they should instill in us all a responsibility to all those who share our blood. Though the foreigner Shih Ghieh-Man has professed himself to be aware of these ties, he is not a follower of the dictates of Kung Fu-Tzu, and for that reason, may not wholly comprehend how far this person has transgressed the tenets. It is true enough that for many years this person was seduced away from these teachings by following the words of the despicable Taoists. He was not aware until recently how pernicious their creeds are, and what chaos they lead us to.

Doubtless the foreigner wonders how it came about that this person became aware of his failings. Certainly it is appropriate that an explanation be offered.

When the documents in the archives were discovered, there was a great furor in the university and there were a great many unfounded rumors spread abroad. As it was implied that the records were placed there by sorcery, and since sorcery is a capital offense, the death penalty was given the missing foreigner, to run from this time until the phoenix rises. When this person, distressed to hear his friend maligned, approached the Magisterial Tribunal and admitted what he had done, he was most strictly admonished by the officers, who were not inclined to see the value of the records in precisely the same light that this person did.

In order to spare his family any greater embarrassment and to remove the terrible blot which he has seen tarnish his own life, but which has discolored and black-ened the repute of those closest and most dear to him, this person has decided on a gesture that will ensure a measure of expiation. Surely the foreigner Shih Ghieh-Man recalls the experiments that were conducted under his instruction in the Year of the Monkey. At that time there were occasional procedural errors which resulted in the substances in question being rendered unsuitable for use. As the foreigner may remember, a few of these substances were preserved, for though they were corrosive, yet they could be contained in various specially designed vessels which the foreigner was good enough to provide for that purpose. The foreigner Shih Ghieh-Man will be interested, for his own sake, perhaps, that there is a use for these substances, and that it is preferable to allowing others to select the time, the method and the place.

This person hopes that the foreigner will not think too harshly of him, for all he has said here is predicated on the obligations and responsibilities of those fortunate enough to have an honored name. He assures Shih Ghieh-Man that the end of their friendship is necessary.

From his own hand, and with his chop,

Kuan Sun-Sze

2

RUBBLE BLOCKED the narrow road, and ten paces beyond, most of the side of the mountain had been carried away by the avalanche.

"There's no going over it or under it or around it, not on this trail," Tzoa Lem said mournfully. "It happened recently—see where the rocks cut over the grass and moss? The moss regrows quickly, very quickly. This happened, at the most, two days ago. Probably during that heavy rain."

Saint-Germain stared at the bend up ahead where the road resumed, as if he could bridge the distance with the power of his eyes. They had been on the road for six days, and each day they covered less ground. It was cold at these elevations, and the storms that swept through the mountains were wild. They had experienced three storms so far, and from the way clouds were gathering overhead, another would be on them by nightfall. "Very well. What must we do?" Saint-Germain sounded neither angry nor discouraged. He looked at the guide expectantly, and the squat man on his equally squat pony sighed.

"There are other ways, of course. At midafternoon, we passed a road, do you recall?"

"Yes."

Tzoa Lem made an unhappy sound. "That is another way. Very steep. There are many rocks."

"As there are here," Saint-Germain said patiently. "No way will be without them."

"Yes," the guide agreed as he turned in his saddle to look back at the string of ponies he led. Rogerio was mounted on the last of these. He was bundled in a cloak of firecat pelts and was bone-weary from the days in the saddle.

"Master," Rogerio called, "do you wish to try to cross the slope? With caution and enough ropes, it might be managed."

"I don't think so," Saint-Germain called back, and was startled to hear a spatter of rocks on the swath. "No. It isn't steady enough. It's too likely to shift underfoot."

Tzoa Lem voiced his glum agreement, then paused to consider the matter. "If we turn now, we will reach the fork in the road before night is completely upon us. Then, in the morning, we may start up that other trail, if that is what you decide we must do. If it is what you wish to do."

"Why should I not wish it?" Saint-Germain asked, brows raising.

"There are many reasons." The guide would not look at his employer.

"You said the way was steep. That is hardly a deterrent, you know." He was aware that Tzoa Lem was being evasive. "What is so wrong with the other trail? Is it haunted? Are there highwaymen? Do they collect extra tolls?"

"Well," Tzoa Lem said, relenting, "that is the way to the old Chui-Cho fortress. It guards the pass. It's been there hundreds of years. Warlord Mon Chio-Shing has it now. He's one of the descendants of the Sui nobles."

"What is it that makes this Chui-Cho fortress so terrible?" He had heard various rumors of rapacious Warlords, but none of them naming the Warlord Mon Chio-Shing.

"Old Mon is not a concern." Tzoa Lem snickered uneasily. "He's fifty-eight years old. No, it's not Mon."

Saint-Germain was getting exasperated with the guide. "What is it, then?"

The answer came in a rush. "They say the place is defended by an ogre, and that everyone who fights against him is defeated."

"An ogre." Saint-Germain rubbed his face with one hand. "Tzoa Lem, though I have never before been in these mountains, yet I have seen much of the world. In my travels I have heard tales of giants, monsters, chimeras, basilisks, phoenixes, gryphons and dragons who have been said to guard everything from the most fabulous treasure to a hillside spring. I say I have *heard* of them, but never have I *seen* them. No," he corrected himself. "Once, I did see giants. It was in a land you have never known, which was called then Mauretania. I saw some men there, warriors of a distant place, who were half again as tall as I am, or very nearly that. They were lean as vines and had skins of tawny black."

"There are no such men," Tzoa Lem declared, glaring at Saint-Germain.

"That is precisely my objection to your ogre." He dismounted with care, for the path was very narrow, just wide enough for a heavily laden pony to pass if he walked on the outer edge of it.

"They say that this ogre kills and eats people," Tzoa Lem insisted.

"Yes," Saint-Germain nodded. "They usually do." He gave a signal to Rogerio and looked back at Tzoa Lem. "We'll have to turn the ponies individually. There's not sufficient room here to do this any other way."

One at a time, they unhitched the animals from the lead connecting each pony to the pony ahead and behind him. Though patient and surefooted, the Spiti ponies were nervous, and the three men had to work with great care, soothing the squat animals with the spindly legs as the turns were made. While they were working on the fourth pony, Rogerio slipped, and for a moment he teetered on the crumbling edge of the trail. But Saint-Germain caught his arm and pulled him back to safety. Neither Saint-Germain nor Rogerio said a word, and so Tzoa Lem was silent as well, though he watched Saint-Germain speculatively from time to time.

It was quite dark when they at last reached the fork in the road. The wind was moaning, demented, along the walls of the gorge, and from the smell of the air, they knew rain was near. Tending the ponies and seeing to their barley gruel filled more than an hour, so that the night had settled darkly around them by the time Rogerio busied himself with a campfire and Saint-Germain worked with Tzoa Lem to put up their night shelter.

Saint-Germain kept night guard perched on one of the three large chests containing his native earth. He was armed with a Byzantine long sword, one of two blades he had brought with him when he had traveled into China many years ago. It was a handsome weapon, lighter and slightly longer than the European broadsword, and having better balance. The hilt was unornamented, with a functional crossbar and quillons to protect the hand. The tapering blade was made of Damascus steel and was razor-honed on both edges. He wore the scabbard across his back, and it dangled against the trunk, for it was thick, somewhat flexible camel leather. When at last the storm broke, Saint-Germain wrapped oiled cloths around the sword and scabbard, but he did not seek shelter himself. He let the rain drench him, welcoming the discomfort, for it kept his mind from turning to Chih-Yü and the revenge he had visited upon the Mongol warriors for her death.

He was silent in the morning, and the drizzling tail of the storm did not encourage the other two men to speak beyond the few necessary words as they broke camp and loaded up the ponies.

That night they made camp on a ridge, and in the morning they were surprised by a small herd of golden takin browsing in the rhododendron bushes growing in the lee of the ridge.

"What are they?" Saint-Germain asked as he watched the animals.

"Takin," Tzoa Lem said. "There are others like them: the serow and goral. It is most unusual to see them."

Rogerio looked at them with unabashed amazement. He turned to his master. "They look like antelopes that were crossed with goats."

Saint-Germain only nodded. "I have seen the tahr goats—are these related?" He had an affection for the tahr, for though it was less impressive than many wild goats, it was sturdy and steady-tempered. Twice, when traveling the Silk Road, he had encountered the russet-haired tahrs and had enjoyed them.

"No, you cannot capture these. The tahr will accept a goatherd, but the takin will not," the guide answered.

The voices had disturbed the unusual animals, and at last an old bull raised his head, made a strange gurgling bugle, and the herd bounded away through the brush.

"They are thought to be good omens for travelers—it is said that the takin keep away rain and rockfalls." Tzoa Lem gave a shrug to show that he did not subscribe to the belief, but did not wholly discount it.

Rogerio had already begun to untie the skins from the shelter poles, and he remarked, "A better omen for travelers would be to get packed properly and on the road again."

"True enough," Saint-Germain agreed, and gave his attention to the Spiti ponies.

It was slightly past midday when they first caught sight of the Chui-Cho fortress. It was an imposing building of tall, squared towers topped with sloping tile roofs. The stone walls were almost smooth, with few windows. The ramparts were high, notched for archers and faced with more tile.

"The gate," Tzoa Lem explained with forced nonchalance, "is on the other side and cannot be approached without passing under the archers on the walls."

"But is there another road on the other side?" Saint-Germain asked, assuming that there was not.

"A small path that one of the wild goats might find challenging. It must be scaled with rope ladders. They say that once a rival Warlord sent his men here, and ordered them to attack by the rope ladders. The fighters of Chui-Cho sat at the top of the ladders and killed the invaders one by one."

Saint-Germain could not refrain from comparing Chui-Cho fortress with Mao-T'ou stronghold. Whereas this huge stone building was virtually impregnable, Mao-T'ou had stood open, more as a guard post than a deterrent to passage. Chui-Cho was made of tall, thick stones; Mao-T'ou had been almost entirely wood. Chui-Cho was certainly capable of housing four or five hundred fighting men, their families and their equerries. Mao-T'ou was crowded when more than one hundred fifty people occupied it. Chui-Cho was clearly the most important building on the road for many li; Mao-T'ou had been less important than the two valleys it overlooked.

"How old is it?" Rogerio asked Tzoa Lem.

"It is believed that it was built in the years of the Han Emperors, but I do not know if that is true or not. Any ancient building is rumored to have been built then." He looked at the fortress. "The ogre is said to defend that little outbuilding there at the bend in the road."

The structure indicated was not really very small, but the towers of Chui-Cho dwarfed it. It was a Z-shaped building, two stories high, fortified with stone and huge standing logs. "Appropriate for an ogre," Saint-Germain observed, and tapped at his pony's ribs to start the animal forward again.

"You're not going to challenge him, are you?" Tzoa Lem asked, urgency driving his pitch up several notes.

"As I understand it, one of us must challenge." Saint-Germain reached over his shoulder and felt the pommel of his Byzantine long sword. There was also a small francisca tucked into his belt. This Frankish ax was not used for striking, but for throwing. Saint-Germain had carried it with him many years, but rarely used it. He was not certain that it would be of any value to him now, but his hand closed on the steel ax head where it joined the leather-wrapped oaken haft. He hesitated for a moment, then dismounted and began to walk up the trail toward the inhospitable ogre's house.

An outraged warning shout broke through the morning. Saint-Germain stopped, holding his hands out to the side to show that they were empty. It was difficult not to look back, but he knew that it was more important for him to pay attention to what made the sound than to see how his companions were reacting to it.

When the sound had finished echoing down the cliffs, another noise, the awesome note of a large hammered bell, rolled through the air, as powerful as a storm-driven sea.

Archers appeared on the walls of Chui-Cho fortress, and the sound of battle drums began their insistent beat inside the high stone walls. None of the archers lifted their weapons, though one of them did throw a ruined shoe at the little party on the trail.

A ram's horn was sounded on the battlements, and at that signal the archers readied their bows, but did not loose their arrows: they stood silent, waiting.

Saint-Germain had learned to appreciate these formalities of battle, and could not entirely dismiss the impression this preparation was making on him. It would be useless to pretend that he did not recognize the threat this display represented, and realized that for a great many travelers, this alone would be sufficient to turn them back, or cause them to pay large sums of money for the privilege of leaving the shadow of those walls unscathed. His right hand closed on the hilt of the long sword as he made sure the upturning quillons would not catch on his clothes if he had to draw the long blade quickly.

The cacophony of the drums and ram's horn grew worse, until the rocky faces of the mountains rang with the sound of it. The noise was nerve-racking: even the steady-tempered Spiti ponies grew restive from the onslaught.

A moment before Saint-Germain would have strode forward himself to bring this bombination to an end, there was a crash, as of falling trees and breaking rocks. In the next moment, an oddly armored figure rushed into view.

He was not an ogre, Saint-Germain realized at once, but he was a formidable warrior. He had seen such armor only once before, and that had been many years ago, before Pei-King had fallen to the Mongols. Then the forces of a visiting foreign noble had worn similar accoutrements. His body armor was made of what appeared to be mats of wood and metal woven tightly with heavy cords. He carried a long, slightly curving sword in an ornate scabbard. Around his brow was a band of plaited and gilded leather which Saint-Germain at first mistook for a coronet, and then realized that the upstanding stellations were in reality the handles of more than a dozen tiny knives.

"What is he?" Rogerio called to Saint-Germain as he watched the warrior hurry forward.

"I think he's from those islands to the east of Korea. One of them is called Honshu, if I remember correctly." Saint-Germain answered calmly, though he did not take his eyes from the strangely armed man.

The fighter took up a stance and shouted in gruff and atrociously accented challenge, "Fight for your honor, for you will die!"

"Commendably succinct," Saint-Germain remarked dryly as he reached over his shoulder to grasp the hilt of his sword.

As the other fighter deliberately drew his weapon, he taunted Saint-Germain. "My katana will make ribbons of your entrails." The steel blade glowed in the light, the sun winking jewellike on the edge.

Saint-Germain knew that his blade was perhaps two handspans longer than this fighter's weapon, but he was cautious. He had heard tales of the swords made on Honshu, so keen that they could slice a man from neck to hip without slowing the speed of their descent. Several of the alchemists he had known in Lo-Yang vowed they had seen such demonstrations, and he had very nearly believed them. Now that he saw this weapon, he understood how the reports might be true, for the slight moiré pattern that glinted on the steel could only indicate a fine layering, a complex laminate tempered many times with salt and leather and blood.

"No man passes me!" the warrior announced, assuming a posture as deliberate as a dancer's. "I am Saito Masashige, grandson of Taira Kiyomori, the hero of Gion and Dan-no-ura; great grandson of the scourge of the pirates, Taira Tadamori. My father distinguished himself at the Battle of Uji and his valor gained him much favor and recognition. I was honored by my ruling lord and sent as a pledge of mutual respect to the great Warlord Mon Chio-Shing at the behest of the Emperor of the Middle of the World, and have been decorated by that August Hand at the Imperial City in K'ai-Feng. It is a privilege to meet death at my hands." The words were ritualistic and obviously required a reply.

With a sardonic smile, Saint-Germain said, "I am Francs Ragoczy, Count of Saint-Germain, son of a King, initiate priest, alchemist, magician. In the Empire of the Middle of the World, I am called Shih Ghieh-Man, and was not given the name lightly. The history of my blood is long indeed, and I will not recount it, for it goes back three thousand years. It is fitting that my opponent is so great a hero, for I do not wish to sully my hands with lesser men." He held the long sword in one hand, a considerable feat.

Saito Masashige gave a growling laugh, not unlike the sound of a cat hissing. He held his sword at the ready. "Son of a King, you call yourself, foreigner, and yet you hang back."

Saint-Germain moved two steps nearer, but not far enough to stand on the gravel of the road. It would be folly to try to fight on such unstable footing. "If you are a great hero, then come to me, Saito Masashige." Now that he knew he would fight, he had to control the reckless anticipation that wakened in him. It was so tempting to throw himself into the battle, to take needless risks for the exhilaration of it, and the possible true death that waited in the katana's lethal touch. The fury and despair that had smoldered in him sought the oblivion of destruction.

The other man grimaced as he stepped to the side of the

gravel. Now he was somewhat closer to Saint-Germain, though there was still too great a distance between them for any real combat.

Too late, Saint-Germain realized that he was being maneuvered so that he would have to fight with the sun in his eyes. A few more paces and Masashige would be with his back to the sun. "If that is your game . . ." Saint-Germain said quietly, then took a few short steps, then leaped over the gravel to land on the same side of the trail as Saito Masashige stood. It took him a moment to recover, and in that time, the other man had reached up to the knives in his headband and flicked one at his opponent. The sting in his shoulder told Saint-Germain what had happened more than what he had seen, and at once he knew that if he allowed himself to be distracted, even to look at the little weapon lodged just below his collarbone, that the katana would flash down, cutting effortlessly through bone and muscle, bringing with it the death that had eluded him for so long.

"Ha!" Masashige cried out, his katana snapping as it turned in his hand to allow for a backhanded slice.

Saint-Germain was already out of range, moving his longer, heavier, less wieldy sword from his right to his left hand. Few men were capable of swinging the weapon with both hands, let alone one, and Saint-Germain saw Masashige hesitate for the flicker of an eyelid before moving toward him, the sword rushing like an extension of his arm toward his adversary.

The rashness which had threatened to overcome him now faded as Saint-Germain jumped back and brought his long sword around in a horizontal arc. He was fully aware that when the point of the blade was at the farthest extent of its swing that he would be vulnerable to attack, and would not be able to bring the sword down quickly enough to stop the katana from sliding through him. He let the weight of his weapon pull him around so that the momentum was not interrupted, lunging forward as he came out of the turn.

Masashige was startled by this maneuver, but made sufficient recovery to take one cut at Saint-Germain's back as he spun with his long sword. He was not close enough to reach his target, and did not have time to move closer before the long sword was whistling toward him, driving him back as Saint-Germain attacked.

Steel rang on steel, once, twice, and then both men stepped

back, the points of their weapons slightly lowered as each regarded the other.

Saint-Germain saw now that the negligent way with which Masashige held the hilt of his katana was deceptive. That loose right hand, above the small guard—for the katana had no quillons—was part of the man's formidable skill. He had seen other men with that curious ease with their weapons, and knew that inevitably those were the most formidable fighters. The left hand, behind the right, was firmer on the hilt and the marked sinews in his arm gave mute testimony to his strength.

"We cannot fight here!" Saito Masashige called out, a little short of breath. "There, the ground is firm underfoot."

"Yes." Saint-Germain looked where the other man pointed, though he knew he risked being struck with another of the little knives. "It is no honor to kill a man because he lost his footing, is it?" he asked kindly, but his face was hard.

"You are not like most of them," Masashige said, as if it were an explanation.

"No."

The area Saito Masashige had indicated was fairly near the fortress walls, a wide expanse of hard, dry earth. The flat space was oblong, and for an instant Saint-Germain was painfully reminded of the Roman circus. This was much smaller, and there were fewer spectators, but it had the same deadly feel of that long-vanished place.

Nothing was said, but both men selected a position that would not force the other to look into the sun. This was no longer a simple challenge, but a contest of both skill and honor. The men watching on the battlements were silent; Tzoa Lem and Rogerio were silent.

"Ready!" Saint-Germain said, lifting his point once again.

Saito Masashige brought his sword up at the same time, grunting his assent. There was a difference in their movements now. They were quick, crisp, cleaner, more dangerous.

Yet neither did more than stand for some little time, sword ready, watching the other. Once Saito Masashige shifted his weight as if nervous, but Saint-Germain was not deceived. He kept his position, and his sword did not waver. He would not be lured by such an opening. His dark eyes were as enigmatic as they were intense and did not leave the hands of his adversary.

The exchange, when it came, happened swiftly. At one moment both men stood apart, waiting, still, and in the next instant there was a rushing, a shining arc as Saito Masashige's katana was deflected by the circle of Saint-Germain's long sword that began above his head and swept downward, shielding his body. The scrape of the swords was the only sound on the hillside. Then the men separated again, each taking up his anticipatory stance.

Saito Masashige planted his feet as if determined to force Saint-Germain to come to him. The long curve of his sword glistened from the sweat that had run down his arms and over his hands. His right foot, somewhat advanced of the left, seemed hardly to touch the ground.

Outwardly, Saint-Germain was as serenely alert as Masashige, but his mind was filled with alarm. He had felt a shudder pass through the long sword as it struck the katana, and he knew that had the blow been direct, the fine Damascus steel would have shattered. He could sweep the other man's sword aside, but could not risk a direct blow from that weapon. How long would it take Masashige to understand the full extent of his power? One more exchange, two at the most, and his opponent would make Saint-Germain's blade his target. The pressure of the francisca under his belt was comforting, though he dared not depend on the little throwing ax.

He was so preoccupied with this problem that he missed the slight tremor of Masashige's hands before he made a sudden leap forward, his sword sliding downward, snapping as it turned to move upward, the bow of the blade pressing toward Saint-Germain's side, exposed now as he brought his long sword up.

Again the blades met and sparks danced where they struck. Both men confined the engagement to one move—attack, parry—and then they were far apart, Saito Masashige less than an arm's length from the walls of the fortress, Saint-Germain almost standing on the low-growing scrub that lined the trail.

Now that he had a moment, Saint-Germain was tempted to pull the knife from his shoulder, though he did not. The blade was painful but there had been little bleeding. Once it was removed, there would be nothing to stop the blood. By force of will he eased the tension in his neck and jaw and back; tightness would slow him down, and against a weapon that was faster, he could not afford the most minute delay.

He moved cautiously, his sword ready, to a place slightly nearer Masashige. His left hand, holding the long sword, did not waver, but he knew that with the little knife sunk in his shoulder, his right hand would be weakened. He paced forward another three steps.

Saito Masashige was poised for a renewed rush, but did not expect Saint-Germain to alter his tactics and sprint toward him, the long, heavy sword aimed squarely at his chest. At the last instant his katana sliced sideways and the long sword nicked the armor covering his hips before Saint-Germain could swing it toward Masashige's head.

Now that he felt the tidelike rhythm of this fight, Saint-Germain was able to move with it, his well-knit body graceful in its power, his sword arm relentless. Five times he and Masashige sped together, their swords flickering over one another like flames, then separated.

On the sixth pass, Masashige faltered, so very slightly, in the speed of the turn of his katana, and Saint-Germain pressed the advantage. His only chance, he knew, was to tire the other man, to outlast him, since he could not match him for quickness. Until this battle, he had thought his Byzantine long sword a superior weapon, but he realized now that it was clumsy and slow. Dangerous as he knew the katana to be, he could only admire it, and the unparalleled skill of the fighter who used it.

Two more swift engagements came rapidly and for the first time Masashige was forced to retreat. Saint-Germain did not make the mistake of extending himself too far when his own position was perilous. He whirled his sword over his head once as he stepped back, and saw that Masashige had darted a swift, apprehensive glance at the knife lodged below his collarbone. Under other circumstances Saint-Germain would have been grimly amused by this, but this combat was far too stark to allow this.

Saint-Germain was ten or eleven paces away from Saito Masashige when he saw the other man lift his hand, and suddenly there was a sharp pain in his thigh. A second knife had been thrown. This time he could not ignore it. He reached down and tugged at the knife, and that was when Masashige ran at him, sword lifting for the ultimate blow.

The Byzantine blade took the full impact of the katana's downward sweep with the sound of breaking walls. Saint-Germain had just swung it aside when the Damascus steel made a sound not unlike a sob, then broke, leaving him holding a stump of a weapon.

Saito Masashige flicked the katana, confident that it would end the battle, but Saint-Germain was out of range. Though there were two knives in him now, though he must surely be in pain, he appeared to have lost none of his strength. For the first time superstitious fear gave voice to the questions that puzzled him. The foreigner in black had announced he was a magician, and his name implied mastery and skill of imposing potency. He approached the man carefully, his sword held up.

Saint-Germain moved with uncanny swiftness. Wherever Masashige struck with his katana, Saint-Germain eluded him. Three more knives were thrown and two found their mark, one high in his left arm, the other grazing his calf as he sprang from the hard-packed earth where they fought, to a boulder standing beside the road. As he gained his footing on the rough stone, he reached for the francisca in his belt, tugging the ax free. It shone as the sun winked on the wedge-shaped blade as Saint-Germain began to swing it.

Masashige was striding nearer, katana rising before him.

The francisca made a disquieting purr as Saint-Germain gave it one test swing. He vaulted onto a rocky outcrop, out of range of the katana.

"What cowardice is this?" Saito Masashige yelled at him, voice cracking with fatigue.

Saint-Germain braced himself, certain that if he remained on the tumbled boulders, he would be picked off with those little knives that served Masashige in place of a coronet. The francisca moaned as he swung it again. "Don't force me to kill you." It was strange to say that, and to know that it was true: he did not want to kill this man. There had been too much of killing, too much of the numbness that denied grief. His compelling eyes were without anger.

For a reply, Masashige threw another knife, giving a sharp, pleased shout as it left a furrow along Saint-Germain's brow.

Saint-Germain was already giving the francisca its final swing when the ram's horn sounded again. He did not allow it to distract him, but felt momentarily disappointed that so fine a fighter as this Saito Masashige should use such a ploy. He was ready to throw the ax when he heard Rogerio's shout.

"Master! The gate!"

At this, both Saint-Germain and Masashige turned. The huge gates of the Chui-Cho fortress were swinging open.

"No!" Masashige yelled, and tried to leap to the boulder immediately below Saint-Germain, where he would be able to get a clear stroke. His yell turned to a scream as he missed· his footing and fell.

Saint-Germain kept to his place on the outcropping, his francisca ready. He watched Saito Masashige get to his feet, shaking his head as he reached for his katana.

"Don't make me kill you," Saint-Germain said quietly.

The realization that he had been completely vulnerable and yet was spared filled Masashige with sickening shame. He stared at the katana in his hands, and then up at Saint-Germain and the ax. Then his eyes traveled to each of the knives protruding from Saint-Germain's body, and he paled.

Eight horsemen had come out of the fortress and had halted at the place where the combatants faced each other. The foremost rider, a balding man with eyes permanently narrowed by failing sight, addressed the two. "I command you to stop."

Saito Masashige's face sagged and he could no longer meet Saint-Germain's penetrating eyes. "If that is your wish, Warlord Mon," he muttered.

"It is. A man who fights as this one does deserves our honor. In all the years you have been with me, Masashige, no one has bested you." He turned his attention to Saint-Germain. "I heard you call yourself Shih Ghieh-Man."

"That is correct, Mon Chio-Shing," Saint-Germain told him, after a troubled glance at Masashige.

"You're aptly named: only a powerful magician could continue to fight with those knives in him." He motioned to one of the other horsemen. "Attend to him."

Saint-Germain bowed slightly, and for the first time felt the full impact of the tenacious pain of the knives. "My servant," he said with a suddenly weak gesture toward Rogerio, "will attend me." To his consternation he saw that this simple statement had appalled Saito Masashige even more. "You are an extraordinary fighter," he said, studying the closed face, but seeing little.

"You are welcome at Chui-Cho fortress," Mon Chio-Shing said with as formal a bow as his saddle would permit.

What was it, Saint-Germain asked himself, that so horrified Saito Masashige? He might have asked the man himself, but then Rogerio was waiting at the foot of the rocks, and the knives seemed to be expanding in his flesh, and it was too much trouble to speak, or to think.

———————◆————————

A letter from Olivia in Rome to Saint-Germain in Lo-Yang. The mendicant friar carrying the letter to the merchant outpost in Turkestan was captured by deserting European soldiers from the Crusade; the friar and the letters entrusted to him were destroyed.

To Ragoczy Sanct' Germain Franciscus in the city of Lo-Yang, which may or may not exist, Olivia sends her most earnest greetings from Rome:

Your letter, which has been on the road more than two years, surprised me, and made me aware of how very much I miss you. Your memory has lain in the back of my mind, dozing, and needed only the sight of your eclipse seal to come fully awake.

Perhaps I should tell you that the last letter I had from you before this one arrived more than twenty years ago, at which time you informed me that you were going east along the Old Silk Road. It was shortly after the Jews were banished from France and that mob in Lyon put three of our blood to the torch. You told me that the knights were spoiling for another Crusade, and that they would probably practice on anyone they could label a heretic. Well yes, you were right about that.

Tell me, have you found the haven you wished for? When you were there before, you said that the people respect learning and put high value on tolerance. But that was centuries ago, my friend. Is it as you remember? I confess that I hope it may be, so that you will not have to bear so much. The suffering endured by those of our blood is terrible to think of, but is isolation the only alternative? I have lived in Rome a very long time and have learned, as you said I would, to live in a way that attracts little notice. Surely you could live here with me. After all, this is your house, and has been for more than a thousand years. Come here to me and return to a familiar place. I promise you that you will be protected—I will let it be known that an eccentric relative will be sharing the villa, and your way will be smooth.

By the way, I think you will like the way the north wing has been rebuilt. You gave me permission to make alterations, and I think that what has been done will please you. The builders were most upset, but followed the orders they were given. The atrium has been widened and is a proper court now. There is a gallery around the second floor so that all the rooms have access to the court. It is not unlike the house we shared in Tyre. You see, I have never forgotten. Though I have not seen you, heard your voice or your footfall for more than four hundred years, yet they are familiar to me, and I will catch myself waiting for them.

You have probably not heard that the English King John has at last submitted to the Pope. Everyone in Rome is busy taking credit for this, and His Holiness is unbearably smug about it. I don't mention it, of course, but I feel sympathy for John. That brother of his was impossible. He put all of his kingdom in debt and went off to war with never so much as a moment's doubt that his debts would be paid. And to make it worse, he never made a wife of his Queen. If Richard Lion-Heart had been able to overcome his inclinations long enough to produce an heir, matters would be different in England. Certainly Richard was a splendid leader in war, very brave, a superb warrior, and so forth. But these Crusades are insanity, and Richard's devotion to war, I think, was at least partly spawned by his reluctance to touch Barengaria. It is an unfortunate prejudice in a king. Other men may have their pages and apprentices and students and urchins, but for a king to spurn his wife, that is another matter. If he could not endure her at all, he could have found her a discreet lover and said the child was his. That has happened often enough before. So England went to John and now Pope Innocent is preening like a cock on a dunghill.

Tomorrow I will give this letter into the hands of a Cypriot captain bound for Thessaly. He has promised to hand it to a merchant or a friar going East. He has warned me that there are not so many travelers now, as there are rumors of great wars in the East and devils coming out of the desert to plunder the land. For your sake, I trust that this is not the case, and that a small band of brigands has been improved upon in the telling until a handful of men have become an army. It will take time for this to reach you, but when it does, know it for what it is, dearest Sanct' Germain—the cry of my soul to you.

Perhaps it is true that we are doomed to live as outcasts much of the time, and perhaps it is true that if our natures were generally known we would be loathed, hunted and killed by those who believe the worst of what is strange. But, Sanct' Germain, no one has loved me as devotedly as you have. The bond that began that night when I watched you come into my chambers and was filled with terror has never been broken. Do you remember how kindly you used me that night? Without the strength of your love, I would have died before I was thirty. And do not remind me with that wry smile I like so well that I did die before I was thirty. It is not the same thing, and you know it. No one, my friend, no one has loved me as you have. That has sustained me for more than a thousand years, and will doubtless continue to do so until the true death claims me.

How morbid I sound, and here I am trying to persuade you to return. Pay no attention to anything I say, but that I love you, have always loved you.

I must end this before I become maudlin. It would not do for me to attend the reception for the King of Aragon in a distraught humor. It is times like these when I wish I had not lost the ability to weep, for tears might cleanse me. But red and swollen eyes will not become me, so I will tell myself that I was fortunate when the change deprived me of weeping, and my soul will mourn. Doubtless someone will provide me a distraction, and, who knows—I may find someone who will want to share my pleasures.

And you, my dearest, have you found someone to share your pleasures, or are you still alone? If there were anything I might do to give you that which you seek, though it ended my life, I would do it. Empty words, with you so far away from me.

I have sent for my servant and have given orders for my palanquin, so I must bid you farewell for a time.

From my own hand on the Feast of St. Matthew, in the 1214th year of Our Lord, in Rome,

Olivia

3

SAINT-GERMAIN opened his eyes. "How long?" he asked Rogerio, who stood beside the chest where his master lay.

"Three days," was the carefully neutral answer.

He paused in his rising. "Three days?" His hand touched the places where the knives had struck his side and his shoulder, and felt only slight tenderness.

"You bled a great deal." Rogerio's features betrayed nothing, but his eyes were not so well schooled and they were dark with distress.

"I must have." He sat up slowly. "This is Chui-Cho fortress?"

"Yes." Rogerio busied himself with putting out Saint-Germain's clothes.

"The old man . . . I remember he asked us in." He put his hands to his temples. "There was a large room, I remember, and archers, but . . ."

"You collapsed there. I asked that you be carried to a quiet room and your chests brought. I told them that you had to perform a certain ritual because of the combat." There was a slight, telling pause. "I . . . I didn't think it would take this long."

Saint-Germain raised his head. "You told them the truth: this is a ritual of a sort. Three days, though." He swung his feet down to the floor and stood gingerly. "I'm weak," he admitted, chagrined.

Rogerio did not trust himself to respond. He placed the black silk sheng liao within easy reach and held out Persian leggings. "The Warlord Mon Chio-Shing has requested you to give him the pleasure of your company as soon as you have risen."

"Indeed." He put his hands to the shenti knotted around

his waist and noticed for the first time that the room was cold. "Has there been snow?"

"The wind has shifted and it comes off the mountains," Rogerio said as he took the shenti, his eyes turned away from Saint-Germain's naked body and the wide white scars that covered his abdomen.

Saint-Germain drew the leggings on, fingering the rapidly fading mark of Saito Masashige's knife. He tied the leggings at his waist and fitted the leather codpiece into place when Rogerio handed it to him. "What hour of the day is it?" he asked as he reached for the sheng liao.

"It is late afternoon. The fourth meal began not long ago. They keep to the old ways here, five meals instead of four." Rogerio had folded the shenti, and had taken a collar of silver links from the Roman chest. He gave this to Saint-Germain and adjusted the pectoral with its black eclipse disk and raised wings on his master's chest.

"I have been struck," Saint-Germain said with an attempt at lightness, "by the thought that I would have certain difficulties without you, Rogerio, since I cast no reflection. How would I be sure that my collar is correctly centered, or that I have not got a smudge on my face if you were not here."

Rogerio knew this gesture for what it was, but could not entirely accept Saint-Germain's affection. "You dress by touch, and need no one to make you elegant." He was busy with the Roman chest, not looking at his master when he felt the small hand on his shoulder.

"My friend," Saint-Germain said kindly, "I am trying, in my awkward way, to tell you that I value all you have done for me. I know that I owe you my . . . life many times over. And of late, my bitterness has . . ." He broke off. He could say nothing more, though he wished that he might find that one, graceful phrase that would let Rogerio know he was aware of the hazards his servant had accepted so readily.

"Without you, those human jackals would have killed me, and my bondholder would have gone untouched by the law and the state. As to your bitterness, how can you not be bitter? I am often amazed, my master, for I think I would be lost to cynicism had I endured what you have." It was clearly his last word on the matter.

"You didn't know me in the beginning," Saint-Germain said, and left it at that. "Have you learned your way around this place?"

"There are stairs at the end of the hall. They lead to the second floor, where the reception rooms are." His face relaxed a bit. "Warlord Mon will be relieved to see you. He has been pestering me since yesterday to send you to him."

Saint-Germain nodded absently. "Then perhaps he should be notified that I am waiting for the opportunity to meet him." His dark eyes were distant. "Why did she insist on dying? What did it gain her?"

Wisely, Rogerio said nothing, but the anguish in Saint-Germain's voice touched him as well. He closed the Roman chest.

As he opened the door, Saint-Germain turned to Rogerio. "What has become of Tzoa Lem and our ponies?"

"They are all well-housed. Tzoa Lem is having the time of his life. There are three kitchen maids competing for his favors and wooing him with food." He was able to smile at this. "He is in no hurry to leave."

"Hardly surprising." He did not ask about Saito Masashige, for he did not want to learn that his superb adversary had been treated badly for not besting him. "I don't know how long I will be," Saint-Germain admitted, and closed the door.

The hallway was narrow and ill-lit. Though the inside of the fortress was largely of wood, there was still the feeling of dank stones, of moss and chill. Saint-Germain walked swiftly, his heeled boots clicking on the worn floorboards, each creating a small hail of echos. He passed only one servant, who stared at Saint-Germain with eager dread. On the stairs, Saint-Germain once again had a moment of giddy weakness, then it was past, and he continued to the lower level, his face fixed with an expression of good humor that he could not feel inwardly.

A houseman bowed Saint-Germain toward the reception room, remaining in the door as Saint-Germain made his way to one of the low chairs by the narrow windows. Then the servant indicated the most profound respect and left Saint-Germain alone.

The reception room was pleasant and uncluttered. Two fine scrolls hung on the wall, and though one was water-damaged, the other was in fine condition. Saint-Germain judged from the style and brushstrokes that the scroll was three or four hundred years old. There were lacquered chests standing by the walls, one of them quite large, the others of medium height. All were fitted with neat-worked brass. There were two couches, both handsomely but not lavishly upholstered, and six chairs. A low table was placed between the couches. It was rosewood and elaborately inlaid. In Lo-Yang, Saint-Germain thought, the room would be regarded as far too plain, almost shabby. Chih-Yü, he knew with a pang, would have liked the room, though it might have been a little too cluttered for her taste. He turned to look out the window, letting his mind wander over the ridges and crests of the mountains. The curious emptiness of grief had gripped him and it was almost more than he wished to do to wrench himself free of it. In all his years, he had never learned the secret, if there was such a secret, of resigning himself to loss. His joy had been purchased with the pain of loss.

He was still staring out the window when the door opened and one of the house servants announced in a dialect Saint-Germain could barely understand. "The Warlord Mon Chio-Shing." Saint-Germain rose at once, forcing his attention back into the room. He bowed formally.

"Ah," said the older man, coming forward with the curious rolling gait of one who has spent more time in the saddle than on the ground. His bald pate shone and the grayed wisps of his mustaches drooped around his mouth. Yet he walked with vigor and his nearsighted eyes were lively. "You are the magician, then." He made a sort of bow, then indicated that Saint-Germain should sit as he himself dropped onto the nearer couch.

"Among other things. This person has been credited with skills and abilities which—"

Warlord Mon interrupted him. "You have beautiful manners, but there is no need for your address form here. Talk like a plain man, I beg you."

Saint-Germain smiled faintly. "Thank you. I did not want to give offense after all you have done—I am grateful, believe me." He might have continued with these courtesies, but Mon waved his hand impatiently.

"Yes, yes. I know the routine as well as you, if not better. One of the reasons I stayed away from Court—there were others, of course, but this was an important factor—was all those ceremonies required for the simplest things. When a man must spend half the morning trying to find just the right way of presenting a lacquered fan, then you know things have gone too far." He sighed. "I was beginning to wonder when you'd emerge. Three days is a long time for a ritual.

That servant of yours guards you as diligently as a dragon guards heaven."

"He has been with me a long time," Saint-Germain explained, though he implied no apology.

"That's as it should be," Mon concurred. "It takes more than a year or two to make good servants. It's not easy to create real trust. It pays to treat them well, but you must know that."

"Yes, that has been my experience," Saint-Germain agreed politely, curious to learn what it was that this old Warlord really wanted of him.

"Take Masashige," Mon went on so casually that Saint-Germain knew the discussion must be urgent. "An excellent servant. I've never had one better. He has defended this fortress for more than a dozen years. The fastest swordsman I've ever seen. No one . . . could touch him."

"Yes," Saint-Germain said dryly, "I would not like to face anyone faster."

Warlord Mon laughed heartily and pounded his knee with his fist. "You foreigners," he said when he could speak again. "What I like about you is your humor. Delightful. A Chinese soldier would feel he had to give me a full report on how he conducted his battle, and all you do is tell me that you would not like to meet anyone faster." His mirth played itself out and he assumed a more serious expression. "He's taking his loss hard. It's never happened before."

"He didn't lose," Saint-Germain said at once. "You stopped the fight."

"You convince him of that. He has told me he could not have got to you before you threw that ax, and a weapon like that . . . He insists that you said that you did not want to kill him. You wouldn't have said that unless you thought you *could* kill him. He told me that he was wholly disgraced because stopping the fight deprived him of an honorable death." Warlord Mon pulled at the ends of his mustaches. "In part, I suppose I was trying to save him—to save you both. I will hardly allow Masashige to get cut down, and if I had wanted you dead, I had only to signal the archers, and you would have been full of arrows. But you see, I was impressed with you."

Saint-Germain had been studying the old Warlord and knew that this bluff manner was assumed. For an instant, he pictured himself shot with arrows, and could not decide how he might have accounted for refusing to die. He had been shot by arrows many times before, but none of the shafts had struck his spine or penetrated his brain, and he had survived. "I will have to say, Warlord Mon, that I felt I did not do well against Masashige. If his sword had been as long as mine, or if he had had more stamina, he would have killed me before we completed the first four passes."

Warlord Mon gave this his judicious consideration. "Quite likely," he said after this reflection. "You are very strong, aren't you?"

It was true enough, and no one was more aware of it than Saint-Germain. He lifted his shoulders in self-deprecation. "I have a certain advantage in my blood. We have great strength—it is a gift."

"As you say, an advantage." The Warlord gave Saint-Germain another long look. "They tell me that you are a powerful sorcerer."

"They?" Saint-Germain inquired.

"Your servant and your guide, naturally, and most of the men who watched you fight." He leaned back in the chair and waited for an answer.

"I have some skill." He said this carefully, not knowing how much the old Warlord might know.

"Your name implies rather more than that, Shih Ghieh-Man," he said testily. "How does it happen that a great sorcerer is on this trail?"

Saint-Germain had known he would have to say this eventually, and now that Warlord Mon had asked, he knew a certain relief, though it was tempered with recognition of his precarious situation. "There are new laws in the Empire that are punitive to foreigners. It makes for some difficulty in gaining employment. For three seasons the Warlord T'en Chih-Yü was my patron. I provided her with metal alloys. She required an alchemist." It was not entirely polite, but Saint-Germain rose and paced down the room. "She had wanted to hire mercenary soldiers, but settled for me, instead."

Mon Chio-Shing's eyes followed Saint-Germain. "Was?"

"The Mongols came to the Shu-Rh District where Mao-T'ou stronghold was. Twenty-two days ago, they destroyed the two valleys she guarded." Was it so little time since Chih-Yü had been cut down? The memory of her was at once strangely distant and achingly, abrasively near. T'en

Chih-Yü, who had wept in his arms, now lay in a poorly made grave, a carrying box for a coffin. His hands tightened at his sides.

"We've been hearing more about these Mongols," Warlord Mon remarked as he pulled a moon-fan from his belt and began to wave it. The room was cool and a thread of wind snaked through it, chilling it more, but Warlord Mon used his fan.

"And you will hear more still," Saint-Germain said bitterly, no longer bothering to observe the proper social forms. "While the men in Lo-Yang and K'ai-Feng debate what is best to do, those warriors will devastate the land."

"Isn't that a trifle overstated?" Warlord Mon asked.

"No. It is the truth. You haven't seen the destruction I saw in Shu-Rh District." He turned to his host. "You believe this is like the old wars, where the Lords evacuated an area and conducted their combats according to rules approved of by Kung Fu-Tzu. Those men of Temujin's have not heard of Kung Fu-Tzu and care nothing for his dicta. They want land. Land, Warlord Mon, not crops and slaves. They have cut trade routes, sacked towns and cities, killed every peasant, artisan and merchant they have encountered. And while the men of the Secretariat of War insist that honorable soldiers would not stoop to such acts, the Mongol warriors continue to pillage and slaughter." His voice had become rough with the depth of his feeling.

"So." Warlord Mon nodded gravely. "Then the dispatches I have read have not been misleading. I had hoped otherwise." He got to his feet, and now he moved like the old man he was. "How long would you guess it will be until they come into these mountains?"

Saint-Germain stopped on the far side of the room. "I don't know. It will depend in part on the Imperial army. If the army can be moved quickly and decisively enough to provide a regular defense, the Mongols will be slowed. Who knows, with proper strategy, they might even be stopped."

"But you do not expect this to happen," Warlord Mon said.

"No. I don't."

Warlord Mon gave a click with his tongue. "Those clerks of the Secretariats and Tribunals, they are like seamstresses. What do they know of these matters? They are in love with minutiae. They will waste months trying to determine if all the new infantry helmets match."

Unhappily, Saint-Germain was forced to agree. "They have been slow to send inspectors, and the petitions for army assistance, as far as I can tell from what happened in the Shu-Rh District, go unanswered. I know that T'en Chih-Yü journeyed to Lo-Yang herself and never got the attention of anyone more highly placed than an official of the Magisterial Tribunal. That was one of the reasons she hired me. She had no opportunity to speak to men who could give her soldiers." He turned one of the chairs around and sat again.

"So it will be unwise to depend upon the capitals." Warlord Mon strode to the window with a trace of his old jauntiness in his step. "And we must fend for ourselves, it appears."

Although Saint-Germain shared Warlord Mon's evaluation, he said, "It may be that the defenses will improve as the Mongols strike nearer the heart of the Empire. It is one thing to ignore the remoter districts, and quite another to leave the major cities open to attack. If there were one or two constant lines of resistance to the invasion, I think it is possible that the tide could still turn."

"And it may be that the Celestial Dragon will appear in the sky and blast our enemies off the face of the earth, but I am not going to anticipate such an event," Warlord Mon said as he stared out the window. "I'm badly manned here," he went on a moment later, his tone quite conversational. "I know how imposing the place looks with the big towers and high walls, but they count for little. Oh, there have been several hundred men quartered here in the past. At the moment, however, I have seventy-two men-at-arms here, and most of them are archers, which is just as well, because there are only fifteen horses in the stables. We can fire arrows from the battlements until we run out of them, which would happen quickly, because we have few supplies, and then we would be exhausted."

"Only seventy-two men-at-arms?" Saint Germain asked, incredulous.

"I don't let it be known generally. And with Masashige defending the approach to the gate, few travelers got close enough to see how pitifully few men I have here, and how little resistance we can offer." He glanced at Saint-Germain. "I don't suppose I could persuade you to remain here, could

I? You fight well and you admit that you have some skill in weapons-making."

For a moment Saint-Germain could not speak. A sense that was not quite sickness, not quite dizziness, churned within him. He wished he knew how much of this could be read on his face. Had he changed color? There was no alteration of Warlord Mon's expression, and so Saint-Germain gave a steady response. "It is an honor—"

"It's nothing of the sort. I'm desperate," the old Warlord interjected.

"But one that I cannot accept," Saint-Germain finished. "I would, believe me, be of little use to you. Most of my equipment was destroyed and I have no means of replacing it. There is nothing I could do for you that a good smith could not do equally as well." This was not entirely the truth, but he did not want to have to answer more questions.

"Nonsense," Warlord Mon said brusquely. "You can fight. I saw you against Masashige, remember."

"That was not my choice," Saint-Germain pointed out quietly, his dark eyes on the old Warlord with their full, compelling weight.

"True enough," the old man muttered, and turned away. "Well, I had hoped, but . . ." He thrust his moon-fan back into his belt. "When you are healed, I will not detain you— you may leave here without hindrance, you and your servant and your guide. Should you change your mind, I would welcome you here. And it may be," he added hopefully, "that by the time you are healed, the passes will be blocked and you will have to remain here until spring."

Saint-Germain gave Warlord Mon an understanding smile. "I am sorry. I will be ready to leave tomorrow."

"Tomorrow? But there were knives in you . . ." The old man's narrowed eyes grew wide.

"The . . . ritual which kept me confined to that room for three days was, in part, allied with healing. It is something like my strength, you see." He rose from his chair. "There is weakness still, but it will pass." He did not add that it would require blood for that to happen.

"I've always thought that the reputations of magicians and sorcerers were more a matter of the credulity of those who allowed themselves to believe than any power on the magician's or sorcerer's part. In your case, however . . ." As he crossed the room to the door, he made a sign that Saint-Germain had seen children make to ward off evil. "It is well that you leave, if that is the way of it."

With great sadness, Saint-Germain gave the old Warlord a full, formal bow. "Mon Chio-Shing, this unworthy person is most grateful for all you have done for him and those accompanying him. It has been a privilege to have met you, and this person wishes to assure you that he will treasure the memory of this encounter."

Warlord Mon bowed and left the room, but said nothing.

A little while later Saint-Germain quitted the room and began the walk back to the quarters he and Rogerio had been assigned. His mind was preoccupied with the unfortunate interview he had had, and for that reason he did not at first notice the powerful figure that approached him along the narrow hallway.

"Shih Ghieh-Man!" the gruff voice called out in barbaric accents.

Saint-Germain looked up and saw Saito Masashige coming toward him, his sword in his hand.

"I have come to your room on eight separate occasions," Masashige said as he drew nearer, and it was then that Saint-Germain saw the misery in his eyes.

"You do me honor, Saito Masashige," he said carefully. He was reasonably certain that the foreigner would not attack him here, though this might be the proper setting for a challenge to finish what was begun under the walls of the Chui-Cho fortress three days ago.

"Honor," Masashige scoffed. "I have none left to me. I cannot have any now."

Saint-Germain regarded him, feeling compassion for this man. "If that was the case, why didn't you attack me on the rocks?" His curiosity was genuine—over the centuries he had encountered a bewildering mass of codes of honor and had learned to respect them, diverse as they were.

Saito Masashige was affronted. "Defy my Lord? He ordered the fight stopped. How could I refuse him? When I acknowledged my dishonor, he refused to let me end my worthless life—"

"What?" Saint-Germain demanded, aghast.

Masashige chose to misinterpret Saint-Germain's reaction as righteous indignation. "Well you may ask. Having ordered my dishonor, he would not let me make the cuts." His clenched hands moved across his abdomen and Saint-Germain realized with deepest revulsion that the man wished to disembowel himself. Involuntarily his hand touched his belt, as if to cover some of the scars that lay beneath it.

"But why?" he asked, when he had recovered somewhat.

"He says that he needs me here. He wishes me to guard the gate for him, no matter what. I have tried to explain, but he is not samurai, though my Lord who gave me to him regards him as an equal. My Lord would not insist that I live with this dishonor." His distressed features grew calmer. "My katana"—he held out his sword on his open hands—"was made for my great-grandfather, he who defeated the pirates and was regarded as the greatest hero of his day. My grandfather carried it in battle, and my father. All of them were good men, true samurai. So was I." His eyes lowered. "The honor of my family is in this sword. It has never been defiled before." At that his words thickened and he could not speak for a little time.

Saint-Germain could find nothing to say. He felt the misery in the other man with suffocating intensity. The katana in its beautiful scabbard drew his eyes. Finally, to end the silence, he said, "It is a fine sword."

Masashige ducked his head. "Worthy of a true samurai," he muttered. "Take it! Take it! *Take it!*" He thrust the katana at Saint-Germain. His eyes were wet.

"I will," Saint-Germain said, his small hands closing on the scabbard.

Fiercely, Masashige went on. "Oil the blade but do not touch it with your hands, ever. There is a scroll in the hilt, under the tang. Put your name there, and tell how it came to be yours. You are a master, Shih Ghieh-Man. That ax would have killed me. It should have killed me. There is nothing I can do now but die, and that has been forbidden. But at least I have saved the katana from my disgrace." He turned away abruptly and stalked off down the narrow hall.

Saint-Germain stared down at the katana in his hands. The scabbard was wooden, with fine carvings, and it had a dull shine in the muted light. Belatedly, Saint-Germain looked up, searching for Saito Masashige, but the man was no longer in sight.

One of a series of routine reports from the border station of Fa-Djo on the Go-Chan road.

On the day of the Descent of the Eighth North Pole King, from the Fa-Djo station, Ox Year, Cycle Sixty-five.

Only eight travelers today. In the morning, a family of herders came through with their yaks. A father and two sons. They have been on this road many times before. They deal with the weavers at Tsum-Ho, and references will be seen in other reports. They are men of T'u-Bo-T'e. They are planning to return in five days, which is standard.

Shortly after noon, two Buddhist monks came through the station, bound for a monastery farther up the mountain. The abbot of the monastery sent notification a fortnight ago that these men would be arriving, and a copy of that notification is included with this report. The men came from Hsia-Yi, far to the north, and have been traveling for some time. They left a disturbing report here, indicating that the attacks by the maurading Mongols are more widespread than we have been told they are. It would be well for the Ministries and Secretariats to investigate these activities.

Two hours before sunset, the guide Tzoa Lem, who is well-known on this road, came through with two travelers, both foreigners. The foreigners identified themselves as Shih Ghieh-Man, alchemist, and his servant Ro-Ger. Tzoa Lem has said that he will take them to the Yellow Hat lamasery and find a guide for them there so that they will be able to continue their journey. Tzoa Lem anticipates that he will be here within the month, as he does not wish to pass the winter in the Country of the Snows. He has stated he intends to return to the Empire by this road. Should he be caught in the snow, he

189

will send word with one of the men who travel at the
dark of the year.

The weather has been holding cold but clear. The
signs are for snow, however, and we are advising all
travelers to be on guard against storms.

Dispatched by messenger at the hour after sunset by
the captain of the station, Jai Di.

his chop

4

THEY TRAVELED less than eight li that day: the rain had become sleet, cutting along on the wind, slicing at their faces
and turning the trail to icy mud that crunched and slithered
underfoot. The jagged tops of the immense peaks around
them were lost to sight as the weather closed in.

"I know of a farmhouse," Tzoa Lem panted as they called
a halt for the fifth time that day. "It's not too far from the
main trail, and the men there are friendly. Not like some,
who would rob and kill you."

Saint-Germain nodded. His bearskin cloak covered everything but his eyes, for he had taken Tzoa Lem's warning to
heart and made sure his nose was not exposed to the freezing
rain and sleet. "How long will it take to get there?"

"Most of the afternoon, at this pace. They will have barley
and lamb for the ponies and a meal for us." He gave Saint-
Germain a curious look. "Unless you would refuse to eat
with them."

"Among my kind," he said at his most urbane, "It is considered improper to . . . dine with more than one person. We
find the act too intimate for more than two." He had been
aware for the last few days that the guide was growing more
and more suspicious of him. He was grateful that Rogerio
had caught game regularly and brought the animals to him,
for what he explained to Tzoa Lem was ritual killing.

"It may be difficult to explain that to these men, who share
everything, including their wives." He glanced back along the
line. "One of the ponies is going lame," he remarked in another tone.

"I was afraid of that. I saw him favoring his off-rear foot
earlier today. Should we unload him?"

Tzoa Lem considered the question. "There is a spare pony, but in this weather, changing loads will take more time than we can spare if we wish to get to this farmhouse before nightfall."

"Very well," Saint-Germain said, though he was not entirely certain it was a wise decision. "How much farther does this canyon go on?"

"Six more li. We will leave it on a goat path in little less than a li." He pressed his pony into the lead again and the party once more set off into the face of the storm.

They had almost reached the goat trail when the pony that had been limping tripped, and with a high, terrified whinny, slipped off the path, his hard little hooves scrabbling on the rocks before he dropped away into the gorge, carrying with him the next pony behind him, who was linked to him by lead-rein. The other ponies stamped and snorted, and one reared, almost going down the cliff face with his fellows.

Saint-Germain had come out of the saddle at the first sound, and rushed back along the line of ponies, breaking the lead-rein as he went so that no other pack animal could be lost. He steadied each pony in turn as he hurried back along the narrow track. When he reached the place in the line where the two ponies had fallen, Rogerio, who had been bringing up the rear, was waiting for him.

"They carried two of your chests. The ones filled with earth. There is only one left," Rogerio said loudly so that he would be heard over the wind.

"Yes." Saint-Germain stared down into the steep, rocky canyon as if, by will alone, he could return the ponies to their places in line.

"The largest chest is left," Rogerio added, nodding toward one of the remaining ponies.

"Get the used barley sacks, and load the earth into them, and put one sack on each of the ponies. That way, if we lose any more, it will not be . . ." He gestured, finding no way to express the utter vulnerability he felt at that moment.

"Immediately." Rogerio had already turned and was trudging back down the line of ponies.

Tzoa Lem was making his way toward Saint-Germain. "It's not good to stay here," he shouted as he got close enough to make himself heard.

"We must unpack my third chest and distribute its contents

to the other ponies," Saint-Germain said, already working at the heavy ropes that held the chest to the crude packsaddle.

"Unpack? Here? You're mad," Tzoa Lem shouted.

"Then indulge me," Saint-Germain snapped, without humor. The rope was stiff in his gloved hands and he eased the knots with difficulty.

Tzoa Lem stared astonished. In all his years as a guide, no one had challenged him in this way. "We must go on!"

"Not until this chest has been unloaded," Saint-Germain responded in a tone that allowed no opposition.

"You hired me to guide you, and I tell you—" Tzoa Lem began but was cut short.

"I hired you and I am paying you. I would not override your instructions unless there was an excellent reason to do so. This is such a case. We will be here less time if you will help my servant and me. Three will work faster than two." He had the first rope freed, and this he tossed away. "Put them on the trail at the break in the lead-rein," he said to Rogerio as his servant approached with the empty barley bags in his hands.

"I've brought some oiled paper as well," Rogerio said, holding up the wide sheets. "It will afford some protection so that little is washed away."

Saint-Germain gave a swift smile. "Thank you for that, old friend." With a sudden exasperated movement he broke the second rope holding the chest on the saddle. Then he reached up and took hold of the huge chest and lifted it off the saddle, ignoring the appalled expression on Tzoa Lem's face. He would think of an explanation later, he told himself as he lowered the chest to the ground.

"It's full of dirt!" the guide said as Saint-Germain opened the lid.

"Yes," Saint-Germain agreed as he held out his hand for a bag and the grain scoop Rogerio offered him.

"We lost two ponies carrying chests of dirt? Was that what was in the chests?" Tzoa Lem glared at them.

Saint-Germain interrupted his work. "What the chests contain is my business, Tzoa, not yours." He was already lining the second bag with oiled paper as he spoke.

"If it is dirt you want, it is all around you." Tzoa Lem was trying to make sense out of what he had seen.

"As any alchemist will tell you, that is not entirely true. All earth has peculiar properties—some is more fertile, some is more sandy, some is filled with clay, some with pebbles, some with leaves. This earth is . . . potent." He resumed his work, filling the large cloth bag swiftly and taking a third sack from Rogerio. "Put those two on the last pony, and then come back for this one."

Rogerio went to do Saint-Germain's bidding while Tzoa Lem stared in disbelief.

"You are not going to unload all that, are you? Why not save a few sacks and toss the rest over the edge? It will be night shortly." The guide's incredulity was swiftly turning to anger.

This time Saint-Germain did not stop his work, but spoke while he scooped up the earth and poured it into the bag. "If you wish to help, it will be done sooner, but I tell you now that we will remain here until this chest is empty and every sack is filled." He glanced up at Tzoa Lem. "This is not a matter open to debate."

Muttering a curse under his breath, the guide turned and tramped up the line of ponies to his mount, at the head.

The earth was turning to mud, but Saint-Germain worked steadily, without dismay. He heard Rogerio's footsteps and silently handed him another two sacks.

By the time he was finished, the canyon was sunk in shadow and though the sleet had stopped, there were a few shards of snow drifting on the wind. Saint-Germain closed the chest and with an odd sense of regret tossed it over the side of the canyon, watching as it bounced off the protruding boulders, and then was lost to sight.

"I've spliced the lead-rein," Rogerio said as he came to stand beside his master.

"Good. We should be ready to go on." He looked toward the front of the line of ponies and his face hardened. "Did you see Tzoa Lem leave?"

Rogerio's face was shocked. "Leave? He's gone?"

"Well, he's not at the front of the line of ponies and his mount is missing," Saint-Germain said with a sardonic lift to his fine brows.

"But where . . . ?" Rogerio did not go on.

"To those friendly farmers, I suppose, the ones who live fairly near the trail." He sighed. "There's no use trying to find him now. We'd only get lost. Which may be what he's counting on." Saint-Germain glanced at the ponies, then said with sudden intensity, "Check their girths. Every single one of them."

Rogerio did not question this order, but nodded once and started toward the back of the line while Saint-Germain began to work his way to the front. There were only seven ponies now, and it took little time to go over them. Saint-Germain was standing at the head of the lead pony when Rogerio came up to him. "Two girths are partially cut. Only on those ponies carrying loads, not those for riding."

Saint-Germain nodded. "Yes. One of the front ponies has a nick in his girth. Those with the heaviest loads were harmed first." He stared off toward the distant peaks. "Now, it seems we must be on guard against traps. Given the hour, I doubt that we'll have any trouble tonight, but tomorrow, Tzoa Lem and those helpful farmers of his may well be back, full of good humor and readiness to aid us. Or they may not bother with the deception, and simply attack." He let his mind drift a moment, then said, "Are you willing to ride through the night?"

"Of course," Rogerio answered at once. "It won't be the first time."

"Indeed it won't," Saint-Germain agreed with the ghost of a laugh on his lips.

Again Rogerio hesitated. "What about the ponies, though? Do you think they'll hold up?"

"They must," Saint-Germain said simply. "We'll rig nose bags and keep to a steady pace. I see well enough in the night that we should not encounter any serious trouble. We can rest after dawn if necessary, but I want to get out of this canyon before anything more can develop." He gathered the lead pony's reins into one hand and set his foot in the stirrup. "It will be best if we do not speak, I think. If you wish to signal me, use the whistle we used in Catalonia, when we were being sought by the Emir's son. Do you remember?"

Rogerio pursed his lips and made an eerie sound, and the nearest pony whickered, ears turning. "Yes, I remember," he assured his master.

"Good. I will use the same with you." He swung into the saddle. "If you hear anything you can't account for, give the signal, and we will stop at once."

"Should we perhaps have a regular signal as well, so that each will know that the other is there?" He watched Saint-Germain.

"You're right," he said. "But it should not be too predictable. If we are followed, all that they need do is learn the signal and the interval for repetition, and we are no safer than we were without it." He toyed with the reins. "The chorus of the hymn to Saint John. In Latin, I think, line by line. At the end of the ten lines, go back to the beginning. You do the first half of each line, I will do the second. If too much time passes, I will do the first half and wait for you to do the second. Once every two li should be enough."

"The hymn to Saint John, in Latin," Rogerio repeated, then started for the rear of the string of ponies.

Night engulfed them before they had gone two li, and the wind came down off the snow like a ravening animal. Any worry Saint-Germain had had of Tzoa Lem's overhearing them was quickly forgotten as he strove to hear the sound of his pony's hooves over the shriek of the wind. He barely heard Rogerio's shouted Latin phrases, and had to turn in his saddle and answer them at the top of his voice.

Sometime later they called a short halt in the lee of a rock-face, and set to making the gruel for the ponies so that they could provide them with nose bags.

"Water, too," Saint-Germain said. "It should be warmed a little or they'll suffer for it." He had succeeded in starting a low fire and was measuring barley into a large iron pot.

"I will attend to that," Rogerio said, rubbing his face with his hands. "The fur gloves help, but the wind . . ."

"Terrible," Saint-Germain agreed as he added water to the grain. He was determined not to dwell on the hazards of their situation, so he said, "Can you recall anything that the soldiers at the border post said about what lies ahead?"

"They mentioned a monastery, quite near, and said that there were others. From the sound of it, the country must be made up of monks. The officer did say that the capital is on the far side of the plateau, and the roads there are often impassable after the snows fall." Rogerio had pulled a wide, deep pan from the pack of the next-to-last pony and was emptying the contents of a waterskin into it.

"I gathered as much," Saint-Germain said. "While the officer was questioning me, he intimated that we were foreign initiates to one of the various orders. I assumed that there was some sort of rivalry developing between two of the largest orders. He seemed to think that the Yellow Hats were the ones to watch."

"One of the guards mentioned them. They also told me the Red Robes had a great deal of influence." He put the pan near the fire to warm it.

Saint-Germain sat beside the fire, shielding it with his body. "We'll have to be cautious, Rogerio. More than usual. I've never been here, and I don't trust anything I've heard."

His servant made a gesture of resignation. "It will happen as it happens," he said. "How's the barley coming?"

"It won't be ready for a while." He patted the damp ground beside him. "Lie down. Get some rest. It's going to be a while before we'll have the chance again."

Rogerio did not object. "When the barley is ready, wake me and we'll see to the ponies and get under way again." Neither man thought it strange that the servant should be giving orders to the master. Saint-Germain nodded his agreement and moved slightly to give Rogerio a little more room so that he could rest in a less-cramped space. And while Rogerio slept, Saint-Germain waited for the barley to come to a tepid boil.

They were moving again well before midnight, climbing steadily out of the canyon and onto the spur of one of the mountain crests. The road here was a little wider and showed signs of recent repairs. Saint-Germain kept his eyes on the most distant parts of the way that he could see, but there was no movement. Once he thought he saw a goat-hide tent pitched in a little gully on the far side of the canyon, but he could not be sure, and it was quickly lost to sight.

Dawn found them near the head of the canyon, approaching a precarious bridge that crossed the plunging river which had dug the gorge over thousands of years. The bridge, held by ropes as thick as a man's calf, swung and creaked with every twitch of wind, and the planking seemed flimsy, but the ponies crossed it unerringly.

When he reached the center of the bridge, Saint-Germain stopped a moment and stared down at the falling water. Spray from the cascade made a freezing mist, and the rising sun struck it, turning the mist to a nimbus of preternatural brightness. As always, crossing water gave Saint-Germain a sensation of vertigo, and he was grateful for the layer of his native earth in the soles and heels of his boots. Then he nudged his pony's sides and completed the crossing.

An old man in lama's robes waited at the far end of the bridge, his begging bowl ready. But instead of holding it up

to Saint-Germain, he bowed low, abasing himself, and remained silent as the little party passed.

"What did you make of that?" Saint-Germain called back
to Rogerio in Greek as they rounded the first bend in the
road.

"The monk? Who knows? Monks are strange. He may do
that for the first travelers over the bridge every morning." He
had, in fact, found the lama's behavior disquieting, but refused to say anything more about it.

"What color robe did he wear, did you notice?" Saint-Germain called back a little later.

"No color. Brownish-gray."

"That's what it seemed to me, too." Saint-Germain glanced
around once, but the mountains were empty. Yet he could
not quiet his thoughts. He had been an object of awe and
veneration before, as well as of fear and detestation. This was
not quite the same, and he could not define for himself what
disturbed him. He told himself that it was the strangeness of
the country that awakened these feelings within him, not the
lama at the bridge.

They came to a spring at midmorning, and halted for a
moment.

"What are those?" Rogerio asked, pointing to three oddly
shaped towers standing beside the spring.

"I don't know," Saint-Germain said, looking at the structures. They were more than twice as tall as he, narrow, with
pointed tops and intricate shaping that looked as if it had
been done on a gigantic lathe. He approached one and
caught a subtle carrion scent. He stood still. "Rogerio, I think
we had better not stay here."

Rogerio, who was preparing to dismount, looked at his
master, great curiosity in his face. "Why not? Because of
those . . . things?"

Saint-Germain answered carefully. "Something is dead
here. It's been dead for a long time. These structures are
probably a warning. The spring may not be potable." He
caught up the reins of his protesting pony. "We'll have to go
on. There are bound to be other springs." As he got back into
the saddle, he added, "A halt would be welcome. Keep alert
for a likely place to camp." He knew it might be dangerous
to camp in the day and travel at night, but he had to admit
that it was what he preferred. At night his powers were at
their strongest and he felt most free.

Rogerio had to tug at the reins to get his pony to leave the spring, but at last they moved on, following the narrow path that cut darkly through the first thick fall of snow.

The sun was high overhead when they reached a fork in the road. Both branches seemed equally well-kept, and both showed some little signs of travel. The country here was less steep, and there was a low stand of trees off to the side of the road.

"Which way?" Rogerio asked as he drew in his pony at Saint-Germain's signal.

"I don't know," Saint-Germain said. He dismounted and drew his pony off the road toward the trees. "We might as well rest here, and in the evening, we'll choose one or the other if we haven't seen anyone else on the road by then who can tell us where they lead." He tugged the pony over to the nearest tree, a scrubby sort of pine from the look of it, and looped the rein around the lowest branch. The other ponies followed, most of them moving with heads low and dragging feet. Saint-Germain set about tethering them while Rogerio looked under the trees.

"There's a bit of a clearing in the middle of the stand. Not much, but better than nothing. It's protected and the ground is flat for a change," Rogerio reported a little later.

"Can we still see the road?" Saint-Germain asked as he lifted the packsaddle from the third pony on the string.

"Yes, some of it." He busied himself with the girths. "These ponies amaze me."

Saint-Germain rubbed the neck of the next one down the line. "They're very strong, but they need to be rested. That traveling last night was more than they're used to." He bent to loosen the girth and frowned. "We'll have to find someone who can replace these. There are only two girths left in our supplies." He lifted the saddle from the pony's back and put it with the others. "You'd think," he said as he straightened up, "that there would be taverns or inns or something else on this road, but I haven't seen sign of one."

"Or of the monasteries," Rogerio agreed, starting to gather various bits of wood for their fire.

"Yes, that's even more puzzling. From what Tzoa Lem said, there should be monks on every crag, and I've yet to see anything other than that one we passed yesterday." He was working on the next pack pony.

Rogerio made no comment, putting his mind to the tasks to be done. The ponies would need extra rations of warm gruel, and he himself was growing hungry. He would have to find meat before too long. He did not want to consider what his master must feel, though nothing he did or said gave any indication of the need that must hourly be growing stronger in him.

"We'd better put up the shelter for the ponies," Saint-Germain said somewhat later. "I don't want to harm them, and after a long day, the cold might be bad for them." He indicated two trees, saying, "If we string the mats between them, that will provide a windbreak and we can rig the cloth shields over the tether line." As he felt his way through the packs, he laughed once. "There's no getting away from it," he said. "The world imposes, no matter what we do."

"Too much so," Rogerio said. He had just failed for the fourth time to get enough of a spark to start a fire in his mound of kindling.

Saint-Germain busied himself with the mats, then said, "It's the oddest feeling, but I can't get over it—we're being watched. I've looked all day, and have seen no one."

"Herdboys?" Rogerio suggested.

"What herds? I haven't seen any." He paused in his labors to scowl. "I'm probably still worried about Tzoa Lem and his farmers. It seems unlikely that we'd escape them without help." He had had luckier escapes down the years, but few so convenient, and it bothered him. He said nothing more.

When the gruel for the ponies was boiling in its pot and the fire crackled like new jokes, Saint-Germain came into the shelter Rogerio had erected. "I think perhaps," he said after a moment of silence, "that it would be best if we travel by day only." He wished it were not necessary, but he was certain that by night they would meet no one who could guide them.

Rogerio nodded. "Probably for the best."

Saint-Germain did not respond, but stood in the entrance to the shelter, keeping watch while Rogerio made the gruel for the ponies.

When the ponies had been fed and the fire banked, Saint-Germain went on impulse to the covered stacks of their baggage and pulled out the katana Saito Masashige had given him. He thrust the scabbard through his belt, checked the hilt of the sword to be sure it was properly in place, then made his way back to the shelter, saying only, "There will be snow tonight."

Though Rogerio saw that Saint-Germain carried the katana, he made no mention of it.

———— ◄●► ————

Text of a report sent from the Rdo-rje DBang-bzhi monastery to the Bya-grub Me-long ye-shys lamasery.

On the morning of the Festival of the Path of True Wisdom in the Eighteenth Year of the King's Reign.

The lama RNying Sbo brought word yesterday morning that while he kept his watch at the Rab-brtan Bridge, he saw two men and their pony train materialize out of the light just as the sun rose. The men came from the north, but were not of that race, but another. The first man was described as having dark eyes of penetrating power, and the man who followed him was quite calm. They traveled with seven ponies, and the significance of this number did not escape RNying Sbo.

Since then, they have been watched. At the Bon shrine by the SGom-thag Spring he dismounted, but neither the man nor his companion nor their ponies drank from the waters. They spoke at that time, and others, in a tongue unknown to us, though it has been described as foreign and flowing, like the wind or water.

They made no religious observances and took no measures to protect themselves against the malicious spirits that haunt the trails, looking for victims to lure to their deaths. The one with the powerful eyes has demonstrated unnatural strength, and though he goes armed, he has not struck one blow. It has been suggested by the oldest lamas at this lamasery that if the man is as advanced a being as we have reason to believe, his sword is merely a symbol, an Attribute granted him by All-Wise Heaven.

They have camped in the Long Shadow Grove, where

no man camps for fear of the ghosts of the brigands who died there a century ago. These men were not afraid and went to the worst part of the grove without incident. They rose before first light and have, in the last few moments, according to the lamas who have watched them, got ready to journey southward.

We are sending the herdboy STam to them, to offer to act as guide. Most of the lamas agree that if these remarkable beings wished our help, they would have come to us and commanded it. As it is, because they have chosen to live in this unassuming guise, we have decided to do what we can to aid them without an unseemly intrusion. STam will act as guide, and if they are willing, will bring them to your lamasery so that they may meet with the Master of our Order.

We of the Rdo-rje DBang-bzhi lamasery send our assurances of devotion to the Master SGyi Zhel-ri and meditate upon his enlightened teachings in the course of every day. Surely the Eightfold Path and Consecrations are fulfilled in him, and we advance in spirituality through the merit of his lessons. May he have a long life, incur no debts and find release from the Wheel.

By the hand of the Abbot Bhota-bris Lung, by messenger, after morning prayers.

5

"THERE!" the herdboy STam shouted, pointing toward the crest of a nearby peak. "That is Bya-grub Me-long ye-shys lamasery." He was far more excited than the two others with him: he bounced in the saddle of his Spiti pony and waved both his hands.

Snow was drifting quietly out of a steel-colored sky. There were almost no shadows to mark the passing of the day, though it had to be midafternoon. Saint-Germain drew up his pony and looked back at Rogerio, addressing him in Greek.

"What do you think, old friend? Shall we chance this monastery?" He was suffering from the curious indifference that deep hunger sometimes visited upon him. At such times, he could not convince himself that he must take action to change this or ravening need would suddenly seize him. He had not experienced that frenzy in more than a thousand years, but the memory of it still had the power to horrify him.

"It might be interesting," Rogerio said cautiously. "We don't know what they might expect of us, but it is probably better than spending another night in the snow."

"True enough." Saint-Germain called out to the herdboy in the few awkward phrases he had managed to learn in the last four days on the road. "We will go there. You lead us."

STam's smile was very broad as he turned off the main road onto a path flanked by low stone fences. "You see, even in the snow, you can find the road," he enthused.

A little of his pleasure communicated itself to Saint-Germain. "You have been here before."

"Once. Then I was only allowed as far as the outer gate. This time they will let me in because I am bringing you." He was so delighted that he did not see the quick meeting of eyes between Saint-Germain and Rogerio.

"Why would that make a difference?" Saint-Germain inquired blandly, his small hands tightening on the reins.

"You are strangers, and the Master is always curious about strangers," the youth answered, suddenly very circumspect.

Keeping his tone genial, Saint-Germain continued in Rogerio's native Latin. "This would be a difficult place to escape from, as you can see. The walls are high and there are apparently two sets of them. If I know anything about monks, there will be someone up at every hour, and moving about in a strange place is always dangerous." He gave a brief laugh and Rogerio dutifully echoed it. "Do not let the boy see your apprehension."

"There may be no reason for concern," Rogerio pointed out.

"You say that, after what the good Brothers did to Ranegonde's lover?" he asked, not quite able to maintain his mendacious good humor. "Or the way the Frankish Benedictines encouraged the good people of Lyon to burn Herchambaut and Javotte and Yolande—have you forgotten that?"

"No, my master. I have not forgotten." His voice was somber and he fell silent.

The outer gates of the monastery were high, massive and without adornment. From high above them a strange horn sounded, and the gates swung open.

"We may pass through," STam announced importantly,

and led the way, saying a few words Saint-Germain and Rogerio could not hear to the small party of robed men who met them inside the gates.

"Impressive," Saint-Germain said dryly, still speaking Latin. "I think we may have trouble leaving, if all the doors and walls are like this."

Ahead of them was another wall, not so high as the outer one, but much more elaborate. It was carved and painted in a variety of bright colors, and there were representation of the Buddha in every conceivable pose and shade. Each of the six doors leading into that building was guarded by huge statues of fierce monsters, most of them in warlike postures and carrying a gruesome array of weapons.

"You must not ride the ponies through the next door," STam said earnestly as he dismounted. "Only men may pass through that door."

"Indeed," Saint-Germain murmured sardonically, dismounting. He looked at the ponies, each carrying precious bags of his native earth. He looked at the herdboy, saying as simply as he could, "I must have what the ponies carry. If I am without it, bad things will happen to me." He was not entirely certain he had said it properly, but STam smiled eagerly.

"I will tell them. They will place the bags in your quarters, do not fear it." He swaggered a little as he walked to the lamas so that he would not reveal too much of the awe that almost overwhelmed him. He spoke loudly so that Saint-Germain could hear him. "The distinguished foreigner requires that all the contents of the packsaddles, without exception, be taken to the quarters he is assigned. It is most important, and he has said that bad things will happen if it is not done."

This pronouncement stirred the lamas to action, and one with a more elaborate headdress than the others turned to Saint-Germain and bowed very low.

"They will do it," STam said merrily, coming back across the courtyard. He beamed up at Saint-Germain. "What bad thing would you do?"

Saint-Germain's expression was wholly bleak with the desolation he had carried within him for all his long years. "Feed." He had said it in his native language, which Rogerio knew imperfectly, but he recognized the pain in his master's face, and put one hand on his arm.

"Don't. Something will be arranged."

Quickly Saint-Germain nodded, forcing his thoughts away from the need that grew in him.

The apparent leader of the lamas hurried up and abased himself. "I am the Guardian, Bsnyen-la Ras-gsal. I bid you welcome to the Bya-grub Me-long ye-shys lamasery on behalf of the Abbot and the Master." He made three ritual gestures, and rose.

"A reassuring beginning," Saint-Germain remarked to Rogerio in Latin, then summoned most of what he had learned from STam. "It is a great honor to be welcomed here. My companion and I are most grateful." He knew that he had not pronounced the words very well, but the Guardian beamed at him and ushered him toward the ornately carved gate.

"Come, then, and accept what poor hospitality we can offer you." He rapped a pattern on the gilded wood, and waited respectfully as the double doors swung inward. He bowed again and indicated that the visitors should enter. "I am not of sufficiently advanced rank to enter by this door," he explained as he stood back.

"I hope that is the true reason," Saint-Germain said softly to Rogerio as they went through the doors, STam trailing behind them with a frankly astonished expression on his face.

Another lama, with more elaborate headgear, was waiting for them, and when he spoke, the eerie horn blast that had accompanied the opening of the main gate was repeated.

"It is my pleasant duty to show you to your quarters," he said, indicating a wide hallway lined with scrolls of painted silk showing various lamas performing a number of feats most of which Saint-Germain assumed were allegorical. In the largest scroll, a man in a lama's robe fended off a flying creature with a double set of horns and fangs, whose twisted green body was covered with eyes. There were a number of pillars along the hallway, each with an elaborately painted capital. The ceiling, too, was painted, each section between the beams having a different design, most of which were repeated geometrical patterns. Here the predominant colors were rust, deep blue, and bright yellow.

In one of the large rooms they passed, fifty lamas sat on the stone floor, their legs crossed, facing an altar on which an enormous gold statue of Buddha seated on a lotus was placed. The lamas were chanting quietly: a few of them held the rattlelike instruments in their hands which Saint-Germain had discovered were called prayer wheels.

"Up these stairs," the lama who was leading them said, and the men at prayer were quickly behind them.

Their assigned rooms faced the north. The walls were thick wood, and the tiny windows were high and narrow, providing a little light. There were two sections to Saint-Germain's quarters, both scantily furnished. To Saint-Germain's surprise, all the bags and the Roman chest were stacked in one corner. It did not appear that they had been opened.

As he started to open the Roman chest, the air was filled with a low, shuddering note—one of the huge temple gongs was being rung. The sound of it was not so much heard as felt. It trembled and echoed once, twice, a third time, and then was silent.

"How often do they do that?" Rogerio asked from the door.

"I have no idea," Saint-Germain answered. He indicated the sacks and his chest. "They said they would bring them, and they did. I'm somewhat perplexed."

Rogerio's blue eyes grew bright with relief. "So they did," he said, coming across the room to have a better look at them.

"Where are your rooms?" Saint-Germain went to the door and looked down the hall. Though there was no one in sight, he said, "I think it will be best if we speak Latin and Greek. Doubtless there are men here who know Chinese, and I would wager a few of the Islamic explorers have got this far. No Persian, then, and no Arabic."

"Latin and Greek," Rogerio agreed. "Latin, preferably."

Saint-Germain managed to smile slightly. "Nostalgia?"

"Convenience," his servant answered. "Do you wish me to make up a bed for you?" he went on in a different tone, indicating the earth-filled bags.

"It would be wise. I don't know how long I will have to go without other . . . nourishment, and so I must rely on my native earth to sustain me." He looked at the raised pallet against the wall. "That is the bed, I assume. You can improvise some sort of a matress with the shelter cloths and the bags, and that should be sufficient."

Rogerio nodded. "It won't take me too long."

"Do you wish my help?" Saint-Germain inquired, knowing the answer as he did.

"No. Of course not." He hesitated, then said, "I understand there is a bathhouse somewhere in this building. When you return I will have clothes set out for you."

Saint-Germain looked at the Roman chest. "You'd better store Masashige's sword in the back panel. There are a couple dozen jewels there, and it might be wise to have a few of them ready, in case we have need of them." He put his hand on the chest. "If we ever find a place to stay for a while, I must build another athanor and replenish our supply of gold and jewels. It's ridiculous to try to set up an establishment on so little."

"Were you planning to establish yourself here, then?" Rogerio asked, startled.

"No, not here. It would not be terrible, however, to have a few months of calm." He shook off the despondency that had begun to take hold of him. "I'll see if I can find the bathhouse." With that he stepped into the hall.

A lama found him a little while later and guided him to the low wooden structure where the baths were. Saint-Germain thanked him and gave himself up to the oblivion of warm water and steamy rooms.

True to his word, Rogerio had set out a change of clothes, and Saint-Germain donned them with relief. He dressed with Frankish elegance, in a long tunic of black wool embroidered at cuffs, hem and collar with red silk. Over that he wore a cote of sable lined with black Venetian velvet. The silver chain with the black-and-ruby pectoral was pinned on his shoulders. His boots were of Byzantine design—reaching above the knees and having tall heels and thick soles. As he finished dressing, he flicked his short, loose curls to dry his hair. Then he sat in the one low chair and waited. He was certain that after such a welcome there would be more expected of him.

The sound of the chanting from the central room had grown louder when there came a knock at his door. Saint-Germain rose and answered it, and found himself facing a bent old man in a shapeless woolen robe. "I am not a lama." he said to Saint-Germain. "I am merely the servant of the Abbot, who would be grateful if you might spare him a moment of your time."

There was little else for Saint-Germain to do, but he responded politely, "I am grateful that the Abbot will see me." He hesitated. "My servant . . ."

"He will be told where you have gone and when he should expect you to return." The old man smiled toothlessly and bowed in the direction of the main hall. "The Abbot's quarters are in the south tower."

Saint-Germain acknowledged this with a gesture and fell into step behind the old man. The sharp report of his heeled boots marked their progress down the hall.

As on the main floor, scrolls and murals covered these walls, depicting spiritual beings in symbolic manifestations. There were three wooden statues along the way, each gilt and painted. Saint-Germain noticed that all the figures had intensely blue hair, and he wished he could stop the old man and ask why. He contented himself with the reminder that he would be here most of the winter, and during that time he would learn much.

The old man paused before plain double doors and knocked once, very softly. An indistinct voice answered at once. "He is waiting to see you," the old man said to Saint-Germain, and stood aside to let him enter the room.

Though several elaborate scrolls hung on the walls, this room was no more elegantly furnished than Saint-Germain's quarters. There was a man seated on a thick mat on the floor and he looked up as Saint-Germain entered.

"Ah!" the man on the mat said. "You are the foreigner. I am the Abbot SNyin Shes-rab." He made the ritual motion that Saint-Germain knew was a greeting, and which he returned.

"My servant and I are grateful for your hospitality." he said, wishing he had a better command of the language.

Apparently the Abbot shared his feeling. "I fear I do not speak the languages of China, but the Master does. I understand that you comprehend most of what is said to you."

"Yes, that's true enough," Saint-Germain said, wondering if he was supposed to stand in the Abbot's presence.

SNyin Shes-rab rose to his feet. He was not very tall, but had an air of command that Saint-Germain respected. "Doubtless you have been asking yourself why we brought you here."

So it had been deliberate! Saint-Germain schooled his features to a confidence he did not feel. "You must have your reasons."

The Abbot bowed. "It was at the order of the Master,

SGyi Zhel-ri, who read the report of you and said that when you arrived you were to be admitted."

"And you obeyed," Saint-Germain said.

"Of course. We are most fortunate to have such a Master, good foreigner." He stopped. "Surely you have a name that you would let me use."

Saint-Germain nodded. "In China I was called Shih Ghieh-Man. It is as good a name as any."

"Shih Ghieh-Man," the Abbot repeated with an odd inflection. "Very well." He sank back onto the mat and indicated the low chair in the corner of the room. "Let us talk, Shih Ghieh-Man."

"By all means." Saint-Germain seated himself, and though the chair was uncomfortable, he contrived to be at ease.

"Our Master is one of the Great Masters," SNyin Shes-rab said when he had gathered his thoughts. "He is far along the Path and his wisdom touches all of us." He gave Saint-Germain a level look. "You are the first one he has ever asked to see. Until now, those who have wished the chance to enter his presence have had to request it, and those requests have not always been granted. Even the King has not been admitted to his meditation chamber."

"Then why should he send for me? Surely there are foreigners enough . . ." He had decided that half of what the Abbot said was intended to impress this foreigner with a sense of the magnitude of his honor, and he was determined to let SNyin Shes-rab know that he was not easily awed.

"You are more than a foreigner, Shih Ghieh-Man," the Abbot said firmly. "Most foreigners are ignorant and pass through our world with as little influence as a leaf riding a mountain stream."

Saint-Germain concealed the alarm he felt. What did the Abbot mean? "We all pass through the world that way, SNyin Shes-rab. Only on rare occasions do we . . ." He could not find the proper word and did not know how to draw a metaphor.

"This is one such occasion," the Abbot assured him. "It was the wish of the Master that you see him, and you shall. You would do well to listen closely to all that he says, for his words are more precious than jewels. Often his teachings are copied down and sent to other lamaseries of our Order so that all may benefit from his great knowledge." He smoothed his sun-colored robe. "He will tell you himself why he wishes to see you. It is not for me to answer for the Master."

"So you have said," Saint-Germain responded. "When am I to be admitted to the Master's presence? Is there anything I should do?"

SNyin Shes-rab looked away. "You must sit at his feet, and you must not speak until he gives you the office to do so. You must not question his words unless he has said that he desires to answer questions. When he dismisses you, you must leave at once, and retire to your room so that you may meditate on what the Master has told you. Do not discuss what has been said until you have meditated on it." He waved his hand, indicating that Saint-Germain should rise. "There is a door at the end of the hall, and it is finished in gold leaf. That is the door you wish. You may enter it when you reach it. SGyi Zhel-ri knows you are coming." His face smoothed out as he closed his eyes. Clearly, Saint-Germain was dismissed.

Saint-Germain smiled wryly as he left the Abbot's room. He was inwardly somewhat amused by this preparation. The lamas of this lamasery were determined to enhance their Master's reputation, of that there could be no doubt. He went quickly down the hall, enjoying the theatricality of the meeting. When he reached the door he lifted his hand to knock, then shrugged. He had been told that the Master expected him, and so he would simply enter the room. Quickly he lifted the latch and stepped inside.

It was unexpectedly dark. If there were windows in the room, they were closed. Three oil lanterns burned behind a fretwork screen, but other than that, the chamber was deep in shadow.

"You are the foreigner," said a voice from behind the screen. It was pure and high. Hearing it, Saint-Germain was taken aback, for he realized that the Master of the Bya-grub Me-long ye-shys lamasery must be a eunuch to sound as he did.

"I am." He stopped, waiting.

"You have come far," the Master observed. "Very far. You have made the journey in more than distance, you have made it in many years."

Saint-Germain tried to convince himself that anyone as European as he would be given a similar evaluation, and would accept it as proof of the Master's perspicacity. Though it was difficult, he reminded himself that startling as the Master's pronouncement was, it was also safe: travelers had to come a long way to reach this place.

The voice spoke again. "How can you free yourself from the Wheel, Shih Ghieh-Man, if you live as you do, without dying?"

Now Saint-Germain was truly taken aback. "I . . . I don't understand . . ."

"Do not say so," the Master went on in Chinese. "You understand me very well, Shih Ghieh-Man. You have learned to be cautious, which is a wise course, no doubt, but in this instance, it is quite unnecessary. I am not one who believes in the demons who prey upon men and drink their blood. Those are tales for frightening gullible and ignorant people."

Saint-Germain, listening to that tranquil voice, was almost lulled into betraying himself. With an effort, he shut out the Master's words, interrupting him. "What do you intend?"

Apparently this rude treatment did not offend SGyi Zhel-ri. "I intend to learn from you. I ask no sacrifice. You will have a willing partner in your bed and the earth you lie on will not be tampered with." The Master was silent, as if waiting for Saint-Germain to speak again. When nothing was said, he went on. "In this land we have long believed in the powers of the great magicians. While I realize that is not quite what you are, I respect what you can accomplish, and what you have endured in your quest. You are on a quest, are you not?"

"Yes," Saint-Germain answered slowly. "I suppose you might call it that."

The Master was somewhat more decisive. "You have long to search. There are many, many years between you and your goal, and much of the world to cross to attain it."

Saint-Germain could not quite laugh. "It had eluded me so far, SGyi Zhel-ri."

"Not entirely. You have known great love, and you have given it selflessly—"

"Not quite selflessly," Saint-Germain put in. "If you know my nature, you know what I require." He told himself that this was madness, to be speaking so in the dark to a serene and flutelike voice belonging to someone he had never seen. His hard-won reserve seemed to desert him entirely, and he feared it might be the result of his hunger making him reckless. He folded his hands together and listened.

"Your requirements do not constrain you to give love, only

to create strong emotion. You know that you might as easily terrify your partners, but you do not do this."

"Not now, not most of the time," Saint-Germain allowed. "How did you learn this?" He had not wanted to ask that question, for it implied the Master's knowledge was accurate, but he could no longer resist knowing.

SGyi Zhel-ri sounded amused. "Wisdom is a great gift, but it can only be accepted without reservation. If conditions are made, then the wisdom becomes dogma and is without use on the Path. You know that as well as I, Shih Ghieh-Man. Why does it disturb you that you are not loathed, when being loathed is the greatest hurt you have known? Loss is not so great as that gulf so many put between your kind and the rest of humanity." The voice was silent, and when he spoke again, there was a mischievous sound in the words. "I am eager to see you, Shih Ghieh-Man. I will not chide you for hesitating, but it would please me to look on your face."

Saint-Germain hesitated. "If you insist."

"Hardly insist," SGyi Zhel-ri said at once. "You may depart now, if that is your wish."

Perversely, because he had been given permission to leave, Saint-Germain took half a dozen steps forward, then rounded the end of the screen.

In the light of the oil lanterns on a raised dais sat the Master. He was dressed in robes shot with golden thread and on his brow was a coronet of gold fashioned to look like an opening lotus bud. He smiled at Saint-Germain's amazed expression and clapped his hands together.

"It can't be you," Saint-Germain said as he looked down at the Master.

The voice he had been listening to answered. "But it is." Then he laughed again with great delight, and for that moment he sounded like the nine-year-old boy he was.

Report to the Ministry of War from the town of Ti-Yuen.

On the eve of the Year of the Tiger, the Fifteenth Year of the Sixty-fifth Cycle, from the Municipal Tribunal of Ti-Yuen to the Ministry of War at K'ai-Feng.

Our District outpost, in accordance with orders issued by the Ministry of War, has been detaining all suspicious travelers in this region and has held them for questioning by the local Magistrate. At this time, the District Magistrate, Jen Jo-Wei, is confined to his bed, as he has been for most of the winter, with a disease of the throat which his physician has not been able to cure. For that reason the Tribunal has been entrusted to us, his lieutenants, until such time as his health is restored and he returns to his duties.

Therefore, in accordance with the duties of the Magisterial Tribunal, we have continued to carry out the tasks of the Tribunal.

A week ago we detained a suspicious man, who called himself a guide to travelers going to T'u-Bo-T'e. He claims to have come from there, though this is hard to credit in the dead of winter. The roads through the passes have been closed for five fortnights and we do not anticipate having them open again until the middle of spring, which is more than nine fortnights away. This man insists that he had the aid of a family living not far from the border, which is, in itself, open to question.

The guide answers to the name of Tzoa Lem and it has been suggested that he may be one of a band of robbers who prey on travelers, luring them into the mountains, then taking all their goods and abandoning them on foot, or simply getting rid of them by tossing them off the trail. If this is so, it is a serious charge, and it is well-known that such jackals do operate in these regions.

212

Therefore we questioned Tzoa Lem at length, and he insisted on saying that he is an honest guide. He said that he went into the mountains in the fall with a foreigner and his foreign servant and that they were separated by an avalanche, so that he can give no report on the travelers.

We then conferred and decided that this man was not telling us the truth, and so we had him beaten with bamboo whisks until his back was round as a melon and of a terrible red hue. During that time, he was questioned again, and at last admitted that he did work with a few of the brigands, but that these men had not fallen victim to them. He admits abandoning the travelers, but further says that he is certain they were wanted men, sought by the various officials in the captials for unknown reasons, and he believes that it was in the interests of the state to abandon such miscreant rogues to their fate.

We, the lieutenants of the Tribunal, have considered these responses and we believe that this Tzoa Lem has concocted a useful lie, for it is an easy thing to say that missing men were enemies of the state and therefore deserved to be left alone in the mountains. Since Tzoa Lem has admitted that they traveled with ten ponies, it is obvious that these were wealthy travelers. Tzoa Lem insists that part of what they carried was three large chests filled with earth, but this is patently not true, and we have come to wonder what it was he took from those chests.

Therefore, we have decided to apply greater force. This man has shown himself to be one of the brigands who are beyond the protections of the law, and surely he has committed other crimes which have yet to be revealed. We have decided to peel the skin from his hands and feet to see what else he will tell us. The Tribunal has three goats who have been trained to lick the hands and feet after flaying. Only the most desperate criminals will resist this.

Submitted to the Ministry of War on behalf of the Magistrate Jen Jo-Wei by his lieutenants, P'a Pao, Hua Tung-Gi, Ching Liang and Ton Hsa-Chuang.

Appended to the report:
The suspicious person, Tzoa Lem, succumbed to the

peeling of his hands and feet. Before his death he confessed that he and his brothers-in-law had long been in the habit of robbing travelers, taking not only their goods, but their ponies as well. He said that he had maintained a good reputation for a long time because he did not actually attack the parties he led until they were well into the mountains, and that he made a great effort to be sure that his parties talked to any and all travelers they met, so that it would be reported that they had been seen on the road and that all was well. He also confessed that he never brought his booty to the town where those he stole it from hired him. That way, there was no chance that the goods he had plundered would be recognized. He said that there were four separate places on the main road where he and his brothers-in-law would waylay the travelers. One of those places is not currently available because there has been a great landslide. However, the other locations have been marked on the map enclosed so that the authorities may send out men to stop them. Doubtless this falls under the jurisdiction of the Chui-Cho fortress, so word should be sent at the thaw to the Warlord Mon Chio-Shing.

On the matter of the travelers he was guiding, the man Tzoa Lem was strangely adamant. He maintained to the last that there was something very wrong and dangerous about the foreigners. We of the Tribunal feel that if it is so—though we have good reason to doubt it—we should consider ourselves lucky in being rid of two potentially harmful men.

The transcript of the confession of the man Tzoa Lem is enclosed, along with the map to show where his gang operates. His body will be buried as soon as the ground can be worked.

For the Tribunal, the lieutenants and the Magistrate Jen Jo-Wei, under his chop.

6

WINTER HAD sheathed the Bya-grub Me-long ye-shys lamasery in brittle snow, sculpted by relentless winds into forms suggesting ships and beasts and castles. Each storm added to the fantasy landscape until all the world was lost to this en-thralling white kingdom.

A portion of the top floor had been set aside for Saint-Ger-main's use as a laboratory and it was here he spent most of his days. The lamas left him alone because the Master had ordered it so. As the snows deepened and the days shortened, Saint-Germain accustomed himself to the limited life of the lamasery, refusing to admit he was bored.

Occasionally SGyi Zhel-ri would climb up the steep, lad-derlike stairs to the room and watch Saint-Germain work with his improvised equipment. He rarely volunteered to as-sist his guest, but he asked a great many questions. After the first month, Saint-Germain began to look forward to these in-frequent visits.

He was mixing eggs with sand one afternoon toward the end of winter when he heard the light tread of the boy, and he set the large wooden bowl aside, turning toward the door as it opened. "Good day to you, Master SGyi," Saint-Ger-main said with the proper ritualistic bow that had no trace of subservience in it.

"And to you, Saint-Germain." He had been using the Eu-ropean version of his name since Saint-Germain told it to him. It came strangely off his tongue, but he would not say any other name.

"Why do you honor me with this visit? And I trust you will forgive me if I keep at my work." He had already picked up the bowl once more and was stirring the mixture.

"Of course you must work. I won't interrupt you. What are you making there?" He came and peered into the bowl.

"I hope that this will hold the bricks so that I may build a bigger athanor that can be heated to higher temperatures. The little one I have now is useless for many procedures. The problem is that this cold makes it almost impossible for the cement to dry properly, and if it does not dry properly, it cracks and is useless." He drew out the wooden paddle he was stirring with. "The Romans used eggs in their cement to prevent just such difficulties."

"Romans?" SGyi Zhel-ri asked.

"I've told you about them before. They lived far to the west and for a time had an enormous empire. They were great builders and they loved spectacle." He was dressed warmly in a black quilted woolen bliaut with his sable cote over it. Though his clothes were decidedly plain they were of excellent quality. He seemed unconcerned about the damage the mixture he held might do to his garments.

"Ah, yes, I remember the Romans. They are the ones who called the sight of men being torn to shreds by beasts 'games.' " He drew up a stool and climbed onto it. "Do you miss it still?"

"Rome?" Saint-Germain stared down into the mixture. "Not precisely."

"But you do miss Europe," SGyi Zhel-ri said.

"Among other things." It was difficult to speak of such matters to this too-knowing child.

"I don't mean to distress you, Saint-Germain," the boy said kindly. "But I am aware that you are not . . . content." He looked around the room. "That chart is new. What is it?"

Grateful for this change of subject, Saint-Germain set his bowl down once again and went to the wall where a newly painted silken scroll hung. "This represents most of the alchemical processes. I know them well enough myself, but there are times, as you're aware, when I require assistance, and this will serve as a guide for those who help me." He pointed out a drawing of a bell-shaped flask in which a silver-skinned woman and a green-skinned man were lying together in a yellowish substance. "When this—that is, silver—and this—that is, a specific acid which is in that jar marked with the sign of the green man—are combined and heated, this yellowish material is the result. If you do it right," he added dryly.

"Why are they shown copulating?" SGyi Zhel-ri asked.

"To imply union, that the silver and the acid must be man—are combined and heated, this yellowish material is the united. When there are diverse elements, this metaphor is the most easily understood." He came back across the room. "Do you want to learn alchemy, after all?"

"It would be enjoyable," the boy admitted as he looked at the apparatus in the high, cold room. "But I fear that it is not for me, this life. My Path is chosen and my feet are upon it." He smiled with that quiet serenity that had astounded Saint-Germain at first, and which he was not entirely used to yet.

"And you could not deviate?" Saint Germain inquired rather distantly.

"Certainly, if I had any desire to." SGyi Zhel-ri said, adding, "You could deviate from your Path, too, but you do not."

Saint-Germain gave a noncommittal shrug. He selected one

of the jars he had set out on his worktable and poured some of the granules it contained into the eggs and sand. When he had stirred this a bit more, he scooped a little of it out of the bowl and smeared it on a clay brick set out on the table. He watched it critically for some little time, then sighed. "It's too cold still."

"You will not be able to use it?"

He looked up at the boy. "Not until it's warmer."

"Then your work will be wasted." SGyi Zhel-ri sounded disappointed. "I wanted to see how you will build a larger athanor."

"Oh, it won't be wasted at all. I will place it in a sealed container with oil around it to keep out the touch of air, and it should be ready for use in the spring." He frowned. "I doubt I will be here then. You may have it, if I'm gone."

"You plan to leave?" The boy studied him without apprehension.

"Yes." He glanced at SGyi Zhel-ri and smiled slightly. "It is nothing against you, Master SGyi. It is simply that your ways are not my ways, and there are things I must do." He was not certain what he meant by that, but he knew that remaining at the Bya-grub Me-long ye-shyn lamasery would be intolerable.

"You will not find what you are seeking here," he agreed somewhat wistfully. "I have spoken to BDeb-ypa at length."

This reference to the woman who had been sent to his quarters on his first night at the monastery, and who has visited him regularly since then, made Saint-Germain uncomfortable. "Have you."

"She is aware that she has not been able to meet your needs as completely as you have met hers. It grieves her." He had tucked his legs under him, balancing precariously with ease.

"It shouldn't. It is not her fault." He had selected a large metal jar and was pouring oil into it. He hoped that this activity would provide him with an excuse to remain silent about the woman BDeb-ypa. "She has done all that she can, and that is . . . adequate."

SGyi Zhel-ri said nothing for a time, and apparently was content to watch Saint-Germain transfer the cement he had made from the bowl to the metal jar. Just as Saint-Germain was preparing a wax seal for the jar, he said, "You were a priest when you were a child, weren't you?"

Saint-Germain looked up, almost dropping the hot wax stick. It was a moment before he could compose his thoughts, and he glanced away on the pretense of attending to the seal as he tried to sort out the emotions that warred in him. He knew that the boy was watching him, and that this was one question he could not defer answering. "I was a child a very long time ago," he said in a tone he hardly recognized.

"But you were a priest then," the boy persisted.

He was silent, then said, "Yes." It was plain that SGyi Zhel-ri wanted him to continue, that his admission was not sufficient. When he was finished with the metal jar, he spoke again. "It was the custom among my people to make priests of the sons of the Kings who were born at the dark of the year, as I was. We were dedicated to the service of our protector god, who was very powerful." He was able to laugh once. "The protector was not, in fact, a god, but a vampire, as I am. Those who served him provided him with . . . sustenance, and in time, if we were selected for this duty often enough, we acquired his power and his life. Most of the priests, when they died, were cremated, but those whom the protector designated his heirs were ritually buried so that they could waken to his life. There were never more than two protectors, and there were occasions when one of them would be beheaded with great ceremony so that his strength would pass into the fields or the walls of the city." He looked down at his small hands, stretching out the long, well-shaped fingers, watching the play of tendons under the skin.

"But that did not happen to you," the child-Master said, his eyes bright with fascination.

"No, it didn't. I died a slave in the land of my enemies." He got up and walked away across the cold room. "And that was a long, long time ago, SGyi Zhel-ri. Those enemies are dust and their city lies deep in the earth. It is, I suppose, vengeance of a sort."

"What had you done?" The boy's voice was calm, and for that reason, if no other, Saint-Germain answered him.

"I won a battle." There was a rough bench beside the alchemical scroll and he sat on it, glad for the distance that let him be isolated with his memories. "Those of us who had been captured when our land was invaded were made soldiers. We were far more expendable than the troops of our captors. In battle the leaders of my company fell and we slaves were left exposed to the full might of chariot attack. I called the other slaves to me, and we were able to defeat the enemies of our captors. When the local ruler heard of this, he had me executed. He was very much afraid of any slave who could command men in battle." He paused as he recalled that hot day in a town of mud-and-stone houses where a stooped man in frayed red robes who was old at thirty-two had shouted out his sentence for his victorious slave, and had then watched in terror as his executioners readied their knives and hooks for their work. Saint-Germain could hardly recall why the man was so frightened of him. "They did not know what they were dealing with," Saint-Germain said dreamily, "and they didn't know how to kill me." He put his hand to his waist, knowing the scars began there, then let his fingers move aside.

"But the old man who condemned you feared you," SGyi Zhel-ri pointed out, as if aware of Saint-Germain's thoughts.

"With good reason, I imagine," Saint-Germain agreed, steel in his tone now. "His title, as I remember, was Ruler of the Earth and Sea. The Sky might also have been included, I'm not certain. His kingdom was a day's journey on horseback in all directions. My father had ruled a land four times that size." He sighed. "It's long past and done."

"But you have not forgotten."

"No."

From the sanctuary far below them the sound of chanting rose to fill the quiet of the laboratory. It was so ubiquitous that neither truly heard it.

"Is it the worship you miss when you lie with BDeb-ypa?" SGyi Zhel-ri asked a bit later.

With some difficulty Saint-Germain shook himself out of the reverie he had fallen into. There were so many things he had put behind him, so many faces and cities and lands. It was foolish, this dreadful glamour that transformed those arduous years into great adventure. His memories played tricks on him, he knew it, so that he could bear himself. SGyi Zhel-ri's question was remote and it was several moments before he answered. "Worship? I've ceased to believe in that."

"But there is something that comes of it," the boy said with his uncanny perceptivity.

"Yes," Saint-Germain admitted, finding a hurt renewed within him. "There is a kind of passion that is not of the body—or not entirely of the body," he amended with an attempt at cynicism he could not truly feel. "When it is present, then I am whole again."

"And the blood?" He braced his elbows on his knees and gave Saint-Germain a steady look.

"Oh, that is part of it. It is the essence of life, for those such as I." He got to his feet and abruptly began to pace. "Why should this concern you? You're a child, SGyi Zhel-ri. I haven't been a child since before the walls of Babylon rose. What can I tell you that you would understand?"

The boy's smile was still serene. "But I do understand, Saint-Germain, for I can feel what you feel." He paused, then said, "When you were a boy and a priest to the protector god who was not a god, how did you serve him?"

Saint-Germain stopped pacing. "How do you think: we gave him our blood and he conferred his strength and his life upon us. It is our nature." Saying it, he felt an echo of the awe that had touched him the first time he was taken to the holy place and earned his name—Saint-Germain—sacred liberation.

"But that was not the embrace of lovers, was it?" SGyi Zhel-ri persisted.

"No. That came later. To be honest, a great deal later. For . . . many years"—he could not say that those years were measured in centuries—"the fear was all I desired. I knew I could inspire the fear easily. Why not use it, when everyone shrank from me? Eventually, that changed." So that he would not have to think of the degradation that led to the change, Saint-Germain resumed pacing, though somewhat more slowly than he had moved before. He stopped to stare down at the gravel-filled basin where he had placed his very small athanor. The little stones dissipated the heat so that the alchemical oven could get quite hot without being a danger to the wooden interior of the lamasery.

"How did you give him blood?" Plainly, SGyi Zhel-ri was not going to abandon the matter.

"All right." Saint-Germain looked down at his hands once more, this time at the palms, where he told himself he could still see a few of the fine scars from that time. "We would go to the holy place of our liberation and would be seated on a special chair—it was little more than a stool with a plank for a back, but it was beautifully painted. The oldest priest then came with a certain knife, used only for this, and nicked the palms of my hands." If he noticed he had ceased to speak impersonally, he did not indicate it in any way. "I would hold my hands together to form a kind of cup as the other priests withdrew. The place would be dark, for these ceremonies took place only at night, and only the oldest priest was entitled to carry a torch. Once he left, there was only starlight. There would be silence as my hands filled, and then there would be motion, and I would feel lips touch my fingers to drink. What happened then . . ." He gazed at the wall, not seeing it. In his mind he was once again a boy not quite alone in that holy place, and a being he could not see clearly knelt before him. "I felt . . . exalted." His voice was soft and his eyes were enigmatic, his face sad.

"Was it you or the other who caused this?" The boy's voice no longer seemed an intrusion.

"I don't know," Saint-Germain confessed. "And at this distance there is really no way I can tell."

"There is one way," SGyi Zhel-ri said. He did not sound excited, though his expression was one of lively curiosity.

"No," he said quickly. "Not that. Not you."

"I haven't said—"

Saint-Germain cut short his objections. "I know what you are intending. You are going to offer to take the place that I filled so long ago. No. It isn't because I doubt your sincerity," he went on more gently as he saw the shock in Master SGyi's eyes. "It has been more than three thousand years since I experienced that. I doubt, after all this time, and all that has happened, that I could recapture what I felt then with anyone." As he said it, he wanted very much to know again that lightness of spirit he remembered from his long-vanished childhood. "What I seek now, you would not want to provide me, were I cruel enough to ask it."

SGyi Zhel-ri thought this over. "You haven't sought what you first found." He got up from the stool and went to where Saint-Germain was standing. "You are in need of restoration. You are no longer willing to impose your desires on others. Why must you also refuse what is offered you?" He did not wait for an answer, but turned and went out the door.

"It's not so simple as that, SGyi Zhel-ri," he started to protest, but heard the door close before he could finish. Feeling strangely bereft, he turned his attention to his worktable and busied himself in cleaning and arranging the containers, apparatus and tools set out upon it. This was comforting work, mindless and undemanding. He could let his thoughts drift, avoiding all those matters that brought him acute discomfort. He compared himself to a helmsman navigating through shoals, mocking himself for the analogy since he was very much aware that he and all his kind were terrible sailors. When at last he banked the fire in his little athanor, his laboratory was quite dark, and the few oil lamps cast only enough light to make the shadows seem vaster.

Saint-Germain was no stranger to the dark, and as he pinched out the lamps, he welcomed the closing in of the night. As he made his way down the stairs, he could hear the night chanting of the lamas in the sanctuary in countermelody to the moaning of the wind over the snow. The heels of his boots were sharp, waking echoes from the walls as he went briskly toward his rooms.

"Your pardon," said one of the old lamas as he came up to Saint-Germain from the hall intersection where he had been waiting.

"And yours," Saint-Germain said automatically, preparing to pass the old man.

"Your presence is required, Shih Ghieh-Man," the monk said, and bowed, indicating that Saint-Germain was expected to follow him.

At first, Saint-Germain wanted to refuse, assuming that SGyi Zhel-ri had sent the lama for him so that they could resume their discussion. He was keenly aware that few of the others at the lamasery wished for his company, as they regarded him with a distaste that bordered on revulsion. Yet he did not wish to defy the old man, who doubtless was only carrying out instructions. "Where do you plan to take me?"

"To the chapel of the Bodhisattva SGrol-ma Dkar-mo," the lama answered.

Saint-Germain could not entirely conceal his smile. SGrol-ma Dkar-mo was the redemptress of the Tibetean pantheon, the personification of compassion. The Bya-grub Me-long ye-shys lamasery had a small chapel to her, as did almost all of the Yellow Hat Order lamaseries "At this hour?" he asked aloud, saving his other questions for his next interview with the Master SGyi.

"The Master has said it would do you well to meditate there for a time, and sent me to be certain that you acted on his instructions." From the tone of the old lama's voice, it was unthinkable that anyone would refuse to follow the instructions of SGyi Zhel-ri.

"Very well. Lead the way." He suspected he would be able to find the small room more easily than the lama, but the old man had lived within the lamasery walls for thirty years and knew it as thoroughly as his fingers knew the seams and planes of his face.

"Through here," the old lama said at last as he opened a narrow door at the end of the western hall.

Saint-Germain bowed, the palms of his hands pressed together just above his wrist. "May you incur no karma and pass from the Wheel," he said politely as he went into the chapel. The door clicked shut behind him.

The room was dark and surprisingly silent, being far enough away from the main sanctuary that the sound of the chanting did not reach it. Even the wind was muted, for this side of the building was in the lee of the mountain where the storm could not carry. There was a faint scent of incense, the same that permeated the walls of the lamasery, offsetting a little the smells of close-packed humanity, yak butter and wet wool.

It was a moment before Saint-Germain realized he was not alone in the chapel. There was a movement on the dais where the presiding lama sat when prayers were said in honor of SGrol-ma Dkar-mo. There was a scrape, a quick intake of breath, then a metallic clatter as something dropped to the floor. Saint-Germain could now discern the other presence, for though there was no light in the room, there was the boy SGyi Zhel-ri: he waited on the dais, his hands cupped, extended, bleeding.

Slowly Saint-Germain approached the dais, moving quietly but without stealth. He wondered briefly if the protector who had come to him had felt the same gratitude he experienced as he moved. It had been one thing to turn away from this gift when it was a matter of debate, but here, in the privacy of the night, he had no will to deny the esurience that gripped him. At the dais he knelt, then bent his head. His lips touched warm fingers.

His childhood was too many years gone for him to recapture that sense he had known then. There had been too much loss and anguish for him to be free of the constraints he had learned down the years. Yet, unexpected and unbidden, a kind of peace touched Saint-Germain in the depth of his loneliness. A solemn elation, at first remote, then magnified, filled him, an annealing homage to the force of life he had not encountered before. The gulf of his isolation yawned a little less; the fetters of his alienation loosened.

When at last he lifted his head, his features were calm: his soul, so long in turmoil, was at rest.

━━━━━━◄●►━━━━━━

A dispatch from RDo-rje-brag lamasery, southernmost of the Yellow Hat Order lamaseries, to the other houses of the Order.

At the coming of the various purifying festivals of the Vernal Equinox, and upon the occasion of the anniversary of the birth of our King, we of RDo-rje-brag lamasery take this opportunity to inform the rest of our Order that during the last three days, travelers have come on the road from the south, and have been able to cross the passes without mishap. Therefore, those seeking to make their way to the lowlands for continuing study and dedication to the Path are advised that this is the most appropriate time for such a venture, as the great heat of the summer has not yet come to the lowlands.

We of the RDo-rje-brag lamasery would wish to be informed if any large parties of our fellow Yellow Hats plan to make this journey, for we will then make arrangements for ponies and guides to be made available to them. We are aware that ten lamas from the chapterhouse in Lhasa intend to leave in thirty days for the Hindu countries, and those wishing to have the advantage of their enlightened company should plan to arrive here within that time.

Our prayer wheels are always spinning and our chants rise up continuously to the source of all being. Let yours do the same.

Zhi Kha-spungs, scribe of the RDo-rje-brag lamasery.

7

IN THE courtyard, a lama in the costume of a tiger-demon chased another lama representing the timorous soul. Bells and drums accompanied this display as the gathered lamas celebrated the arrival of spring.

Two of the King's sons had come from Lhasa to witness this ceremony to extend the annual royal blessings to the lamas. They had come with a large train of servants and had set the entire Bya-grub Me-long ye-shys lamasery in an uproar.

"It's because I kept the King waiting once," SGyi Zhel-ri said to Saint-Germain as he stood in the dismantled laboratory. "They want me to know that they will not allow a similar affront to themselves."

"Which is why you are up here?" Saint-Germain suggested as he looked for rags to wad in around the jars he was loading into a large basket.

The boy laughed. "That is part of it. The rest is that I am sorry that our Paths diverge here." He pulled up the stool and began to sort vials and packets. "Their train leaves for Lhasa in three days. It would not be difficult to arrange for you and Rogerio to leave with them. You would have the advantage of royal escort, and would not be unduly delayed on the road. Those traveling with Princes, though they are foreign, have certain privileges."

Saint-Germain was surprised. "I thank you, SGyi Zhel-ri."

A burst of noise from the courtyard claimed their attention for a few moments as the tiger-demon roared and howled.

"They do this every year," Master SGyi said when things were quieter.

"Does that bother you?" Saint-Germain had found the rags and was wrapping a number of glass jars with them.

He shrugged. "There is little harm in it, but not much growth, either. The lamas who place their belief in such rituals do not comprehend the real nature of the principle of Yab-Yum. Most of these seasonal rituals," he went on more prosaically, "are left over from the Bon traditions. Many of the lamas refuse to admit it, but it is the truth. The old magicians would take time to placate or encourage all the forces

225

around them because they did not understand that all force is one force."

Saint-Germain paused in his work, brows raised. "Were you taught that, or did you find it for yourself?"

"I found it for myself, as you did. That's the only way anyone ever learns anything." He opened a small box and looked inside. "What are these?"

"Rubies and diamonds," Saint-Germain answered.

"Did you make them?" He had picked up one of the stones and was staring at it, watching the light play through it.

"Yes." He gave the basket he was packing an experimental heft to be certain he could balance it properly when he had to carry it down the stairs. It was, he decided, tricky but not impossible. He took another basket from the corner and began to load the last of the jars and vials into it.

"It will be strange to have this room empty once more," SGyi Zhel-ri said. He took rags and conscientiously began to wrap the more fragile items in them. "Don't take it amiss when I tell you that no one has ever treated me as an equal before, Saint-Germain."

"You're an extraordinary boy," Saint-Germain observed. "It would be strange if you were treated otherwise."

"But you know about loneliness, better than anyone I have ever met," SGyi Zhel-ri protested. "It's difficult to live so far removed from all those around you. I can say this to you, because you have endured far more of it than I have. And you won't respond with more veneration, which is what the lamas here do. The Abbot encourages it." His voice had grown shrill, and he made an effort to calm himself. "I understand my responsibilities, and I know what I am to do. But I wish that there were others to carry the burden with me. Not all the time, just once in a while." He sat still, dejected, suddenly out of words.

Saint-Germain put his packing aside and gave his attention to the boy. The usually tranquil features were distorted with unhappiness. "SGyi Zhel-ri," he said kindly, "I have no way to aid you, though I wish it were otherwise. You have your Path, as you told me at the first." He considered the young Master. "If you would not disdain it, let me give you a warning: the Abbot, SNyin Shes-rab, is an ambitious man. I doubt he sees himself in that light, but it is true He wants to see this Order rise in importance, which naturally would bring an increase of power for himself. You, SGyi Zhel-ri, are his most persuasive asset, and he will use you to attain his own ends."

SGyi Zhel-ri made an impatient gesture. "I am aware that SNyin Shes-rab longs for power. He sees the day when the King himself will bow to the Yellow Hats. I don't wish to be bothered with this."

"You may not wish it, but it will come to you." Saint-Germain thought of the fragility of youth. How could he find adequate words to convince a nine-year-old boy, no matter how perceptive, that he had been designated a player in a game of which he had no making? He put one small hand on the child's shoulder and realized it was the first time he had touched him, except to put his lips to SGyi Zhel-ri's fingers. "You are unique—"

The boy interrupted him. "That's not quite true. The Yellow Hats have a long tradition of child-Masters. I am not the only one."

"Perhaps, but you are likely one of the most genuine." He knew that SGyi Zhel-ri could not challenge that, and he waited as the boy's face grew somber. "The very fact that you are what you are is advantageous to your Abbot. He will draw others into his influence because he will try to control the access to you. It may seem that this cannot happen, but unless you take measures to stop it now, it will. He has too much to gain through that control."

"He has said that he doesn't want me talking to the Princes today or tomorrow. He said it was because there are other ceremonies that would be more appropriate for the Princes to attend." SGyi Zhel-ri sighed. "I suppose he's told them something else."

"Ask them," Saint-Germain said at once. "Send one of the lamas to the Princes, and when they come to you, ask them what they have been told, and compare it to anything he may have told you. If the two don't agree . . ."

"SNyin Shes-rab has been very good to me," the boy said, suddenly unsure of himself.

Saint-Germain felt a terrible sympathy for this child who had shown him such great humanity, and he wished he could shield the boy from the isolation and pain he felt. "Yes, he has been good to you."

"I know why, Saint-Germain. You're reluctant to tell me that there was little caring in his decision. I know that because I can't not know it." He bowed his head, and at that moment seemed aged.

There was one thing, Saint-Germain realized, that he could tell SGyi Zhel-ri, and he offered it as a gift. "Don't shut yourself away. It is more . . . painful this way, but the other is worse than death. I . . . lived that way for too many years, and I paid the cost of it. It is seductive, the shutting away. Others with your ability have turned away from it because it demanded too much of them, but in doing that, they crippled themselves. That crippling"—he closed his eyes against his memories—"all the pain that compassion can bring is nothing compared to that withering of the soul. If your Abbot is an opportunist, you don't have to let him contaminate your work. You have the power, not he, and you can choose the course you wish to take. SNyin Shes-rab's position depends on you, and little though he may like it, he will accommodate your demands because if he did otherwise, he would lose everything." He stopped, watching the boy's face. "It's little enough, SGyi Zhel-ri, but there is nothing else I can do. Even if I were to stay here, I could not protect you. In time SNyin Shes-rab would be rid of me, and then he would have a weapon to use against you."

SGyi Zhel-ri nodded, his face closed. "I'm aware of that. It's just that I wish it weren't so." He tugged at his robes, and looked at Saint-Germain. "It will be best, I think, if I go down to the courtyard now. I will see you before you depart." He hesitated. "You did not have to help me."

"Nor you me," Saint-Germain reminded him, bowing formally to the boy.

His bow was returned. "I won't forget you." With that he turned and went out of the room.

The crowd in the courtyard was singing an apparently endless and repetitious song when Rogerio came up the stairs to help carry down the last of the baskets.

"How much longer, do you think?" Saint-Germain asked as his servant came into the room.

"The guides say that they will be ready to depart in three days' time, at first light. They have agreed to allocate us an extra pony. That, with our own, will carry everything we need. I've asked about the purchase price of the pony, so that we may take it when we continue on." He tactfully did not mention where they were going, for neither of them truly knew.

"Excellent." He went to his little athanor, which was now cool. He opened the door and brought out a small crucible. "I haven't been able to make much gold, but here"—he held out a few gleaming nuggets—"use this to pay for the pony and our passage. Do we have any strings of cash left?"

"Four or five of copper and brass, one of silver, one of gold." Rogerio watched Saint-Germain expectantly. "Not very much."

The sum was, in fact, quite large, but considerably less than what Saint-Germain had become accustomed to. "I'll have to use the jewels, then. There aren't very many of them left." He went to the window and stared out at the mountains. "I wish we knew what has been happening in the world. Once we reach my house in Shiraz, there will be no difficulty. My laboratory there is well-equipped. Also, there is a considerable cache of gold and jewels hidden in the walls of the library. But until then . . ." He touched his fingers together. "We must be cautious until we reach Shiraz."

"I will attend to it," Rogerio assured him, looking around the room. "It's all ready but the athanor and the scroll," he remarked.

Saint-Germain's expression had become remote. "Leave them," he said quietly. "We can't use the athanor while traveling, and I will need a larger one in any case. The chart . . . I know what's on it." He left the window as the sound of the singing went on and on.

That night there was feasting at the Bya-grub Me-long ye-shys lamasery and the revels lasted long into the night. Saint-Germain stayed in his quarters, hearing the revelry around him while he painstakingly translated a few of the texts SGyi Zhel-ri had lent him from Tibetan to Latin and Greek. He knew that he lacked fluency in the Tibetan language, and occasionally felt the frustration of it as he struggled to determine the exact meaning of a phrase. Shouts and songs echoed along the corridors as he wrote, though the lamasery fell silent long before he had finished his work.

The next day was devoted to religious ceremonies of a graver nature. Special tents were erected in the courtyard, and the lamas, in ceremonial vestments and headdresses, sat beneath them, prayer wheels turning, the reverential chants punctuated with the sporadic ringing of the gong. Toward evening SGyi Zhel-ri addressed the gathering, speaking on the wisdom of noninterference, pointing out that those who seek achievement and advancement through others would end by harming themselves as well as those they had used as tools.

"He's being very forthright," Rogerio said as he listened. "I still can't catch it all, but it sounds as if he's giving that Abbot of his a warning."

Saint-Germain had not discussed the matter with his servant, but was not surprised that Rogerio had seen the problem. "It's wise to stop that kind of jealousy as early as possible," Saint-Germain agreed.

"The boy has a difficult life ahead of him." He stepped back so that he leaned against the wall. "I was thinking of the parents of such a child. Were they grateful or sad when he came here? When my son died, I was glad that he had escaped his suffering, but there was a hole in my life that nothing can change. With a boy like that, what do his parents feel?"

"He's not dead, that's something," Saint-Germain pointed out.

"But he's gone far beyond them."

"Yes." Saint-Germain motioned Rogerio to be silent so that he could hear the rest of what SGyi Zhel-ri had to say.

That night a fast was kept by all but Saint-Germain. For the last time the woman BDeb-ypa came to him, and though their lovemaking was no different from any other night they had passed together, Saint-Germain was no longer troubled by it, and accepted what it was that she could give him when her pleasure reached its peak.

Before sunrise, Saint-Germain made his way through the halls of the Bya-grub Me-long ye-shys lamasery for the last time. His heeled boots gave sharp reports as he walked, interrupting the chanting that rose from the sanctuary. He and Rogerio had already loaded their ponies, taking the extra precaution of supplying each animal with a new packsaddle and girths. Now, while Rogerio finished the final negotiations with the guides, Saint-Germain returned to their quarters to get their traveling cloaks and individual saddlebags.

He stood in his room and found it oddly unfamiliar now that his things were gone. It was merely a chamber with white-painted walls and a minimum of furniture, a lama's cell like any other monk's cell in the world. Already he found it more like a memory than the room in which he had slept so few hours before. With an impatient gesture he caught up the two muffling fur cloaks and threw them over his arm, and was reaching for the saddlebags when he heard a sound behind him.

SGyi Zhel-ri was in the door. "I said I would talk to you again before you left."

Saint-Germain smiled at the boy. "You did. I assumed you would come to see the party off."

"No. You are the one I want to speak with, and I would rather not have to worry about what the lamas might say to the Abbot if I distinguished you so much. He's not at all pleased with my speech to the visitors." He came into the room and sat on the pallet. He looked tired, with smudges under his eyes and a listlessness in his movements. As if in confirmation, he yawned.

"You haven't had much rest these last few days." Saint-Germain sat on the plank table and watched SGyi Zhel-ri. He liked the boy, respected him, knew that he could do nothing that would spare him hurt.

"Very little. The celebrations are always like this. It's as if we're all mad for a time." He blinked and forced his sleepy eyes to clear. "I have something for you."

"For me? Why? If anyone should—" He was silenced by a gesture from the child.

"I have thought it over carefully, and I know that it is appropriate for me to do this." He reached into the voluminous folds of his outer robe. "This is not from the lamasery. It is my own, and I want to give it to you." In his hand he held a small bronze statue of the white Tara, Bodhisattva SGrol-ma Dkar-mo. The figure sat with folded legs, her left hand raised, her right extended. On her forehead, her palms and the soles of her feet were eyes painted the intense blue of the pacific manifestations.

"The Lady of Compassion," Saint-Germain said quietly as he took the little statue. He recalled with an intensity that snagged the words he would have said in his throat the night in the darkened chapel to SGrol-ma Dkar-mo.

"Take her with you," SGyi Zhel-ri said. He smiled as he got to his feet. "We will not meet again in this life, I think. This way each of us will have cause to remember."

"I don't need a piece of metal to remind me," Saint-Germain said gently.

"But take it, anyway." He bowed. "I should say that you should incur no karma and depart from the Wheel, but that is not your Path. I will only wish that you find what you are seeking." He watched while Saint-Germain bowed to him. "Good-bye," he said when their eyes met.

"Will you take anything from me?" Saint-Germain asked, unable to think of what in his possession the child might want.

"No. You will have more need of gifts than I." With that he turned away and left the room.

The rising sun had turned the snow to rainbows of gems as the train of thirty-four ponies passed through the high outer gates of the Bya-grub Me-long ye-shys lamasery. Saint-Germain, riding toward the rear of the line, turned in the saddle to look back once, and then set his face to the south.

◄●►

A dispatch from a merchant of Herat to his brother-in-law, a merchant in the city of Rai.

It has pleased Allah, the All-merciful and All-wise, to bring a terrible scourge on his impious people, dear Khuda, and for that reason I take time to warn you of what has befallen us here in Herat.

Surely you know, as all of us do, of the misfortunes that have been visited on those far to the east of us, whom we, in our pride, thought deserving of such a visitation of disasters. The Old Silk Road has been most unreliable for more than six years, and we have thought that it was fitting that those who have not heard the call and acclaimed Allah as the One God should be made to suffer, and so we consoled ourselves. But this is not how it chances now.

The great numbers of Mongols we have heard of and have dismissed as the ravings of terrified men are not any more than the truth. I have just this day returned, thanks be to Allah, from a short expedition into the mountains to meet with traders, as has been my custom, as you know, these past twelve years. This time I arrived to find a smoking ruin and the people hacked to bits and the bits stacked up for the carrion birds. The creatures who did this, for of a certainty they are demons and not men, are moving westward with the rapidity of a storm, and it is a deluge indeed that they bring with them.

In the past six days a pitiful few survivors of that village, and of other villages treated with similar ferocity, have come into Herat with little more than their skins as wealth. Yet for that they are grateful and send up true praises to Allah for sparing them from the deaths they saw visited upon their friends and relatives. Every one tells tales of such brutality and horror that the listeners are stupefied by the magnitude of it.

As it is now certain that these invaders are most certainly determined to invade our country, I propose to journey with my family to your city of Rai, for is quite apparent to me that Herat will have to face these murderous warriors before too many months pass. I do not intend, Allah willing, to see my wives and children fall victims to the Mongol horsemen. Therefore I pray that you will be pleased to welcome us into your house until this terrible evil has been driven from our city and our land. As my second wife is your sister and we are brothers for her sake and for the sake of our trade, do not turn us away, for it is clearly apparent that to remain here is courting death.

We have been told that all of Persia will rise to hold off these men, but I am not convinced that there will be enough time to present real opposition here at Herat. Already we hear the name of the Mongol leader, Jenghiz Khan, used as a standard for describing the worst that can be wished upon any living being. He is more terrifying than earthquakes and floods, and when his men come over the land, either of those natural catastrophes is preferable. The Mongols will darken all the earth with our blood. May Allah preserve us from their predations.

Look for us to come to you in a month. We will require four days to pack the most essential of our household goods and make proper arrangements for business so that our trade does not suffer unnecessarily. It is my intention to make all due speed in our journey, but as it is summer it will not be possible to press on as quickly as I would wish possible. I have sent word to various way stations and requested that they have accommodations for us when we arrive. After all these years of doing business with them, it is little enough to ask that they find a place for us at this time.

All is in the hands of Allah, yet the wise man acts with prudence in the face of danger, and it is not the way of the coward to abandon that position which is clearly untenable. There are warriors who will face the Mongols and most assuredly defeat them completely. For those of us who are not capable of feats of arms, it is sensible to get out of the way.

Pray that when we meet we have lost no more than our houses and some of our goods, as truly it is from the men of Shaitan that we flee. If all we must lose is a portion of wealth, it is cheaply enough purchased.

By messenger at sunset, twelfth day of Rajab, the 595th year since the Hejira.

8

At Lhasa five of the lamas left the party, going to join their fellow Yellow Hats at the main chapterhouse. The guides ordered a resting period of two days in the royal city while they searched for others traveling south. There was a curious grandeur to Lhasa. It sat in a long river valley betweeen two massive ranges of mountains. Though the whole of the country was very high, these peaks reached even higher. Climate dictated sturdy, simple houses, and for the most part Lhasa was a mass of high thick walls and sloping roofs. Only the royal palace stood out, for though it was much the same design as the other buildings, its roofs were elaborate, the cornices and roof beams ornamented and lavishly painted. Three lamaseries clustered at its feet, silent indicators of the increasing role religion played in the life of the court.

Four days later when the party once again set out to the southeast, it consisted of fifteen men, twenty-eight ponies and six yaks. They went slowly, rarely covering more than thirty li a day, and on days when the wind sliced off the snow at them, less than twenty.

At night the party made camp and mounted guards against robbers, though few such bands were so intrepid as to haunt these ice-bound crags. Saint-Germain won himself a degree of acceptance from the rest by volunteering to stand guard in the latter half of the night.

Near the crest of the range they were surprised by a storm and spent four days huddled in a pilgrims' house attached to a small lamasery of the Red Robes Order. When the worst had passed they dug themselves out and continued on over the shoulder of the mountains whose crests were lost in the mist and clouds.

It was more than a month after their journey began that the party at last started to descend. The slopes now, while formidable and clad in permanent snow, were less imposing than the peaks behind them. Now the way turned, winding westward. Rock and ice now grudgingly yielded patches of sheltered footing to scrubby trees. Finally, fifty-three days from Lhasa, they came across their first roadside shrine. The guides exclaimed over this, telling the members of the party that it was dedicated to the spirits of the snows, and admonished them to come no farther down the mountain.

A day later they passed a goat boy with his flock, who waved and called out in a strange language which baffled the guides as well as the rest of the party. Gradually flowers appeared on the slopes, a few sparse buds at first, then larger, more luxuriant blossoms. The way was marked by low-growing shrubs, and in the protective crannies and clefts of the stone face of the mountains, trees grew. Now the fur cloaks were necessary only at night, for the days were cool but mild and the wind that blew from the valleys below them was warm, green-smelling, promising a fertile, drowsy summer.

When they reached the second village, the yaks left the train to return with strange-garbed traders to the Land of Snows; these great beasts did not thrive in lower altitudes and heat. The foreigners were glad for the animals, for they had a great deal of goods to carry to Lhasa before the onset of autumn. The guides haggled a reasonable price, and in the morning when the train pushed on, the great long-haired oxen were left behind.

Six days later, nine of the lamas left the train for a Buddhist monastery set back in a deep gorge. The lamas were eager to expand their studies and had promised to peruse the texts kept at that fabled monastery so that they could carry the teachings back to the Yellow Hat four or five years in the future, when the texts had been read and understood. With them went thirteen of the ponies and one of the guides.

Now there were taverns and inns to welcome the travelers and provide them with food and drink as well as the shelter of a roof. Villages mushroomed on the hillsides, squalid, dusty and noisy, a pleasure to see after the frozen majesty of the mountains. Here there were many more men on the road in a wonderful diversity of garments. Often the guides would stop to talk with those coming from the west, and exchanged news with them. More and more were seen the shoulder-slung triple strands that marked members of the Brahmin caste, as well as the distressing wretches known as Untouchables.

"Tomorrow," the chief guide told Saint-Germain a few days later as they stopped for the night at a good-sized inn near a famous market town, "we must leave you, for our commission now takes us to the south, which is not the way you have elected to go. You will not continue with us, since you have said you desire to press westward back toward your homeland." He could not entirely conceal the relief he felt at this. "If you require another guide, I will do what I can to be certain you have an honest one."

Saint-Germain, recalling Tzoa Lem, shook his head. "If my servant and I travel the much-used roads, we should have no trouble going north and west."

"Let it be as you wish," the chief guide said, acknowledging this with a graceful gesture.

"I am in your debt for your service," Saint-Germain went on smoothly. "I realize that you were not entirely pleased to have me travel with you."

"You are . . ." The chief guide glanced off toward the spires of the mountains. "You are not like us. We were told by the Yellow Hats that you have great magical powers."

"And you dislike magicians?" Saint-Germain suggested, unable to keep the sadness out of his voice.

"It is not that, precisely," the chief guide said, still unable to meet the foreigner's eyes. "You did not eat with us."

"That is the way of my kind," was the gentle reminder.

"And you brought no food," the chief guide added, making it almost an accusation.

"True enough, but my servant hunted. Once or twice he brought fresh meat to you." He permitted himself to give the man a thin smile, enough to make it seem that the guide was acting foolishly.

Apparently the strategy succeeded, for the chief guide rose and gave Saint-Germain a formal bow. "It is unfortunate that our paths diverge here," he said with dignity.

Saint-Germain returned the bow. "You did well. In gratitude I have left a token for you." The token, he thought, would more than satisfy the guide, as it was a topaz, the size of his thumb. "Do me the honor of accepting it for the service you have rendered me."

The chief guide nodded once, then started away from the table. Then he paused and turned back. "Revered One," he said somewhat shamefacedly, "you are not familiar with this place, and there are those on the roads who profess themselves to be willing companions upon the road, but who are there to make sacrifice."

"Indeed?" Saint-Germain raised his brows, recalling such an encounter many, many years before. "You wish to warn me of the Thuggi?"

"You know of them?" the chief guide asked with a curious mixture of relief and disquiet in his voice.

"Something of them, yes." He folded his hands on the rough table. "Do you seek to warn me that they are active again?"

"Yes." The chief guide moved a little closer to the table. "The trader I spoke with yesterday on the road told me that to the west there have been many incidents of travelers garroted. It is because of the invaders from the West, they say, those who are part of the Delhi Califate. The ones who worship the true gods wish to avenge the insults done to their holy ones, and so the sacrifices increase."

"And the nearer to the Delhi Califate one comes, I suppose the greater the danger?" Saint-Germain gave an enigmatic smile. "Well, I thank you for your concern and the warning. My servant and I will take great care, I assure you. Again, I have you to thank for guiding me to safety."

The chief guide still hesitated. "You will go where, Revered One?"

"Eventually, I will go to Shiraz in Persia, and from there I will make my way to Damascus, and from there I will go into my homeland." His expression for one instant was remote.

"There are rumors that Persia is at war," the chief guide warned him.

"I will be on my guard." He rose, indicating that he no

longer wished to discuss the various dangers of travel. "I fear, chief guide, that you are seeking to persuade me that traveling with you would be the safer course."

There was a kind of horror in the man's eyes. "No. No, that is not my object." He recovered quickly and made a self-deprecatory gesture. "It is simply that one who is a teacher of the Yellow Hats and a great magician cannot simply be abandoned in an unknown country."

"Not quite unknown," Saint-Germain promised him. "I have been in these lands before." It had been a long time, though, and Saint-Germain could not entirely free himself from apprehension.

"You will know to be on guard then." The flicker of relief was in the chief guide's eyes again, and he stepped back, eager to be gone now that he had discharged his obligation to the foreigner. "There will be four ponies to carry you, and the innkeeper will provide you with . . . whatever supplies you might need." He turned quickly then, glad to be gone from the perplexing stranger who had earned the respect of the Yellow Hats.

When the chief guide was gone, Rogerio came out of the inn to the table where Saint-Germain sat. "We continue west?"

"Yes." Saint-Germain gestured to the bench the chief guide had vacated. "Sit down. This may be the last chair you see for some time." He was slightly amused, but there was a more somber set to his face than there had been when he had talked with the chief guide.

Obediently Rogerio sank onto the bench. "I've arranged for grain for the ponies and three waterskins. Though neither you nor I have much need of them," he added in Greek.

"Better to have them," Saint-Germain responded in the same language. "It raises less suspicion. The ponies might use them. Be certain that we have proper bedrolls, as well. I don't know what manner of housing we will find to the west." He gazed along the rising slope of the mountains, into the haze that turned the distance an oddly yellow-tinged blue. "In Shiraz we can rest. Next year, or the year after, we will go to my homeland."

Rogerio nodded, his eyes turned toward the west with his master's.

"Do you miss it?" Saint-Germain asked some little time later.

"Yes," Rogerio admitted. "And you?"

"Yes."

When they returned to the earthen-walled inn, the shadows were long and the breeze had become chilly. In the largest room the travelers who had stopped here for the night were gathered around a central fire pit where chunks of mutton fat sizzled on spits. The landlord greeted them with inviting smiles.

"You come," he said, pointing toward the company gathered to eat. "Very good. Food." He patted his belly, grinning and gesturing to indicate how much the fare would please them.

Though Saint-Germain spoke few words of the local dialect, he was able to decline politely, indicating that it was not his custom to dine in the presence of others. He acknowledged the others around the fire pit with a gracious half-bow, then passed on to his rooms.

"How long has it been since you have . . . dined?" Rogerio asked once they were in their rooms.

"You know the answer as well as I do." He leaned back on two of his few remaining bags of earth. "I fear what might happen when these are gone," he said, frowning. "Without them to sustain me . . . I think perhaps it will be best if we travel at night, my friend."

Rogerio turned and regarded Saint-Germain. "At night?"

"It will help conserve my strength," he said, with a look of distaste. "There is no one to take me as a lover, and no one I desire, not here. The blood of animals, well, you understand the limitations. So we will travel at night." He started to sit up, then dropped back on the bags. "I have nine of these only. It has been more than a thousand years since I've been quite this vulnerable." His mind went back to a squalid cell under the stands of the Circus Maximus. He had been imprisoned there, and could recall being grateful for the dark.

"And the ponies?" Rogerio was arranging their few spare garments in the red Roman chest. "Will you wish to use them?"

"For the time being. We still have high country to cross, and they manage well in this terrain. Later, we'll replace them with other animals. Horses perhaps, or mules." He stared up at the low ceiling. "I think it will be best if we settle with the innkeeper tonight. I will handle that. He might ask questions of you, but he won't of me." There was a suggestion of a smile on his wry mouth.

"When do you wish to leave?" The chest was almost in order and Rogerio set out two woolen cloaks. "There are rents in the lining, but I haven't the materials to repair them."

"No matter," Saint-Germain said. He closed his eyes and endeavored to make himself comfortable on the bags of earth. "Wake me at moonrise and I will deal with the innkeeper."

When he rose, some hours later, the inn was quiet but for occasional snores, and the muffled cries and tussle of lovers from a room down the hall. Saint-Germain dressed simply in his accustomed black, and at the last moment, belted on the katana Saito Masashige had given him. Even as he chided himself for being overcautious, he tested the blade in its scabbard to be sure he could draw it swiftly.

The innkeeper was shocked to see his foreign guests preparing to depart. Distress contorted his features, and he did his best to try to explain to Saint-Germain why it was unwise to leave. "Night demons," he insisted, spreading out his arms and hooking his fingers like talons. "Attack travelers. Steal money. Drink blood."

Saint-Germain's sad laughter horrified the innkeeper. "I am not afraid," he said gently, and gave the man a silver coin.

"The Revered One will be . . ." He did not know the words, but he made a bludgeoning motion with his joined hands.

In answer, Saint-Germain put his hand to the hilt of the katana. "I do not fear demons. And this will take care of robbers."

With a lifting of his arms that was clearly intended to let the gods know that he had done all that he could, the innkeeper went to the door, assuming his usual servile eagerness. "If the Revered One so wishes."

"Distressing though it may be, I do wish it," Saint-Germain said in a very high-caste dialect. He motioned to Rogerio. "My servant has a number of things to load upon our animals, and then we will be gone and will not trouble you again." He motioned to Rogerio to follow him as he stepped outside.

It was chilly, but not unpleasantly so. A few night birds were singing, and aside from one crashing sound in the woods, nothing disturbed the hour. Saint-Germain stood looking up at the sky, marking out the constellations, thinking back to all the various names he had heard them called over the years. He traced out the way north, looking for the Pole Star, but the rising bulk of the mountains cut him off. On the high, frozen plateau of the Land of Snows, he had spent one or two nights watching the slow wheeling of the stars overhead, and had marveled at the clarity and brightness of them. Here the stars seemed less distinct. He smiled slightly, enjoying the darkness.

"My master . . ." Rogerio said at his elbow.

"Are we ready?" Saint-Germain asked without turning.

"Yes. I have taken the liberty of dividing your sacks of earth between all the animals. That way, should anything happen . . ." He nodded as Saint-Germain turned to him.

"Very wise," he said to Rogerio after a moment. "When have we been reduced to these straits, Rogerio?" He did not let the man answer but went on. "Twice with Aumtehoutep I was very near despairing. In one instance, I was in prison. That cell in Rome was enjoyable by comparison." He flinched inwardly as the memory returned to him with more force than he thought possible after so long a time. There had been rats at first, and then a voracious stupor and a prison guard whose foolishness had ended so horribly.

"My master?" Rogerio said quietly, disturbed by Saint-Germain's appalled silence.

At once the dark eyes regained their familiar ironic expression. Saint-Germain shrugged and busied himself with the fastening of his cloak around his shoulders. "We'll manage it somehow, old friend. Do not fear it. Though perhaps it will not be entirely pleasant." He touched his brow with one small, beautiful hand: he did not want to face such privation again, for he had come to loathe what he became at such times.

"Are you ready to ride, my master?" Rogerio knew that Saint-Germain was still held by his memories, and had not entirely broken free. He started toward their waiting ponies.

Saint-Germain followed him slowly, letting his thoughts drift. He stopped before the first of the ponies and reached up for the lead tied to the bridle. "I will walk," he said quietly to Rogerio. "It's better if I walk." He patted the pony's muzzle and murmured a few reassuring words to the animal before he led the way out of the innyard.

The village was sleeping, and no one except a very old

man who spent his nights sitting and waiting for death saw them go. The road wound between the clusters of houses, then out onto the rising slope of the mountain. Soon the night was being measured in steps and the steady sound of the ponies' hooves on the rutted trail.

The first night passed uneventfully enough, and toward dawn Saint-Germain found a ruined temple above a spring that had run dry many years before. "There's grass for the ponies—with broth and grain that should be adequate. I'll take care of watering them." He looked at the toppled stones of the largest part of the ancient building, noticing that there was a gigantic face carved into one of the fronts. "From the tongue sticking out, I'll guess this was Kali. She must be very pleased. Why Kali at a spring, though?"

"She's in charge of fecundity, too, as well as destruction, isn't she?" Rogerio asked as he began to hobble the ponies.

"Certainly sexuality. One of her other manifestations is in charge of fertility and growth. I forget the name." He regarded the balefully, ruined face. "It was probably dedication to her other form, but she was represented this way, as well." He glanced into the smaller portion of the building, which was untouched. "Be on guard for snakes, but I don't think we'll be bothered."

Before the sun had risen, the ponies had been watered and left, hobbled, to graze on the new grass which had sprung up around the wreckage of the temple. Saint-Germain and Rogerio lay asleep in the part of the temple that was still intact. The snakes that ordinarily inhabited the place avoided it that day.

Night found them once again on the road. They made good time, for here the way was less steep, though the mountains were no less formidable. The trail had been cut along the side of the range, and though at a fair elevation, it was almost flat.

"In the day, I would guess that the view is impressive," Saint-Germain said to Rogerio as they stopped somewhat after midnight to rest and water the ponies. "Yet, do you know, for all the size and majesty of this range, I would prefer the mountains of my homeland."

Rogerio said nothing, but shared some of the emotions of his master. They had been gone too far and too long, and although he did not share Saint-Germain's need, he understood the affections of the older man. But what, he wondered, would Gades be like now, since the Moors had come to Spain? He had heard a Crusader call it Cadiz, twenty years ago. Gades, when he had lived there, had been predominantly Roman—now it was quite different. Would he recognize the place, he asked himself, or would too many of the buildings be gone, and the sense of home be lost?

A few nights later, near the village of Nawakot they were confronted by a number of men, all of them armed with long knives and clubs, who blocked the road.

"We are peaceful foreigners," Saint-Germain said in a dialect he hoped they would understand. "Why do you detain us?" He put his hand to the hilt of the katana, very much on the alert.

The spokesman for the men stepped forward, folding his arms on his chest. "Where have you come from?" he demanded, saying the words awkwardly.

"From the southwest today. Before that, from Bod, the Land of Snows. I have traveled widely." He allowed himself to sound slightly perplexed.

"You are not of Bod," the spokesman said confidently.

"No," Saint-Germain agreed, and volunteered no more.

"You travel at night. Demons travel at night." The man gave an unpleasant laugh, and said something to the men with him. They echoed the laughter. "Demons cannot be killed with knives and clubs."

"But robbers can. If you beat us and we die, we are thieves. If we do not die, we are demons, and you will cast us into the flames." Saint-Germain could not forget that similar arguments had been used in Europe not long ago to condemn those of his blood to the flames for heresy.

The spokesman seemed somewhat startled that a foreigner should be able to follow his reasoning. He regarded Saint-Germain closely. "Who are you?"

"A traveler, as I have said. In the Land of the Snows I was regarded as a magician. I am an alchemist." He hoped that these isolated men had heard the term. "It is my desire to return to my home, far to the west of here."

Again the spokesmen addressed the others, and they burst into laughter once more, this time more boisterously. "If you are what you say, then it would be rude not to have you stay with us. If, in the morning, there are no signs of more robbers or you have not assumed another form, then we will show you the respect that a magician deserves." His gesture for Saint-Germain and Rogerio to follow left them in no doubt that they would have to fight these men or accede to their wishes at once.

Rogerio was somewhat surprised when Saint-Germain agreed without question. "My master . . ."

Saint-Germain began a singsong kind of chanting, making curious gestures. His words were in Greek. "Do not oppose them. They could do as much harm, and neither you nor I have the strength to spare for a fight. If these men are satisfied that we will do them no harm, we can use their goodwill to advantage. There's bound to be a certain amount of communication between these villages. If these men speak well of us, we'll be spared similar delays."

Rogerio chanted his answer in the same language. "We must be on guard, but this may be the wisest way."

The spokesman had stopped and was watching the exchange between Saint-Germain and Rogerio. "What are you saying?"

"I told you I am a magician," Saint-Germain said arrogantly. "I have put an enchantment on the bags I carry. If anyone other than myself opens or moves them, the gold in them will surely turn to earth and will never become gold again." He tapped one of the bags strapped to the nearest pony's saddle.

"Gold?" The spokesman could not bring himself to scoff at that. "Those bags contain gold? All of them?"

"For me they do," Saint-Germain said, correcting him sternly. "If any other person were to open them now, they would find only earth. When morning comes, then if the bags have been undisturbed, perhaps I will present you with some of the gold they contain, and I give you my word that it will remain gold forever. If you and your men tamper with the bags in any way, you will not have any gold at all, and I will be left with sacks of earth." He called over his shoulder to Rogerio, this time in Latin, "How much gold do we have left in the chest?"

"A fair amount. There are also a few jewels," was the answer, but said as if he were responding to a most stringent order.

"I'll need a dozen gold pieces when we leave. And put the rest into the tops of the sacks of earth. Do it carefully—these men will probably put a guard of some sort on us." He looked back at the spokesman. "My servant will be on watch throughout the night."

With a glance at Rogerio, the spokesman said, "You are the master and he is the servant, you say, and yet it is he who rides and you who walk." He added something to the men with him, a few of whom gave Rogerio a quick, curious look. "Perhaps," he went on, "it is he who is the master and you the servant."

Saint-Germain raised his fine brows imperiously. "It is for the master to guide the servant. At night and on such roads, it is fitting that I should lead. And it is wiser to lead on foot, would you not agree?"

Impressed now, the spokesman addressed the others, apparently repeating Saint-Germain's comment. "You say you have traveled far, foreigner," he said as they neared the entrance to the village.

"Farther than you know." Saint-Germain sighed, speaking his native language, then gave the man his attention. "To the north and east there is savage war being fought. In the west men have taken up arms against their fellows. I have tried to find . . ." He stopped. What had he sought through all this? Peace? Stability? Sanctuary? The village spokesman was looking at him with curiosity. "Pardon. I could not remember the correct word. I have looked for a place where I could pursue my work without interference. War, you will agree, is an interference." This was not entirely honest, he knew, but it was an acceptable answer.

"Those in the north and the east," the spokesman said at his most knowing, "they are men of strange customs."

"Indeed," Saint-Germain agreed dryly. They had entered the village now, and Saint-Germain saw that it was fairly good-sized, with a place for a granary, which indicated a fair level of prosperity.

"There is a house for travelers," the spokesman was saying.

And undoubtedly, Saint-Germain told himself, it had provision for observing the travelers who stayed there. "Most commendable," he said without a trace of mockery.

When they had arrived at the guest house, the other men departed, but the spokesman regarded Saint-Germain for a bit, and then said, "My wife's younger sister will share your bed, if you wish it."

Saint-Germain had long since ceased being startled by such offers. "You compliment me, leader." So that was to be his

guardian and spy. The sister of the wife of the village spokesman. He assumed that the men here were polygamous and
that the woman in question was some sort of inferior wife to
the man.

"She's a clever girl," the spokesman assured him. "She's
slept with other foreigners, and has learned many things."

"You are a fortunate man," Saint-Germain said, adding,
"The traditions of my magic forbid me entering an uniniti-
ated woman," he improvised, "but there are ways that we
could seek satisfaction of each other. If that is acceptable to
her . . ."

"She's slept with other foreigners," the spokesman repeated, and opened the door to the guest house. "There are
servants who will aid you with the ponies. I will send my
wife's sister to you when you are ready to retire." His face
creased in smiles, and he started to move away.

"There is one other thing," Saint-Germain said just as the
spokesman began to stride off into the dark.

Caught unexpectedly, the man turned, his confidence sub-
tly diminished. "What is it, foreigner?"

"In the morning," Saint-Germain said evenly, "if there is
one of your village who would be willing to guide me and my
servant through the mountains, there might be more than one
piece of gold for you and this village." He had been toying
with the lead-rope of the first pony.

"I will let it be known, foreigner," the spokesman said, unable to conceal the greed Saint-Germain's offer awakened in
him.

As Saint-Germain carried the earth-filled sacks into the
guest house, he thought about the spokesman's wife's sister,
who had slept with other foreigners. He hoped that she was
not another passive woman, who would allow him the use of
her. He wanted, he needed, more than that. Sternly he reminded himself that any contact was better than none, and
knew, with profound sadness, that this was not true.

Text of a letter carried by Saint-Germain from SGyi Zhel-ri, Master of the Yellow Hats. The letter is written in Tibetan, Chinese, Hindi and Tamal.

From the Master of the Yellow Hats at the Bya-grub Me-long ye-shys lamasery to those distinguished persons to whom this message is presented.

Long have we of the Yellow Hat Order treasured knowledge and learning. It is the pursuit of these qualities that set the steps on the Path, and lead to the release from the Wheel and the attainment of Inner Light. Those who are capable of great learning are surely to be honored and revered by all who seek to end their travail in this life as well as in those to come.

The bearer of this, a man from the West who has been called Shih Ghieh-Man by the scholars in China, has shown himself worthy of such a name, and for that reason, if no other, should be received with courtesy in the courts and homes of all lands where understanding is treasured. Be sure that Shih Ghieh-Man has a profound respect for the value of study, and a true love of all the attributes of knowledge, and for this reason, if no other, is capable of adding much to any discussion that he enters. You who read this are most fortunate to have the chance to avail yourselves of this remarkable man's experience and learning.

This man, I assure you, is not a pedant or a mere cataloger of information, but one who has taken to heart the essence of what he has learned. Though he does not describe himself as a philosopher, there is more philosophy in him than there is in most of the men who have taken that title for their own. Shih Ghieh-Man has not only erudition, but great literacy, and you will find that the hours spent in his company will be filled with remarkable conversation. Whether he provides you with allegory or the example of history, you will come away from him with enriched perceptions and increased wisdom.

It is not appropriate for me to speak of those things he has shared with me, but you should know that I hold his confidence, which he reposed in me with the highest esteem. Nothing I can say would be adequate to describe the value of his friendship. Should you be fortunate enough to have the honor of his affection, you will have the rarest of opportunities, and one it would be folly to turn from.

Though I address you as leader to leader, and with the formality that is born of respect both for you, though unknown, and for Shih Ghieh-Man, who is my friend, and my words are those of one who speaks in public to a multitude, there are no idle compliments here, no flattery or polite deception. Shih Ghieh-Man, or Saint-Germain, is the most remarkable man I have ever known, and my life, I know, would be the poorer had I not met him. If you are willing to receive him, you may eventually share my appreciation. It is very much my hope that you will.

May your life incur no karma, and may you pass soon from the Wheel, and return to the state of unity with the Source of all Bliss.

Your kindness to this man Saint-Germain will bring you my prayers to aid you to that excellent state.

SGyi Zhel-ri
from his own hand
at the Bya-grub Me-long ye-shys lamasery
Order of Yellow Hats

9

TODAY THE merchants and vendors had moved their bazaar nearer the river in a vain attempt to escape the heat that lay over the city, moist and stifling as a wet cloth. As it was almost sunset many of the awning-covered booths had been taken down, but there were those who hoped to earn a few more bits of copper before retiring for the evening. Behind the bazaar there were shops, and perhaps half of these still stood open.

The old jeweler was about to close his doors for the night. No one had set foot in the dark interior of his shop since midafternoon, and the oppressive heat, redolent with the scents of spices, sandalwood and excrement, had made him drowsy. It was time to be at home with his family, sipping a cooling mixture of fermented milk and fruit juices. The thought of it made him hasten, and he was in the act of closing his doors when the stranger appeared.

"I realize it is late," he said in oddly accented but high-caste dialect. "If you would spare me a little time, it would, I think, be of benefit to both of us."

Though it was late and the evening particularly hot and still, the old jeweler was curious. The stranger was clearly a foreigner, for the color of his skin and the way he walked proclaimed him so as much as his black clothing. Around his neck he wore a silver chain and from it hung a pectoral in the shape of a black disk with raised, spread wings—the sign of the eclipse. The stranger's dark, compelling eyes rested for a moment on the jeweler, and then he smiled wryly.

"Truly, it is late, but I find it hard to bear the full weight of the sun. If you would prefer, I will return tomorrow at first light, but it would be just as well for us to settle this now, if you are interested." His voice was beautiful, musically modulated and low. He put his hand to the wallet fastened to his belt. "I admit that I have come to sell, not to buy, but that may not disappoint you."

The old jeweler stiffened. "It is quite late, good stranger. If you will tell me what you have, then perhaps tomorrow . . ."

"Look for yourself," the foreigner said as he held out his hands. There were six stones in his palms, four of them the size of the man's thumbnail. But the other two—the other two were magnificent. One, the jeweler could see though the light was poor, was a straw-colored diamond more than twice the size of the Rajah's. The last gem was slightly smaller, and rather uneven in shape. The old jeweler reached out to touch it.

"A ruby? This size?" he whispered as he felt the curious, slightly greasy texture of the stone.

Now the stranger permitted himself to smile. "I came here only a few days ago, and inquired of the traders here for escort west."

The jeweler gave a scoffing laugh before he could stop himself. The stranger, being a Westerner, might not wish him to mock the plight of those distant lands.

"Yes," the stranger said unhappily, but with steel in his tone. "I wàs told of what has happened in Persia. Jenghiz Khan has brought his Mongols there, and is conquering the land." For a moment he was back in that narrow valley, near a pile of shattered bodies, searching for one . . . He forced his mind back to the old jeweler. "For the time being, I would be wise to stay here, and for that reason I will need a house and servants. Selling these will enable me to live reasonably well for a time."

It was the opinion of the old jeweler that a man possessed of such jewels could live better than the Rajah for more years than any man could reasonably expect to live. He thought perhaps that the stranger was possessed of a large family and many slaves, but the impression was dispelled at once.

"I would also wish to know where I might hire servants. I would prefer not to buy slaves." The stranger glanced at the three oil lamps in the shop. "Here. Take them. Look at them." He held out the jewels to the old man.

Had these stones been religious objects, the jeweler could not have handled them with greater care. He took the small stones first. There were two diamonds, one quite clear, one with a slightly bluish cast. The smallest stone was an emerald, a blue light winking in its green interior. The fourth stone was a sapphire with a large star gleaming against its blackness. He held each of these to the lamps in turn, and each time he was filled with the kind of awe that stopped the words in his throat and made him wish to weep. He was not certain he dared to touch the larger stones again.

"Please," the stranger said persuasively, handing the two largest stones to him. "Examine them."

The old jeweler nodded, lifting the diamond and then the ruby to the light. Both stones glowed with that uncanny luminosity that distinguished all superior gems. "They are . . . amazing," he murmured. In his many years as a jeweler he had never seen such fine stones, and to have six of them at once! He gave the jewels back to the stranger. "They are most remarkable."

"Yes," the foreigner said as he returned the jewels to his wallet. "It was good of you not to try to tell me that the quality was poor or that you would not be able to find any interest in these gems just now."

"Ah." The old jeweler darkened with embarrassment. "You have been to Chandri before me." He could not meet the stranger's dark eyes.

"I asked him to believe that these were not pebbles I had found in the road," the foreigner said so politely that the old jeweler was touched with fear.

"A man with such stones would know their worth," the old jeweler said, sighing in spite of himself. "And for that reason, I do not know if I may purchase them. It is not that I do not want them, for it would delight me to have these stones, if only for the time it would take me to find a buyer. But you will wish money at once, and though I am not a poor man, yet I cannot put my hands to sufficient amounts in little time."

The stranger did not seem perturbed by this. "How long would it take you to find enough to make me a reasonable offer?"

"And who is to judge the reasonableness of the offer?" the old jeweler said with a chuckle. "You or I?"

"I am willing to strike a bargain with you. But I dislike haggling. This is not your way, I know. But keep it in mind when you make your evaluation." The stranger let the old jeweler consider this. "How much time will you need?"

"By tomorrow I should have had an opportunity to speak with my brothers and cousins. At this time tomorrow, perhaps, you will return and I will tell you what we have decided." He was determined to have the jewels, and both he and the stranger sensed this.

"Tomorrow at sunset, then." He turned toward the half-closed door. "I would wish to warn you that if you send one of your nephews to follow me, I will have no more dealings with you." He said it casually, and his voice was still beautiful to hear, but the threat was most certainly genuine.

"It did not enter my mind, Excellency," the old jeweler lied.

"Did it not." He stepped out of the shop and away into the deepening shadows.

The old jeweler stood alone in his shop for some little time, asking himself if he had dreamed the whole. Yet he knew he had touched those stones. He could recall the weight of them. As he remembered the jewels he felt suddenly cold.

The stranger would return the next night, and he would have to make an offer, one that was not demeaning. He clamped his teeth together, for no matter what he said to his brothers and cousins there was no way they could find enough money to pay for more than two of the smaller ones. He would have to find other means. At once he thought of the Rajah Dantinusha and wondered if he had the courage to approach the Prince on the matter.

It was now almost fully dark, only a violet bar lay along the western horizon as a reminder of the day that had fled. The old jeweler fingered his neat beard and wished for a sign that would indicate what was best for him to do. Dantinusha was known as a reasonable man, but when presented with news of a foreigner possessing such gems to sell, he might behave differently.

A half-grown goat, which had been tethered to a stall at· the far end of the bazaar, suddenly broke away and ran in the direction of the main road, turning toward the Rajah's palace when he reached the crossing.

This was a plain sign, the old jeweler recognized at once. He bustled to the back of his shop to the iron coffers bolted to the wall. Swiftly he opened these chests and drew out a number of wide golden chains and bejeweled bracelets. He already wore several rings, but decided to add a handsome band of red gold set with black pearls. There were those who would consider such a ring unlucky, he thought, but in the years he had worn it, his business had increased and none of his children had died. A most fortunate ring. He closed and locked the coffers, then hurried out of the shop.

Rajah Dantinusha's palace was not as large as it seemed, but it was sumptuous, and its setting was magnificent. With a grove of trees and the rising mountains behind it and the river below its wide terraces, it was a fabulous beacon to all those who lived in this high valley of the upper Chenab River. Though the little principality extended some distance beyond the valley, this was the heart of it, and the palace of the Rajah was its treasure.

The old jeweler was detained at the gates by four pike-carrying guards in splendid military outfits. The senior guard asked a number of insolent questions, but in the end he called for a slave to take the old jeweler into the presence of Rajah Dantinusha. At the entrance to the royal quarters, the old jeweler was handed over to a dignified chamberlain and taken through a number of beautiful chambers, coming at last to a circular room that glowed like burnished gold in the torchlight.

The chamberlain paused in the doorway of this magnificent apartment. "The jeweler . . ." He turned back to the old man, waiting.

"Nandalas," he whispered.

"Yes." Again he raised his voice to announcing pitch. "The jeweler Nandalas." Then he stepped aside to allow the old man to enter the presence of the Rajah.

Dantinusha sat on a dais, his low couch so covered in pillows that it was almost impossible to see the furniture that supported it. On a low table at his elbow a number of simple refreshments had been set out, and the Prince was just pouring himself spiced and honeyed fruit juice as the jeweler entered and abased himself. Dantinusha looked at the old man, saying after a moment, "Well?"

Nandalas lifted his head. "I must speak to you, Rajah. It is of the utmost importance, or I would never have dared—"

"—to insist on this audience," Dantinusha said in slightly bored accents. "It seems that the only reason my subjects approach me is for reasons of the utmost importance. Go ahead." He leaned back on his cushions and brought the elegant little cup to his lips. He was an attractive man, with a strong, thick body and deep-set, intelligent eyes. His hair and oiled mustaches were glistening black; his skin almost matched the dark honey that flavored his drink.

Though he was somewhat puzzled, the jeweler Nandalas determined to speak. "Great Lord, I am a jeweler, an honorable one, and the trade has long been in the family—"

"So I understand," Danatiusha interrupted him. "You, your brothers and your cousins have excellent reputations."

Nandalas was momentarily diverted. "You do? How does it come that so great a Lord—"

"First," Dantinusha explained painstakingly, but without any particular interest, "you are aware that I and my household buy more jewels than most, and are apt to know who gives the best value. While it is true that it is my chamberlain who deals with your cousin, nonetheless, I know where the jewels are bought. Second, my treasury has a record of assessments made on businesses for the last eight generations, and the name of your family is a prominent one." He put his cup down. "Perhaps in vast kingdoms it is possible for a ruler to know nothing of those he rules, for there are so many of them. It is not a luxury I can allow myself, not with the followers of Islam nipping away at my borders." He stared down at the jeweler. "Why did you come, then? What is this important matter?"

"Uh . . ." the old jeweler found it difficult to recapture his thoughts. "It seems . . ." He cleared his throat and forced himself to begin again. "This evening, at sunset, when I was preparing to close the shop we keep near the bazaar, a man came to me with jewels to sell." He could see the polite but bored expression in the Rajah's eyes, and went on hurriedly. "He was a foreigner, from the West, though he has traveled far, I gather. Yes. He had jewels to sell, as I have said . . ."

"I am at a loss as to why you bring this to my attention. There have been foreigners here before. Men have sold jewels. Were they counterfeit?" He replenished his cup and held it, but did not drink.

"No, they were not counterfeit," Nandalas said with such a change in his tone that Dantinusha's attention was caught at once. "Great Lord, they were wonderful, these jewels. There were six of them: a black sapphire with a star, of moderate size but great perfection; an emerald with a fine blue flash; two small diamonds, one clear, the other faintly colored. Then there were the larger stones. One is a yellow diamond, larger than the one in your state jewels—

"How much larger?" Dantinusha asked. "Significantly?"

"Yes." Nandalas faltered after he had spoken. "I didn't see it in bright light, and it may not be as fine." He knew that this was not true, and apparently the Rajah recognized the fiction.

"And the quality? Surely you did not rush here to tell me of inferior jewels." He brushed his curling mustaches, not quite smiling.

"The quality was excellent. The last jewel," he went on doggedly, "is a ruby, the size of a small hen's egg. The diamond is slightly larger than that." He fumbled with his sash, suddenly embarrassed. "I would buy those jewels if I had sufficient funds for them, but, alas, I do not. My brothers and cousins would say—and certainly they would have reason on their side—that even if we had the money for such gems, aside from yourself there is no one to whom we could easily sell them. All these considerations occurred to me as I held the stones . . ."

"Yet you've come to me," Rajah Dantinusha pointed out.

"And none of them made a difference, not when I saw how beautiful the jewels were. I would have ruined my family, I think, if I could have possessed those gems." He looked at once suppliant and defiant.

Dantinusha studied the old man. "Why do you say that?" he inquired after some little time.

Now the old jeweler stumbled over his words in trying to frame an answer. "I do not know . . . You must love the stones, Great Lord. If there is a love of the stones, then . . . they are more than brothers and sons. They are vital. They are more than flesh and blood. To see the dark light in the heart of the ruby . . . I am as ardent as a young lover when I think of it. Don't you see, Great Lord, most gems are flawed. They are not well-shaped, or their inner light does not shine truly, or their polish is marred, or there are chips missing, or the color is not good. There is hardly one stone in a thousand that is not in some way flawed. It is rare to see one such stone, and I have held six this very night." His words came fast and he felt his heart race within him. "Any one of them would be remarkable, but six! . . ."

"Six," the Rajah repeated slowly. "Who did you say this person was? A foreigner?"

"Yes," Nandalas said fervently. "He brought them to me as the sun was setting. I thought at first that he was counting on poor light to disguise bad stones, but that was not the case. He encouraged me to look closely at the jewels, to hold them to the light so that I might see how fine they were." He felt tears in his eyes as he remembered the way light had seemed to be caught and magnified deep in the ruby.

"And the man, what of him?" Dantinusha asked with a greater show of impatience than he had permitted himself yet.

"A foreigner, as I have told you, Great Lord. He was from the West. He was dressed in black and wore a heavy silver chain about his neck, with a black emblem on it. I could not see it clearly, but I had the impression of raised wings. He speaks with an educated and very high-caste accent, but it is clear that he has learned the tongue from another. His pronunciations and phrases are old-fashioned."

"His teacher may have been one of the various exile families that have gone to the West," the Rajah suggested. He knew that as the Delhi Sultanate expanded, there were many who fled the followers of Islam, though the Sultans had shown themselves to be fairly tolerant of the Hindu teachings, though they had disliked the Buddhist pacifistic doctrines. There were many families in the various principalities and kingdoms on the borders of the Islamic territory who had come from those conquered cities and towns. It was a difficult business, the Rajah knew, for he did not wish to risk antagonizing the Sultan, but at the same time, he could not turn away high-ranking Hindus. He sighed, and saw at once that the old jeweler misunderstood.

"Truly, Great Lord," Nandalas said hurriedly, "there was little I could have learned from the man. It is fair to say that I was more concerned with the gems he showed me than I was with him, but I did not intentionally ignore him. I would certainly recognize him again. If I saw him in the dress of our people, I would still know him, as he is distinguished in appearance, even for a westerner."

Rajah Dantinusha assumed an interest that he did not entirely feel. "Describe this man to me, so that my guards may be told of him."

Nandalas pressed his eyes closed, and the wrinkles of his face stood out. He had not paid enough attention to the man, he knew he had not, and now he strove to recall as much as he could. "He is about the same height as you are, Great Lord, though not as ample of body. That is not to say that he is a stick of a man, for I noticed that his chest is deep." He made a greater effort to recall the stranger who had brought the jewels. "His hands are beautifully shaped—the fingers are comparatively long, though his hands are not at all large. His hair is dark, and curls somewhat. His eyes . . ." As he spoke, he remembered the impact they had made on him. "His eyes are quite extraordinary."

"How do you mean?" Dantinusha demanded. "Are they of unusual color or . . ."

"They are dark, but I did not see their color. No, it's not that. His eyes are arresting. I have never seen such eyes." He abased himself again, fearing he might have offended the Rajah.

Rajah Dantinusha looked down at Nandalas, and was saddened. The old man was behaving as if Dantinusha were a powerful ruler, and the Rajah knew it was not so. It had been more than four generations since his family were reduced to ruling a principality instead of having the august title of Maharajah, with the lands and the wealth and the power that were the justifications of that title. It was unfortunate that he ruled now on the sufferance of Delhi, but he supposed he was more fortunate than many of his uncles and ancestors had been, for he was alive with a sliver of a country to call his own. He was careful of his safety, and had so far been lucky. His one source of despair was that he had had no son who lived past his ninth year, and it seemed that this scrap of an ancient kingdom must pass to his daughter, who would surely be forced to surrender it to the Sultan at Delhi. He realized with a start that Nandalas was frightened by his long silence, so he said, "Most unusual. I doubt I have ever seen that man—not as you describe him."

The old man could have wept with relief. "I have never seen one such, Great Lord."

"Then you will, as you have said, know him when you see him again."

"I will. He said he would come to my shop again tomorrow. That is why I approached you," he reminded the Rajah timorously. "If I could make a reasonable offer on even one of the jewels . . . It must be a reasonable offer. He knows what the stones are worth. He showed that in his attitude as well as his words."

"If you had to make a guess at the true worth of the stones, what would it be?" Dantinusha was rubbing at his lower lip, a gesture that was well-known to those who knew him—the Rajah was weighing alternatives.

"Perhaps four or five grain-measures of gold." He said it softly, for it was an enormous figure, but a reasonable one as well.

"Four or five grain-measures of gold," Dantinusha echoed. "They must be amazing stones." He folded his arms "Four or five grain-measures of gold . . ." He fixed his eyes on the far wall. "Tomorrow, when this foreigner returns to your shop, *if* he returns to your shop, then you will tell him that because of the great worth of the stones you have seen, you have told me of his treasure. You will then instruct him to visit me at once. Tell him that though my invitation is cordial, I do not wish to be disappointed. I shall expect him to call upon me at once, and should he not do so, I will assume that he is not here as my friend or the friend to my country, and will act accordingly. Do this, Nandalas, and there will be both recognition and reward for you. Also, it is my wish that you tell this foreigner that I am willing to pay him the reasonable sum he demands, should his jewels be, in truth, what you have reported." He made a languid gesture with his hand as a sign of dismissal.

Nandalas scrambled to his feet and backed out of the Rajah's presence, feeling light-headed with awe and curiosity. He was met at once by the chamberlain, who indicated that he would escort the old jeweler from the palace.

"What do you think?" Rajah Dantinusha said, apparently to the air, when the old man had gone.

There was an answer from behind the screen. "I confess to a certain curiosity," was the answer, and in a moment the Commander of the palace guards strolled around the end of one of the elaborate wall panels. His uniform was much grander than those his men wore. "A foreigner with such jewels."

"That's not impossible," Dantinusha said, trying to pour more of the juice and finding, to his disappointment, that none was left. He put his cup aside. "But it may be a very clever trap, or so it seems to me."

"Ah. It seemed so to me as well." The commander sat on one of the cushions near the foot of the low dais. "A man, sent by the Sultan, might be able to bring a few inferior or counterfeit jewels, excellently made, and by defrauding our merchants, lessen the monies in the treasury, so that an invasion would not be too much resisted." He hooked his thumbs in his sash. "Such strategy has been successful elsewhere."

Rajah Dantinusha gave this careful consideration. "And if the jewels are genuine, and of the quality the old man describes, then it might be beneficial to have them. Guarding the borders is expensive, as you often point out to me." Again he rubbed his lower lip.

"There would be no advantage in paying him," the commander said with a cold smile.

"A man with such wealth may have more gems to offer, and we may have need of them in the future. I will barter with him . . ." He was already considering the various honors and pleasures he could offer the unknown stranger.

"A few hours with Sibu would gain as much, and for nothing but a little sweat." It was apparent that the commander preferred this solution.

"No." The Rajah spoke sharply. "No abuse, no torture. If the man is wealthy, he is probably powerful, and we may need his goodwill. I allowed you to use such methods with the Egyptian who came here, and I remind you that we never found the treasure he had. He lied to us because we had done our worst and nothing would have saved his life." Dantinusha felt a touch of shame at this memory. "I will not tolerate a similar mistake."

The commander smiled again, and with the same amount of sincerity he had shown before. "If that is your wish, then it is how it will be. I trust that you will not have cause to regret your leniency." He got to his feet. "I have given orders that the jeweler should be followed. If the foreigner returns and is not anxious to answer your summons . . ."

"Yes, very well," the Rajah said testily. But do not harm him, Guristar. It will not redound to your credit if the foreigner is treated badly." He joined his hands over his fashionable paunch and fixed the guard commander with a reprimanding eye. "We must deal in good faith."

"As you wish," Guristar said, annoyed, as he turned to leave the room.

"I will not believe convenient tales of the man disappearing, either," Rajah Dantinusha added as Guristar reached the door. "And I have those who will tell me anything you hope to keep private."

Guristar glared at the Rajah for a moment. "I had never considered lying to you, Great Lord." Though both men knew this, too, was a lie, the Commander left his Prince without being challenged. Now truly alone, Dantinusha stared at the door and wished he knew a way to deal with Guristar. Foreigners, restive people, the soldiers of the Sultan at Delhi—those he could deal with easily. The Commander of his guard was quite another matter.

————◆▶————

A letter from Mei Hsu-Mo to Nai Yung-Ya and the Nestorian Christian Church of Lan-Chow. Never delivered: the messenger bringing this and over two hundred other letters from Lo-Yang was one of five thousand persons killed by Mongol raiders at the town of Sai-T'u.

On the Festival of the Hungry Goats, the Year of the Tiger, the Fifteenth Year of the Sixty-fifth Cycle, the one thousand two hundred eighteenth year of Our Lord, to the Pope Nai Yung-Ya and the faithful congregation of Lan-Chow.

Doubtless you are curious why it is I instead of my brother who sends this message to you. It is my sad duty to inform you that Mei Sa-Fong died of a tenacious and wasting fever rather more than a month ago. I have postponed informing you of this tragic event while that dreadful man Chung La decided what he wished to do. He has left now, in the company of men from Delhi, and has sworn that he will renounce his faith and take up the banner of Islam as his own. While my brother lay suffering, this man made many advances to me, saying that so long as we were far from those of our faith and our families, it was proper that I should assuage his loneliness with the embraces he desired. This man left four wives in Lan-Chow, and until this terrible thing occurred, he had behaved most properly. On one occasion, he became so adamant that I was only able to discourage him by breaking a crockery jug over his head. In the next room, my beloved brother moaned and babbled in his sleep. It was shortly after this night that Chung La began to take up with the men of Islam who have a small temple in this city.

Perhaps I should tell you that we have reached the place called Tum-Kur and had intended to take the road to Pu-Na as soon as the weather permitted safe travel again. It is still my intention to travel, but I have not yet found one willing to be my guide. I will pray for guidance, and for the patience and wisdom that come of waiting. Your prayers will be of great solace to me, and I hope that you will remember me when the drums call you to worship.

Before his body succumbed to the ravages of fever, my brother spent much time trying to find others of our faith here. He did not entirely succeed, though he was told that there are those who worship Christ in the city of Pu-Na, and for that reason, he determined that we

should next go there. So far there have been many who
have heard of Christian worship, but few who have seen
churches and even fewer who have met those practicing
the faith. It may be as we fear, and I will have to journey into the west to seek out those of our faith.

It may not be entirely becoming of me to continue
this search, but now that my feet are on the Path, as
those who follow the Buddha say, it is not for me to
turn aside. I only hope that you will not cast me out of
your hearts for this act, which may appear rash, but
which, I must assure you, comes from my soul. Surely
the work that my brother began must be finished, and it
is appropriate for me to do so, as there is no other to
continue. I will endeavor to keep you informed of my
travels and my discoveries, but there may be long peri-
ods when it will be difficult or impossible for me to send
you word, such as when I am aboard a ship, if it becomes necessary for me to travel by water again.

There has been other, disquieting news that I must
tell: the Mongols are rumored to have come to the lands
west of here. One man we met shortly before my
brother fell ill said that he had heard that much of the
land he called Persia was even at that moment under assault from these inhuman warriors. He said that all of
the country of Persia goes in terror by day and night,
and that they all expect to be slaughtered by these men.
Persia is apparently the country we have known as Bu-
Sa-Yin. The man claimed to come from the city of Sie-
La-Shi, which he called Shiraz. Though he has not been
in his native city for several years, he told us that he
had had word from his brother a few months before and
his brother had said that even then the city was in danger
and would not be able to resist much longer.

We were distraught to hear of this, and though I have
made inquiries, there seems to be no doubt that his report was honest, and the Mongols have indeed come to
Persia, intent on conquest. We have heard, also, that
these Mongols have brought disaster to much of the
Golden Empire, but this does not seem possible. Though
I am aware you will not be able to send me word until I
have reached the end of my journey, still I trust that
your news will be reassuring. Certainly the Imperial
army is more than a match for these scruffy men on po-

nies. Surely God and Christ will champion those who
strive for knowledge and peace and will turn away from
those who make war.

With my prayers and my love to all of you, and the
hope that your blessing will bring comfort to my
brother's soul, I commend this to the merchant from
Braddur and the Will of God, at whose behest all things
are done.

Mei Hsu-Mo
sister to Mei Sa-Fong
on the road to Pu-Na

10

WHEN THE soldiers reached the throne room, they stood aside
in a respectful manner and let Saint-Germain enter alone.

"Ah," Rajah Dantinusha said slowly as Saint-Germain approached him. "The jeweler told the truth."

"I would assume so," Saint-Germain answered with a sang-
froid he was far from feeling. He dropped to one knee in the
European fashion, then rose, regarding the man on the
throne. "If you desired to speak with me, you needed only to
send a message." He was taking a chance making this gentle
rebuke, but if he had any intention of keeping his independence, he knew that he must assume he had it from the first.

Dantinusha hesitated, his eyes flicking over the stranger,
noting the heavy silver chain and the quality of the black silk
robe he wore. Then he turned to the four men who flanked
his throne. Nearest was the commander of his guards, Guristar. Beside him the Brahmin holy man Rachura, who regarded Saint-Germain with contemptuous curiosity. On the
other side of the throne was Jaminya, the greatest scholar and
poet in Rajah Dantinusha's small kingdom. The fourth man
was quite old and dressed in the clothes of a traveling merchant. Dantinusha selected this last man, saying, "Well,
Qanghozan, what do you think?"

The merchant was startled to be the first to speak, and he
began awkwardly. "Great Lord, certainly there is . . . there
can be no doubt that this man is from the West. . . . The
eyes, the skin . . . most assuredly, he is not . . . ." He stared
at Saint-Germain.

"Yet you do not know how far west," Saint-Germain said ironically in Persian, repeating his observation in classic Arabic and Greek, and was rewarded by the amazed expression the merchant showed him.

Qanghozan mastered his astonishment, and spoke in Arabic. "Do you follow the Prophet? Are you of Islam?"

"No, that is not my faith," Saint-Germain said, continuing in the elaborate courtesies he had learned from earlier followers of Islam. "It is a great misfortune that one such as I must give offense to you, and I pray that you will realize that it was not my intent. Surely those who have put themselves in the hands of Allah need fear nothing from the doubts of those less learned and blessed."

The merchant nodded, saying carefully, "I have not, myself, taken up the way of the Prophet, though three of my brothers have. It is well that you honor his word, for Delhi is close and there are those who hear what is said in this place."

Rajah Dantinusha interrupted the merchant. "You will speak in our tongues or not at all."

"I had not meant to be discourteous," Saint-Germain said at once. "It is my custom to speak to men in their own languages, if I know them. Hindi is acceptable to me. I have some Kashmiri and Tamal, but my command is faulty." He looked back at Qanghozan, but continued to speak in Hindi. "You were good to tell me of these things."

Apparently the poet Jaminya had understood the Arabic, for he could not hide his slight smile. He regarded Saint-Germain with awakening interest. "We were informed that you have traveled far. Where is your homeland, then?"

"In the West," Saint-Germain answered promptly. "In what is now the Kingdom of Hungary. I have not been there in some time, and it was my hope to return there within a year. If, however, the Mongols are indeed spreading through the cities of Persia, then it may be some time before I can undertake the journey." He paused, considering. "I could cross the Arabian Sea and land in Egypt or Africa and from there make my way to the Mediterranean and embark on a Venetian ship bound for Trieste or Constantinople, but that presents a great many problems, particularly since I am a very poor sailor."

"He knows the routes," the merchant said at once. "He does not speak as one who is ignorant."

This time the Rajah himself asked the question. "Where

have you come from? You have given us an excellent idea of where you are going, but where did this homeward journey begin?"

"I left my home in Lo-Yang about two years ago," he said, his compelling dark eyes meeting the Rajah's directly. "I went into the west of China and fought there against the Mongols until we were overrun and I was forced to flee. I made my way into the mountains, coming through Bod, the Land of Snows, where we passed the winter with Yellow Hat monks. Once out of the high mountains, we have come west and north along the mountains."

"We? You did not travel alone?" Guristar demanded, his hands braced on his hips. He was not prepared to accept anything that Saint-Germain told him.

"I have traveled with my servant, Rogerio. He has been with me throughout my travels, in fact, for many years before that." Saint-Germain read anger in Guristar's swarthy face and decided to add a cooperative note. "Send for him, if you wish, and speak to him privately. He will confirm all that I have said."

"Then he is well-coached," the Commander snapped as he turned toward the man on the throne. "Great Lord, any man may claim he has come from far away, and when the man is plainly a foreigner, as this one is, it is the more plausible. He may tell us that he has been in the Land of Snows and there are few who could disprove him. It is a convenient lie, Great Lord. He is much more likely to be a spy for the forces in Delhi. The Sultan is anxious to extend his realm, and you know as well as I that this principality would be welcome addition to the Sultanate. Listen to the man. He speaks the language of the men of western Islam. What could be easier than to send such a one among us, posing as a traveler, needing only to tell ever-more-fantastic tales of his adventures to turn us away from real vigilance? Consider this, Great Lord, I beseech you!"

"Very eloquent," Saint-Germain said softly, and as all five of the others stared at him, he reached into the wallet buckled to his belt. "I have here a message from the Master of the Yellow Hat lamasery called Bya-grub Me-long ye-shys, where my servant and I passed the winter. The message is in several languages, and one of them must be familiar to you." He took the scroll from the wallet and offered it to the man on the throne.

But it was Guristar who took it. "Do not think that we are unwary, foreigner!"

"Naturally not," Saint-Germain murmured, and watched while the Commander of the guards opened the scroll with exaggerated care.

"Tell me," Rajah Dantinusha said to Saint-Germain while Guristar pored over the words, "why did you want to sell those jewels? One I can understand, and perhaps two, but six?"

Saint-Germain raised his brows, answering in a philosophical tone, "Since it is apparent that I will not be able to reach my homeland this winter, or quite possibly next winter, I must have a place to live. I have studies to pursue, and I would prefer to live pleasantly." He did not add that well-paid servants were less likely to carry tales than poor men with a strange neighbor.

"You wish to buy a house? With these jewels you could have half of this palace." The Rajah's manner was less formidable now.

"I doubt it," Saint-Germain answered truthfully. "A room or two, no more."

"Perhaps," Dantinusha allowed. "Guristar, what have you learned?"

The Commander of the guard looked up from the scroll. "I can read one of the sections, and it is as he says, though, of course, there is no way to prove that this is genuine." He started to hand the scroll back to Saint-Germain, but was stopped by the poet Jaminya.

"Let me examine the scroll, Great Lord. If there is forgery, I will know it." He held out his hand for the scroll, and after seeing an approving sign from the Rajah, Guristar reluctantly gave Jaminya the scroll.

The room had grown silent as the poet read. Saint-Germain hoped that the man's claim was justifiable, or he might find himself wrongly denounced. It would not be, he reminded himself, the first time. Or the tenth.

At last Jaminya glanced at Saint-Germain. "The Yellow Hats are quite an important sect, aren't they?"

"So I understand. I didn't see much of other Orders, but in the middle of winter, it was not likely that anyone would be traveling, and so I must take their word for it. Their chapter-house in Lhasa is quite large." Saint-Germain was wary, though he answered the question easily enough. The questions would test him and he would have to satisfy the poet.

"They have an ancient tradition of masters, do they not?" Jaminya was holding the scroll negligently, but his eyes kept moving over it.

"That was my understanding, yes." Saint-Germain did not dare to look at the Rajah, for fear that such a move would be interpreted as insolence.

"And this one, this SGyi Zhel-ri, is a man of great wisdom, wouldn't you say?" Jaminya was not looking at Saint-Germain at all.

"You must pardon me—certainly the master is wise, but I would not call him a man. He is less than ten years old." The first of the traps was past, and Saint-Germain hoped that the rest of the test would be of a similar nature.

The others listening were startled. "Absurd," Guristar said quite loudly.

"Well, Jaminya, is it absurd?" the Rajah inquired.

"He is correct," the poet assured his prince. "Two years ago I spoke with a number of Buddhist scholars who were returning from a long retreat in Bod, and they told me then of this child, who had only recently entered the lamasery, and who was regarded with reverence and awe even then." He opened the scroll again.

"Let me see," Dantinusha said, holding out his hand for the scroll, accepting it quickly from the poet. "But this is most surprising," the Rajah said as he read.

Guristar laughed unpleasantly. "Do you expect me to believe that the Master of the Yellow Hats would speak highly of a foreigner, one who is not part of the country or the faith of Bod? He has hired some forger in a distant city to do this, and he has asked a number of questions of the men coming from Bod, and has learned enough to impress those who seek marvels."

Saint-Germain did not raise his voice, but the quality of command grew in him so that he was more forceful. "If it were my intention to deceive you and the Rajah and, indeed, anyone else, there is no reason I should choose such elaborate and easily discredited methods. I would only have to say that I was a merchant from the West who had been driven out of a distant city by invaders or a corrupt ruler. There would be no way for you to verify my claim. I would only have to show you the jewels and tell you my tale of misfortune. Instead I have spoken to you honestly and openly, and for that you have accused me of deceit."

Dantinusha looked up from the scroll. "You're a most clever man, foreigner. You have an answer for any reasonable objection."

"Great Lord," Saint-Germain said evenly, "what am I to do, if everything I say is regarded with suspicion?" There was no challenge in his words, and no apology. He looked from one man to the next, his eyes betraying no feeling.

Dantinusha let the scroll roll closed. "You are said to have great understanding. The Master of the Yellow Hats commends you for your wisdom. Most unusual, isn't it?"

"I do not know, Great Lord," Saint-Germain answered honestly. "It was nothing we discussed." He could see that the Commander of the guard was getting restive again.

The poet Jaminya spoke before Guristar could. "If you have wisdom that the Master of the Yellow Hats acknowledges, then reveal it. A wise man may remain silent all his life, but once discovered, then it is important that he find a way to bring his knowledge to others." He was looking not at Saint-Germain but at the Brahmin Rachura.

The somber holy man nodded. "True wisdom will make itself known. If the message on this scroll is genuine, then all will benefit from his teaching. If the message is not genuine, those of us who have advanced far in learning will know it at once."

Guristar almost smirked. "Excellent. Let the fool bring himself down by his own temerity."

Rajah Dantinusha hesitated, watching Saint-Germain carefully. "If I make this demand of you, foreigner, will you agree that it is just?"

"I will accept your terms," Saint-Germain said carefully.

"That is not quite the same thing," the Rajah admonished him.

"No, it is not." His eyes were on Dantinusha's and he did not look away.

"Very well," the Rajah said at last. "You will not agree that it is just, but you are willing to accept the terms." He held out the scroll to the black-clad foreigner. "What do you wish to teach us?"

Saint-Germain glanced toward the window. "I will tell you a tale, Great Lord, and you will judge its wisdom." He thought this whole interrogation was foolish, but could not afford to antagonize these men. He had no desire to have to travel westerward until he had made careful preparations.

"What will be the thrust of the tale?" the Rajah asked, beginning to enjoy the foreigner.

"I will not tell you that, Great Lord. If there is wisdom, you will not have to have it pointed out to you." His expression was gently sardonic. "If there is some doubt, you may wish to confer when I have finished."

"And if there is no agreement," Guristar said haughtily, "then you can claim that we were incapable of understanding."

"Be silent, Guristar," Rajah Dantinusha ordered in a tone that tolerated no contradiction.

The Commander of the guard fell silent but from the set of his features, he did not intend to listen to anything Saint-Germain said.

"There was a boy," Saint-Germain began after a moment, "who may have been a Prince, but did not lead a princely life. He was given to the leader of a caravan and taken into the mountains, to a place far from his home, and it was apparent that he was to remain in this distant and isolated place his life long. Though the men of the caravan were without malice toward the boy, they did what they had been paid to do, for otherwise they could not continue to trade with the boy's homeland."

"Traders will tolerate anything if there is profit in it," the Brahmin said to Rajah Dantinusha. "We have heard this often."

"Let him continue," the Rajah said, raising his hand for silence.

Guristar looked away from the throne and from Saint-Germain. There were scented oil lamps hanging about the room which had been recently lit, and these held the Commander of the guard's attention with rapt and mendacious fascination while Saint-Germain went on.

"These traders were the only link the boy had with his home and his people, and because it was late in the season, the boy was able to persuade his hosts to let the traders remain through the long winter. The hosts were kindly men in their way, and did not too much resist the request made of them: the traders were secretly glad to have found shelter for the winter, as the mountains were treacherous. Now, these men in this mountain citadel had many animals, especially cats, and the boy often found himself the companion of a large soot-colored cat with topaz eyes, and having no other real confidant, he gave all his thoughts to this aninal. And the cat watched him with his topaz eyes, in the self-contained manner of his kind,"

"Buddha spoke against cats," the poet Jaminya observed.

"He is not the only one to do so," Saint-Germain responded urbanely. "Cats are curious beings." He met the Rajah's eyes and went on. "In the spring the traders prepared to move on, and the boy was filled with anger and fear, for now he would be truly alone. It seemed to him a great betrayal that these men would leave him and perhaps never return. He climbed to the parapet of the citadel and poured out his fury to the cat, saying that he could not endure the isolation. And in his wrath, he hurt himself. The cat fled swiftly and silently; far down the mountain the boy could see the caravan falter. His ire faded at once and he wept joyously, for though he knew that the caravan must have experienced some misfortune, he knew, also, that he would not be left quite alone."

"Did this boy have a name?" the Brahmin Rachura inquired, not quite politely. He touched the threefold cord of his rank and waited.

A face rose in Saint-Germain's mind, a face he had not seen for more than a thousand years, but the memory of loss was still sharp within him. "I will call him Kosrozd," Saint-Germain said quietly. "It may or may not have been his name."

"Persian?" the merchant Qanghozan asked, startled.

"Yes." He was still for a moment as the recalled impressions of Rome faded. "As it turned out, within the hour the cat had returned, and not far behind him came the caravan. The guide had fallen and was quite seriously injured. The good men of the citadel took the party in and ministered to the guide. By the time his broken bones had knit and the guide was once again able to travel, winter was upon them, and the boy was able to enjoy the company of the traders through the dark of the year. He deceived himself willfully, pretending that the traders would stay at the citadel forever and he would not be entirely alone among strangers. He told this to the soot-colored cat during the long night, and the cat watched him with his topaz eyes.

"Of course, spring came, and the caravan once again made ready to depart. The boy, who now had the downy cheeks of approaching manhood, was thrown into the darkest despair, so that all his life stretched before him as desolate as the Arabian sands at night. He could take pleasure in nothing; learning, dance, the delights of the table and the flesh had no lure for him. He thought only of the terrible solace of final silence, and on the day the caravan was to depart he climbed to the watchtower of the citadel and held the black cat, telling it of his misery, saying that he wished he had the courage to jump and dash out his miserable brains on the stones far beneath his vantage place. At this the cat leaped up and sped away."

"What consolation is there in his leaving?" the Brahmin asked.

"None," Saint-Germain responded at once. "But almost at once there was a sound of thunder in the mountains, and a great avalanche rumbled and shattered down the slopes, destroying the road on which the caravan had to travel. And so, for a second time, the kindly men of this citadel took the traders in, and side by side they worked to rebuild the road that led out of the mountain fastness to the fertile plains. The youth worked with them most diligently, for he could not escape an inner chagrin; he blamed himself for the misfortunes that had kept the traders with him even as he took delight in their presence. He was so industrious that many looked to him for leadership, and praised him for his efforts, which filled him with shame. By the time the road was completely repaired, winter had come again, and the traders had to delay their departure until spring arrived. The youth was much in their company, savoring every hour, hoping to assuage the long years alone that were to come, for he knew that he would soon have to say farewell to them, no matter how much he wished them to stay. Though he could not harden his heart, he tried to persuade himself that the loss of his countrymen would not be intolerable. He poured out his confusion to the soot-colored cat, who watched with topaz eyes.

"In course of time it was spring and the caravan made ready to depart. The youth was filled with sorrow, for he knew without doubt that when the traders were gone, his last link with his own kind would be broken. He took the cat and climbed to the peak of the highest roof in the citadel and watched as the traders made their way down the new road. The soot-colored cat regarded him, ready to spring away at a word."

Rajah Dantinusha leaned back against the pillows of his throne and allowed himself to smile. Wisdom or nonsense, he liked tales of this sort, and remembered fondly the ones he had been told as a child. He noticed that Saint-Germain had stopped, and motioned him to resume the tale.

Saint-Germain inclined his head to the Rajah. "At last the caravan passed from sight and the youth wrenched his tear-filled eyes away from the empty road. He reached out gratefully to the soot-colored cat, finding solace in the presence of the animal. The cat allowed the youth to stroke him for a few moments, blinking his eyes slowly in his contentment. Then he rose, stretched, and bounded away over the roofs of the citadel, and was never seen again."

The room was quiet. The merchant Qanghozan shifted uneasily on his feet and tried to avoid notice. Jaminya smiled knowingly as the silence lengthened.

"Yes?" Rajah Dantinusha said impatiently when it was clear that Saint-Germain was not going to say more until prompted. "What happened then?"

"I don't know, Great Lord," Saint-Germain said rather apologetically. "That is all of the tale there is."

Guristar gave a snort. "It was as I predicted. There is nothing in the story, and what you wish to make of it is the only wisdom it can offer."

"It has been my experience," Saint-Germain said diffidently, "that this is true of everything. Whatever meaning it has is what we give to it."

Jaminya grinned. "So I have often thought," he agreed, eyeing Guristar covertly. "If there is a meaning and a form, it is known only to the gods, who reign for millions upon millions of years."

Rachura was clearly offended. "There is karma and the attainment of perfection. The Enlightened Ones perceive it."

"It is possible," Saint-Germain conceded. "Yet there are few who are enlightened: most of the world walks in darkness."

Before Rachura could speak again, Rajah Dantinusha interrupted him, and the others in the throne room were still. "I have been considering what I have heard, and this is my decision: you, Shih Ghieh-Man, or Saint-Germain, whatever you call yourself, may remain here in my principality for the space of a year, at which time I will review your accomplish-

ments. Guristar may be right, and you are clever with words
that hint at much, but reveal nothing. It may be that you are
one of those whose merit is not known until long after you
teach. I will not decide that for some time. In that time you
will live here, for I cannot allow you to be unobserved—"

Though it was unheard-of, Saint-Germain interjected a
comment. "Great Lord, I know it is a most desirable honor
to be close to you, and I am profoundly grateful that you
should extend your hospitality to me. However, there are
those who will not speak kindly of you for taking a foreigner
into your house. They will fear that you are being influenced
by those from beyond your borders. You know far better
than I how perilous these times are. I would be loath to bring
any misfortune to you because my presence here caused
needless suspicion to fall on you." He did not add that he
had no desire to be closely watched. Household spies were
inevitable, but he was determined to maintain as much privacy as possible.

Dantinusha's face had hardened. "What you say is true,
and it is, for you, quite convenient."

"On the contrary," Saint-Germain said at once. "You live
in a splendid palace with more slaves and servants than any
other person in your principality. My studies are arduous and
nothing would suit me more than having access to the records
and the assistance of those who serve you." That, he told
himself, was true enough. "However, it would benefit neither
you nor me, Great Lord, to have rumors spreading that
would override any advantages that my presence might
have."

"So you maintain," Guristar snapped, his eyes kindled with
anger. "And you wish to do your evil work where none may
watch you. You think to conceal your intent with this pretty
lie, but it will not work, foreigner."

Saint-Germain turned to the Commander of the guard,
hesitating in order to master his temper. "If you are offering
me servants to spy on me," he said in a dangerously even
tone, "I will not refuse them. I have assumed that there will
be reports made of my activities, no matter where I live, or
with whom." His small hands were tight at his sides, but
there was nothing in his face now that would reveal how near
he had come to giving way to his rage.

"Both of you: stop at once," Dantinusha ordered, sounding

more tired than incensed. "I have trouble enough without you bickering in this petty way." He rubbed at his lower lip. "I have said that you, Saint-Germain, may stay here for a year. I will not rescind my offer. I have suggested that you live here at my palace, and the disadvantages you have mentioned are genuine—they are, Guristar, and you would be the first to warn me of these consequences of having a foreigner here if Saint-Germain had not mentioned it before you had the opportunity." He looked up at the elaborately ornamented ceiling. He wished that the old jeweler Nandalas had never told him about the jewels or the foreigner who had brought them. It was not possible to ignore either of them, but he wished that instead of conducting this tedious interview, he was in the company of his new concubine, spending the evening not in debate but in the varied pleasures of the body. He had few of the luxuries his grandfathers had enjoyed, but he still had women and boys in abundance.

"You cannot allow him to live away from you!" Guristar exploded.

"I realize that," Rajah Dantinusha said, his attention once again directed to the matter at hand. "Something must be done."

"There is prison," Guristar said nastily.

The idea had occurred to Dantinusha, but he had rejected it, for if this foreigner were a spy, his masters would learn soon enough what had become of him, and would send others in his place, others who would be less easily detected. "And if I order him to prison, or have him executed, what do I gain? There is no peace of mind to be had in this affair, no matter what I do." He glowered at a space on the wall and set his teeth. "It is of no matter. Something must be done." He directed his gaze at Saint-Germain and was both relieved and disappointed that the foreigner did not quail under the force of his eyes. "Suppose I made one of my country estates available to you? What then?"

This was becoming even more difficult, and Saint-Germain chose his words with care. "Whatever you, Great Lord, decide is the most appropriate solution. I, as a foreigner and guest in your country, will comply with your wishes with gratitude. The objections I raised previously might still pertain, for I would be, in effect, a guest in your house. You might prefer to send me to one of your brothers or cousins . . ."

"Never," Dantinusha muttered, thinking of the bloody uprising his younger brother had led three years before. "I have no surviving brothers or cousins," he explained in a carefully neutral tone.   .

"Then perhaps one of your ministers might be willing to receive me into his home." Saint-Germain had not missed the tension that had filled the room at his casual mention of cousins and brothers. He determined to find out as quickly as possible what had become of the Rajah's male relatives. "It might be better to send me to one of your ministers' country estates."

"Who would be such a fool as to let you so far out of his sight?" Guristar demanded, unaware that his outbursts were working contrary to his interests.

Rajah Dantinusha did not smile, but there was a lighter turn to his full mouth. "My sister."

"What?" Guristar shouted as Jaminya laughed.

"My sister," Dantinusha repeated. "I may be able to persuade her to accept this foreigner into her house. Surely no one would accuse her of subversion." The more he considered this, the more he found it an excellent plan. "Yes. I will send a messenger to her at once."

"She may refuse," the Brahmin Rachura warned the Rajah.

"She may, but I doubt she will. She's an educated woman, and the opportunity to have such a companion . . ." He regarded Saint-Germain somewhat more speculatively. "Would you be willing to go to the home of my older sister?"

The proposition was unexpected, but Saint-Germain sensed that it was the best alternative to staying at the Rajah's palace. "If my presence will not compromise the woman, it would be an honor to stay at the house of your sister for a year. I will defray the cost of any expenses she may incur in providing me proper quarters." He added this for Guristar's benefit, for he sensed that the commander of the guard was eager to find objections to this plan.

Expense was rarely discussed with the Rajah, and the others were shocked to hear Saint-Germain mention the cost of housing him. Rachura was embarrassed and averted his face. Guristar chuckled scornfully. Rajah Dantinusha looked perplexed, but said, "She may agree to that. She's an unusual woman." His discomfort—and he was clearly uncomfortable—was shared by his companions, so that Saint-Germain began to be apprehensive about the woman. He concealed his doubts and bowed in the Western fashion.

"I look forward to her acquaintance," he said, though he was not at all certain that he did.

———— ◄●► ————

Report to the Sultan Shams-ud-din Iletmish at Delhi, from his representative at Rajah Dantinusha's court, Ab-she-lam Eidan.

To the Sultan Shams-ud-din Iletmish, in the seventh year of his reign, and by the Will of Allah, this from Ab-she-lam Eidan in Natha Suryarathas, the principality of Rajah Dantinusha.

To the beloved son of Allah, just ruler and wise judge, greetings.

This is to inform you of the activities in Natha Suryarathas and the doings of the court of Rajah Dantinusha. Tributary payment in gold and gems accompany this message. You will notice that there is a particularly fine emerald among the jewels, which lately came into the hands of the Rajah. I could wish it were the Will of Allah that all Princes on the borders of the Sultanate were as reasonable and sensible as Dantinusha. I fear that if we ever have to deal with his daughter it will bring misfortune to all of us. She has the soul of the screech owl and is said to worship unclean things. I have seen her but once—she is a young woman, lovely after the beauty of these people, and made for voluptuousness, and if it is true that she consorts with demons, it is a double tragedy, for we will no longer have a thoughtful man to deal with, but a dangerous and willful woman, from which Allah preserve us.

Rumors continue that the Rajah will order the construction of an artificial lake in the little valley near his palace. I have in the past described this to you, and I will say that the setting is quite soothing. There is al-

ready something of a garden there, which is above the
low ground where the lake would be. Two builders have
come to consult on the matter with the Rajah, and although nothing has been announced, I feel certain that
he will soon decide whether or not to embark upon the
project. It is my intention to encourage him in this. As
long as he is building lakes, he will not be thinking of
war.

Rajah Dantinusha's Commander of the guards, Sudra
Guristar, is not so tolerant in his attitude. He frets under
what he imagines to be your tyranny, and longs for a
bloody uprising. He did not participate in the rebellion
the Rajah's brothers attempted, and feels cheated. It is
understandable that he should wish for the honor of
battle and the opportunity to kill his enemies, yet I hope
that he will not decide to rouse Natha Suryarathas. I
have developed a fondness for this place and it would
sadden me to see it destroyed. Surely if it is the Will of
Allah, then it must be, but my prayers are that I will not
have to see it, if it must come to pass.

A messenger has recently been sent to Dantinusha's
sister, Padmiri, who is sometimes called Manas Sattva
for her reputed dedication to study. I have never had occasion to meet this woman, for she lives retired from the
court, and since the uprising of the brothers and cousins,
has not seen her brother. It has been maintained that she
had no part in the treachery, but we are wisely taught
that all the evil in the world lies between a woman's
thighs, and I find her refusal to see the Rajah indicative
of her native female cunning. Apparently the message
has some relation to the foreigner who has recently arrived in this principality, but I have learned nothing
more either of him or why Padmiri should be concerned
with it.

A periyanadu has been ordered for two moons hence.
That is the country-wide village assembly that is called
at the whim of the Rajah, when grievances are heard
and the state of the country is discussed, so that all the
villages may understand their roles in the development
of the country, and the wishes of the Rajah may be
made clear to all. For the most part these are peaceable,
and this one will doubtless be the same unless Guristar
attempts to light the fires of rebellion once again. This

will be the first periyanadu in well over a year, so the Rajah anticipates a long meeting, perhaps as long as forty days. Much will depend on the weather, but the worst of the rains should have ceased by the time of the periyanadu. There was quite a bad storm ten days ago, and the farmers say that there is another one coming, but all agree that the rains will have ceased by the time the village leaders gather. There has been relatively little flooding this year—Allah is merciful even to these infidels—and the Rajah has said that he plans to expand the dike system he has begun on the various brooks that feed the Chenab here. There is no protection but Allah, and his precautions are those of a wise but faithless man.

When you next send a messenger to me, I would appreciate knowing more of the news of Persia. I have heard that the warriors of Jenghiz Khan have swarmed over the country, worse than all the insects that feed upon the dead, and that the stench of the carrion they have left behind them rises to heaven throughout the land. If this is indeed so, it is a great catastrophe, and one that demands vengeance of all those who trust in Allah. This Jenghiz Khan cannot be a man like other men, I fear, since it has been said that his warriors have also conquered half of the Yellow Empire, and how can it be that he should do that as well as destroy the cities of Persia? I pray that your response will put my mind at rest. Doubtless there have been a number of border skirmishes, and these have been repeated with additions in the telling, and what is a minor incursion has been magnified into a full invasion.

May Allah grant that your life be long and filled with honor, the devotion of your women, and many sons. It is my privilege to serve you here in the principality of the Rajah Dantinusha, and any other place you may desire to send me. There is no will greater in my life than yours, save that of Allah, who is All-powerful and All-compassionate.

From the hand of Ab-she-lam Eidan, in Natha Suryarathas on the Chenab, at the end of summer.

11

THERE WAS a cold, wanton light in her enormous eyes as Tamasrajasi opened the door to Sudra Guristar. At seventeen, she had not yet reached the full flowering of her body, yet the Commander of the guard could not look at her without being gripped by intense lust, for the girl was magnificent.

"Be seated," Tamasrajasi said, indicating a pile of cushions. "I have given orders for refreshments."

Guristar had to clear his throat before he could answer. "It is not wise to let the slaves know I visit you."

Tamasrajasi had a clear, cruel laugh. "They will say nothing. My slaves are better schooled than that."

As Guristar sank onto the cushions, he reached out to touch her. "Will you deny me?"

She allowed him to caress the flaring rise of her hips, turning provocatively away when he sought greater liberties. "Not yet, Commander. There are matters we must discuss before we do . . . anything else."

"Very well." He felt his hands tremble as he brought them to his sides. His greedy eyes lingered on the line of her buttocks, then the swell of her breasts as she made herself comfortable on the other side of a low table.

"Sudra Guristar, you are devoted to me, are you not?" She had leaned back, offering him a tantalizing view of her body.

Guristar rubbed his palms on his short sleeveless jacket, and felt the embroidery as if it were the new lines in his hands. "Most assuredly, Rani." He should not give her that title, not while her father lived and she remained unmarried, but he could not stop himself. He did not want to stop himself.

"Excellent, Commander. I wish you to remember this in days to come." She clapped her hand sharply and said as an inner door opened, "Bring the refreshments at once."

"Yes, Shakti," murmured the voice.

"They call you Shakti?" Guristar asked, thinking that the essence of female power was an appropriate name for her.

Tamasrajasi only smiled, and said, "I will have need of your devotion, Sudra Guristar. The time is drawing near when there are many things I will require of you. I must be certain that you will do them without question."

"I have vowed to aid you," Guristar reminded her, trying not to gaze too long at the place where her sheer chamber robe folded between her legs.

"Are you still determined?" There was a sharper note in her voice and she watched him closely, her elegant head held imperiously.

"I am." He determined to give his attention to their words, not to surrender to the distraction of her splendid flesh. "The insult to the gods must be avenged, and the kingdom restored. We have tolerated the presence of the Islamic dogs too long. Your father—I know I may say this to you—is on a course that will only lead to disaster. Only two days ago money and jewels were sent to Delhi to the man who calls himself Sultan. In the time of your great-great-grandfather, the boundaries of Natha Suryarathas were farther than any man could ride on a swift horse for ten days. Cities that now bow to the Sultan called your great-great-grandfather Maharajah, and it was right that they did so. Now, your father is permitted to call himself a Rajah, but he pays tribute to those curs in the south. We are reviled, and your father does nothing."

"You speak with conviction—"

"It is not feigned."

Her brows snapped together; she did not wish him to interrupt her. "But I do not know that you will stand by me when I summon all of my subjects to aid me in casting off the yoke my father wears like an ox." Her nails were long, and as she drew them down the heavy silk of the cushion, they made a faint, eerie shriek.

Guristar shifted uneasily; his groin was tightening, stiffening. Perhaps he should not look at Tamasrajasi, he told himself, but could not turn away from her. "Yes," he agreed hazily. "The yoke . . . must be thrown off."

A slave girl came into the room and placed a tray of honeyed fruit on the table, then made obeisance to Tamasrajasi.

"You have done well," Dantinusha's daughter said sweetly, motioning for the slave to withdraw.

The girl scrambled up from her position on the carpet and hastened from the room.

"All your slaves mind you," Guristar said after the door was closed.

"It's best for them if they do." She leaned forward and inspected the fruits on the tray. "You may take what you like," she said to him, her voice promising him more than the refreshments on the table.

"Most certainly," he said, feeling slightly drunk. He selected a peach, and found that its shape, its scent, the waxy honey that clung to it, all aroused him unbearably. He put the fruit back on the tray and licked his fingers. "Perhaps later."

Tamasrajasi laughed again, this time low in her throat. "You would prefer me to the peach, wouldn't you, Sudra Guristar?" She ran one hand along the curve of her hip.

At that moment, Guristar wished to sheathe his flesh in hers though it cost him the world. "Tamasraj . . ." he began, then stopped breathless, as the girl drew her robe up, revealing all her body to him. This, he told himself sternly, was the Rajah's daughter and he, as Commander of Dantinusha's guard, should be the last man to pursue this girl. Even as he thought of these objections, he was moving toward her, loosening the sash at his waist. After the most perfunctory of caresses, he knelt between her thighs and lifted her hips to him. As he went into her, she made a strange sound, half a sigh of satisfaction, half some more sinister emotion. Then, in a swift, powerful motion, she had risen, and straddling his legs, held his face to her breasts as she urged him on fiercely. So intense was his pleasure that he did not feel her nails on his back when she had torn away his tunic.

"Guristar," Tamasrajasi murmured when she had finished with him, "you are dedicated to me, aren't you?"

"Yes," he said slowly, now curiously numbed. He gathered his clothes about him in a mechanical way.

"You would never betray me or my cause, would you?" She was reveling in the power she had over the man. It was an effort not to laugh at him now, but she recognized how vain he was and controlled herself.

"I would never betray you, Rani," he answered. He was concentrating on tying his sash, not looking at her.

"Eat some fruit," she suggested impishly. "It will restore you." Her tongue flicked over her lips.

"I'm not hungry, Rani." Nevertheless, he reached out obediently and picked up the peach he had not been able to eat earlier. Juice dribbled over his chin as he bit into it, honey ran down his fingers, but he could taste nothing.

She watched him as he chewed on the peach, and her lustrous eyes darkened. "You must not think that I will permit you to change your mind, Commander Guristar."

His mouth was full of peach, so he said nothing. The child of his Rajah had begun to frighten him.

Apparently Tamasrajasi understood this. She lowered her head and gazed at him from under her thick lashes. "You have given me much pleasure, Sudra Guristar, and you are sworn to my cause. You will be first in my favor when my father has gone. It will be you who will lead our men into battle, and it will be your arms I will lie in when the victory is ours."

It was so easy to believe the lie. Guristar had no wish to question these extravagant promises. Such avowals, coming from a man, he would regard with deep suspicion, but he knew that every woman was a slave to her passions, and accepted her words. When he had licked his fingers, he said to her, "I am almost your father's age, and in time you will desire a younger and more stalwart lover. When the time arrives that you take a consort, it will be fitting that you choose from among the sons of the Rajahs who have reason to feel as we do about the Sultan in Delhi. Then it will be best that you take the younger man. In the meantime, nothing will give me more delight than to know the joy of your touch and the secrets of your body."

"I have already been offered marriage with three Rajahs' sons and I have refused them all. My father will not force me to marry against my will, or contrary to the good of the country."

"Your opinions and his must be strangely divided," Guristar said lightly.

Tamasrajasi stared at him, and he felt the same disquiet he had earlier. "My father is still Rajah, and though he is weak and foolish and a tool of Shams-ud-din Iletmish, I will not hear him spoken against by you or anyone else at this court. To do so is dangerous. Let my father learn that you have made a common cause with me, and you will give your bones to the vultures, if you are fortunate. Let my father learn what you have done with me, and you will pay the full penalty for despoiling a noble virgin. And I will not speak on your behalf. I will watch you die as if you deserved it." She saw the arrogant expression Guristar had worn take on a comical terror. "It is more important that our country be free of the Sultan than that you and I spend more entrancing hours together, Sudra Guristar."

He croaked out a few words of agreement and huddled back in the cushions. "It must be the country that is first in our thoughts," he forced himself to say.

"And you must be willing to act on short notice, for when my father is gone, there are others who will try to seize our land, not the least of whom is the Sultan himself. They will all claim that because I am female I am incapable of ruling though my father has designated me heir until one of his sons should live to adulthood." She smiled easily. "That, naturally, must not happen. My brothers and half-brothers have not survived, nor are any of those unborn likely to survive."

Guristar looked at her, bemused. "You are not telling me that your brothers and half-brothers died . . . unnaturally."

"There is nothing unnatural in dying after consuming poison," Tamasrajasi said so nonchalantly that Guristar could not tell whether she was being serious.

"It's not wise to suggest such things," he admonished her nervously. "Jests of this sort are often misconstrued."

"I had not planned to discuss it," she said, somewhat bored now that her purpose was accomplished. She indicated the fruit on the tray. "You should have more."

"No, gracious Rani. I will have a meal soon with your father. He will remark on my poor appetite." It was time to get into his clothes again, though it was awkward to do so. He held up his tunic and saw the rent in it. "I will have to wear another." Secretly he was pleased that he had awakened such passion in the girl that she tore the clothes off him. He was forty years old, he reminded himself, and had caused a beautiful woman of seventeen to surrender to him completely.

Tamasrajasi guessed the nature of Guristar's thoughts as she studied his face. Let him think that he had mastered her: she knew who had won their encounter. All she need do was feign delirium and Guristar would do anything she demanded of him. She sighed. "Sudra Guristar, when will you come to me again?"

He turned toward her. "It cannot be at once, Rani. There are too many who might remark on it, and then we would be in great danger."

"True," she said, relieved that he was willing to let her have time to deal with the others she would need to put her plans in motion. "How soon do you think it would be wise?"

"Ten days?" It was longer than he wanted, and less time than was wise.

"So many days?" She filled her voice with disappointment. "Can't it be sooner?"

He could not disguise the pride he felt. "It's best to wait that long, Rani. It is not only our delights that concern me, but the men I must seek out before we can make more plans. By the time Dantinusha presides at the periyanadu, I will have found the key village leaders and spoken to them of the shame the Sultan visits upon us."

"The periyanadu will be held at the end of the rains, won't it?" She knew the answer, but thought it was wiser to conceal this. His response would indicate to her how much trust she could put in his information.

"Yes," he said. "There will be a festival at the end of it. There has been no proclamation yet, but the Rajah has confided in me"—he was clearly pleased by the confidence— "that he intends to have six full days of festivities after the periyanadu so that the village delegates will be inclined to think well of him and to be well-disposed to regular periyanadus."

"A festival lasting six days," she repeated thoughtfully. She had heard that there was to be a feast, but had not known how grand an event her father intended. "It may be to our advantage more than his. During a six-day festival, anything might happen."

Sudra Guristar was chilled by the tone of her voice. He tried to assume his swaggering manner, but it was not successful. "Anything? It sounds to me as if any action then would quickly turn chaotic. It's not sensible to take action then."

"Isn't it? Well, you are the commander of the guard, and I am only the Rajah's daughter, so I must defer to your knowledge." From her expression it was plain that she did not mean what she said. Sudra Guristar was not looking at her, and took her words as spoken.

"That will be best. I'll guide you, Rani, and we will have the vengeance that this country has been denied for so long. That's not to say that the periyanadu will be wasted. It won't. I have said that we will make progress with the village spokesmen, and we will. Let me act as I judge most discreet. We might yet be denounced by the men of the periyanadu if we do not go cautiously. Your father will be much approved for the festival. If I can make it seem that he spends his time in debauchery rather than tending to the affairs of Natha Suryarathas, every day of festival will bring men to our cause. The representatives of the Sultan will be at the festival, and I doubt it will be difficult to make it seem that they are encouraging the Rajah in luxury and excess in order to weaken him." The notion had not, in fact, occurred to him until he began to talk, and as he outined his plan, he decided that it was not only plausible, it could be very workable.

"How will you do this so that my father does not suspect you? In such a gathering, any duplicity might easily be brought to light." Tamasrajasi surprised Guristar by noticing the only real flaw in his idea.

"I . . ." He thought a moment, then said with enthusiasm, "I will not speak to criticize, but out of concern. I will say that my Rajah has always had my allegiance, which everyone knows is true, and that I am worried that the influences of Delhi have become so strong that Dantinusha has become slow to act on behalf of his subjects."

"Will any of the other officials agree with you?" She waited impatiently for him to answer.

"If I work very carefully, I think it is possible," he said when he had weighed the matter carefully. Now that he was truly embarked on a plan for rebellion, the light-headed anticipation had passed. He was aware of the dangers of the enterprise, and, belatedly, decided that it was unwise to join his interests to those of Tamasrajasi. He had no need of her. A girl was no ruler for a country on the verge of war. He would have to find a way to control her until her father was no longer Rajah, and then she could be dealt with. Tamasrajasi, in spite of her glorious body, was little more than a child.

"Remember that my father has already triumphed in one uprising. He is not entirely without courage." There was a trace of mockery in her eyes. "You may command the guard, but they have all sworn loyalty to the Rajah on the names of the gods."

"I will remind the soldiers that it is the gods themselves who have been most affronted by Dantinusha's conciliatory dealings with the Sultanate. If they honor their vows, then they must see the justice of rebellion." He stood and began to pull on his clothes, adjusting them as best he could. "When I dine with your father, I will try to learn what entertainments he plans for the festival. If he has any special celebrations in mind that would compliment Ab-she-lam Eidan, I will be certain that the guard hears of it, and see to it that they are properly outraged."

"And when the Rajah learns that it was you who told them of the event, what then?" She was drawing her nails over the silk again and the sound distracted Guristar.

"What then? I will see . . . I will see that the blame is placed elsewhere. There are a few soldiers in the guard who will . . . Rani, let me beg you to stop—the noise raises the hairs on my neck." He did not say this loudly, though he would have had great satisfaction in giving the girl a sharp order.

Tamasrajasi drew her nails over the cushion, quite deliberately, one last time, then folded her hands, waiting for him to continue.

"I was saying about the guard . . ."

". . . that there are a few soldiers who will or will not do a thing for you?" she suggested.

"Not precisely." He disliked her tendency to assume authority, and was more brusque with her. "There are those guards who will speak for me. I need only suggest a few things, and they, being hotheaded, and their honor smarting from the presence of the Sultan's representatives, will say all that is necessary."

"It is good to hear it." She rose and went to him, rubbing her opulent young body against his when she was close to him. "Ah, Sudra Guristar. How long the time will be, how slowly it will go. I will lie awake and think of your member like a staff, a pillar within me. I will dream of being bathed in your seed."

Guristar had heard amorous talk from his wives, but never anything as stimulating as this. Swiftly he clutched the girl tightly to him. "Hush, Rani, Shakti. I will not be able to leave you if you continue, and it is imperative that I go."

"I wish it were not so," she said in a small voice, turning her head so that she would look into his eyes. "Ten days will be a thousand years. I will wither and grow old and the flesh will fall from my bones in that time."

He was glad her need of him was great, and her impetuosity was very flattering. A woman who wanted so much of him would be subject to his will when it was necessary. "No, no, Rani. You will become like the peach, ripe and full of nectar, and I will desire you more than ever."

"If I were the daughter of a merchant or a farmer, I would have been married three years ago. I would have practiced all the arts I have been taught for so long. There are three years of passion I must reclaim." She lifted one leg and wrapped it around his thigh, drawing him closer.

"So you shall," he told her thickly, his vanity denying the alarm her words gave him. It was painful to release her, to refuse the bounty she offered him. "In ten days, Rani. If I remain here, we are in danger that I will be missed. It is not wise that anyone should seek me."

She lowered her leg and stepped back from him, pouting a little. "If, in the evening ten days from now, you have not come to me, I will seek you, and that will be dangerous." She nodded her dismissal and went back to the cushions where she had lain.

For a moment Guristar was tempted to remonstrate with her for this unseemly treatment, but he recalled that she was very young, and the only child of the Rajah. It was natural that she should have learned this unbecoming manner. In time he would teach her to give him his due respect. "In ten days I will be here, Rani." He favored her with a bow, then left the room. Next time, he thought, he would bring unguents so that she could anoint his body.

Tamasrajasi waited until she was certain that the commander of the guard was gone from her quarters; then she clapped again, and one of her slaves appeared. "Bring the cloths to clean me," she ordered, and waited in stillness until the young woman returned with two scarves of red silk. As Tamasrajasi spread her legs, the slave girl knelt and wiped what Guristar had left. When this was done, Tamasrajasi rose, beckoning the slave to follow her.

The room was in a remote part of Tamasrajasi's quarters. It was small and deliberately dark. At the far end of the room was a statue, in black stone, of a dancing woman. Tamasrajasi approached the statue reverently, chanting the ritual words as she held out the stained red silk in offering. Finally she put the cloths on the embers in a brass brazier standing before the statue. There was a brief stink in the air as the scrap of cloth flared, flamed, and was gone.

"Caress me!" Tamasrajasi ordered the slave without looking at the woman. She stood facing the statue, gazing at the rapacious face carved in the stone.

The slave performed her task impassively, having done it many times before. There was neither pleasure nor repugnance in the act. But Tamasrajasi abandoned herself to the ministrations of the slave. Her breath became deep, then harsh. Sweat shone on her flesh as the slave removed the sheer robe Dantinusha's daughter wore. When the slave woman crouched between her legs, Tamasrajasi had to steady herself, touching one lifted foot of the black statue. Her eyes were more feverish, her movements more frenetic than they had been when she had permitted Sudra Guristar access to her. That had been a convenience; this was an act of religious sacrifice.

For Kali was goddess of sexuality as well as destruction.

A letter to the Rajah Dantinusha from his sister, Padmiri.

To the favored of the gods and champion of the kingdom, the Rajah Dantinusha of Natha Suryarathas, most beautiful of lands.

Great Lord, my sincerest greetings.

It has been a considerable time since a messenger has come from you, and as you have not always trusted me, I confess that the sight of the man gave me a moment of fear. All of us are aware of the dangers visited upon this country, and it is not impossible that in order to secure the land, you would give orders that might otherwise be repugnant to you, and contrary to the laws you yourself have instigated. Yet I saw that my apprehension was in vain, and the scroll brought to me was the polite request that I receive a guest in my house. You tell me that the man is a foreigner, from the West, and not, I gather, a follower of Islam. The scroll says that this foreigner has but one servant and yet possesses the finest of jewels. By that alone, I will admit, my curiosity is piqued.

When our brothers and cousins rose against you and there was so much death that I feared I might never cease mourning, my decision to remove myself from all aspects of the court was comforting. I preferred to make myself an exile on my own terms than to risk banishment on yours. My life here goes peacefully. I see no one but scholars and teachers and occasional musicians. I am of an age when this no longer disappoints me. Had I been a young woman when the uprising occurred, I might have felt these privations, such as they are, more keenly.

I am saying this so that you will understand why I am willing to have this foreigner share my house. I have come to miss the company of others, but I don't think I can bear to be reminded of the losses we have all endured. While it is true I lost no husband or son—having none to lose—when the battles and executions were carried out, there was much that I had valued that was gone. So I will not take in my own kind. Your foreigner, though, is another matter. My days, though pleasant, are much the same, and I am as subject to boredom as anyone. It would please me to have the company of a man who is intelligent and well-traveled who might be persuaded to recount some of his travels to me, so that I will have a taste of what he has seen and done. I do not desire to speak to him of Natha Suryarathas or any of our relations. You may be certain that I will reveal no secrets—I know none, and there is nothing but grief in remembering what is past. I ask that you tell this man of my conditions, and if he is still inclined to share this house of mine, then he will be welcome.

When the rains have stopped, I will allow another wing to be built onto this house, but until then, it is useless to attempt alterations. I will allocate six rooms for his use and another two for his servant. This should be sufficient unless he plans to enlarge his household considerably. As the rooms are in an unused part of the house, it will be a day or two before my staff can put them in order. It will be inconvenient for him to arrive during the next two days, but after that, I will be pleased to see him when it most suits you and him.

Your offer to supply me with additional guards is doubtless well-intended, but I will refuse them. I am already filled with a sense of being in prison, and so it would not reassure me to have armed men here. My eunuchs are good fighters and have guarded me from worse things than two men far from home. Should I change my mind, I will send a messenger at once. A rider leaving here at midday will easily reach your palace before sunset, and I am sufficiently isolated that it would be difficult for anyone to flee this place before your guard could arrive here.

Tell your foreigner that I hope he will accept my hospitality. Until your message came I did not realize how eager I am for a little novelty in my life. My stipulations will not, I trust, prove too demanding. A man who has seen as much of the world as you claim this foreigner has will have more to talk about than treachery in a remote principality on the northern border of the Delhi Sultanate. It is for that and for your request that I will be pleased to have him here.

May the gods protect you now as they have before, and may your reign continue free from strife. Of all our family you and your daughter are the only ones left to me, and though I see you rarely, my affection and loyalty remain true and unchanging. I am pleased to be able to comply with your instructions, and will always be pleased to do so, as much as I am capable of doing.

Your sister,
Padmiri

PART III

Tamasrajasi
daughter of
Rajah Kare Dantinusha
of Natha Suryarathas

◄●►

A letter from the merchant Loramidi Chol to Saint-Germain.

Revered and honored guest of Rajah Dantinusha, and esteemed traveler, my most humble and respectful greetings.

It is with profound regret that I inform you I have not been able to learn of any ships that will take you down the river to the sea. Too many of those who trade on the river fear that the warriors of Jenghiz Khan who are harrying their way through Persia will next turn their mounts toward the Delhi Sultanate. For that reason, few will make the journey at all, and those that will, have no intention of going as far as the sea. Were it possible to do so much, yet no captain would accept a foreigner onto his vessel at this time. You must realize that they all believe every foreigner to be capable of spying for the Mongols, and my sources tell me that this rumor is more prevalent in the Islamic territories than it is here, farther upriver.

Let me assure you that I will continue to search out river captains to learn if any of them will take you. After the rains have stopped there may well be more traders on the river, even this far up the Chenab. At that time I may discover that there are trustworthy men who will take you with them on their return voyage. They will doubtless not wish to leave until very near the spring rains, as this may be the last opportunity they will have to trade here for some time. If it is true that the Mongols are planning to attack the lands of Shams-uddin Iletmish, there is much sense in what they do. Merchants, as you must know, are cautious men in their way, and because they gamble with their fortunes are reluctant to gamble with their lives. As I have told you, this is not a thing that can be arranged quickly. It is my

293

opinion that you will not be able to depart for at least two seasons.

In the other matters, however, there has been more achieved. The substances you have requested will be provided. Powder of cinnabar is not easily available, and it will be a while before I can deliver it to you. My agents in Delhi have found the azoth, fine carbon, and salts you have requested. They will be in your hands by the time the periyanadu convenes. It will take a bit longer for the woods you asked for to be brought, but I have been assured that they can be had. The question of Hungarian earth is another matter. A magus in Kanpur is reputed to have some, and word has been sent to him that it is required. You specified that the earth must come from the mountains of the Transylvanian region. It is not known if the Hungarian earth he has is from that region, but if it is, the offer you have authorized will be made. I am aware that you stressed alacrity in this instance, and I assure you that I am proceeding as quickly as I am able, but with the rains and these uncertain times, it is not always possible for me or my agents to procure all the materials desired by those who come to me, and to the rest of the travelling merchants.

I have in hand the gold you promised, and let me praise the high quality of the metal. Nothing has debased it, nothing has lightened it. How rare such gold is in these times.

In the hope that I may continue to be of service to you, now and in the future, and may the gods look with favor on all your endeavors,

Loramidi Chol
merchant
by the hand of the scribe Indukar

1

IN THE northern corner of the room the athanor was almost complete. Casks, sacks and boxes made islands and obstacles all over the floor as Rogerio busied himself with labeling, cataloging and storing all the supplies that had been delivered. He was inspecting one of the smaller boxes when he observed to Saint-Germain, "This box of salts is of very poor quality. Chol said it was the finest he could buy. What must the worst be like?"

"Can we purify it?" Saint-Germain inquired. He was busy with the Roman chest which had been stood by the wall farthest from the windows.

"Probably, but it is a nuisance." Rogerio marked the box and made a notation on the scroll he carried. "Do you think Chol will be able to supply you the earth you need?"

"I hope so," Saint-Germain said with feeling. "It's not just a question of the earth. What I have will last me for a while, and if there were a way to reach Shiraz, I would not be concerned. However, I think it will be wisest to hold two of the sacks in reserve. If we do get transportation downriver, I will need the earth." He finished making his adjustments in the chest, then tugged at the lock to be certain it was still firm.

"And for the other? Will you purchase a concubine?" Rogerio had set the scroll aside and was stacking the boxes he had cataloged.

Saint-Germain sighed. "I suppose I must, but I would rather not. When pleasure is bought, it is a superficial . . . nourishment." He fell silent, staring out the window at the enormous purple clouds that would soon empty rain over the mountains as fieldwomen emptied the great loads of grain from their aprons at the end of the day. The air was already thickening with damp. "I could lie quiescent on what little earth I have left. I would prefer not to."

Rogerio opened the largest of the sacks. "Carbon dust. This is superior."

"As it comes from Delhi, this isn't remarkable. The Muslims have practiced the Great Art for several hundred years, particularly the processes with metals. Their carbon dust ought to be superior."

"There are three vessels of azoth," Rogerio remarked.

"Good. I'll concentrate on jewels instead of gold. The results will be more reliable, I think." He picked his way across the room to the athanor. "This will be finished soon. Then I will see how it turns out rubies. If they do well enough, I'll make diamonds."

Rogerio was only half-listening. "Diamonds?"

Saint-Germain smiled wryly. "Diamonds. You have seen them before, I think. Most often they are clear, but a few have a tint to them." He laid one hand on the bricks of the incomplete athanor. "It will be good to practice the Great Art again. It's been too long."

"You had an athanor at the lamasery," Rogerio reminded him as he made another notation on his scroll.

"That was a paltry thing. Hardly worthy of the name. This is better. It will be able to be heated hot enough for the jewels." He spoke with a curious affection. "Music and alchemy," he said quietly, as if talking to the athanor. "Those two have sustained me." Then he gave a crack of unhappy laughter. "That is not entirely correct. I require other things for sustenance. Perhaps, philosophically, there is truth in it, but that is all."

The first drops of rain spattered into the room, and Saint-Germain moved quickly to close the shutters. Once the rain began to fall, it increased steadily, making a sound not unlike the sea.

"The rains are almost over, they say," Rogerio said, after looking up toward the ceiling once.

"If the weather holds true to pattern, that's correct." Suddenly he recalled another time, long ago, when he and Rogerio had been in Asia during the rains. "That temple on the Irrawaddy . . ."

Rogerio looked up, then grinned, which was rare in him. "Yes. There was almost no way to tell where the river ended and the land began. All the offerings were bobbing about in the eddies and the priests were on the shoulders of the idols shouting at the clouds."

This time Saint-Germain's laughter was genuine. "That child in the little boat, gathering up anything valuable that floated by him? He nearly capsized when he tried to haul that waterlogged bolt of silk on board." His face became more sober. "We were fortunate to have that barge. I would not want to be in such a flood now with only a few sacks of earth to protect me." Suddenly he shook his head. "I am becoming morbid about this. I suppose it is from disappointment. Not just that we have come so far and to so little purpose, but . . . I had thought that after China it would be a simple matter to reach Shiraz, and from there return in easy stages to my native land. It was unwise to assume we need only cover the distance and all would be well." He put his hand to the silver chain and pectoral hung around his neck. "What more must I lose?"

"My master," Rogerio said as he straightened up, "not

even you can live without mourning. Perhaps you mourn more than others do. You left horror behind you in China, and now you find that it is waiting ahead for you in Persia. While the others hear rumors of what the Mongol warriors do, you, and I, have seen it. And we may have to look upon their slaughter again."

"And it is different for you, old friend?" Saint-Germain asked lightly.

"I am not the same as you. My losses are not your losses."

"No," Saint-Germain agreed.

The silence between them was not awkward; they had known each other too long for that, but Rogerio could feel his master's self-imposed isolation become stronger. "What do you suppose a magus in Kanpur wants with earth from Hungary?" It was a safe-enough question, and one to which he truly wanted an answer.

"It's probably going to be used for spells to help the Muslims conquer Europe." He ran one small hand over the wall nearest him. The room had not been occupied in some time, and there were fine strands of spiderwebs holding dust under his fingers.

"Earth for spells?" Rogerio asked, rolling up his scroll for the moment.

"I'm guessing. He may require it for other reasons." He pulled his hand away and rubbed his fingertips and thumb together, testing the gritty residue from the walls. "The walls had best be scrubbed with vinegar water. Otherwise, who knows how much contamination we'll have to filter out of everything we do?"

"Why would earth aid spells?" Rogerio persisted, bending to move a number of the sacks he had cataloged into a tighter pile.

"I doubt the earth does aid it, but if the magus believes it does, it will be essential to him. You remember that sorcerer in Britain? He was a man about fifty, a fair healer and good with herbs." He saw Rogerio nod. "He had earth from all over the island, and before every campaign, he would perform certain rites that used the earth so that his leader would triumph. It may have helped. As I recall, they held that beleaguered kingdom together for more than fifteen years." Saint-Germain folded his arms. "Perhaps it's because I'm so far from home, and may not get back to it, that I spend so much time remembering."

Whatever Rogerio was about to reply was interrupted by the arrival of Bhatin, the eunuch who was the chief steward of the household. He was somewhat taller than Saint-Germain, with a clever face. His hair was clubbed at the back of his neck and he wore a sleeved linen tunic that almost reached his ankles. He favored Saint-Germain with a polite gesture of greeting.

"It is my honor to tell you that my mistress has come to see you." There was no indication, either from the inflection or the words he used, how he viewed this.

Saint-Germain had spoken to Padmiri, but had not yet seen her. As was proper, she had received him in a chamber divided by an ornamental screen. This departure from custom puzzled Saint-Germain.

"I have no screen here, and the room is as dark now as I may make it," he said to Bhatin, and noticed there was a subtle alteration in his attitude.

"She wishes to see you," the eunuch said in his high, clear voice. "Your servant and I will remain here." This was an order, and Rogerio bowed his acceptance.

There was a light, firm tread in the hall, and then Padmiri, sister of the Rajah Dantinusha, came into the room. Her eyes, clear as dark amber, found Saint-Germain at once, and she bent her head to him, as if she were meeting a distinguished teacher or scholar.

Saint-Germain returned her greeting. "Rani—" he began.

"No," she corrected him in a musical, low-pitched voice. "I have renounced all claim on that title. It has brought me little but sorrow." She met his eyes frankly. "So you are the foreigner I have admitted to my home. Welcome, foreigner."

"You are most gracious. Your introduction the other evening was more than I had expected or hoped for." She had told him then that he would be permitted to set up his workroom as he saw fit, that he could hire servants or purchase slaves and that so long as he paid for their maintenance, she would place no restrictions on him.

Her laughter was the sort that came only at the end of long suffering. There was a freedom in it; her laughter was for its own sake. "We are both aware of how remote this house is, and how little diversion I am able to offer you. When my brother informed me that you had much knowledge, learning and skills, it was too tempting to refuse him. You must think of this as a part of your home." From the fleeting pain in his face, she knew she had erred. "Perhaps not your home."

"Forgive me, Ra . . ." He stopped. "What shall I call you?"

"Padmiri." She ignored the admonitory hiss Bhatin gave her. "And you? What do I call you?"

"Saint-Germain will do." He turned toward the various piles and stacks littering the floor. "I would show you what I can produce here, but as you can see, I am not ready to begin."

"But you will permit me to come here, on occasion?" Her handsome face brightened as she asked.

"Naturally. It is your house." He had not intended to offend her, but he saw that he had.

"It is not my wish to be tolerated, Saint-Germain," she said stiffly. "If you would rather I do not come here, I will respect your wishes."

Saint-Germain made an impatient sound in his throat. "No, that was not my intention. You have the right to come here at any time and you have my invitation to do so. It was your kindness that has made it possible for me to be able to work." His formality reassured Bhatin but puzzled his mistress.

"Tell me, Saint-Germain, why would my brother make this request of me for you?" The iridescent silk of her gold-embroidered skirt was the color of carnelian, and the short, loose jacket she wore was a deep red-brown.

"I'm not exactly sure," he said after a moment, "but I think that the jewels he has bought from me had something to do with it."

"Jewels?" From the way she said it, she felt that her brother had been bribed.

Saint-Germain was quick to explain. "I believe he wants more of them. He hinted as much when he sent me here."

"And you have more jewels?" She seemed disappointed now, and raised her hand to signal Bhatin.

"I will have," he said without amusement.

She stared at him. "You *will* have? How?"

"Why, with this," he said, looking around the cluttered room. "I am an alchemist, Padmiri. There is more to alchemy than making gold for greedy Kings and better steel for warlike ones." He saw that he had recaptured her interest. "There is a secret to jewels. I am not speaking of counterfeit gems, but real ones. It's a tedious process, and most of those who practice the Great Art would rather make gold. There are more rewards in it. But there are many other achievements. There is a most effective remedy that begins with nothing more than moldy bread, which can be made relatively simply. There are pigments of rare luminosity that can be blended with certain powdered shells. The jewels are another such achievement."

Padmiri heard him out, tension in her face. "Does my brother know this?"

"He suspects it." He knew that his answers had disturbed her and wished to make amends. "I hadn't intended to send him reports, Padmiri."

"He will know of it, though. The household spies will tell him when you have made more jewels. Then he will seek you out again and will try to coerce you into doing more for him." She shook her head and stared blindly at the window shutters. "If he does not, one of the others will and it will all begin again!"

Rogerio cast Saint-Germain a worried look, but Saint-Germain motioned him to be still, and approached Padmiri gravely. "Would you rather I leave? I have no wish to repay your generosity with trouble."

She did not respond at once. "You don't know what it was like when our brothers and cousins rebelled. The streets were so filled with blood that sheep and cattle could not be driven across them. I think of my uncle, who was a kindly man, and had done nothing more than take his oldest son into his house during the rebellion. He was dragged out and put on a wheel and his hands and feet sheared away. Then he was sawn apart with ropes. This man was old! He was not part of ,the rebellion, except that his son participated. He insisted that he was loyal to my brother and supported the truce with Delhi. It was after that that I left the court. Never have I been so grateful that I had no husband or children. Doubtless they, and I, would have been taken to the execution ground as well." Her face was wet and there was a tremor in her voice, but she sighed and went on. "For one who insisted that you not discuss court life in any way, I have a poor opinion of my own strictures."

Saint-Germain came near her, his dark eyes—dark in a way hers were not—full on her face. He read old anguish there, and resignation that preferred this lonely life to further hurt. "Padmiri, this is not my country, but I know what it is to lose those of my blood. You may speak to me or not as you choose, of this or any other matter. Perhaps, because I am a stranger, you will find it easier to talk."

Padmiri wiped her face. "I don't know if I will do so, but I know that your offer is given in kindness."

"As was your offer to me," he said at once, touched by her candor and her dignity.

She said nothing, turning toward the door and motioning for Bhatin to follow her. When she was at the door, she turned back. "Saint-Germain, though my brother did not ask this of me, I would have been pleased to have you here. I trust you will not regret your decision to stay here; I am glad that you have come." With a polite lowering of her head, she was gone, and her eunuch closed the door behind them.

"An interesting woman," Rogerio said into the silence.

"Yes," Saint-Germain responded in a very neutral tone, and did not mention Padmiri again until two days later while he was setting the last of the bricks into place on the athanor. The storm had not passed, and there were one or two damp patches showing on the shutters as well as moisture on the floor. "Padmiri," Saint-Germain said as he tested the shutters with a long, thin knife for rot, "told me that these shutters are three years old. She's offered to replace them if they should require it."

"She's a generous hostess," Rogerio remarked. He was putting the last of the sacks and boxes into their places on the new shelving which he had installed the day before.

"The floor is all right," Saint-Germain went on. "I tested it yesterday. Though I think I might make up some of that sealant and apply it to the floor and walls: it will protect against stains as well as wet."

They both continued to work; when Rogerio finished his work, he drew up one of the two rough stools in the room, and, as he sat, said, "I gather from what the grooms were saying earlier today that there were messengers from the Rajah here last night."

"That's hardly surprising," Saint-Germain said as he painstakingly fitted one of the last three bricks into place. He spoke rather distantly, his concentration on his hands, not his words.

"Actually, from what they said, it *is* surprising. There is little communication between Dantinusha and his sister, apparently. That's been her choice. The servants know that regular reports are exchanged, but this was unusual." He bent over to tug the soft shoes he wore into a better fit. "Most of the servants attribute this to your presence."

"They may be right," Saint-Germain said, not truly listening.

A gust of wind rattled the shutters, making the wood shiver in the frames. Rogerio looked up sharply.

"I don't know how these people get used to these storms," he complained, but more with irritation than ill-usage. "Last night I thought the wind would lift off the roof."

"It did damage one of the walls of the slaves' quarters," Saint-Germain said, standing upright and looking away from the athanor.

"When was that?"

"Late last night, apparently. Two of the slaves were badly hurt when a beam fell. One of them died." He spoke quietly, icily. "From what Bhatin said this morning, he views the whole incident as inconvenient. Slaves are necessary to a household this size, and having two die unexpectedly upsets the order of the house."

"Did Bhatin wish your aid?" Rogerio straightened up.

"No. He is of the belief that if he aided these slaves, he would have karma with them in a later life, and he cannot bear the thought of having to deal with Untouchables. When he came to my room this morning, it was to deliver a message from Padmiri."

"Why does she send a message to you? Why not carry it herself or ask that you come to her?" Rogerio found many of the ways of Hindus difficult to understand, and despite two journeys through Hindu countries, had never learned to deal with the formalities or the customs.

"Apparently it is not fitting that she come to me, and requesting that I come to her is little better. She lives alone and has never married, and there are many restrictions on such women." He gave his manservant a tight smile. "Do they know that you understand them, the servants?"

Rogerio shrugged. "They know that I understand a little, but they think that if they speak quickly, I will not be able to follow what they say."

"That's a useful ruse," Saint-Germain approved. "Don't let them learn otherwise. We may have need of servants' gossip before we leave here."

One of the shutters banged open on a fierce gust of wind. Rain streamed into the room, spattering and darkening the floor. Rogerio moved quickly to secure it as Saint-Germain threw rough sacking onto the spreading pool. When the water had been mopped up and the shutter protected with a double twist of wire, Saint-Germain pulled the other stool away from the wall and straddled it.

"Padmiri is curious about what we do here, but I doubt she will intrude. I will invite her to visit here regularly, which will lessen the suspicions of the household a little." He stared, unseeing, at the opposite wall. "I wish I knew which of the servants were spies, and for whom."

"Is there any way to discover that?" Rogerio did not think that there was, but hoped that Saint-Germain might know a method to obtain that information.

"It might be done by accident. Spies are natural to a court, and it isn't impossible to find out who supplies information, at least trivial information. In a household such as this one, I don't know what must be done to unearth the spies. You're more apt to stumble on spies than I am, as the servants may be bolder around you." He put his hand to his forehead. "It's . . . disquieting to be here. This is a prison without bars. Very pleasant, certainly, but still a prison."

"Is that why the Rajah sent you here?" Rogerio got up from the stool and began to make measurements on the wall, using a length of knotted cord.

"I think so, in part. Though what his sister makes of this, I can't say. If she were younger than he is, he might be able to command her at will, but since she is older . . ."

"When will you speak with her again?" Rogerio began making notes on a narrow paper scroll. The numerals he used were Roman, though Saint-Germain had often pointed out that the Arabic system was faster, more adaptable and useful; Rogerio had learned his figures the Roman way and he preferred to continue to use them.

"Later today, I hope. It's awkward, because of our irregular position in society. From what Bhatin said this morning, no one is quite sure how you and I are to be treated. Bhatin delivered her message and I asked him to tell her that I could not reply as I would wish to the question, and told him that I hoped she would be willing to receive me so that we might discuss the matter. Bhatin is not convinced that I have any right to make that request, or that Padmiri should grant it, but I'm fairly sure he'll repeat what I said." He looked around the room. "I think we'll be able to do serious work fairly soon. If the weather changes, it will go more easily. It will take at least two days after the rains stop for the road to be passable to wagons. Once we get the next consignment from Chol, we will do well." His face lightened at the prospect of working again. He had missed the excitement of alchemy, the discipline and the discovery which had fascinated him for more years than he cared to count. His work and his music had sustained him—he had been without both for too long.

"Do you think he'll be able to get you the glass you need?" Rogerio had resumed making measurements, and was kneeling now, setting the knotted cord against the foot of the wall.

"Probably not, but if he will supply me the sands I've required, I will be able to blow my own utensils. I'd have to do that for the athanor vessels in any case." Then he added inconsequently, "I doubt if Chol can get white brass. I must be prepared to make that, as well."

Rogerio got to his feet. "I have taken two sacks of your earth and put them behind the others in this cabinet." He spoke in Latin, and very quickly, in the atrocious accent of the Ostia wharves that had not been heard in more than eight hundred years. "Of the rest, half is under your mattress, the other half in the false back of your Roman chest. I'm planning to move one of the sacks to the stables after you are given permission to have horses."

"Excellent," Saint-Germain said. "I have disposed of the portion I had in ways I think I had better not describe. You will be able to plead ignorance, if you must."

They had been through too much together for Rogerio to question the wisdom of this. He went back to his measuring, and stopped only when Bhatin entered the room.

The eunuch bowed to Saint-Germain, ignoring Rogerio entirely. "Esteemed guest of my most-favored mistress," he said in educated and poetic accents, "it is my privilege and honor to bring you a summons from Padmiri, sister of the Rajah Dantinusha, she who is known as Manas Sattva for her great devotion to learning and truth. It is the wish of this most-favored lady that you come to her reception room with me at this time so that it is possible for you to discuss the matters that are of interest to you both. It is the will of this most-favored lady that you be prepared to enlarge upon the earlier message that you sent through me, and which, in humble duty to this most-favored lady, I reported wholly and without alteration. Therefore, be good enough to ready yourself at once so that Padmiri, daughter of the Rajah Kare Dharmasval, sister of the Rajah Kare Dantinusha, may not be insulted by unseemly delay."

Saint-Germain was not familiar with the proper form of ritual courtesy, but he knew that his acknowledgment of Bhatin's address should be elegantly expressed. "Good eunuch, be assured that your summons on behalf of your mistress, the most-favored lady Padmiri, crowns my day with honor. Let me give my servant brief instruction so that he will not be idle while I avail myself of this unhoped-for opportunity." He turned to Rogerio, speaking now in Greek. "As you probably guessed, Padmiri wants to see me. If she grants my request for horses and a boat, we may yet find our way downriver, and from there, board a ship for Egypt or the port of Safwan."

Rogerio bowed deeply. "May it be so, and before the rains begin in the spring," he responded in Greek.

"There," Saint-Germain said to Bhatin, once again speaking in the high-caste manner he had learned long ago. "My servant has his instructions. I await only your guidance on how best to comport myself in the presence of your most-favored lady."

"It is fitting that you inquire, foreigner," Bhatin said unctuously. "It is not uncommon for strangers to be unbearably insulting to great ladies." He led the way to the door and started down the neglected hall, not looking to see whether or not Saint-Germain followed him.

As he fell into step behind the eunuch, Saint-Germain pondered the outcome of the interview ahead.

Text of a letter from the commander of the Rajah's guard, Sudra Guristar, to the village elder Damilha.

To Damilha, village elder, who will be delegate to the periyanadu of Natha Suryarathas forthcoming, the commander of the Rajah Dantinusha's guard is pleased to send his greetings and wishes for safe and swift travel.

Let me assure that all preparations for the great periyanadu are well in hand, and the occasion will certainly be a most fortuitous one for all of the country. I am filled with delight that a meeting of this nature should be held now, for I am confident that it will reveal once again how great the strength of our people can be and how puny the men from Delhi compared to our own. There are many who rely on you, Damilha, and those like you, to demonstrate that our might does not come from the whim of the Sultan Shams-ud-din Iletmish, but from our people, our gods and our blood.

It is with sorrow that I have observed, as have many others, the changing ways of some of those of high rank. They seek to placate the Sultan in the south and emulate his decadent ways, forgetting the land and the gods that are the glory of Natha Suryarathas. Such men, though often acting from goodwill, are, nonetheless, seduced by the promises and luxuries of the Sultanate, and they forget that it was not very many years ago that the land they tread now was ours, and the men they profess to despise ruled for ages in the place where they have spent so little time. Doubtless you will see evidence of this and it may pain you to realize that there are those who feel that this is the course of wisdom, and counsel delay, tolerance, and subservience rather than encouraging all those here to rise against the foreigners who oppress us.

When you speak at the periyanadu, it may be that you will mention your concerns, and it may be that others will discuss this with you when the gatherings are less official. At either time, in either place, it is well to remember that there are those who seek to curry favor with the men of the Sultan and will provoke you to speak rashly. Let me urge you to be circumspect in all things, for it would be most awkward for your Rajah to be faced with unpleasantness while the men of the Sultanate are his guests. Rather watch and evaluate for yourself. Then later, if it should seem to you that there is truly reason for concern, it might be wise to bring the whole question up at your local meetings, so that a true consensus may be achieved before any action or recommendations are undertaken.

How you must contemplate with joy the opportunity to bow before the gods and offer them the splendors of this great celebration which will follow the periyanadu. If there is a way to offer the gods recompense for the insults they have endured from the men of the Sultan, this must be the way. The Rajah has shown great perspicacity in this, for it is wholly appropriate that he should invoke the gods at such a time, and yet he has chosen to do it in such a way that the ambassador may not say to those in Delhi that Rajah Dantinusha has forgotten himself and offered us a challenge that will lead to war. Other, more hotheaded men might decide to attack the party of the ambassador, and it would not be badly thought of in many quarters. Yet Dantinusha sees beyond this, and for that reason it is well that we appear complacent, no matter how bitterly our hearts burn within us.

To you, and the men who will gather for the periyanadu, the gods smile upon your journey, and may your sacrifices be received with full acceptance and favor. The festival will be a tribute that any man may be proud to take part in, and may afterward boast that he participated in a most auspicious gathering.

> Sudra Guristar,
> Commander of the guard
> of Rajah Kare Dantinusha,
> the nineteenth year of his reign,
> third year since the defeat of the uprising,
> the forty-fourth year of his life

2

As Ab-she-lam Eidan approached the elevated dais where Rajah Kare Dantinusha sat in state, he and his party made low salaams to him, calling down the blessings of Allah upon him, though he was a Hindu infidel. The ambassador placed his foot on the bottom step, then knelt and bent in the full courtesy one Hindu Prince might give another. "From the Sultan Shams-ud-din Iletmish at Delhi, whom Allah protect and guide, to you, Great Lord, the most respectful and profound greetings."

Rajah Dantinusha had shaded his eyes against the sun, for the great open tent of striped silk faced the west and offered no protection now that it was midafternoon. "Rise, rise, Ab-she-lam Eidan, and come nearer so that a true greeting may be exchanged." He did not rise, as he might have for the Sultan himself, but waited until the ambassador had reached the top step. They kissed each other's cheeks and lips, and spat into the shade to ensure protection against the manipulations of demons.

"A glorious beginning to your festivities, Great Lord," Ab-she-lam Eidan assured the Rajah. "Surely my master, the Sultan, must count himself unfortunate to have missed this fine display."

"Surely so great a ruler as the Sultan has seen festivals of greater splendor and magnitude than this one, for the expanse of his kingdom is great, as my distant fathers knew, and the riches of the plains far exceed what we have here in the mountains. The entertainment we offer is poor in comparison to the magnificence of the Sultan, but it is given to delight the gods and bring favor upon us as well as to express the satisfaction in the completion of the periyanadu which has brought such pride to the country."

This was the signal for the Muslim ambassador to step down from the dais and rejoin his party, who clustered around the platform's base. He salaamed again, and made his way down the steps backward, going cautiously, and wishing that Rajah Dantinusha would grant him the favor of walking down the stairs facing to the front. As he reached the bottom step, the whole party bowed deeply, and turned away.

A great crashing of cymbals and beating of tuned drums got the attention of the crowd who had gathered for the festivities. The thumping and clashing effectively silenced all conversations, and the people on the small field faced toward the tall open tent of striped silk, their faces expectant.

Dantinusha had risen, holding his gem-inlaid silver elephant goad high. This symbol of his authority was recognized throughout Natha Suryarathas, and was regarded with awe by Dantinusha's subjects. At a gesture from the Rajah, Rialkot, his herald, came to stand beside him. Dantinusha turned to the burly man, saying quietly, "Commend them all for being here."

Rialkot placed his hand over his heart to indicate he would obey, and then his enormous voice boomed out over the field. "It is the wish of the Rajah Kare Dantinusha that each of you take deep and abiding satisfaction from your presence at these festivities.You may all know that you have been commended for attending, and for this reason, you are most favored by the Rajah and the gods." As he finished, the drums and gongs and cymbals set up a dreadful racket.

"Tell them that on this occasion I am going to present them with my heir, so that they will all know who it is, and will uphold the claim." He remembered the uprising as he said this, and knew that it was necessary to ensure there would not be another such insurrection.

"The Rajah Dantinusha," the herald announced, "wishes all here to share in his pleasure at the choice of his heir. The gods have given him forty-four years of life, and have been allies in his battles, and it is fitting that he show you, the world and the gods, his choice of succession. You are to have a distinguished favor today. Rajah Kare Dantinusha will present you his heir for your acclamation."

There was a mixed reaction to this revelation, and many of the elders who had attended the periyanadu looked toward the Muslims with open hostility even while they gave voice to their approval of this presentation.

"Remind them that I have no living sons," Dantinusha murmured to the herald.

"It has pleased the gods to send no long-living son to the Rajah. Surely this is the price they have exacted for their aid in dangerous times. Worthy is the Rajah who is willing to give up his sons in order to protect the country."

This was met with all sorts of hoots, cheers and cacophony from the drums and gongs.

"Remind them that I do have a grown daughter." Dantinusha was rubbing his lower lip, quite concerned now, for this was the greatest test he faced. The periyanadu had been minor in comparison. If the people, particularly the elders, were willing to support his heir, there would be no convenient civil war, no ruling gap that the Islamic generals might construe as an open invitation to seize power in Natha Suryarathas.

"The Rajah is fully mindful of the favors the gods have done him, and all here have seen evidence that he is much favored. Therefore he has taken great pride in as much of his family as are left to him after the predations of rebellious conflicts. He has a daughter, full in flower and of great reputed wit and beauty." The herald had to raise his huge voice even more toward the end to be heard over the buzz of sound that swarmed through the gathering.

"Remind them that I have not given her in marriage," the Rajah said quietly, watching the sudden movement in the various groups of people below him. It was an effort not to scowl. In other times, he thought, there would have been many sons and nephews to the Maharajahs of the kingdom, but those days had fled. Had this been such a time, he would not have hesitated to scowl, or to order Sibu, the executioner, to dispose of those who appeared to be talking disapproval.

"The Rajah, treasuring his daughter as a jewel beyond price, and knowing how fragile the chain of rule may be, has kept her near him rather than made her the wife of any of the Princes or sons of Princes in the lands bordering Natha Suryarathas. So fair and beloved is this daughter of Dantinusha that she is placed first in his heart and it is not possible for him to coerce her into taking a more subservient role than the one she has here." Rialkot, the herald, stopped to clear his throat.

"Tell them that it is my will that she be my heir until such time as she bear a son, who will then be Rajah." He folded his arms. wishing that the sun were not in his eyes. His head throbbed from it.

"Fully mindful of the obligations to his family and his country, it is the will of the Rajah that his daughter be recognized as his heir, to rule after him, until such time as she bring forth a son of her own to be your Rajah." He waited while the roar from the gathered festival-keepers began to subside, saying quietly to Dantinusha, "What more should I tell them, Great Lord?"

Rajah Dantinusha hunched his shoulders. "I'm not certain. Tell them that I will shortly present my daughter to them."

"They may not wish that," the herald warned him.

"Yes, I realize that," the Rajah said testily. "But I'd better do it now. There won't be another periyanadu for three years, and by that time, the Sultan might be more militant, or we might be driven by other concerns."

Rialkot coughed once; the forced volume was beginning to tell on him. As the gale of words began to abate, he raised his voice once more. "How blessed are all of you here! It is your excellent opportunity to see the cherished daughter of the Rajah Dantinusha before the sun sets today. Those who are here will see her, in her beauty and her skills, and will be able to tell the rest of the world how fully capable she is, and how dedicated to the country."

This time the drums, gongs and cymbals were joined by the clamor of bells. It was an awesome crescendo, drawing from the people an enthusiasm that neared frenzy.

Rajah Dantinusha turned away from the milling, shouting, surging crowd and descended the steps into the tent.

Tamasrajasi had been pacing the far end of the tent, her long, rolling stride like a tiger confined. She was magnificently attired in cloth-of-gold fashioned into a skirt and jacket. Earrings heavy with jewels brushed a collar of gold and polished stones. "Well?" she said as she saw her father come toward her.

"You can hear them, my child," Dantinusha said, indicating the hysterical outpourings that made it necessary for both of them to speak fairly loudly.

"Yes, I hear them, but that tells me nothing!" she snapped, then looked contrite. "I did not mean to say something so undutiful. It is my greatest pleasure to serve you, my father."

"I know." He smiled with pride. How many fathers, he asked himself, could regard their daughters with the same delight that they would a son? Since his male children had not lived, he was surely protected by the gods, who loved Tamasrajasi.

At that moment, Sudra Guristar came into the tent. He was resplendent in his most impressive ceremonial clothing. Hardly an inch of his silken garments were not embroidered elaborately. Beside him, the Rajah seemed almost plain, though he was dressed in cream-colored silk sewn with jewels. "Great Lord," he said at once, then turned and acknowledged Tamasrajasi.

"Is there trouble?" Dantinusha demanded, thinking suddenly how unprotected they were in this silken tent.

"No, no, no trouble." He nodded toward the guards who ood at the two entrances to the tent. "This is a most joyous occasion. And it is a pity that the men are not allowed to participate in the festival. There are other soldiers who are willing to take up their posts if you will give them permission to leave."

Rajah Dantinusha looked slightly shocked. "Were they supposed to stand here from midday until sunset? That's stupid, Guristar, and you of all men should know it. Keep a guard at such a duty and he will fail you. By all means bring your other soldiers and let these men celebrate." There was a time when the loss of a guard or two would have seemed minor, and a good example to the other men, but that was a profligacy that Rajah Dantinusha could not afford. He dismissed the irritation he felt as senseless.

Tamasrajasi glared at her father. "That's a mistake, my father. Let the soldiers know that they may be allowed liberties and you will find they have deserted you in your hour of need. Strap one of them to an elephant's foot and let the others watch what happens. Then they will stand guard over you night and day with loyalty, knowing that the elephant's foot waits for those who are lax." She turned toward Guristar. "Would you agree, Commander?"

"It is a wise precaution," he said, inwardly cursing the child for showing her claws so plainly. Her father might decide to chastise her, or provide her a husband before the change of power occurred. He reprimanded her. "At times such as these, it is best to be circumspect. There are enemies all around us."

"So there are," Tamasrajasi agreed, her eyes widening. "You are correct, Commander. It is a thing too easily forgotten."

Guristar smiled knowingly. "It is well that you, who must one day rule, should remember that." He enjoyed the respect she gave him, thinking that later in the night she would give him much more than that. He made obeisance to the Rajah.

"There are dancers arrived from the temple in Phutra. They are ready to begin once the field is cleared."

"Good, good. How many of them are there?" Dantinusha asked, glad to have some other matter in his thoughts,

"There are over twenty. They sent most of the sacred troupe. They are in the smaller pavilion now, and their musicians have already joined the drummers on their platform. If you will signal the beginning of the dancing, they are ready to perform." Guristar dared to look once at Tamasrajasi while he spoke to her father. He was aware that the dancing would last for some time, and could not deny that he would want to spend that time in lubricious dalliance with Tamasrajasi. It was not possible, and he accepted this. Perhaps later, when the festival was at its height and couples writhed together, then he might find the opportunity to embrace the Rajah's daughter again. He did not know what exhilarated him more—the prospect of plundering her flesh for pleasure, or asserting his control over her that would lead to his future power.

"If they are ready, it is as well that we begin now. At the end of their performance, Tamasrajasi will be presented to them, and they will see her as my heir." He was rubbing at his lower lip. "It might be well," he added after a moment of hesitation, "to tell Eidan to attend the presentation. It would look well if he could be seen here. Dispel some of the doubts that have been voiced at the periyanadu about the attitude of Islamic Delhi to our integrity."

The noise outside had degenerated to a kind of howl, though it rose from more than a thousand throats, and was composed of cheers, cries, shouts, and attempts at ordinary conversation.

"I will tell the dancers it is time," Guristar said, bowing deeply and leaving the enormous striped tent.

"Why do you defer to Eidan?" Tamasrajasi demanded as soon as the commander of the guard had left. "You are not a puppy to have to wag your tail to a master."

Her father did not answer her directly. "In the time of my grandfather, he made it a point never to answer a question that was put to him in less than ten days. If the matter still required his attention, then he would give his answer, and if not, he would abandon the issue. He had a Captain killed because he insisted on an answer in four days, which was not to be thought of. Those days have gone as the Wheel turns, and now I am flattered that they bother to ask me. I do not want it said of me that I provided the Sultan an excuse to ravage this country." He started toward he narrow stairs that led to the throne above them. "You think I am being foolish, my child, but there is wisdom in what I do. Where are the thousands of elephants, the millions of horses my great-grandfather took into battle? Where are the men-at-arms, the weapons, the slaves?"

"If you truly required them, the gods would give them to you," she said, her head raised commandingly.

"You did not see the executions after the uprising. It may be that you should have. I've lost my desire for slaughter, Tamasrajasi. There is more karma in battle than there is in finding peace."

She wanted to lash out at him as she would at a recalcitrant slave. "You are Rajah here. It is your right to demand the lives of those you rule. To do otherwise insults the gods and makes you less than the ant in the road to them. Yes!" Her eyes became brighter. "If your people cannot die in battle for you, you condemn them to the ignominious fate of losing their country and their gods, and offer them instead the sword of Islam to cut away their manhood and pride."

"Tell me that when you have seen battle, my daughter, and I will listen to you with respect. Until then, you must abide by my word. I want to hear no more of this from you. It's dangerous, for you create desires, expectations and discontent in others." He looked up toward the back of his throne. "They will be disappointed, those who hope for war. I've heard some talk, during the periyanadu that distressed me, my daughter."

"You mean it frightened you," Tamasrajasi countered, turning away from her father. "You say that to keep what little we have, we must placate the Sultan in Delhi. That's all any of your men ever hear from you, and it diminishes them."

"War would diminish them more." He spoke wearily, his face looking suddenly aged. "I used to wonder why my older sister was satisfied to live away from the court, but now I share her longing."

"That is the voice of your honor, which is filled with shame at what you have done." She came up to her father. "You will see how the men approve me. They will hail me with joy because I am not afraid of the forces of Islam, I will not bow to the Sultan, I will show them a stern face. The men will praise this." She paced away with that long, rolling, tiger's stride that caused many to follow her with hungry eyes.

"You will be presented and you will behave in a manner appropriate to your station, the occasion and your sex. Anything else, and I will instruct Guristar to return you to the palace under guard." Plainly he had reached the limits of his endurance. He was scowling fiercely as he trod up the steps to the throne from which he would watch the temple dancers perform their ancient, intricate movements. His fine garments felt heavy now and he had to blink rapidly to keep tears from his eyes. How could he make Tamasrajasi see that the course she found so exciting would bring destruction to what little was left of the great kingdom his great-great-grandfather had ruled?

The dancers had taken their place on the field and most of the crowd had withdrawn to the edge of the ceremonial ground. The air was fairly still now—an anticipatory hush welcomed the dancers as they stood in their gaudy, archaic costumes in the traditional postures.

Rajah Dantinusha sat down and tried to turn his attention to the music that began its sinuous tale. He had seen this dance a dozen times and usually was uplifted by the legend, which told of how Rama came to Shiva and planted the love of Parvati within him, so that he was torn from his ascetic life. It told of the union of Parvati and Shiva in their benevolent forms, then enacted the other faces of these two deities—as Shiva the Destroyer and Kali, Goddess of Destruction. From destruction came renewal, and the dance ended with the expression of fecundity as Shiva and Parvati embraced to renew the world.

This afternoon, Dantinusha could not keep his mind on the dance, or on the truth it taught. The steady beat of the drums, reminding the people that Shiva's dance on the Burning Ground was marked by the inexorable tempo of time, contributed to the ache that had been building up behind Rajah's eyes. As the dancers moved and postured below him, he wished he could leave the throne and return to his palace. It was not possible, of course, and should he do anything so foolish the restlessness that had been apparent at the periyanandu would burst into the open. He looked once for the Islamic party and saw Ab-she-lam Eidan deep in conversation with his aide, Jalal-im-al Zakatim, the youngest member of the Delhi mission. The young man was reputed to be a scholar, Dantinusha remembered, and had received various reports from noted Muslim teachers. The Rajah decided to send his poet Jaminya to visit this supposed scholar and discover if the man was what he had claimed to be.

There was a movement beside him, and Dantinusha turned to see his daughter on the high platform. Her eyes were downcast and the small crown she wore seemed suddenly inappropriate. "My father," she said in an undervoice, "I am grieved to have offended you. It is only my love of Natha Suryarathas that led me to speak in such an inappropriate manner. I know that I am too young to have found wisdom, but I offer sacrifice to the gods so that their wisdom will keep me from the follies of youth."

It was a pretty speech, Dantinusha thought, and obviously rehearsed. He wondered how long she had sat in the tent by herself putting those apologetic phrases together. He smiled at her. "You are son and daughter to me, my child. You are the one who will be left with the burden of this country in your hands when I have gone from the world. Your dedication is most praiseworthy, and I know that in time you will learn judgment. Your sacrifices will bring your desired ends," he assured her as an afterthought. "Come. Take the cushion beside me and watch the dancers. It is rare that we are privileged to see them, and there is great truth in their art." He leaned back in his throne, attempting to let the presence of his daughter put an end to the doubts that jumbled his thoughts.

On the far side of the field, Ab-she-lam Eidan pointed to the second figure on the dais. "That's the one you will have to deal with, and I thank Allah's compassion that you, and not I, will be here when she reins."

Jalal-im-al Zakatim stared at the girl. "A beautiful creature," he said quietly.

"Beautiful, and if one is to believe the tales about her, she is as dangerous as the cobra. They say that she worships the demon Kali and is encouraging the men of her country to rebel against the Sultan, whom Allah protect." He turned away from the dais, adding in a whisper, "There are slaves around her who cannot be bought, so terrified are they of her wrath."

"Are they afraid, or merely devoted? A girl so lovely—it would be a pleasure to make a woman of her," Jalal-im-al said wistfully.

"There are tales the slaves tell of slaves whipped to death in offering to the goddess Tamasrajasi adores." There was a note of skepticism in his voice now. "I will make allowances for jealousy and intrigue, since it is certain that her father would not allow her to practice such excesses. He is drawn more than ever to the contemplative life, which is to our advantage. We must do what we can to foster it."

Jalal-im-al did not quite laugh, as that would be poor manners, but he did grin fleetingly. He was, though he did not know it, slightly tipsy. The honeyed fruit juice he had been drinking from a gourd most of the afternoon was slightly fermented and had gone to his head in a subtle, exhilarating way. "Surely the Sultan can find a teacher who would make himself useful, say, by instructing the Rajah in the virtues of submission."

Ab-she-lam Eidan frowned at Jalal-im-al. "This is nothing to play with, young man. If our mission is handled skillfully, this principality will be under the rule of the Sultan before Tamasrajasi's first son is circumcised."

"Why not offer her one of the Sultan's—whom Allah grant many blessings—sons? It seems the simplest way." He looked again at the girl on the dais, and for an instant he was chilled. As a true Muslim, he told himself sternly, he had put away all superstition and placed his trust in the Will of Allah. But at that moment, whether it was the alcohol fumes in his head or something more, he trembled inwardly on this warm, bronze afternoon.

"That is too obvious. An infant, an idiot, would see through such a ploy. There is no way that the Sultan could more quickly alienate all the favor of the Rajah. It must be done otherwise. There are sons of Princes who lean toward Delhi for guidance now. Let one of them make Tamasrajasi his first wife and then you will see how things will change." Ab-she-lam Eidan directed his attention to the dancers on the field, who were reenacting the coupling of Parvati and Shiva when they caused mountains to move with the violence of their lovemaking. "Wanton people," he muttered.

"I've been told that those living in the east are far more lascivious." He was not able to show the severe disapproval that his superior demanded, and for that reason he added, "It is said that such women, schooled as they are in pleasure, make superb concubines, for they are raised with men, not kept in isolation as virtuous women are."

Ab-she-lam nodded toward the dais. "You need not look to the east to find wantons. Tamasrajasi is one such, or I have learned nothing in my life." He started to walk away, but added a last instruction to the younger man. "Those at Delhi who sent you here have said that they wish that you, with your scholarship, find a way to talk with the sister of the Rajah, and win her favorable opinion. She is known for her learning, as you know."

"Her favorable opinion? She lives half a day from the palace. How will I reach her?" Jalal-im-al protested, starting after Ab-she-lam.

"That is not my concern. This is your task and you must do as you think wisest." He stopped. "That foreigner who was sent to her—he may be one path to the woman. You must ingratiate yourself with her, so that when Rajah Dantinusha is dead, she will speak on our behalf and the continuation of the truce."

Jalal-im-al felt a tremor of alarm through his giddiness "Ingratiate myself? The woman is fifty-two years old. How am I to ingratiate myself with such a creature?"

This time there was no response from Ab-she-lam, who quickly vanished into the crowd. Jalal-im-al tried at first to follow the ambassador, then glared petulantly toward the dancers on the field, who were now beginning the portion of the performance that described the powers of destruction and Shiva on the Burning Ground.

A message from a spy in the household of Padmiri to Tamasrajasi, daughter of Rajah Dantinusha.

Revered mistress and favored child of the gods, humbly I seek to fulfill the task that you have set for me, so that the great time will hasten when the yoke of the unbelieving men of Delhi will be taken from us and the former glory of this country will be restored in greater splendor than before.

The sister of your father has continued in the same course she has taken for three years. She lives retired from the world, as you have been told many times before. She has received a few scholars and two traveling musicians since the rains have ceased. There was nothing remarkable about any of them, and the time she spent with them was much the same as she has given to others who were similar. She has shown no interest in the teachings of Islam, though she has three times in the past spoken with scholars of that erroneous creed. No person of military caste has visited her except for the Commander of the guard, Sudra Guristar, who comes regularly to see her servants here, inspect their weapons and be sure that Padmiri is properly guarded.

Your concern about the foreigner whom your father ordered here would seem to have little foundation. For the most part the man stays in his quarters and lives quietly, spending the greatest part of his time in the room he has filled with his alchemical apparatus. No one has anything to say about him, except that his servant knows so little of the language that it is difficult to get him to understand the most basic instructions. The master, as you know, has our tongue and several others, which greatly pleases Padmiri. She has said that she would like to learn more of the languages of the West, but no arrangements have been made. As you may perceive, a woman of your aunt's age is no longer prey to the demons of the flesh, and her way of life does not lend itself to the conduct that you feared. Be at ease, great lady—you stand in no danger here.

The guards are, as always, capable men, careful of their reputations and devoted to the Rajah and the preservation of Natha Suryarathas, and none of them have behaved in any manner that would make me or any other doubt this.

What devotions to the gods Padmiri undertakes are performed, for the most part, in private. She makes formal sacrifices at the various feasts, and insists that those in her household who are not slaves do the same, which is what one would expect of the Rajah's older sis-

ter. She keeps a shrine to Ganesh, which is to be expected of a scholar, of course, and there are those to
numerous minor gods and goddesses, but she is not
single-minded in her devotions. She has shown no particular favor to any of the deities you were curious about.
Other than that, I have noticed that her reading material
is not limited to one sect or period of writing. What she
may read in private is impossible to determine, at least
for one in my position, and I fear I will arouse undue
suspicion if I ask too many questions regarding her reading. Be assured that should I learn anything of interest I
will inform you at once through the kind offices of the
grain merchant who brings this to you now.

As you see, it is much as it has been for the last three
years. Padmiri does not wish to see any more of her
family harmed, and she, herself, does not wish to stand
in harm's way. You have nothing to fear from this
woman, even from her womb, as she has passed the time
when she might bear children who could challenge you
or your heirs for the right to rule here.

Ever in your service and the service of the gods who
will bring to an end this humiliation we have all endured
too long.

Your friend

3

AFTER SUNSET the air became cool and the breeze over the
fields was not oppressive. Padmiri stood on the terrace beyond her reception room and looked up at the sky as dusk
deepened around her. The silken robe she wore was perhaps
a little too thin, for she shivered once as she glanced back
toward the extensive bulk of her home. She could see the
slaves working in the reception room, lighting the oil lamps
and setting out low tables and cushions.

She was not being entirely wise, she told herself for the
ninth or tenth time. Again she offered this sop to her doubts:
you are too old to bear children, and there is no question of
a permanent liaison, should the man be interested in you at
all. That was the most daunting prospect of the coming evening—that he might not wish to do more than enjoy the

friendly conversation she had proposed to him. It was strange that after so many years she would feel herself responding like an inexperienced girl, and to a man who was a complete enigma to her. She drew her shawl around her shoulders, delaying as long as possible the moment when she would return to her reception room and take her place on the cushions. She put one hand to her face, and felt the lines under her fingers. Lacking vanity, she knew that now, at fifty-two, she was a more attractive woman than she had been at twenty. Then her strong features had seemed too overwhelming for her youth, too emphatic. With age, she had grown into them, and now there was a majesty to her face that was not a question of caste or rank. There were wraiths of white in her heavy black hair, and lines beside her mouth, underscoring her eyes, tracing the width of her forehead. She dropped her hand to her side, thinking that it had been a mistake not to wear her jewels.

"Padmiri?" He had come into the reception room and she had not noticed, so lost in thought had she been. Now he stood in the door to the terrace, a sturdy figure in a strange garment of black.

"Saint-Germain?" She felt a quiver run through her and she chided herself for being silly. "I wanted to let the slaves work in peace so I stepped out here."

"They've finished," he said, not moving from the door. "Would you prefer to stay on the terrace?"

"No," she said quickly, trying to master her confusion. "It isn't . . . appropriate." She came toward the door, feeling as if she were moving through water. It was difficult to look at him. He stood aside for her, and she hesitated, unfamiliar with this courtesy he had learned in Rome, more than a thousand years before. "Please," he said, with a gesture to indicate she should precede him. He did not remind her to cross the threshold on the right foot as he would have done for a Roman; that superstition did not exist here.

Padmiri smiled tentatively, going slowly through the door as if she was entering a room she had never seen. All of it seemed new—the lamps, the rosewood-and-alabaster inlay on the walls, the carpet which showed its brilliant colors here and there, but for the most part was muted by the night.

"The cushions there were set out for you," she said, pointing out the smaller of the two piles. A number of oil lamps hung around it, their little snouts of pale yellow flame like minute shards of sunlight. More lamps were hung behind the ornamented, filigreed screen and cast patterned shadows through the room. She wished the reception chamber were brighter so that she might see his face more clearly, but oil lamps were a luxury, and those that were lit now were almost twice the number she usually burned in the evening.

Saint-Germain took his place, reclining on the cushions with practiced ease. He had noted the lamps and the enticing scent of sandalwood when he had come into the room, and his fine brows had lifted in surprise. He had been aware that Padmiri had intended this to be a formal occasion and he had assumed that there would be others joining them. For that reason, if no other, he had dressed with care in garments he had not put on since he had left Lo-Yang. It was ironic, he thought, that these should be the only truly elegant clothes he had left. He wore his black Byzantine dalmatica over a knee-length red shengo go. Black silken trousers of Persian cut were tucked into his only remaining pair of high Chinese boots. Though he did not have his silver belt any longer, he had put his silver pectoral on the heavy silver chain around his neck and knew that his appearance was acceptable for this evening, and for similar evenings from Normandy to Pei-King.

"You refused my invitation to take a meal with me," Padmiri said as she arranged the cushions under her for her greater comfort. "I am curious why."

"It was not intended to slight you, Padmiri." He admired her directness as much as he respected her independence, and he knew that for those two qualities she had had more than the usual difficulties in her life.

"I thought that perhaps it was not permitted for women and men to dine together among your people. I have heard that such restrictions are not unknown in Islamic countries."

"I am not a follower of Islam," he reminded her without rancor.

"Yet you may have similar traditions." She had not intended to be diffident, but she had no arts to conceal her intent.

He looked at her sharply. "Not precisely."

She made no argument, though she wanted very much to ask him to explain himself. In time she might learn what he had meant, she thought. For the moment, she was more pleased than she had thought possible to learn that he had not meant he was offended when he had refused her invitation. "You have been quite willing to live with our customs. I've noticed that."

"How do you know that they are not my own?" He stretched his legs out before him and crossed them above the ankles.

"My servants have told me that you make inquiries through your man, Rogerio. He claims to be inexpert in our language, but from what you do, I assume that he is more fluent than those in the servants' quarters know." There was a tray of sweetmeats beside her on the table but she did not touch them.

"You are most astute," Saint-Germain said dryly. "I hope that you will not give Rogerio away. His feigned ignorance has aided both of us a great deal."

Padmiri stifled her burst of pride. "I did not intend to gossip with my servants."

To her amazement, Saint-Germain laughed softly. "Of course you gossip with your servants. Any sensible person does. You doubtless have another name for it, but you are intelligent enough to know that servants know more than all the wise men in the land."

Her expression softened. How good it was to entertain someone who did not insist on all the petty deceptions of the upper castes. This man, foreigner that he was, understood far better than most men she had met how necessary it was to listen to servants. "Yes, I do have another name for it. And it is true that I ask for specific information from my servants," she went on in a rush of candor, trusting that she would not overstep the bounds of what was proper to her guest.

He said no more, and for a little time their silence was not uncomfortable. Gradually, however, Padmiri began to feel the strength of his presence and stiffened under his remote scrutiny.

"It is not usual for women to have men as their guests," she remarked, finding it suddenly very difficult to explain herself to her companion. "Yet it is not impossible or wholly inappropriate. Here, living retired as I do, I often take my meals with those who have honored me with their company." But not, she added to herself, alone at night, in a room smelling of sandalwood. "You may think that this is remarkable, but I assure you there are few who would be affronted to see you and me as we are at this moment."

"Are you certain?" He knew otherwise, but offered her no more challenge than this.

"Naturally," she said, evading his question, "if you and I were of less mature years, it would not be wise, but given the circumstances, there can be no objection."

Saint-Germain said nothing, but his compelling eyes never left hers.

"You have been here more than a month, and I have been most remiss in my duties toward you. I have felt you might be insulted." She had a moment's desire to send him away from her and end this useless talk, but she plunged on, heedless of the caution that had risen in her mind. "This house is not like my brother's court; I am not constrained as he is to observe strict rituals. Protocol has no importance here."

"I have not felt insulted, Padmiri." His voice was low and filled with compassion. "You have been a haven to me."

She was so startled by this that she could not think of any reasonable remark. She saw her hands close in her lap and watched them as if they were wholly unknown objects she had never before encountered. "I am most pleased to hear of it," she said finally, finding that traditional response wholly inadequate.

"I hope you will feel that way when I leave here," he said, and the sadness in his tone made her throat close with pity.

"Why should I think otherwise?" She did not want him to leave, no matter how awkward she might feel. No one she had known before had treated her in this way, without subservience or superiority.

"That is rather difficult to explain," Saint-Germain said lightly, sardonically. He hoped that she would not insist because he did not want to leave this house, not only because it was a welcome and necessary respite from his travels, but because he genuinely liked Padmiri.

"I hope that someday you will," she responded, matching her attitude to his. She knew it was her right to order him to tell her anything she wished to know, but she could not bring herself to do this. She smoothed one silken sleeve. "Saint-Germain, who are you?"

"How do you mean?" He was very much on guard now, though his demeanor did not change.

"I mean what I ask. You are a Westerner, an alchemist, obviously educated, obviously traveled. Even here in Natha

Suryarathas we hear rumors now and again. Kings are deposed and imprisoned, countries rise and fall, borders change. It is much the same here. Has your country fallen to an enemy? Of a friend?" She could recall the rebellion here three years before and hoped that this man had not lost so much.

"My country has fallen," he said truthfully, "but that is not why I travel." He knew that he could give her a few convenient lies and she would accept them; he could be very convincing. But he did not want to deceive this woman who had provided him with safety.

"Very well, Saint-Germain. I will not prod you." The nervousness she had felt earlier was fading as they spoke. She no longer felt that she ought to bring their conversation to an end.

"Do you know, Padmiri," he said with a rueful smile, "I don't wish to be provoking. In all candor, I will say that when your brother suggested I come here, I was not very pleased, but I knew it was wisest to do as he ordered. You've been generous to the point of indulgence and I am grateful. That's not why I accepted your invitation this evening."

Padmiri had learned to put little trust in gratitude and so she said, "This was curiosity, or amusement?"

"No."

Her honey-colored skin grew rosy and she felt both absurd and excited. It had been years since anyone had stirred her this way and she was relieved that there was so much life left in her. "What was it, then?"

"Affection." He looked through the light and shadows to her eyes again. "If I wished to express gratitude, I would give you a jewel or a book and that would be the end of it. Your company, however is another matter."

"I've had four lovers in my life," she said as if she were discussing a question of literary style or an obscure line of poetry. "It's one of the few advantages of being unmarried and of my rank. My brother has not disapproved as long as I have selected those lovers from among musicians and poets. Those who aspire to military and political power he will not tolerate. There was one such man, and they say he was killed by Thuggi, though I doubt it."

"I am no poet, but I know music and love it," he said quietly. "I give you my word that I have no interest in attaining political or military power." He had had both in the past and found that there was more risk in them than advantage.

Though she had wanted him to say something of this nature to her, she was so startled that she blurted out, "I am not a young woman."

"I am not a young man," Saint-Germain responded calmly, thinking that after all the years he had walked the earth, young and old were trivial words to him: with thirty centuries behind him, the difference between age fifteen and fifty was hardly significant.

"No, but I think you are younger than I am." This was disastrous, she told herself. He would become disgusted with her if she said more.

The desolation in his face surprised her. "I am . . . somewhat older than I appear." His next question was asked with gentle sincerity. "Are you curious about my age, Padmiri? Or is there something else you want of me?"

Had she been younger and less conscious of her dignity, she would have fled from the room. It had been going so well, and now she was on the verge of panic. In the names of all the gods, what was it about this man that affected her so? She looked away in confusion.

"If all this—the beautiful lights, the deep shadows, the scent of sandalwood—is to tempt me, I'm flattered, but it is not necessary." He rose quickly, fluidly. "Believe this."

She knew that if she were truly frightened, she had only to call out and Bhatin would come to her aid. She was in no danger whatsoever. Her breath quickened as Saint-Germain crossed the room toward her. "You are too . . ." Her voice stopped.

"You may tell me to go and I will," he said softly. He was close enough that she could reach out and touch him, but she was still. The shadows from the filigree screen masked his expression.

She hesitated and he took a step backward. "I don't know," she murmured.

"I have misunderstood you, I fear." He was polite, and she felt this made it worse. "Will you forget my importunity?"

"No," she said, a bit more loudly than she had spoken before. "I have not been importuned."

Saint-Germain did not move. "Well, Padmiri?"

She looked up at him. "My mother died with eight other wives on my father's funeral pyre, and I thought it was a terrible waste. She was a sensible woman. She studied the Vedas and made regular sacrifices to the gods. She lived as my father wanted her to and died as he wished. I promised myself that I would not put myself in a similar position. My uncles were horrified, but my brother made no argument. Dantinusha once admitted that it helped to have an unmarried sister when he bargained with neighboring Princes. After a while, when I still had no husband, I left the court, for I was becoming an embarrassment. I had taken one lover while I lived with my brother and he was most distraught. He threatened to banish the man, or have him castrated. When my brothers and cousins rebelled, they tried to convince me to take their part, and I refused." This came out quietly, as much of her anguish had faded to a remote ache which she could bear. "I have my studies and my music, which are more than I had hoped to have."

"Ah, Padmiri," Saint-Germain said as he reached out his hand to touch her hair.

"My mother schooled me well, and my uncles often asked how I came to be so undutiful a daughter. I don't know." She turned her face up to him. "I don't know."

He went down on his knee beside her. "What benefit would there be in doing as your mother had done?" With swift, easy motions he smoothed her hair back from her face. "Long, long ago in Egypt it was the custom for men to be buried with their slaves so that there would be servants for them in the afterworld. Ages later many of these tombs were rifled and looted, the skeletons and mummies of the slaves thrown away or taken and ground up as medicine. What did that do to the men they were supposed to serve? How did the death of your mother lessen that of your father?"

"I have spoken with many great teachers and they have told me that though I have achieved some competence as a scholar, I have betrayed myself for refusing to live as virtuously as women of my caste ought." She liked the way he touched her. It had been a long time since a man had brought her such a feeling of newness. Surely, she thought, he feels the lines of my face, and yet he is as patient and gentle as a wise man is with a bride.

Saint-Germain leaned back against her cushions. "An easy thing for them to say. They did not have to face a burning pyre." He put his hand on her shoulder. "Come. Lie beside me. If I offend or disappoint you, tell me."

"Why?" A vestige of reluctance held her back.

"So that I may give you pleasure," he answered.

"No—why should you do this?"

He met her eyes. "You ask, when your own holy books have complicated instruction in gratification?" He saw her make a slight movement that was almost indiscernible. "You have done such worship, haven't you?"

"Not for some time," she said in an oddly muffled voice. "I am unmarried and there are certain matters . . ." She dropped back against the cushions. "I am being an old woman. I am afraid of what you offer."

"You don't know what I offer." His voice was less beautiful, and the sorrow was back in his face.

"You are a man." She sighed as the illusion of newness left her.

"Not quite as other men. You wished to know why I wish to give you pleasure. Very well. My pleasure, my *only* pleasure is in your pleasure." He waited while she considered what she had heard. "If you do not wish to have that pleasure, then send me away."

"And you? Is pleasure all you require of me?" She looked at the shadows on the ceiling, which wavered as a finger of wind passed over the oil lamps.

"Not quite all," he admitted. He rose, bending over her as he took her face in his hands. "Padmiri, yes, I will take something from you. But only when you are fulfilled."

She did not entirely believe that this was happening to her. It was too much like a dream or a memory. Neither of her last two lovers had been so persuasive, so determined. She had thought at the time that they had been mature in their dealings, free of pretense. Now she thought that she had forgotten too much. "It's been some time since I've experienced that. I don't know if it is possible in someone my age. But, Saint-Germain, I would like so much to know that satisfaction again."

He smiled, his dark eyes warm. "Then let me try, Padmiri."

She had learned from her other lovers that this was the moment to put her hands behind his neck and draw him down to her. She had almost made a ritual of this over the years. She hesitated, and then lowered her arms.

"Padmiri?" Saint-Germain said without alarm.

"I've done that too many times before. I do it without thinking, or feeling; it's a habit." She closed her eyes, her mind unwilling to stop making comparisons. When was the last time she had made love in this room? Which of her lovers had preferred this place, or any place but her bed? She felt rather than saw Saint-Germain's small hand smooth the frown from her forehead.

"You haven't let go," he said, sinking onto the cushions beside her and propping himself on his elbow.

"I . . . I know that." She rubbed her temples.

"Don't be concerned, Padmiri. Despite what your erotic scriptures say, there is no prescribed course this must take. For the time being, we can talk, you and I, and when you would like, there will be more we can do." He put his arm across her, just below her breasts.

"Why don't you go ahead and do as you must?" Her resignation was a disappointment. She had hoped to sustain that new feeling for a little longer, or to be able to recapture it.

"I've told you, that's not possible, or practical." He rolled a little nearer, and his hand slid down to the rise of her hip, there was no urgency in his movements; when he was comfortable he lay still.

"Have you been disappointed with women before?" she asked some while later.

"Often. And they in me." He cast his mind back to the concubine he had had in Lo-Yang, so lovely and so passive. He would have preferred outright refusal and rejection from her in place of that gelid acquiescence.

"You have had many lovers?" She was fairly certain that he had. If what he had told her of himself was true, there would have been many women in his life.

"Yes." There was neither guilt nor boast in the word.

"Men as well as women?" There had been a time when she had had a Bengali slave who had claimed to love her and had performed a number of unexpected acts on Padmiri's body, but that was some time ago, and no other woman she had met had awakened similar longings in her.

"Yes."

"Why?" It was a question she had always wanted to ask and had never dared to.

"These thing happen, Padmiri." He bent unhurriedly and kissed the tail of her eye. Then, very slowly, he opened the fastenings of her silken robe.

Her eyes were almost closed, and she shivered as his hand brushed her shoulders. Let it go, let it go, she told herself, and discovered that this time it was easier. She wished that her body were firmer and more opulent, but Saint-Germain made no complaint. His hands came down to her breasts. Skillfully, fondly, he caressed her, never rushing, never demanding. "Not, not there. Not yet." She was startled to hear how husky her voice was. He began to kiss her, now on the mouth, now on the eyes, on the shoulder, the breast, the thigh, the throat.

Padmiri had not been shaken by passion in several years and had thought that she had lost the capacity for such excitement. Yet when Saint-Germain had parted her thighs to touch her in glorious, subtle ways, she felt the first joyous tremor pass through her, and it seemed to her that there was a greater intensity than she had ever known. Her arms were around him and she tangled one hand in his loose curls so that when he pressed his lips to her neck as the wonderful, shattering spasms shook her, she felt her own fulfillment echoed in him.

It was so good to know that she was not beyond this sensual triumph! Padmiri released him at last, giving his ear an affectionate tweak as she began to laugh.

◄◆►

A letter from Jalal-im-al Zakatim to the Sultan's adviser in Delhi.

> To Musfa Qiral from Jalal-im-al Zakatim. May Allah smile on you, give you his protection and blessings.
>
> I have not long to write this, and so must use unseemly haste. First, I wish to report that the fears for Ab-she-lam Eidan are groundless. He has not in any way that I can discern compromised our position here in Natha Suryarathas. He has carried out his duties and instructions with care and tact and has won a degree of confidence from the Rajah Kare Dantinusha that is quite remarkable, given the circumstances here.
>
> Second, I wish to say that it is not likely that Rajah Dantinusha will take arms to oppose us. There are those

in his principality who are speaking in favor of such action, but he has resisted all such efforts and doubtless will continue to do so, for which Allah be thanked.

Third, it is quite true that the Rajah is completely serious about making his daughter, Tamasrajasi, his heir. He has presented her to his subjects and they have hailed her with great enthusiasm and pleasure, and as the Rajah has no living sons, his edict that her firstborn son will inherit from her has been acclaimed as wise and honorable. There has been no public mention of who it is who is to father this son on Tamasrajasi, but that, I suppose, will be taken care of before too much time has gone by. With so much support from the people, Dantinusha has much to offer any Prince who would wish to marry the girl, though I will add that it seems a poor accomplishment for the one who gets her. That woman is filled with poison or I have learned nothing in my life.

My superior Ab-she-lam Eidan, whom Allah reward, has given me instructions to become acquainted with the sister of the Rajah, the woman who lives apart from the court and is said to be a scholar. While I will do as I am ordered, I am not pleased with this. I have met Padmiri once and found her an admirable woman, of self-contained and reserved mien. To use her against her brother is contrary to everything I have believed is virtuous conduct. It is one thing to enlist her sympathies, but quite another to attempt to suborn her. The Prophet warned us of the deceit and wiles and untrustworthiness of women, but he has also lauded the honor of women. If women are given to vice by the nature of their sex, then when one is found without that vice, it is doubly reprehensible in any man who attempts to awaken it in a chaste woman's soul. Understand that I will do as I have been told, but my heart is against it and I wish it had not been asked of me.

You have already received the report on the periyanadu, so I will not belabor the event. What was and was not accomplished has been described to you.

There have been reports that the Thuggi are active here again. I have seen no direct evidence of this, but I have spoken with a few of Rajah Dantinusha's guards and they say that garroted bodies have been turning up on the more remote stretches of road. Those devils with their silken scarves and their wires are claiming victims for their demon again. I have no reason to doubt what the guards have told me, but I intend to ask of merchants what they know of this, for they will be even more reliable than the soldiers. If it should happen that the Thuggi are at work, I will send you word of it at once, and have the messenger travel under guard. I have already informed my superior of this rumor and he has others of the mission investigating the claims.

May Allah bless you and your seed and your endeavors. And may he guide my judgment here.

Jalal-im-al Zakatim

4

ONE OF the musicians had lent Saint-Germain his bicitrabin and ivory plectrum, and though he had never played this odd zitherlike instrument, he had retired to a window embrasure to experiment. He had forgotten how much he missed music until he touched the unfamiliar strings and heard their slightly buzzy sound magnified by the large resonating gourds at either end of the fingerboard. Luckily the bicitrabin was fretless so that he could play in Western modes and scales as well as their Indian counterparts. Most of the other guests ignored him.

"That is a Western melody, isn't it?" asked one of the Islamic delegation.

"Yes," Saint-Germain said. "It comes from Rome." He did not add that it was the Rome of the Caesars he remembered and the melody was a hymn to Jupiter.

"A disquieting sound," the young Muslim persisted.

"If you're not used to it, I suppose so." He did not want to set the instrument aside, but he knew that he should not be unkind to the man beside him.

"You are the foreigner, are you not?" the man went on.

"I thought that much was obvious," Saint-Germain said sardonically. He was wearing a long Frankish houppelande over chausses of embroidered cotton. As always, the garments were black. His wide-linked silver chain was around his neck, and his black eclipse pectoral depended from it.

"Oh, certainly," the other man agreed. "But you will agree that it is more polite to ask than to announce such things." He gathered his robes about him and sank onto the floor. "I was wishing to speak with you. I am Jalal-im-al Zakatim."

"I am Saint-Germain," he said, reluctantly setting the bici-trabin aside.

"I have been informed that you are an alchemist," Jalal-im-al said with great cordiality.

"This is correct: who told you?"

Jalal-im-al chuckled. "The poet, Jaminya. He has been most informative. Not to the point of treason or dishonor, but he is an observant and talkative man."

Privately, Saint-Germain thought that much the same thing could be said of Jalal-im-al Zakatim. "And he told you that I practice the Great Art."

"Yes. I have also learned from the merchant Chol that some of your supplies come from the Sultanate. This is most interesting to me." He touched his beautifully groomed beard, knowing that its lustrous chestnut brown was rarely seen and often attracted attention.

"And did Chol tell you what these supplies are? I fear that I should explain that I will not allow you or anyone to compromise me and will not be anyone's spy." His expression was one of goodwill and his voice was pleasantly modulated, but his resolution was steely.

"Oh, no, no, no, you misunderstand me completely. Let me assure you at once that I have no such intentions. If I wished a spy, I should be wiser to find one of the slaves to work for me. You, being foreign, would not be in a position to have the information I wanted. You see, I wish you to know that my curiosity does not include subverting you on behalf of the Sultanate." He had a wide, brilliant smile which he turned on Saint-Germain.

"If you don't want to make a spy of me, what *do* you want?" He had long ago learned to be wary of that too-open charm that Jalal-im-al displayed.

"Two things. First, I want to meet Padmiri. She is very hard to see casually, living as she does. I know that you have been given a wing of her house for your own use, and I hope that you will be my introduction to her." He looked through the anteroom to the hall where a banquet was in progress.

"There are two things," Saint-Germain reminded him, his voice quite emotionless.

"The second, yes. This is more difficult." The young Muslim bent forward. "In my family it is considered tradition for all of us to put ourselves in the service of our rulers. Sadly, this is not where my true interests lie. Would you, being a foreigner, be willing to teach me the Great Art? I studied for a time in Aleppo, but my father was not willing to allow me to continue my studies." There had been a change in him. His former practiced elegance had been replaced with unmistakable sincerity. "It would not be easy for me to have time away from Ab-she-lam Eidan, but I think he would give me some time for the work."

"And of course, the fact that you would have to be at the house of Padmiri, whom you admit you wish to meet, is only coincidence," Saint-Germain suggested.

"Not entirely, no," Jalal-im-al said at once. "It would be helpful for me to know this woman. It would be better to learn alchemy. If I can do both, then my way is much easier."

"And you will have greater access to the Rajah, perhaps." He put his hands on the narrow fingerboard of the bicitrabin, feeling the almost imperceptible thrill of the strings as he touched them.

"It may occur," Jalal-im-al said, dismissing the matter with a wave of his hand. "She is not the one who is of great interest to Delhi, after all. It is Tamasrajasi who intrigues them."

"Because she is the heir," Saint-Germain said, and picked up the bicitrabin once more. Very softly he began to pick out a curious tune he had learned in Britain nearly seven hundred years before.

"You wish to be left alone," Jalal-im-al declared, no hint of offense in his voice. "I perceive that you do not attend the banquet."

"No." He played the melody a little more loudly.

"There are restrictions on your people? I admit that I find it very strange to be dining with women, even royal women. It seems that Rajah Dantinusha has brought all his wives with him and they are seated around him on the dais. A most lax custom. It leads to most lascivious conduct, I am told." His words were scandalized but his tone was richly appreciative. "The fruit juice they serve is fermented. These people are truly debauched."

"And you smoke hashish, don't you?" Saint-Germain inquired gently.

"That's another matter entirely. You have smoked it, haven't you?" He had known a great many foreigners who were both repelled and fascinated by the dream-inducing substance.

"No." He knew that there was no euphoria for him in the acrid fumes, no visions.

"Then, being an infidel, you must drink wine," Jalal-im-al said, with the unctuous rectitude of youth.

"No. I do not drink wine."

Jalal-im-al knew that he had made an error with this foreigner, but was at a loss to know how to recover himself. He plunged on, fearing that his silence now would not be wise. "Are you amenable to teaching me? If it is a question of money . . ."

"It is not," Saint-Germain murmured as he continued to touch the strings of the bicitrabin.

"Then you will consider instructing me?" He made a move as if to get to his feet.

"I did not say that." He stopped playing and looked at the young man. "You admit that you wish to meet Padmiri. All right. This much I will do. If you will come to her house, I will see that you meet her. Beyond that, I don't know what more you will want of me. If you have any interest in studying the Great Art"—his tone indicated that he doubted this was the case—"you may speak to me then. But I warn you, Jalal-im-al Zakatim: if there is the least hint that you are seeking to use or harm Padmiri, you will not be allowed near her again and you will regret your action. My word on it." His very calm made his words more frightening. Saint-Germain studied the face of the young Muslim when he had finished speaking and was soberly glad that Jalal-im-al had taken his promise to heart.

"You will introduce me," Jalal-im-al said, scrambling up. He had moved too hastily and his foot caught on the hem of his djellaba so that he nearly stumbled. "I will come within ten days." That was as little a time as propriety required for such introductions.

"As you wish." He began once more to play, and he did not look up when he heard the soft, retreating steps of the young man from Delhi.

He was still playing when the banquet was finished and a few of the guests came into the reception room. They were men of high rank and caste, most of them part of Rajah

Dantinusha's court, although there were a few representatives
from other principalities in attendance. Everyone was gor-
geously attired and the conduct was formal and as abstract as
a dance. Saint-Germain glanced up occasionally, and the
plaintive melody of a Norman love song came from the bicitrabin as he watched.

In a short while, Jaminya drifted over to the window embrasure and nodded down at Saint-Germain. "You are surprising," he said with good humor.

"How?" He attempted to play a run of chords, but gave it
up after a few jangling mistakes.

"You have admitted to knowing alchemy, and Padmiri has
said that you have great erudition, but I did not know that
included music." The poet leaned on a nearby pillar, his lined
face amused.

"I have always loved music," Saint-Germain said rather remotely. He began to adjust the treble strings, which had been
losing pitch.

"You play Western music on the bicitrabin," Jaminya
pointed out, as if Saint-Germain might not have noticed this.

"Yes." He recalled an anthem he had heard in Lombardy
fifty years before. "This may please you, though it is
Western."

When the notes died away, Jaminya cocked his head on
one side. "Yes, it goes well enough. It is too simple for my
tastes, but that is not necessarily detrimental."

"If you prefer, I will play you music I learned in China."
He was curious about the poet, sensing that the man wanted
more from him than simple diversion.

"No, I have heard that noise—nothing but plunk-plunk
and wailing. Your Western music is more interesting." He
folded his arms and waited, not quite meeting Saint-Germain's eyes.

So Saint-Germain played awhile longer, drawing melodies
from his memory as well as letting the music invent itself as
his hands roamed over the strings. When he had done a fair
amount of this, he set the instrument aside. "You wish to say
something to me."

"No, nothing of import. There are a few minor matters
you may wish to discuss, and I have a question about
Western poetry. Nothing that can't wait." The intensity of his
eyes said otherwise.

"Perhaps if you joined me. I was thinking of strolling in

the garden." Saint-Germain stood up as he spoke. Whatever it was that Jaminya wished to tell him, he would not do it here.

"The garden. Yes, the garden is quite pleasant." He no longer lounged against the pillar. "The Rajah will not wish to hear any of my work declaimed for some time yet. Poetry is truly the breath of the gods, and for that reason should not be offered until the mind is free of the table." He went to the nearest door and opened it. "This way is quickest."

And least observed, Saint-Germain added to himself as he followed the poet out onto the terrace above the gardens.

Rajah Dantinusha had lost a great deal of the grandeur of his forefathers, but this little country estate could not have been improved by wealth. Two streams had been diverted to run through its lush gardens and there were flowering shrubs everywhere. The house sat in a pocket on the mountain slope and seemed wholly isolated from the capital until the crest of the ridge was reached, and the city could be seen stretching out below, a day's ride away. Now at sunset the hillside was drenched in a pinkish glow that gave the garden and the extensive villa a glamour and an enchantment that those in the gorgeous reception room missed.

Jaminya breathed deeply. "That is a perfume I prefer to incense," he remarked fairly loudly.

"Splendid," Saint-Germain agreed with a wry twist to his mouth.

"And the flowers I mentioned to you are this way," he went on as they crossed the terrace and descended to the pathways of the garden. "What I wanted to say to you," the poet murmured as they set off along one of the walkways, "is that there are spies in Padmiri's household and one of them at least will do what he can to discredit you."

Saint-Germain was not alarmed by this news. "I assumed that there were spies. But what would any of them want with me? You say that I am in danger of being discredited—how?"

Jaminya stopped by a large bush which was covered with fading blossoms no larger than a thumbnail. They were a soft red in color and their fragrance was almost overpowering. "These are among my favorites, small as they are. Dantinusha likes the enormous blossoms and Tamasrajasi only wants flowers for sacrifice and holy things. I like flowers for what they are, not for their show or their other uses, but as beautiful, short-lived treasures." He looked around, and added, "I don't think we were followed, but be careful in what you say and how loudly you speak." He bent over the bush and breathed in the scented air.

There was a question that had been bothering Saint-Germain since the poet had come up to him. Here, in this deliriously scented garden, he felt it cruel to test his companion, yet he asked, "Why do you warn me, Jaminya?"

The poet gave him a swift, sharp glance. "Do you truly wish an answer?"

"Yes, I do." Saint-Germain took the sting out of his response with a hint of amusement. He stared away over the bushes, watching the sun's rays turn from rose to amber.

"Very well, I will tell you." Jaminya grew tired, less effusive, with grimness behind the shine of his eyes. "First, it offends me to see one who has given hospitality generously used so as a reward. I don't hold you responsible for this—anyone would have provided the excuse. Second, I have long been a friend of Padmiri, and she has been one to me, and this insults her, so that I, too, am insulted. Third . . ."—he lowered his voice again—"I am afraid of Tamasrajasi." He picked three of the flowers and put one in his hair, holding the other two in his hand as he strolled on. "When the rebellion occurred three years ago, I thought that half the country was being bribed to watch the other half. I see this starting again, all the lying and intrigue, and I am worried."

Saint-Germain kept pace beside the poet. "Is that the whole of it." He knew beyond doubt that it was not.

Jaminya faltered and the flowers in his hand dropped unheeded to the pathway. "Padmiri has been kind to me and those I have loved. There are not many at court who would risk such generosity. She has let me use her house when I have wanted to be private, and she has consoled me when the love ended."

Saint-Germain said nothing. He had not thought that Jaminya had been one of Padmiri's lovers, but this confession did not trouble him. He listened to the calling of birds and waited for the poet to go on.

"I am one who loves men, not women. I have not taken a wife, though the Rajah has asked me to do so. Padmiri helped me when I refused Dantinusha's request. He listened to her, at least that time. She has given me more than he has, I think."

They had come to a fork in the path and Jaminya indicated that they should go to the right. The track followed the course of one of the streams for a little way, meandering through banks of flowers. Here and there clouds of insects rose humming like miniature storms. This Jaminya waved away and Saint-Germain ignored. A bit farther on there was a glade, idyllically situated.

"If I were to love a woman, it would be Padmiri," Jaminya said as they came into the glade.

There was the distant sound of a breaking branch and Saint-Germain turned toward it, his senses acute.

"There is a herd of deer in the garden. They often wander at this time of day," the poet said.

"Are you certain that was a deer?" Saint-Germain asked, being reasonably convinced that it was not.

"Of course." Jaminya's laughter did not ring quite true and he moved more quickly. "How like a foreigner—give you a warning and you see menace in every tree branch."

"An old habit," Saint-Germain said, his voice once more becoming sardonic.

"Perhaps it's Thuggi. They say that the killings are happening again." This time his laughter was distinctly nervous. "It is growing dark," he said gratefully. "It might be wise to start back."

"Indeed it might," Saint-Germain said, remarking as they made their way somewhat hastily through the garden, "It was good of you to warn me. I doubt anyone else at this court would be concerned."

"It is not you, foreigner, it's Padmiri. I've told you that." He fell silent again and by the time they returned to the terrace, his expression was brooding. He stopped Saint-Germain before they went into the reception room. "Have a care. There are those who will want to harm her through you. If that happens, I will be your enemy." His attractive lined face was harsh and many of the court would not have recognized the ferocity of his voice.

"I would not want to bring any harm to Padmiri," Saint-Germain said, holding the poet's eyes a moment. "I thank you for the warning. I will heed it."

A movement behind Saint-Germain distracted Jaminya, and he made a smile that was like a wound in his face. "Say what you want about your Western gardens, I still maintain that these are finer than any other."

"Your passion for gardens!" Guristar scoffed at Jaminya as he came up to the two men. "I admire beauty, and I value the loveliness of this garden, but Jaminya is like a man preparing to sacrifice to the gods. Only the most perfect is appropriate."

"You are so with your horses," Jaminya pointed out before he bowed and moved away from the door.

"A most gifted man," Guristar said to Saint-Germain as he watched the poet make his way through the crowd.

"I have not yet read his work," Saint-Germain said diffidently, hoping to forestall an argument. "The poetry of your language is beyond my learning; it is more subtle than my understanding, though I very much admire the forms your poets employ."

Guristar managed a polite answer. "It is a great compliment to say so, for one of your wide experience must be formidably educated in such matters."

"Not so formidably as all that," Saint-Germain said, ending the matter. He started toward the window embrasure where the bicitrabin waited, but Sudra Guristar was not finished with him.

"A moment, foreigner. I need a word with you." He made sure that Saint-Germain had turned back toward him, then ambled up to the stranger, all studied arrogance. "You don't know our ways well enough to know when you are being insolent, Saint-Germain."

"I thought that I did," Saint-Germain said urbanely. "Strange how a man may be misled."

Guristar glared at Saint-Germain, then forced his features into grotesque goodwill. "Earlier this evening one of the Sultan's men was speaking with you."

"Yes. He's interested in alchemy," Saint-Germain said promptly, thinking that Guristar's intent could not be as transparent as it seemed. He studied the Commander of the guard without seeming to. The man was filled with a jittery tension, an ill-concealed and ill-omened excitement. "He wants to study with me."

"What did you tell him?" The demand came quickly, and Guristar, recognizing an error, tried to minimize it. "You understand, we are anxious to see the Rajah's sister protected."

"Are you." Saint-Germain brushed his dagged cuffs as if ridding them of lint or vermin. "I haven't given the young man my answer. Unless I am satisfied that his interest is genuine, I will refuse his petition."

Only a dread of magic kept Guristar from bursting out in anger at this impossible stranger. He dared not risk curses or other malefic influences on the eve of so dangerous an enterprise as he was embarked upon. "Be aware, foreigner," he said, almost choking on the words, "be aware that you are here on sufferance. As a demon may enter a house and bring disease, so there are other demons that might rise against you to punish your impiety."

"But alchemy is not impious," Saint-Germain protested, all innocence. "If it were, the Rajah would never have sent me to his sister."

Guristar wanted to challenge the foreigner in black. He contented himself with the vow that when the time came for his end, Saint-Germain would not die quickly or cleanly. He showed his teeth. "Say what you will now, Saint-Germain. And be warned that no man escapes his fate."

"I will remember," Saint-Germain promised him, then turned away from the Commander of the guard and strode to the window embrasure.

This time the music would not come. Saint-Germain seated himself between the two large resonating gourds and placed his fingers on the strings, plucking slowly. The sounds that came from the instrument were discordant and Saint-Germain told himself that the treble strings had slipped again, though he did not believe this. He stared at the pegbox and began to turn the tuning pegs, fingering the strings, and each tone seemed worse than the last. He sighed and moved the bicitrabin away. His thoughts were too divided now. Reluctantly he rose, not wishing to rejoin the party, but no longer having the excuse of playing to keep him away from the others.

Ab-she-lam Eidan approached him first. He was magnificently robed, but he had carefully avoided using jewels that might be more impressive than Rajah Dantinusha's. His eyes were grave but he had been at court far too long to allow his gravity to show on his face. "My young assistant tells me that you are reluctant to teach him alchemy."

"That's correct," Saint-Germain said. He wished now that Padmiri had agreed to come to this feast. She had said that she had endured enough court functions to sate her for the rest of her life, and was delighted that Saint-Germain would make it possible for her to refuse this summons gracefully.

"Why is this? Let me speak to you a moment on his behalf." He gestured authoritatively toward a low, padded bench.

Saint-Germain declined to sit. "Ab-she-lam Eidan, I appreciate your determination, but nothing you can say will force me to reach a decision until I have seen how the young man conducts himself with my apparatus. I will make no judgment until then."

"Do not be hasty, Saint-Germain. The wise man reflects on his decisions and seeks guidance from Allah." He placed his hand on his chest, and a large stone glowed on his middle finger.

"I will not be capricious," Again he moved away, seeking some inconspicuous place where he could watch the other guests and sort out his thoughts. There were too many currents running in this river, and it seemed to him that they would result in a whirlpool if they converged.

Beyond the reception room were a number of alcoves, most of them overlooking the garden, nine of them with low couches and perfumed lamps. In one of these alcoves there was an elaborate brass chest standing open, and Saint-Germain discovered a number of scrolls in the chest. After signaling for a slave to bring flint and steel, he looked through the scrolls until the slave returned and the hanging lamps were lit. It was more of a precaution than a need, for Saint-Germain's vampiric eyes could read as well in the dark as the light. The scrolls were faded and in an ancient script that he deciphered with difficulty.

The night was far advanced when he at last set the scrolls aside. All but one of the lamps had guttered and the rest of the alcoves were dark, though from the sounds, two of them were occupied. Saint-Germain returned the scrolls to the chest and sat back on the narrow couch, his mind drifting to other times, other places. He remembered walking in Athens in a bright spring rain, looking up to see the gaudily painted frieze on the Parthenon. In Nineveh there had been a priestly ceremony when gongs had been sounded in the streets all through the night so that no one would sleep and thereby insult the gods. Rome, with three of his blood lying broken on the sands of the Circus Maximus, and Olivia's arms around him as he hung in fetters. The Temple of Imhotep and healing. A desperate ride out of Milano when Barbarossa was through with it the first time. Tunis ravaged by a plague that turned faces slate-color before gasping, shivering death. And then, so quickly that he was not prepared for it, the face of T'en Chih-Yü when he had found her after the battle, and the absolute loss of her. Grief sank into him, sword-sharp. For his kind there were no tears, and only his soul could cry out in the sorrow and acceptance of loss. The pain that had ravened him, denied, at last began to diminish. Slowly he stood up and went to the window, staring blindly out over the garden as he felt T'en Chih-Yü slip away from him, to join his other memories. He decided that he would leave Rajah Dantinusha's estate that day and return to Padmiri. There was solace in the woman, and a curious empathy.

He was jarred from his thoughts by a sound, a terrible sound that rose from the remote lake in the garden. So agonized was the cry that at first it did not seem possible that it could be human, but Saint-Germain knew it was, and he felt his skin turn cold. Out there, in the fragrant night, among the blossoms and the loveliness, a human being shrieked in dire and ultimate torment.

———◆———

An anonymous note delivered to the Rajah Dantinusha by a mendicant Brahmin.

Good Rajah, blessed ruler,
I am a friend though you do not know me. As part of that friendship, I write now to warn you. It has been said that the worship of the Black Goddess is increasing again, and if what we hear of the fate of travelers is true, we must believe it. The Thuggi prey on those who are unwise enough to trust them. Yet the Thuggi are not the only ones to be undone by trust.
From various sources it has reached my ears that you are marked, good Rajah, and that you will not live to

see the sun return. If you are to avoid the fate that has been decreed you, be wary and assume that all you have trusted is a lie.

If it is your karma to fall in this way, there is nothing that you may do, however prudent, that will spare you. Yet not all deaths are of that nature, and truly there is much a circumspect man may accomplish. You may warn me that in taking this course I have interfered with your Path and for that reason will have to assume responsibility for what befalls you. This is what scripture teaches us and what our people believe, and if it is so, I will accept that burden and whatever payment it brings, though it bind me to the Wheel for a thousand thousand years.

I do not know who it is near you who seeks your life, but believe that one does. Had I learned the name of the traitor, I would tell it to you so that you might decide how best to deal with the vile one. On this particular matter those I have spoken to are strangely silent. They have even said that those who have such knowledge may be found strangled in ditches. You must be guided by the wisdom of the gods and your own precautions.

Whatever may come of this, know that one of your subjects was loyal. Should you fall, on that day I will take my life, though I return to the earth as vermin for such an act. If you must go into the realms of death, you will not travel there alone.

Guard yourself and those nearest you. There are dangers all around you. May the gods give you safety.

One who is your friend

5

LORAMIDI CHOL stood by the crates he had delivered and turned a woebegone face to Saint-Germain. "Alas, Revered One, it has been most difficult to procure those materials you requested. These, I know, are hardly sufficient, but they are all that I have been able to obtain. I beg that you will not chastise me too severely for this failure, for most earnestly I did try."

Saint-Germain was keenly disappointed, but turned a calm

face to the little rotund merchant. "It is not what I would have wanted, but I don't doubt that you have done your best."

Chol wiped his forehead with his sleeve. "It is even so, Revered One. There were many whom I approached who were unable to procure the things I requested on your behalf, though they have been able to do so in the past. Times are uncertain, and they are not willing to take risks that might . . ." He became lost in the excuse and he lifted his palms to indicate how beyond him the whole thing was.

"I see," Saint-Germain said quietly, walking across the room he had almost completely turned into a laboratory. "When do you think you might be able to get the supplies for me?"

Now Chol looked wholly miserable. "I do not know, Revered One. I have asked, indeed I have asked, and all I hear in reply is that possibly before the rain, or perhaps after the dark of the year. I don't know where to turn, yet no one speaks of the need for these things but me, they say, and I have little I can use to persuade them." He put his thick-fingered hand to his eyes. "I have asked other merchants, and they say that there has been much trouble, much trouble."

"You have not got the earth, or the powedered horn I want," Saint-Germain said, and watched to see how Chol would react.

"Alas, no. Anything coming from the lands of the Sultan, Revered One, are quite impossible to obtain. I have tried, and on all sides I am met with refusals." He sat down on the low stool and fanned himself, though the day was somewhat cool.

"Most lamentable," Saint-Germain agreed. "How long do you anticipate these problems will continue? Is there no one you might deal with?"

The little merchant clasped and unclasped his hands and stared at the window with puckered eyes as if wishing to escape. "I know of no one, Revered One," he conceded unhappily. "It is the times, and there are those who insist that all requests going to the land of the Sultan bear the approval of his emissaries—"

Saint-Germain cut him off. "I see." He looked at the crates and laughed once, bitterly. "Yes. Of course."

Now Chol was perplexed, and though he was not so ill-mannered as to ask outright, he did say, "One of your station, Revered One, should be able to approach those who might aid you."

"Doubtless," Saint-Germain agreed, thinking of the young Muslim who had spoken to him at the Rajah Dantinusha's country house.

"Ab-she-lam Eidan would hear your petition, if you cared to address him directly," Chol said, gaining confidence as he spoke.

"Or Jalal-im-al Zakatim," Saint-Germain added, a certain disgust in his tone. He had been bested, he knew, and it rankled.

"He is also a highly placed man," Chol said, not comfortable with the chilly reserve that colored Saint-Germain's manner. "The Rajah has extended many courtesies to you and would doubtless be willing to see that these men receive you."

Saint-Germain folded his arms on his chest. "Very neat," he said quietly.

"Revered One?" Chol asked, sensing the anger in that cool, foreign face.

"It has nothing to do with you, Chol. You have done all that you can and I am satisfied with your efforts." He began to pace the length of the room. His stride was swift and clean.

Chol watched him, apprehension growing in his heart. These foreigners were an unreliable lot, he knew, and those with powerful friends were apt to be capricious. This man had been most generous, certainly, but sad experience had taught Loramidi Chol to be chary of generosity. "Revered One," he ventured after a little time, "perhaps there is someone else who would assist you?"

"Of course there is," Saint-Germain answered promptly as he continued to pace. "That is precisely what is expected of me."

Each new remark by the foreigner was more baffling than the last. "Then why do you not go to this person?"

"I dislike being forced, good merchant. It galls me." He stopped suddenly, and the room seemed to move around him, so strong had his movements been.

"The aid of powerful men is a great benefit," Chol said, though the old triusm rang false in his ears.

"Is it." Saint-Germain shrugged eloquently. "You may be right and I am frightened by shadows. But this is too neat. I give a man a refusal and within the month I am in his hands."

There was nothing Chol could say to this, but he was touched with cold as he listened. "There is much deception in the world, for Maya is a strong goddess."

"Indeed she is," Saint-Germain agreed, realizing now that he had needlessly alarmed the little merchant. He made himself smile and spoke more lightly. "You have done well, Chol, and I have not expressed my appreciation. Be assured that nothing you have done has disappointed me." How many times would he have to repeat that sentiment before Chol lost the whiteness around his mouth? "You have been most responsible in your tasks. You will be rewarded for your care."

"It is not necessary, Revered One," Chol murmured, though his eyes grew round with greed.

"Nevertheless, let me give you a token of my approval of your work." He clapped his hands sharply, and Rogerio stepped into the room. "I want a small bag of silver," he announced, then added in Latin, "Make it four or five Byzantine coins, fairly old, if we have any left."

"There are a few," Rogerio answered in the same language. "Also we have two or three of the Moorish silver coins."

"Choose for variety, I think," Saint-Germain said, then returned to the dialect of Natha Suryarathas. "My servant will see that you are paid."

Chol was not entirely confident of this. He had listened to the strange, meaningless words that man and master had exchanged and he feared that this was to be his formal dismissal. Revered men did not give themselves the distasteful chore of ridding themselves of unwanted minions. He knotted his hands together. "It is not important that I am rewarded," he choked out.

What ails the man now? Saint-Germain asked himself. "You will honor me if you will accept my poor gift," he said. "If you will follow my servant . . ."

Chol's shoulders sagged. "Very well, Revered One. I do as you wish." He turned slowly and went in the direction Rogerio indicated.

For a moment Saint-Germain looked after the squat, retreating figure of Loramidi Chol, then put the merchant out of his thoughts. He went to the crates and began to unpack them, sighing once at the inferior quality of the powdered cinnabar.

Some little time later, Rogerio returned to the workroom. "I think that Chol believed that you were going to send him away empty-handed," he remarked as he closed the door.

Saint-Germain clicked his tongue impatiently. "Why should I bother to call you, if that was my intention?"

"Apparently that is how such things are arranged here," Rogerio said as he opened the last of the crates. "Do you think he told you the truth?"

"That there are no supplies to be had without approval from the Delhi mission? Yes, I think it likely. Jalal-im-al hinted as much when he asked if he might study with me. And now it seems that I must get his help if I wish to have my required materials." He straightened up, frowning. "It is awkward. Not only for me, but for Padmiri. Any dealings with the Muslims will be to her discredit, I fear."

"How is that?" Rogerio began to stack the empty crates in the corner of the room.

"The Muslims are not trusted here, and small wonder. Padmiri, being the Rajah's sister, is one way to Dantinusha's ear, and so if there are Muslims here, what is their purpose but to influence the Rajah?" He put an alabaster jar out on the table and carefully pried the wax seal off it with a little knife.

"But if the Muslims come to you?" Rogerio picked up the last of the crates. "Do you want me to save this one? It has a hole in the side."

"No, dispose of it." He was about to continue when he heard Rogerio curse in crudest Latin. "What is it?"

Rogerio had moved away from the last crate. "There's a scorpion in the crate. Quite large."

"A scorpion? Well, now we know what the hole was for." Saint-Germain moved quickly, reached for the crate and overturned it, trapping the arachnid beneath it. He could hear the faint scuttling sounds of its legs on the polished floor.

"What now?" Rogerio asked in a hushed voice.

"I'm not sure." Scorpions, as he had learned most painfully centuries before, were dangerous to him and those like him. Only once had he suffered the sting of the creature and it had given him literal years of agony: the memory of it made him flinch.

"Should we kill it?" Rogerio was already searching for a glass receptacle.

"Undoubtedly. Keep the body, though. There are uses for the venom." He turned back to the crate. "I wonder who wished this thing on me?"

Wisely, Rogerio kept silent. He found a long-necked beaker with a heavy stopper and held this out to his master.

"That will do," Saint-Germain said quietly as he took the vessel from his servant.

"Where should I wait?" Rogerio asked.

"Get a metal collar—one of the high ones—and put it around the outside of the crate. Then get me my leather gauntlets." His attention was concentrated on the irritated clicking the scorpion made inside the crate. Without looking up, he held his hand out for the gauntlets as Rogerio approached. He drew the heavy metal-studded leather gloves on while Rogerio positioned the metal collar.

Rogerio braced the metal band with the legs of two stools. "I think it's ready now."

Saint-Germain's grip on the beaker was awkward now that he wore the gauntlets, so he allowed himself a moment to be certain that his hold was secure. "Now, I think."

Swiftly, but with care, Rogerio raised the crate and set it aside.

The enraged scorpion, thinking itself exposed and free, scuttled forward, tail raised and quivering. It was a fairly large specimen, longer than Saint-Germain's small hands could span, and of a shiny dark brown. Its rush ended abruptly as it collided with the metal collar, and it began again to click with irritation.

"It's one of the more poisonous varieties," Saint-Germain said in a rather abstracted tone. He had positioned himself above the scorpion, readying the beaker.

"Why not just crush it?" Rogerio suggested as Saint-Germain hesitated.

Saint-Germain gave a minute shake of his head that effectively silenced his servant. He hung poised an instant longer, then moved with amazing speed. In a single graceful motion he seized the scorpion and thrust it into the beaker, bringing down the stopper before the arachnid had righted itself in the glass container. "Because," he said coolly, "I think this creature may be useful. The venom is most potent." He held the beaker up and looked at the scorpion through the glass. He was not quite able to conceal his distaste.

"Is there a chance that the scorpion simply crawled into the hole in the crate?" Rogerio ventured.

"There is always a chance," Saint-Germain said in his driest tone. "But I doubt I can afford to believe that."

Rogerio nodded mutely, then bent to retrieve the wide metal strip that had served as a collar to the crate. His expression betrayed none of his fears, but Saint-Germain had learned long ago to read the man's silences well.

"You think that I should leave now, don't you?" He put the beaker on the nearest table and began to pull off his gauntlets.

"It might be wisest." The metal, a lightweight alloy produced in the athanor, was rolled into a loose ring.

"Though the Mongols are in Persia and I have little of my native earth left?" He asked the question easily, almost without concern.

"Is it better to stay here and look for scorpions?" Now there was worry in Rogerio's voice and he met his master's dark eyes with his light ones.

"Under the circumstances, do you think we would simply be allowed to leave?" Saint-Germain regarded Rogerio patiently, and when there was no response to this, he went on. "True, it may be palace intrigue and nothing more. Bhatin may be a eunuch, but he is most possessive of Padmiri. I've seen how he looks at her. He may not be pleased that she has shown . . . favor to me. And, as you say, it may be that the scorpion crawled into the hole in the crate."

"And if it isn't palace intrigue?" In spite of himself, Rogerio stared at the scorpion as it attempted to climb the walls of its glass prison.

"Then we will know it soon enough." He placed the tips of his fingers on the table. "If Jalal-im-al arranged this, he has overreached himself. If he has not, he may be of use to us after all." He saw the quickly concealed alarm in Rogerio's eyes. "He will be able to help us, if he is not actually working against us."

"Why should he?" Rogerio had torn his eyes from the scorpion and gave his master his determined attention.

"Because he wants to study alchemy, or so he claims," was the urbane answer. "And if he wants to spy on Padmiri, I would prefer he do it where I may observe him." He went quickly across the room to a new chest, from which he removed a few sheets of rice paper and a cake of ink. "Where are my brushes?"

"What are you going to do?" Rogerio asked, although he knew the answer.

"I am going to send word to Jalal-im-al telling him that I have reconsidered. I will allow him to serve as my apprentice if he is willing to come here every other day to study." He smiled slightly. "That will keep him on the road most of the time, and will minimize any harm he might try to do."

"He will want to stay here," Rogerio said fatalistically.

"But that will not be possible. Padmiri will forbid it because she does not want to compromise herself. And I will agree with her. Jalal-im-al is a good Muslim and he will accept this decision." He was looking in a covered box of inlaid wood as he spoke. "Here they are." He took out his brushes. "I haven't much skill in the script used in Delhi. I hope that he or someone in the mission reads Persian."

Rogerio watched Saint-Germain as he began to moisten the ink cake with water from an earthen jar. "He will be suspicious."

"Good." Saint-Germain moved his brush experimentally over the ink cake and added a bit more water. "That will serve my purpose well enough. Let him question everything. That way our protection is greater." He touched the brush to the paper and began to write in the scholarly style, the words resembling Arabian script, but more curved in their form.

"Do you think he will accept?" Inwardly, Rogerio hoped that the young Muslim might find the invitation too questionable and refuse it.

"I think it likely," Saint-Germain said as he continued to write. "I will want this handed to him, and remain with him until he has read the whole of it. Say that I require an immediate answer." He knew that Rogerio disliked the plan, and he added, "My friend, we won't escape danger, it seems, so it is best that we anticipate it. Your caution is admirable, but in this instance, it could be deadly."

Rogerio accepted this unhappily. "I will wait for the answer. Is there anything else?"

Saint-Germain's smile widened though there was no glint of humor in it. "I have appended to this letter a request for earth from Transylvania, among other items. If the Muslims are determined to use me, I will return the compliment." He read over the message, frowning a little at his phrases then rolled it carefully and wound a length of cotton ribbon around it. "Where is my seal?"

"In the silver box, in the Roman chest," Rogerio said, and went to fetch it and sealing wax. While Saint-Germain set about fixing his device on the wax, he added, "What if I am denied access to the Muslims?"

"Go at once to the palace of Dantinusha and tell him that I have need of supplies from the Sultanate and have been informed that I must deal with the emissaries of Delhi. The Rajah is not a stupid man. He will be willing to get you admitted to Ab-she-lam Eidan or one of his men. From there it will be a simple matter to speak to Jalal-im-al Zakatim. Unless I am badly mistaken, you will not be unexpected." This last was said sardonically: Saint-Germain held out the sealed message to his servant.

Rogerio took it reluctantly. "I will do as you wish," he muttered.

Before he could turn to leave the room, Saint-Germain touched his arm. "Old friend," he said gently, "I understand your fear. I share it. But we must either cower in the corner and hope that we are not discovered, or we must act with audacity. I truly believe that our only protection is in surprise."

"You are not the only one who thinks so," Rogerio said with a nod toward the beaker and the scorpion.

At once Saint-Germain's expression became grim. "Yes." He turned away and walked to the shuttered windows. "And next time, what will it be, and where? Oh, it's senseless to flee from shadows and branches tapping on the walls, but . . ." He recalled the horrible sound he had heard in the garden of Rajah Dantinusha's country estate.

"I will see that this is delivered," Rogerio said quietly.

"And I will wait for his answer." He saw Saint-Germain incline his head before he left the room.

The next afternoon was well-advanced when Rogerio returned to Padmiri's house. The horse he had been provided was somewhat winded and had made poor time on the road. By the time Rogerio left the stables he was grouchy from fatigue and frustration. He hurried to the wing of the house which had been turned over to Saint-Germain and entered by the side door. His boots and leggings were smirched with dirt and his linen garments were grimed with dust.

Saint-Germain was in his laboratory stoking the athanor. As the door was flung open, he looked up. "Difficulties?"

Rogerio dropped onto one of the stools. "At first. Then it was quite simple." He spat and dragged his sleeve across his face. "I feel as if I've dined on earth. The roads are unspeakable."

"Tell me." Saint-Germain closed the front of the athanor and gave his full attention to Rogerio. "You were away longer than I thought you might be."

For a comment, Rogerio nodded. "There were wild rumors of Thuggi again, and I waited until I found a vendor going to the nearest village to travel with. The poor man spent the entire journey stopping at every shrine and reciting sacred verses in a loud voice. If there were Thuggi about, he did everything he could have to bring us to their attention." His faded blue eyes grew icy with anger. "There was one village, about half a morning's ride from the capital, where they are now stoning travelers because the elders have said that there are demons invading the land."

"Were you hurt?" Saint-Germain asked at once.

"No, but the poor vendor received a cut on his arm. I wrapped it in part of my sash." He stopped and regarded his master more calmly. "I did get to speak to Jalal-im-al Zakatim. You were right: he's accepted your terms. He was quite eager."

"Did he say so?" Saint-Germain drew up a stool.

"Yes, at length." He was silent a moment. "He said also that he will come here in five days' time."

"Five days?" That was the barest minimum time for courtesy. "Did he say why?"

"No. He only asked that I tell you he would be pleased to talk with you then. He remarked," Rogerio added with disgust, "that he could not understand how it was that you had not been getting the supplies you require for your work, and assured me that any request made through him would be sent with the official messengers of the Sultan."

Saint-Germain gave a cold chuckle. "How obliging of him." He looked at his servant, seeing the exhaustion in his face. "Come. I will have the slaves prepare a bath for you." Before Rogerio could protest that this would cause a great deal of scandal among the members of the household, Saint-Germain added, "Being foreign, I am allowed my idiosyncrasies. Let them gossip about your bath rather than your errand. Tell them tales of the arrogant Muslims and let them know that they will be able to see one of the invaders for themselves. That way it might be possible for me to discover who it is in this place who is our enemy."

"Enemy?" Rogerio had caught the steel in Saint-Germain's tone.

"Last night there was another scorpion in this room. I destroyed it, sadly. This morning I asked the slaves how they dealt with the creatures and I was told that scorpions are rarely found here. When I showed the crushed carapace to the slaves, they were very frightened, more than I thought they would be." He paused, then went on in another voice, "Bhatin heard about it, of course, and told me that since this wing of the house had not been occupied for some time, it was to be expected that scorpions would be encountered."

Rogerio got to his feet. "Is it possible?"

"It is," Saint-Germain said softly. "And, as I have not been eager to find another, I took the precaution of examining this part of the building. Don't fret," he interrupted himself as Rogerio began to protest. "I wore my leather armor. And I found no evidence of scorpions, though there were quite a number of bats and spiders. As additional precaution, I prepared a fumigative vapor. The slaves were convinced that I would bring the entire house down with the odor."

"Are the scorpions dead, then?" He began to unknot his sash.

"If there were any, they are dead," Saint-Germain answered at his most urbane. "Come. You must bathe."

Rogerio knew that Saint-Germain would say no more on the matter, for the present. "A bath would be most welcome," he told his master as he followed Saint-Germain into the hall. There was a chill in his spine now, and an unadmitted dread. Had his heart been like those of other men, it would have leaped with terror.

Saint-Germain sensed the fright in Rogerio but dared not acknowledge it. Instead, he remarked, "It's a great temptation to falter, but that is the first way to ruin." Then he clapped his hands, and as slaves ran toward him to answer the summons, he gave brisk instructions regarding Rogerio's bath.

---◄●►---

A proclamation by the Rajah Dantinusha.

To the court and country of Natha Suryarathas, by
my hand as Rajah and by the mouth of Rialkot, my herald, I, Kare Dantinusha, decree and proclaim that there
will be a new structure in this land.

All who have been here have admired the beauty and
luxury of the gardens and vistas of this most gloriously
favored country, so it is appropriate that we who live in
this most favored place adorn it so that its loveliness
may be better revealed.

Therefore, I have given orders that a dam shall be
built on the Kudri, at the last cataract before it joins the
Chenab. Where now there is a rocky marsh, there will
be a beautiful lake, and it will be surrounded by gardens
and elegant houses where those of rank and understanding may retire to be inspired by the splendor they find
around them.

Conscriptions of labor from the appropriate castes
have begun and it will be a great honor to aid in this
work. Only those most strong and fit will be selected and
the recording of this activity will be meritorious. Let no
one ask to be part of the building who is not young and
strong, of good name and suitable caste. This is not for
the hands of slaves, except the most basic quarrying and
digging. The rest must be done by those who have true
knowledge of the worthiness of beautiful things and the
suitability of constructing such a place.

We are fortunate indeed that the Sultan Shams-ud-din
Iletmish has offered us fine stone to face the dam so that
it will stand for ages and ages, showing the entire world
the magnificence of this country.

In the lake there will be a number of islands, constructed so that kiosks may be built upon them, and with
the aid of shallow boats, worthy men may retire there

for meditation, religious exercises and the enjoyment of
their wives.

Work is to begin at once on this lake. By the dark of
the year, the first parts of the dam will rise, so that when
the spring thaw and the summer rains bring water cascading along the Kudri, there will be firm walls to withstand its might. Offerings to the gods will be given for
the protection of the walls and there will be sacrifices as
the construction continues. When the dam is complete, it
will be an honor to the gods as well as a monument to
the builders.

Let everyone lend his aid to this. Money, grain, sacrifices to the gods, supplies for the builders, spells to ward
off demons and humiliate them in their efforts even as
Lord Vishnu did; all things are needed and will do much
to progress the soul as well as benefit this excellent
work.

This is my will—let it be done.

> Rajah Kare Dantinusha
> Natha Suryarathas

6

EARLIER IT had been still, but now there was a wind off the
mountains carrying the breath of the first snows. At the edge
of the garden the trees shivered as the light turned brazen in
preparation for sunset. On the terrace slaves played a sarangi
and two tuned drums, the tabla and bhaya. Their music was
wandering, repetitious and drowzy, the beat lazily pulselike.

Padmiri had donned warmer clothes late that afternoon, a
heavy woolen tunic over her deep-pleated skirt, and now, as
she sat on a low bench at the far end of the terrace, her face
was framed by an elaborate shawl. She smiled at her black-
clad companion, allowing him his silence as the day deepened
toward night.

A gaudily plumaged bird flew overhead, its cry sounding
above the gentle music of the slaves. It dipped once above
the garden and then was lost to sight over the trees.

Saint-Germain watched the bird, then let his eyes rest on
the musicians, though he did not truly see them. "Padmiri,"
he said after a time as if her name alone would tell her all

his thoughts. They were complicated, and he had not found a way to express them well. He let out his breath heavily. "You have said nothing of the other night." It had been more than ten days since he had lain beside her in that sandalwood-perfumed room. His desire had not diminished, though it was once again becoming acute. Yet he had not reconciled himself to his own need.

"What should I say?" She was not taunting him, and there was no coyness in her.

"That you were pleased, that you—"

"I was more than pleased," she interjected.

"—were horrified."

"How should I be horrified?" She wanted to touch him but held off, realizing that he was troubled.

He turned away from her, looking through slitted eyes toward the setting sun. For him, the glare was as bright as it was for others at the full brightness of noon. "Many have been," he said quietly, remotely, waiting for her to respond. When she did not, he went on. "No. That's not it."

"What is it, then?" Padmiri was not yet alarmed, though his suffering touched her.

As he turned back toward her, the musicians fell silent. Now he was between her and the sun, impossibly dark, his face unreadable. "I will not lie to you about . . . what I require. It would be useless, wouldn't it?" he added with wry sorrow.

"Yes, it would be useless," she answered, her eyes never leaving the shadow of his face.

"But I have not . . . I was not . . . Padmiri, you have been solace for me, and I have needed solace." This was more difficult to say than he had thought possible. Now he was glad that she did not question him, that she was apparently content to hear him out. "When I loved you, it should have been entirely for yourself. And it wasn't." He touched her with one finger, tracing the curve of her upper lip. "I did not want to say this."

"And why did you?" She was hurt a bit, she thought, but only a bit.

"Because I want to make love to you again, only for yourself." He was peripherally aware that the slaves had gathered up their instruments and gone into the house, leaving him alone with Padmiri on the terrace over the garden.

Now she caught his hand in hers. "Who else were you thinking of, before?"

Saint-Germain hesitated. "She's dead. Does it matter who she was?" His grief was too old to be despair, but there was more than sorrow in his voice.

"It matters," Padmiri said, though she did not entirely believe it: she wanted to know what haunted Saint-Germain.

His small, long fingers tightened on hers. "It was more than a year ago, in China. There was a woman there. I was her lover. The Mongols killed her." He held out his other hand to Padmiri and was oddly grateful when she took it. "When I loved you, I was using you, not substituting you, but . . . escaping from her memory."

"Have you accepted her death?" She said it evenly enough, hiding the dread she felt.

"Accepted her death," Saint-Germain echoed. "What has that to do with it? My acceptance won't change it. Chih-Yü is dead. It's not a matter for debate."

"Even for you?" she asked before she could stop herself.

"For me?" He was startled, and there was an intensity in his unseen eyes.

"You are one of Shiva's creatures, who have been touched by death and refused its hold, aren't you?" Had she dared to say this ten years ago, the words alone would have terrified her, but now, feeling the reality of age with her bones, she could not be afraid.

Saint-Germain's voice was enigmatic. "It was not argument that made me what I am but a far more compelling force." He turned slightly, and the fading light of the sun painted a brilliant line down his brow, along the edge of his eye, the rise of his cheekbone and the arch of his nostril, the line of his mouth, the edge of his jaw, the strong bend of his neck. When he spoke, his small, even teeth shone. "She was not like me."

"And I?" Padmiri was not sure what she wanted his answer to be.

"No," Saint-Germain said in a low tone. "And you need not be, if that is your wish."

Padmiri did not react to this, but instead asked, "You said that you wanted to escape her memory with me. Did you?"

He came one step nearer. "Yes. I will not forget her, but . . . her loss is no longer an open wound in me." He released her hands, but only to turn her face up toward him. "Do you forgive me?"

"For what?" She rose from the bench and walked away from him down the darkened terrace. "For thinking I had enough worth that you would be able to end your sorrow with me? For loving me through your grief? Where is the offense, that you ask forgiveness?"

Saint-Germain had not followed her, listening intently as she spoke, watching her as she moved. "And for yourself?"

She faced him, needing the distance between them, her thoughts crowding in on one another. "With me it is different. I've learned to look beyond the things I was taught, but the lesson was not easily acquired."

"No," Saint-Germain said. "It never is."

"When my brothers and cousins rose against Dantinusha, I was certain that my studying would show me wisdom, and when the rebellion ended and much of my family was put to death, I searched for comfort that was not to be had. I, too, have bandaged my grief with the pleasures of the flesh, but blindly, blindly." There were tears in her eyes and she dashed them away. "I have read some of the teachings of the West, so when you speak of forgiveness, I remember reading of expiation. Is that more reasonable than karma, where forgiveness and expiation are part of the turning of the Wheel?" She had reached the terrace balustrade and now she leaned on it, gazing toward the irregular darkness of distant trees. "Why should I forgive you, when I wanted you? Why does it matter that you were mourning a dead woman? Who of us reaches the middle and the end of life without a few ghosts?"

Saint-Germain felt his memories stir, and faces, bodies, touches, blood, came back to him like the flickering light of torches. He had forgot none of them, could not forget them. Some were filled with amusement and delight, some with tremors of fear or desire, some with passion, a few with poignancy intense and aching. So few were left to him, so few! Even those who had changed and wakened into his life were vulnerable, and he had lost many of them. He tried to speak, but could not express the desire and the anguish in him.

"It doesn't matter what you are. At one time it might have. If I had known before you came here, I would have refused to have you stay. I admit that." She looked at him with the last vestiges of defiance in her eyes. "And perhaps, had I discovered the truth about you some . . . other way, I would have asked that you go elsewhere. I couldn't do that now." Padmiri felt the cold of night on her, and tugged her shawl tighter. "So you see, you are not the only one who has sacrificed to Maya. She is a most persuasive goddess. You, who ask for forgiveness, will you forgive me?"

In seven quick strides Saint-Germain closed the distance between them. He felt her arms tighten around him as he embraced her, and the worst of his hurt faded a little. "Padmiri," he whispered, making a litany of her name.

Padmiri had never expected to find such palliation in a lover. For her, his kisses were anodyne, healing her of wounds that others could not see. She was startled that she still wept, and sought to explain this, without understanding it herself. Saint-Germain stilled her jumbled protests and held her securely until she had cried herself out.

"Don't force yourself to stop," he said as she pulled back from him. "I have no tears—I often envy those who do."

She had taken the hem of her shawl and was daubing at her eyes with it. "No, I'm through. I don't know why it happened." Her words were still muffled. As much as she took consolation from him, she wished that he would leave her time alone, until her thoughts were clearer. She wanted to pause before her shrine to the elephant-headed Ghanesh and ask his aid in clarifying her thoughts.

Saint-Germain released her. "I will go to my laboratory. If you should decide you want to see me, my servant will bring me word of it."

"Your servant? How?"

He looked down at her. "Send word to your slaves that you wish for certain books of poetry, ones that you do not have readily to hand. Rogerio spends part of every evening in their quarters, and tonight I promise you he will be there until midnight. If you make such a request, he will hear it and understand. And if you should prefer that I keep away . . ."—he shrugged sadly—"I would prefer to be with you, but not against your will."

"Rachura, the Brahmin who serves my brother, would tell you that will itself is only another manifestation of Maya, and that all is nothing but the turning of the Wheel." When had she turned away from the great teaching? she asked herself. Her brother had said that she was setting her will above that of her family when she came to live in this house. Rachura predicted then that she would not stay long in such isolation, but time had proved him wrong. There had been a scholar from Aleppo who had visited her once and read to her from the various scriptures and commentaries of the West as well as from Islamic texts. That visit had been brief and for some months thereafter Padmiri had had to endure her brother's displeasure.

Saint-Germain could see that her thoughts were drifting, and so he waited before he spoke again. "It may be only the turning of the Wheel, but there are times you must choose. If the choice is nothing but illusion, does it matter? You will still have to decide. Rachura deplores the successes of the Sultan Shams-ud-din Iletmish, and claims that the encroachment of his forces insults the gods. If there is only the Wheel, how may the gods be insulted?" His voice was kind, and his dark, compelling eyes were warm. "Padmiri, Padmiri, do as you wish to do."

Her laughter was not easy to hear. "How simple it sounds," she said to him, moving a few steps away. "No, no, don't argue with me. Let me decide for myself. If you speak again . . ."

Saint-Germain bowed slightly, watching her with concern. He had paid the price of delitescence too often to wish a further alienation on her, and he was aware that he could use all his compelling strength to dismiss her uncertainties—yet that seemed to be an unconscionable intrusion. All her life, Padmiri had been cheated of her will. Any coercion he used would tarnish him in her eyes, and ultimately poison their association. His eyes did not leave her as she reached the end of the terrace where the musicians had been and looked back at him.

"Let me have time to myself, Saint-Germain," she said. "I will let you know my decision." She put her hand on the latch of the nearest door. "I will try not to keep you waiting too long."

Saint-Germain neither moved nor spoke, but his dark eyes held hers with such intensity that it seemed he touched her.

Padmiri had barely stepped into the terrace room and closed the door when Bhatin appeared beside her. She was startled to see him and might have demanded what he was doing there when he abased himself and spoke.

"When the musicians came in and you did not, there were those of us who were concerned. I was coming to see if you required my aid, mistress. There is danger attendant on that foreigner. The scorpions show that this is true." He stood up, his oddly youthful face impassive.

"Yes, the scorpions," Padmiri said, and could not entirely suppress a grue. No one had been able to explain the scorpions, and Saint-Germain had asked her that an issue not be made of it. She was not convinced that she would not be wise to beat the truth out of her slaves, and only the certainty that Saint-Germain would condemn such tactics prevented her from ordering a general flogging.

"He should be sent away, mistress," Bhatin murmured, his eyes respectfully averted.

Until a moment before Padmiri had thought that this might be the best course, but now she said, "He has been commended to me as a guest by my brother, the Rajah. He is a man of wide learning and experience. As it is unlikely that I will be allowed to travel, I am determined to listen to all he tells me of other lands." She rarely used her most regal manner, but she did now. Her head was high and her dark eyes glittered. "If I should hear of any insolence offered to him, it will be the worse for you and the rest of this household."

Bhatin crossed his hands on his breast. "It is your right to do so, mistress. We are yours to do with as you see fit." It was true: they both knew it, but he had never acknowledged this aloud.

"Yes," she declared. "Because I live in seclusion, I am sometimes lax. But I have not forgotten my rights, Bhatin." The warning was clear, and she used it to end their speech. She went past him into the hall that led to her quarters, and did not look back to see whether or not Bhatin followed her.

It was almost midnight when she sent word to the slaves' quarters that she wanted the volumes of Bengali philosophical rhymes. She had sat by herself in the intervening hours, mustering arguments for and against seeing Saint-Germain. In the end, it was not her intellect but her isolation that won.

Saint-Germain came into her room through a tall window some two stories above the ground: he was a shape, a darkness against the stars, and then he stepped into the soft light of the oil lamps and became himself again. "I had almost lost hope," he said to Padmiri as he approached her.

She stopped him with a gesture. "And I." As befitted her rank, she wore a robe of thin muslin that did not provide enough warmth on this chill night. Her long hair was plaited and bound up with strands of silken cord. "I have been pondering," she went on, indicating that he should be seated. "I was remembering my mother and her immolation, and I have realized that I have followed her example, which was what I wanted least to do."

"Padmiri, you need not—" he began, but she interrupted him.

"Rather than give myself to a husband and the anonymity of a wife's estate, I have banished myself and surrendered to scholarship what I might have given to children. There is no escape from the turning of the Wheel, but complete extinguishing of self. Those who have taken the teachings of Buddha say that they relinquish all desire, including the desire to be free of desire, and then they are one with the god. I can't do that. How much I have lost, thinking that I gained!" Her hands covered her face but she did not weep.

Saint-Germain rose and went to her. "Scholarship is not the same thing as a funeral pyre." One small hand pressed her to him, the other loosened the silk that held her hair so that the long plaits fell down her back, reaching the top of her hip.

"I am nothing. I am less than my eunuch Bhatin!" Her hands dug fiercely into his shoulders and she trembled as she spoke.

"No, Padmiri, no." The scent of her perfumed hair was in his nostrils, and the fragrance of her flesh.

"What have I? What?" She looked up at him and her face was tragic.

"Life, Padmiri."

She saw the ancient despair in his eyes and could not mock it. Life seemed paltry to her, and without meaning, but she was unable to say so with those penetrating dark eyes on her. Slowly her hands relaxed and dropped to her sides. To fill the silence, she said, "I'm . . . distraught."

His lips brushed her brow. "Be calm, cherished one. Do not torment yourself for this." He lifted her hands to his lips and kissed them, the backs and then the palms.

Within her, a welcome, familiar warmth ignited, filling her with a restless lassitude. She admitted, if only to herself, that she had made her decision when she sent for the books, and these last protestations were nothing more than the deprecatory lessons she had been taught all through her life. And compared to the joy his first touch promised her, they were nothing. "Wait, Saint-Germain," she murmured, then chuckled wistfully. "When I was younger, it did not matter where I loved, but now, I would prefer the comfort of my bed." She moved back a few steps and reached to draw the curtains around her low bed aside.

Saint-Germain's hand fell over hers, and he held the curtains parted for her. He waited until she had knelt on the blankets before stepping into the tentlike enclosure of the bed and kneeling beside Padmiri, not quite touching her.

"I'm cold," she said, her hands chafing her bare arms, though she knew it was not the frosty night that brought the frisson to her skin. "Warm me . . ." Her holy books had advised her that this was a night to kiss and fondle the right side of the body, and to adorn the flank of the beloved with patterns of bites like passing clouds, to lie still with legs entwined like climbing plants. Padmiri's last two lovers had been punctilious in observing these dicta, but Saint-Germain was not constrained by such instructions. His hands, light and fondly persuasive, were sliding lightly over the thin fabric of her robe, and the heat they brought came from within her.

As he moved on his knees, Saint-Germain was able to lift the edge of the bedcover and draw it up. "Lie back, Padmiri," he whispered, and as she bent, he lifted her robe from her, then lay beside her in the sweet-scented gloom.

The bedcover was smooth on her skin, but his hands and lips fired her with the onset of her passion. His loosely curling dark hair brushed her breasts, her abdomen. Padmiri's breath came faster and once she made a soft sound like the cry of a night bird. There had never been instructions in scripture for the riot in her soul—how she wanted to touch him, show him the full extent of her gratitude. But he was clothed. A little wildly, she wondered how much hair grew on his body, and where? Were his nipples taut as hers? He was male: surely he must want to have her fingers ready for him . . . for what? For the demands her flesh was eager to answer? Then the questions were gone and there was only the reality of his mouth and his seeking hands.

The bedcovers trembled and surged and once the hangings billowed as Padmiri flung her head back, caught now in a rising tide that consumed her with rapture. Perhaps she called his name when her amazingly sustained release began, and perhaps it was that she was no longer aware of anything but him and her ecstasy.

A letter from Mei Hsu-Mo to Nai Yung-Ya and the Nestorian Christian Church of Lan-Chow. The ship carrying this letter and a cargo of pepper and cotton sank in a squall six days out of port.

In the fortnight of the Bright Frosts, though I have not seen such here, near the end of the Year of the Tiger, the Fifteenth Year of the Sixty-fifth Cycle, the one thousand two hundred eighteenth year of Our Lord, to the Pope Nai Yung-Ya and the congregation of Lan-Chow.

I have been in Pu-Na for some weeks now, and have made contact with a trader from the city he calls Constantinople, which we know as Ki-Sz'-Da-Ni. He speaks a little of the languate of Pu-Na, and I have learned it a little, so we have been able to discuss a few matters. This man, who is called Hemedoris, has said that he might be able to provide passage to Egypt, and from there I would be able to find my way to his home, even as he will. I am not eager to travel with this man, for though he claims to be a Christian, he has neither wives nor concubines, as a good Christian should, but cohabits with the lowest prostitutes, which he says is a sin and which he says that he confesses on his return to Christian countries so that he may be absolved. It is as we have been told, I am discovering, and the Christians in the West have chosen quite a different path, if this man is any example, though I most earnestly pray he is not.

There have been rumors again about the predations of the Mongols. Everywhere one hears of this atrocity and that disaster. May God preserve you from them! I do not know how it may be possible for these appalling men to be in China one day and in Persia the next, but apparently this has happened. Even the sailors I have spoken with fear them and say that they believe it is only a matter of time before the Mongols will ride their demon horses over the sea to plunder ships on the water. This may yet come to pass, though we have been taught that it is only those versed in the ways of God who may stand on the waters and not be wet.

I was fortunate in my companion on the road, a man of some years, and a distinguished Buddhist teacher. We spoke a great deal of our faiths and I am certain that each of us was well-pleased by the understanding we have gained. I see that it is possible for those who follow the teaching of Siddhartha to be in accord with good Christians on many important matters. He, I must tell you, has warned me of this Hemedoris, for he has heard of those who seize upon travelers and sell them into slavery. It would be an easy thing for this Hemedoris to do, as I am so far from home and there are none to guide me, or who await me at the end of my journey. I must assure you that I am taking his advice very much to heart, for it would not please me to have this venture end so poorly. I have also explained to Hemedoris that I am not willing to pay him with my body, however much he may agree to do for me if I should accept his bargains. Be assured that I will take no pleasure with this person, as that would be insulting to this mission and our faith.

It is fairly dry at this time, the rains coming through the summer. Here it is damp, and when my brother died, the air was steaming, so hot and wet it had become. There are fresh breezes off the sea, which take away some of the particular scent of this place. I have been told that in the north it is often very cold and the worst of the rains are spent before they reach the mountains, so that this enveloping heat touches them less. I did not think that I could learn to long for the sight of snow, but so it is. Humble frost would be a delightful thing to me this morning, for although we are near the dark of the year, yet there is a fruit tree bending over the roof of this inn, and I can hear birds singing and chattering nearby.

Sadly, the money which was provided us, and which seemed so lavish an amount when we set out, is now gone, and I am somewhat at a loss as to how to

proceed. I have done a little fine needlework for the innkeeper, and he is willing to pay me for this and supply
me with my passage money when I leave here, but what
I will do after that, I have not yet considered. I have
prayed for guidance and for fortitude, and there is comfort in prayer, though, as yet, no solution. I have still
two pendants of my brother's which I know could be
sold for a considerable sum, but I am loath to part with
them. It would be dishonorable to treat his things in so
shabby a way. If there is absolutely no other recourse
but prostitution, then I will sell the pendants, and offer
recompense to his memory when I arrive in Constantinople, at the great church there.

It is not my intention to make a claim upon the congregation, but if it should happen that it must be done, I
will send you word and ask for what assistance you may
provide. Doubtless, the distances being now so great, it
will be longer than a year before any aid might be provided, yet I fear that I must prepare you for that possibility. Had my brother lived, and had our companion
not revealed himself unworthy of the name Christian,
there would be no need for me, or any of us, to make
such requests of you. I am alone now, and in this world,
that can be most unpleasant. Forgive me for this unseemly petition, but do not turn away from my need because it is not appropriate for me to address you thus.
Think of your wives and daughters, and imagine what
their plight could be in this place, were they as alone as
I am. I have not the money to return to you, and I
promised my brother that I would press on and finish
what we have begun. I do not intend to change that, or
to renege on my word, but I would be more confident in
my task if I did not have the specters of starvation and
degradation as company in my thoughts.

There is a legend here that the Apostle Thomas
preached here and was buried not too great a distance
from this place. I have asked to see the burial place, but
everyone indicates a different direction and a different
hill or mound for him, so I will not be too hasty in assuming that the legend is true. I have been told that
there were Christians here for some time, and that there
are a few still, but no one knows precisely where they
are, or how to find them. It would please me to see an-

other Christian besides Hemedoris, yet I doubt that it will be possible for me to find these people, if they do exist. I fear that it is simply another legend, and that there may have been Christians here once, but now they are vanished. I have been assured that everyone in Constantinople is Christian, even the Emperor himself. Doubtless, when I reach that city, I will be among friends again and the fears that haunt me in the night will not harass me in that city.

You are always in my prayers and thoughts, and if it is fated that we will not see one another in this life, I will greet you in the Gardens of Paradise, which, I tell you most sincerely, Pu-Na is not.

Mei Hsu-Mo
sister of Mei Sa-Fong
in Pu-Na

7

RACHURA HAD been reading from scripture, but Dantinusha now waved him into silence. Here, where the sun lanced through the half-open shutters, it was warm enough, but the wind was cold and where the shadows fell, the heat was leeched away.

"I have a few new verses—minor things, but you might find them intriguing," Jaminya said to the Rajah. "Melancholy is not useful in a ruler."

Ordinarily this bantering tone would evoke a smile from Dantinusha, and he would have given the poet his attention. Today, however, his mouth tightened with distaste. "I wish for silence. If that is not acceptable to you, then leave."

Taken aback, Jaminya retired to a corner of the room and made a show of examining a scroll with critical eyes. His thoughts were far away and he was only remotely aware of the script in front of him. Fear had sunk its claws into his chest and he was striving to master it. He twisted the ends of his mustaches, trying to appear nonchalant,

Rachura had got to his feet and went to stand before the Rajah's throne. It was unacceptable for him to feel distress and so his demeanor was restrained and he called the chill that went through him a breeze instead of alarm. "I will withdraw, if the Rajah permits this."

"The Rajah does not," Dantinusha snapped. "The Rajah intends to keep as much of his court in sight as possible." He rose suddenly and began to walk toward the windows. The sunlight gleamed on the brilliant green silk of his long jacket. "Someone," he said in a steely undervoice, "someone has started a conspiracy against me. I thought we had done with that three years ago, but there are fools everywhere, and the thing has begun again. I will not have it. Understand me. I will not have it." His voice had grown louder and he ended on a shout.

Jaminya shot one frightened look at Rachura but could discover nothing in the Brahmin's composed features. More than anything else, he wished he could leave the room. His hands, he realized, were trembling and he rolled the scroll he held and thrust it into his sash. He tried to speak, but could think of nothing to say.

"This palace is filled with spies, riddled with them. It might as well be a marketplace of secrets. I have ordered that five of my slaves have their tongues cut out. It won't end it, of course. Nothing will end it." He was at the window now, and he pushed the shutters wider. "It was a warning, only a warning. If it is not successful, then there will be executions again, and I am so tired of them."

Rachura did not move from his place before the throne, but he spoke to Dantinusha deferentially. "Great Lord, you are too mild. If there are those who have chosen to move against you, then it is your obligation to cut them down. How else will chaos be kept out of the world?"

Dantinusha was not listening. Something had caught his attention, and he leaned forward to have a better look. "The blind beggar with the slit nose—you know him? He sits in the marketplace and steals vegetables. He was lieutenant of the palace guard three years ago. He was not killed, not being one of my brothers or cousins. There are many like him. This evil is all-pervasive. Limbs may be struck off and tongues cut out and eyes burned away, but there is still rebellion." Quite suddenly Dantinusha came away from the window. "I am sick at heart, but I will order deaths and maiming until I am certain that the throne is protected!"

Guristar appeared in the doorway to the chamber. He was magnificently garbed today, in clothes of silk and fur. He

abased himself and straightened up in one practiced movement. "Great Lord, your daughter desires the opportunity to
speak with you."

"I left word that she was to stay in her quarters. You know
how unsafe the times are," Rajah Dantinusha said with
asperity.

"For that reason, she wishes to see you. She has begged me
to tell you that her place, as your heir, is at your side." The
guard commander touched his long sword.

"So that we may both be struck down?" Dantinusha demanded furiously. "Tell her that she is not to leave her quarters, not until I come personally to lead her away from there.
This is not a minor threat, Guristar. You were the one who
championed swift action, and I delayed. Now, you are courting danger, because of Tamasrajasi's whim." His face darkened and he glared around the room.

"She said," Guristar persisted, "that if you must fall, then
she would rather have a clean death with you than suffer as
she might have to later."

Dantinusha was quiet, his face grave. "They would not use
her well, whoever they are." He looked at the window. "She
would not die quickly, it is true, but she would escape the
debts I have earned in this life. A hot knife is quick, much
quicker than rebels in the hall. Be sure that she has a knife."

"I will tell her," Guristar said, and added, "She will not be
content with that."

"Tell her also," Dantinusha said as if he had not heard
Guristar's warning, "that the slaves who will not defend her
will be taken and flayed alive, and left in the sun for carrion
birds!"

Jaminya had retreated even farther and he tried to shut out
the Rajah's words. How long would it be until suspicion fell
on him and he was dragged to the execution ground? He reminded himself of the various scriptures which preached acceptance, but his spirit was not quieted. There was death in
the air, as if an invisible corpse rotted in the center of the
room. "Great Lord," he said in a stifled tone, "I am not a
brave man. I am a poet. If there is to be conflict here, let me
go."

"Afraid, Jaminya?" Guristar asked, full of mockery.

"Yes, I'm afraid," Jaminya admitted, and felt no shame in
this. "If I were trained for battle, I would want to comport
myself as befits a soldier, but all I know is the making of

verses." He turned away from Guristar, back to Dantinusha. "I cannot aid you, Great Lord. If I remain here, I will not be an asset to you. Nothing will be gained by keeping me here."

Dantinusha sighed. "Leave, then. I would rather have men who can defend me standing with me now. You are not willing to, and there is no reason for you to stay." He gestured dismissal to the poet and then appeared to forget the man was present.

"We might send word to Ab-she-lam Eidan and request that he send what few troops he has brought with him to add to the guard here," Rachura suggested.

"And if the unrest comes from the men of the Sultan, what then?" Dantinusha asked. "We would make it easier for them to have the conquest they desire, but what would the advantage be? Can you tell me that it is impossible that the Sultan has ordered this disruption?"

Guristar stared fiercely at Rachura. "I have not learned who is the enemy in this. However, only an idiot would appeal to the Sultan in this case. There are men he might send to protect the Rajah, and once the protection was provided, it might never be withdrawn." He drew himself up with pride. "Our guard is not large, but I know that the men are loyal to this country and will defend it to their deaths."

"And while you prate here about their loyalty," Dantinusha cut in, "who has come through the gates? If the men are true, give them the orders to stand to their weapons!"

Guristar accepted this rebuke with poor grace. "I did not wish you to be uninformed of the guard's work. I will not stay to talk more, since you have no wish to hear my words." The Commander of the guard stepped back, turned on his heel and strode from the room.

Rachura looked up at Dantinusha. "His ill-will may harm you, Rajah." It was the only rebuke he delivered.

"I had hoped that I had seen the last of rebellion and blood and execution," the Rajah murmured, his hopes fading. On the far wall was a carving of Vishnu Trivikrama, his leg raised high in token of the Three Steps with which the god had strode over the sky, the earth and the lower world. Surely Vishnu would remember the sacrifices he had accepted in the past and would give his support to Rajah Dantinusha rather than let him fall to the men of Shams-ud-din Iletmish. The Rajah approached the carving and looked into the smiling, indifferent face of the young god.

Then there was a commotion at the door and Dantinusha turned to see Rachura speaking to one of the eunuchs who guarded Tamasrajasi. The Brahmin gave Dantinusha a quick glance. "He has been sent to tell you that your daughter desires you receive her."

"Impossible," Dantinusha said quickly. He had begun to feel the citric tang of danger in the air, not unlike heated metal. "She is not to come here. I have heard her concern for what may happen to her, and you must tell her that she is not alone in her fear. I will give orders that she is to be dispatched if there is any . . . difficulty." Belatedly, he remembered his sister. "I will also give orders to send riders to Padmiri at once if there should be real trouble here."

The eunuch was still distressed and for that reason dared to speak to the Rajah. "Your daughter, Great Lord, is a child of great warriors, as you are and your father was. She said that she cannot sit idly by, waiting for the blow that will end her life. She begs that you will let her come to you, so that the household may see what faith you have in the strength of your line." The eunuch's moon face was waxy-colored and his body smelled faintly of fear under the perfume.

"Tell her that if there is no overt attack by nightfall, I will send for her and we will dine together in the banqueting hall. That much I am willing to do, but more is too dangerous." He admired her bravery, but recognized that she could not know how much she courted disaster. "You may inform her that I take pride in her fearlessness."

"I will do that, Great Lord." The eunuch abased himself, closing his eyes as he thought about the ire he would face when he returned to Tamasrajasi's quarters. In desperation he added, "Would it be possible for a messenger to be appointed, one who would carry word between you and your daughter?"

Dantinusha sighed, and though he was aware it would be most wise to refuse, he did not wish to treat his child so harshly. "If that will quiet her fears, then it shall be done. Tell her to choose one of her household to fulfill this office." He did not wish to speak to the eunuch any longer. "Leave me."

Outside in the stableyard Guristar was shouting orders to the guard, doubling the armed men at the gates and insisting that no one was to be given permission to enter until he himself had approved. The Commander's voice was high and harsh, and those hearing it were unwilling to question him. Occasionally the guardsmen would shout back answers as Guristar grew more insistent.

Jaminya, who had withdrawn to the antechamber, now came back into the throne room and made formal abasement to Dantinusha. "You may set a guard at my door, but let me leave here." Before, he had felt no embarrassment, but now there was a twinge of remorse in him. "I will ride to your sister with a guard, if that would be acceptable to you. She must be warned in any event. You have said as much. If I brought her the news, she would be less apprehensive than if it came from one of the guardsmen alone. You could stipulate that the guard was to stay with me at all times, or order that once I arrived at Padmiri's house I be locked into the slaves' quarters. Anything."

"You may ride with the messenger to Padmiri. That much I will allow. You will tell her how it was here when you left, and you will not return until you have heard from Guristar's men that it is advisable to do so. There is a thing I must add," Dantinusha went on, his voice hardening. "Once you leave my presence today, you will never again be admitted to it. Make your farewells now, poet, and depart from here."

"It isn't necessary . . ." Jaminya started to protest, then bowed his head. "I will do as you will, Great Lord."

"Very wise," the Rajah agreed, saying nothing more until Jaminya had retreated from the room.

Rachura was not so foolish as to watch Jaminya go, but he did hesitate once the poet had gone. "It is true enough that such men are not useful in conflict," he remarked.

"True," Dantinusha said quietly, "and had it come to that, I would have sent him away. What is most distressing is that he wished to go. For that alone he has forfeited my trust. The gods do not look with favor on those who will not bow to their fate."

"Perhaps it was his fate to run," the Brahmin suggested. "He will go to your sister and she will be certain that he is protected. In time you may be pleased that he left. It is true that his death would not benefit you."

Dantinusha scowled. "Yet I wish that he had wished to stay. No doubt I am under the spell of Maya, and wish to see the world through her glamour." His gestures had grown heavy, weary. "Whatever is coming, let it be quickly settled. I have no stomach for long battles. Let them come here and end it here."

"That may not be your privilege," Rachura said quietly. "It is best to accept the turning of the Wheel, and make sacrifice to the gods. There is nothing else of merit."

One of Guristar's lieutenants came to the door and abased himself. "Great Lord, it is my honor to stand guard at your door. My brothers in arms are stationed along the corridor so that none may pass without great harm, and so that should there be danger, you will be warned." He was straight and young and his face shone with purpose.

"Excellent," the Rajah said, making no attempt to deny his fatigue. "I trust you will keep me informed of occurrences."

"Most certainly, Great Lord. Sudra Guristar, our Commander, has set up a chain of messengers so that none of us need leave our posts, and will nonetheless have all the news there is." He took up his post outside the door, his shimtare held up at the ready, its slightly curved blade facing outward.

To Dantinusha all these preparations seemed a travesty. What true enemy, he asked himself, would be discouraged by a few guardsmen in the hall, or an increase in the number of guards at the gate? Were he the one wishing to attack, this would not discourage him at all. Rather, he would take heart at the sight, for it would tell him that those in the palace were afraid. "That's not so," he said aloud. He was not afraid. There were others who were afraid for him, but he, himself, had left his terror behind.

"What is not so, Great Lord?" the Brahmin Rachura asked deferentially.

"Nothing, nothing." He stood a moment, then took a restless turn about the room. How long would he have to live this way, frightened by shadows? It would be a relief to tell his guards to arm themselves and send orders to the stables to prepare the warhorses. But whom should he attack?

One of the Tamasrajasi's women stood in the door, her face averted in respect to the Rajah's power. "My mistress," the slave said when she knew that Dantinusha had seen her, "your daughter, asks that I bring her greetings to you."

"Yes," Dantinusha answered, thinking that there were times his daughter was a difficult child. "You may tell her that you saw me well and impatient."

"I will do that," the slave murmured, prostrated herself, then crawled from the Rajah's presence.

"What was that?" Dantinusha demanded of the air. "Slaves have not had to crawl in Natha Suryarathas since my grandfather's time."

Rachura, too, had been puzzled, but he felt it was important that he comment on this. "It may be that since the slave abases herself to her mistress, that she felt she must do more to acknowldge your greater rank."

"It's possible," Dantinusha said, already putting the matter behind him. He took his place in the throne again, but could not make himself comfortable. The cushions were no longer soft, but seemed to have been filled with sharp stones. His clothes were tight, as if made for some other man. Dantinusha recalled the unspeakable days before his brothers and cousins had risen in revolt, and was possessed by the same inner sinking that he had known then. Time was moving far too slowly, he told himself. He was certain that hours had gone by, but the track of the sun through the room belied this. When he was ready to shout with exasperation, he rose again. "I wish to walk in the gardens. See that guards are sent to me. It's stifling here."

The guard at the door stared. "I will have to give word to the messenger. Great Lord, your Commander of the guard would doubtless prefer it if you would remain here, in the throne room."

"Doubtless," Dantinusha agreed. "But I wish to walk in the garden. Tell your messenger and let Guristar find a way to arrange this that will satisfy him."

With an unhappy glance at the Rajah, the guard made a signal, and a few moments later a boy with a military sash tied around his waist over his understeward's clothes ran to him. The guardsman relayed the instructions, the boy bowed and hastened away, and then the room was still again.

Some little time later another one of Tamasrajasi's eunuchs came to the door. "Great Lord," he said as he abased himself. "Your daughter has bade me come to you with her greetings."

"Yes, yes, many thanks to you and my daughter. Her concern is touching, most touching," Dantinusha said brusquely.

"She has asked me to give you a warning, for one of her slaves has said that she overheard two guardsmen speaking, and what they said was not to your good." The eunuch had lowered his voice and once looked nervously over his shoulder. "Let me approach you, Great Lord, and tell you the words that my mistress has entrusted to me."

"You cannot simply say them aloud?" Dantinusha demanded.

The eunuch grimaced miserably. "I can, if that is what you order me to do, but it is not wise that others should hear. You are in the most grave danger, Great Lord, and not all those who fight beside you are your friends."

"How do you mean? Are there others involved?" He had thought all along that there must be some who had professed themselves his friends and were not. It was tempting to hear what the eunuch had to say. He did not want the slave to return to Tamasrajasi and tell her that her father had not wanted to hear her message. The child was anxious, he knew that, and wished to show him how much she valued him. "You say that one of her slaves overheard this. Where was the slave, that she should hear guardsmen?"

"Near the courtyard east of the garden," the eunuch said uncertainly. "My mistress had sent her to fetch blossoms."

"I see. And the guardsmen were there?" Reluctantly he admitted to himself that the information might be important.

"They were posted at the gate between the courtyard and garden. They did not see Tamasrajasi's slave until she was quite near them, and once she was in sight, they were silent." He wrung his hands, staring beseechingly at the Rajah. "Let me approach you, Great Lord. How can I bear to see you in this peril and do nothing to aid you? Your daughter would surely slay me, or I would take my own life."

Dantinusha kept the irritation out of his voice. "Very well, since you are determined. You may approach me and tell me what the slave in the garden overheard."

The eunuch scrambled to his feet. "In this life and in all the lives to come, I am grateful to you, Great Lord," he said as he neared the throne, then came up the steps, stopping less than an arm's length from the Rajah. "The slave in the garden heard the guardsmen talking, and they said that your greatest enemy is within the palace itself, and has been plotting your downfall with the Commander of the guard. This enemy is ruthless and dedicated, Great Lord, and feels unending shame that this kingdom should be reduced as it has been by the predations of the Sultan at Delhi."

Dantinusha started to rise, a protest already forming on his lips, when the eunuch gripped his shoulder, and in the next moment had plunged a small dagger into the Rajah's abdomen, pulling it upward, rending the clothes and flesh of the man impartially, grinning as Dantinusha tried to scream. At last the Rajah gave a strange, guttural cry, and Rachura looked up from his scrolls. Before Dantinusha could make another sound, the dagger was jerked out of him and then plunged into his throat. As he died, the Rajah saw blood cascading onto the throne and could not believe it was his own.

The guard in the hall had shouted with alarm, and Rachura was on his feet. There were running footsteps in the corridor and a few cries were being raised.

With the body of the Rajah at his feet, the eunuch turned to face those who came into the room. His clothes were drenched in blood and his face was spattered with it. He grinned hugely as guardsmen poured through the door.

Rachura had turned pale, unable to bring himself to move forward or speak aloud. He saw the hot, red stain spreading around the throne and the slumped figure there. He heard the laughter of the eunuch as he faced the men in the doorway. He tried to call to mind the holy words for the dead, but his thoughts were empty.

The eunuch was overjoyed. It had been easy, so much easier than he had thought it would be. His mistress had told him there would be no difficulties, and so it had transpired. He waved the ensanguined knife above his head as more of the palace guard came to the door, to look in horrified amazement at the blood on the throne and the body of the Rajah. He shouted incoherently, ready to fight with any who might come up the dais.

A few moments later, Sudra Guristar ran into the throne room. He was somewhat out of breath and his patience was exhausted. He pushed through the guardsmen and stopped at the foot of the thone's dais. There was blood everywhere, he thought. The toes of his boots were stained with it. He had been ready for this, but had not thought that it would come so soon. Tamasrajasi had said that she would not be hasty, and then her father was dead. Uttering an oath to a number of the gods, Guristar started up the three steps toward the eunuch, drawing his sword as he went.

Now the eunuch was confused. He had been told he would be rewarded, yet here was the Commander of the palace guard coming toward him with a blade ready. He howled out a protest, turning on Guristar. "No! No! This is a holy act! You do not understand!"

Guristar had his shimtare out of the sheath, but he hesitated. He had not been given any instructions about the assassin, and did not know what Tamasrajasi expected. "Give me your weapon."

The eunuch waved the dagger in defiance. He grinned ludicrously. This was glorious! He had killed the Rajah. He felt omnipotent, his mind crowded with praise. Never had anything elated him so. He could smell the blood and other tokens of death. In a short time the room woud be rank with them. "I will kill you, Guristar," he sang out.

Again the commander of the guard hesitated, though he knew he was expected to pursue the murderer. He lifted his shimtare and was about to lunge with it when there was another disruption.

Tamasrajasi had come into the room, forcing her way through the guardsmen and household slaves. Her young, sensuous face was a mask now and she spoke sharply. "Is that the man?"

The eunuch grinned. Now he would have his reward and recognition. It was for his mistress that he had killed her father, and surely she would give him the honor she had promised him. "He is dead, mistress. He is dead!"

There was no indication that Tamasrajasi had heard. "Seize h·m," she said, her tone so cold that there was an instant of complete silence after she spoke. "Guristar."

It was all the order that the Commander of the guard required. He took the last two steps in a rush, his shimtare up.

"Don't kill him. Yet," Tamasrajasi said sharply. "For the moment, cut out his tongue so that we will not have to listen to his oaths and lies." She whisked the hem of her skirt aside so that it would not touch the pool of her father's blood. "Do that now."

Guristar nodded, and grabbed the eunuch's head in an imposing lock. "You, and you," he said, nodding to two of his lieutenants. "Assist me. Hold his head, and keep his jaw open."

The two lieutenants obeyed at once, climbing the dais stairs with care so as not to walk in the Rajah's blood.

"No," the eunuch shouted, but the sound was garbled by the way his head was caught. "No, mistress. What is this?

You assured me that I would be rewarded. I did this for you."

"The man is mad," Tamasrajasi muttered. "His tongue."

There was a scuffle on the dais, a few half-voiced curses, the swift descent of a knife, and then the room was filled with a gurgling scream, and Guristar stepped back with a bloody snippet of flesh between his thumb and fingers. His lieutenants held the eunuch so that he could not fall.

Tamasrajasi had been looking at her father's body, but now she turned her eyes toward the standing men. "Good. You have it." A frozen smile crossed her face and her eyes were fervid. "Now you may kill him. Slowly." She stood at the foot of the dais as the eunuch was dragged down, her face emotionless.

◄●►

A covert report from Bhatin to Tamasrajasi, sent under seal.

Most glorious Rani, esteemed mistress, foremost priestess, this comes with the full devotion of your servant Bhatin.

You have asked to know what transpires between your late brother's sister and the foreign alchemist she has taken into her household. It is as you suspected: the two are lovers. They are much in each other's company, but most of the time is passed in his alchemical room where he makes gold and jewels and speaks to her of the great mysteries of that Art. Padmiri is most curious about this study, and has said that she hopes to continue instruction with this learned man. She has given orders that when Saint-Germain departs, his laboratory is to remain intact for her own use.

It has been most difficult for me to discover what passes between them in bed, but I have twice been able to watch them, unseen, and I will now tell you what I observed. This Saint-Germain came to Padmiri's chambers quite late in the night. He was wearing a curious long robe of black silk and there were high boots on his feet. Certainly this was not the usual garb of an expectant lover, nonetheless it was his mode of dress and I make note of it. He entered her quarters with some degree of stealth, being careful to see that no one was about—he did not know of my hiding place, or he might have left—and closed the door quietly.

Padmiri awaited him in her outer chamber in a long robe of fine-woven linen. She had perfumed herself earlier and her hair had not been braided for the night. There were a few lamps in the room, and over the cushion on the floor Padmiri had flung rugs made of fine pelts. Cedar incense was burning. The two of them embraced once, and then sat and talked like old friends for a while. Eventually, this Saint-Germain approached Padmiri, opened her robe and caressed her in a variety of ways. Padmiri gave every indication of the most profound pleasure. She reclined on the fur rugs and let the foreigner touch her and arouse her most shamelessly. She encouraged him to kiss her and to use her body fully. She was disappointed that he did not do as she had asked. When she had reached the culmination of her desires, she urged him to take his pleasure of her.

Now, this was what astounded me. I have seen men and women couple many times and in curious ways, but that is not what this man did, As Padmiri cried out her achievement, this foreigner set his lips to her neck, and in some strange way, he seemed to take her fulfillment into himself. Certainly he was satisfied.

The second time I observed them, he did not set his lips to her neck, but the encounter was substantially the same. Saint-Germain aroused Padmiri's passions to the utmost and then pressed her to him and gave her that same deep kiss he had before.

You expressed curiosity about the nature of this foreigner. Did I not know it is impossible, I would think this man a creature of Shiva, preying upon the living. Yet it is not reasonable to assume that Padmiri would not recognize him if such he were, and send him away from her. She has not done this, and the delight she takes from this man is not what she could expect from the creatures of Shiva. She welcomes him, and is happy to be in his company. Her fascination is not that of the flesh alone, which is surprising. Were this man one of Shiva's minions she would be filled with disgust and would be revolted by him unless she sought out his embraces as a sacrifice, which she most certainly does not. Here is a desire of joy, and what she receives from him does not meet with repugnance.

I will make every effort to watch them again, and I will tell you what I observe then. I know not what else to tell you, for this foreigner has me greatly puzzled. I am convinced that he is dangerous and that it would be wise to be rid of him, but upon this subject, Padmiri and I cannot speak. Her lusts for pleasure have too much power in her, and she is drunk with her satisfaction. Also, she is intrigued with the man's learning, and wishes to expand her studies.

Send me your commands and it will be my greatest joy to obey them with alacrity. You are sublime, my Rani, and you alone will be the splendor of my life.

This by my own hand,

Bhatin

8

MORE THAN half the night had wheeled overhead when the tapping came at the shutters. Saint-Germain looked up from the copper vessel he had been agitating carefully, and listened.

The sound came again, more urgently.

"By all the forgotten gods . . ." he swore, setting the vessel aside and resigning himself to losing that batch of azoth. He crossed the room quickly, grabbing a metal-topped staff as he went. The staff, intended for particular alchemical rituals, would also serve as an excellent cudgel.

Again the scraping sounded, and at that moment Saint-Germain pulled the shutters open.

"In the Name of Allah!" Jalal-im-al Zakatim whispered, holding up one arm to block the blow.

Saint-Germain lowered the staff and looked at the man who clung to the narrow balcony with some surprise. "What nonsense is this?" He held the shutters open and extended his arm to the young Muslim.

Jalal-im-al scrambled into the room and closed the shutters at once. Even in the muted light it was possible to see he was pale, and there were bruises on his face. His white djellaba was torn, and although a scabbard hung from his wide leather sash, it was empty. He panted, from more than fatigue, and when he spoke, his voice was ragged. "Not nonsense. Not that. Allah! Allah! It happened so quickly." He had spoken more loudly, and at once hushed himself. "We did not expect it. Who would think such a thing might happen?"

"What is it?" Saint-Germain asked, keeping his tone low. Jalal-im-al's appearance had alarmed him, and for that reason he was most cautious.

"Our mission. Gone." He put his hands to his eyes. "They came in quickly, so quickly, and they fought so surely. They are not human."

Saint-Germain put his hand on Jalal-im-al's shoulder. "Tell me what has happened. Who came in?"

"The men of Kali. There were so many of them. They entered the house from all doors. They brought knives and their garroting scarves. They worked swiftly. No demon could have been faster. Half of us had been watching a troupe of jugglers, and the commotion meant nothing to us until the men had come into the reception room. It was a slaughterhouse there. And the men of Kali were happy in their work. One of them whistled. I heard it." The young Muslim dropped to his knees and began to sob.

"The men of Kali," Saint-Germain said to himself. Were these the Thuggi, or some others, perhaps more sinister? Since Rajah Dantinusha's assassination twenty days ago, much of Natha Suryarathas had been uneasy. There had been rumors circulating that the Rajah's death was a signal of some sort, and that it presaged a time of destruction.

"They were glad that they killed," Jalal-im-al said unsteadily.

"How did you escape?" Saint-Germain had moved one of the lights nearer and he sat down on the floor beside Jalal-im-al, tucking his legs beneath him and bracing his back against the wall.

"It was the Will of Allah," the Muslim said at once.

"Naturally, but you must have done something," was

Saint-Germain's unruffled response. "If the men of Kali were as ruthless as you say, escape must have been very difficult."

Jalal-im-al trembled, then mastered himself. "Yes. Allah gave it to my mind. When I saw what the men of Kali were doing, how all of us who serve the Sultan were being cut down, I was provided a vision, and I acted on what Allah had shown me. I was near a door onto the terrace, and rather than run, and thereby attract the attention of those who had come to kill us, I rolled there, going fairly slowly. I was able to push the door open with my feet, and by that time the . . . butchering was at its height, so that I could crouch low and make my way across the terrace. There, I went over the balustrade and hung from it over the garden because I feared that these upspeakable men would have guards posted to prevent just such an escape as mine. Allah gave me the strength to hang there until the screams and . . . other sounds"—he could not find the words to describe the hacking that had come from the reception room—"had stopped. The men of Kali gathered in the room to chant their praises, and that was when I fled. I dared not go to the stables, for I imagined there would be guards there, too. I caught one of the horses in the pasture behind the house and I made a rough bridle of my boot lacings. I rode her to the edge of the pasture, and there was a guardsman there who tried to cut me in pieces."

"A guardsmen?" Saint-Germain asked, interrupting him for the first time. "Are you sure?"

"I have seen enough of them to recognize them. He had the green jacket and the broad sash. Also, he wore a standard shimtare and carried a light pike. Who else is so armed in this country?" He had let his voice become loud again, and he glared at Saint-Germain. "It was not an evil spirit. My sword cut him down, but I could not get it from the body. I rode the horse until he dropped, and then I came on foot. I dared not ride for the frontier. If the guardsmen were fighting with the men of Kali—"

"Yes," Saint-Germain said quickly. "If the guard is part of this, you would not be allowed to leave." He regarded his visitor with curiosity. "Under the cirsumstances, I am not entirely sure what you expect of me."

Jalal-im-al stared at him. "What do you mean?"

"I mean, since you know you are a marked man, how do you think I can assist you?" He was not angry, and there was no worry in his words or his face. "Do you want me to aid you? If so, how?" .

"I had not thought . . ." Jalal-im-al began, coloring slightly.

"Perhaps it would be wise if you do so now," Saint-Germain said calmly, though he was growing troubled. "How did you approach this house?"

"From the side, through the garden. I didn't want to go near the slaves' quarters, in case one of them might still be up, or there might be a guard on duty." He was mildly upset to admit this. "I have come like a thief in the night, it is true, but I pray you won't refuse to hide me. I know I would not live an hour on those roads now." Again he hesitated. "You haven't any reason to help me, and I have not behaved in a way that would give you a respect of me. I realize that. But I never thought—"

"That the tables might be turned," Saint-Germain suggested. "It is a fairly accurate description of the situation." He looked at the young Muslim's haggard face. "You fear for your life, Jalal-im-al, for what I assume is the first time."

Jalal-im-al nodded and could not look at Saint-Germain. "I've been on maneuvers, but never . . . nothing like that."

"Yes." There was genuine sympathy in Saint-Germain's dark eyes. "You believed that it would not happen to you, and tonight you discovered that indeed it could." How long ago he had learned that sobering lesson! Yet, remotely, he recalled the invaders with their swords and torches and whips, and the things they did. "There is no shame in fear."

"But I trust in Allah, and I am subservient to Allah's Will," Jalal-im-al protested.

"That does not mean that you must want to have a shimtare in your guts." He got to his feet. "I am here on sufferance myself, and there are spies here. I cannot promise you that you will be safe with me, but I will do what I may for you."

Relief filled Jalal-im-al and his vision swam. After the long hours of horror and fright, there was safety. "Allah is merciful," he said, and started to get to his feet.

Saint-Germain motioned him to stay where he was, and then walked to the door. For one dreadful moment Jalal-im-al was convinced that Saint-Germain would give him away, but almost in the same instant he heard the foreigner call to the night steward. "You may hear an occasional commotion here," he said to the salve. "I am involved in some delicate procedures that require supernatural aid, and anything that disturbs me, and consequently them, will be most dangerous for everyone in this household. I would appreciate it if you would warn the other night guards so that they will not break in while I am working and do themselves harm."

The slave, listening in awe, bowed slightly and gave his word that he would not enter the laboratry if he saw demons and devils cavorting around the whole building.

"I am grateful to you," Saint-Germain told the man, and gestured to dismiss him. When he came back into the room, he said, "That will keep them away for a little while, but not long. And Padmiri won't believe it for a moment. Therefore, you must be secure before morning."

Jalal-im-al did not entirely follow what he had been told, but he rose unsteadily. "I will go where you wish."

"Well, for the moment that will not be too difficult. I will send you to my sleeping quarters and put you in the care of my manservant, Rogerio. You know him. But after first light, we will have to find a better place for you. There will be slaves all over the house, and some of them, doubtless, are spies. If it is even hinted that you are here, not only will you no longer be safe, but I, Rogerio, and Padmiri, as well, will be in grave danger. I say this so that you will not take risks or be tempted to press your luck. Allah may protect you, but not from your own folly." He began to pace around the room. "There is a small amount of room above this ceiling. It would be possible to hide you there, I think, but it would require that you lie still all day. You would not be able to eat until dark, and you must avoid making noise of any kind. Can you do that?"

The young Muslim was about to make extravagant promises, but there was something in Saint-Germain's penetrating gaze that stopped him. "I think I might be able to. With Allah's aid."

"Of course," Saint-Germain said dryly. He went to the largest of his worktables and without warning banged two metal pots together and let out a whoop that sent a shudder up Jalal-im-al's spine. Saint-Germain replaced the pots and said, quite conversationally, "I promised the night steward some unearthly noises: it's best that he hear a few."

Shortly thereafter, as Saint-Germain was shaking a wooden tub filled with pebbles, Rogerio came into the room. He was neatly dressed, and there was nothing in his manner that implied Saint-Germain was behaving oddly. "There was a noise," he said.

"Yes, and there are apt to be more for a while," Saint-Germain said in Greek. "We have a visitor, as you see. He tells me that the worshipers of Kali are abroad. When he arrived he told me that the entire Delhi mission had been slaughtered. In the morning, you will find out if this is the truth, as I suspect it is." He had left the tub alone and was blowing down the neck of a thick glass cone. The noise it made was eerie, and Jalal-im-all pressed his hands to his ears.

"And the visitor?" Rogerio was also speaking Greek. "What of him?"

"We must hide him, and well. As soon as it can be arranged, he must be sent away from here." He struck one of the brass chests with a large stone. "That should be enough for the moment." Then he gave his attention to Jalal-im-al again. "Do you know Persian?" he asked in that language.

"A little. Well enough," came the answer, strongly accented but quite acceptable.

"Speak no other language until we're away from here," Saint-Germain warned him. "There will be those who know the tongue of Delhi, but they will not know Persian, or will not expect to hear it from a Sultan's man." Saint-Germain caught his lower lip between his small white teeth as he looked from Rogerio to the Muslim and back again. "I think that Loramidi Chol might be the best one to ask. He knows I have a student, and has not seen him."

"Who is this man?" Jalal-im-al demanded. "What person do you speak of?" He fought a rising panic as decisions were made for him.

"This man is a merchant, very well-respected. He does a great deal of trading with the lands of the Sultan, and it would not be impossible, if you were willing to disguise yourself, that you could leave this place with him." Saint-Germain read Jalal-im-al's offended expression correctly. "Better to go disguised and live than to keep a proper dress and die," he pointed out.

"But a merchant, and an Infidel . . ." His objection faltered as he recalled the charnel house he had left behind. "I will wear a disguise."

"And speak Persian," Saint-Germain reminded him gently.

"I have lived much longer than you have, Jalal-im-al, and I have learned that too much pride is a dangerous luxury."

For once Jalal-im-al did not wish to dispute the matter. He gestured his acceptance as the last of his strength deserted him. "I will do as you tell me to do."

"Good. For the moment, I tell you to rest. Rogerio, take him to my quarters and make up a bed for him in the corner, away from mine. I will want it removed before the slaves come to sweep in the morning." He gave the young Muslim a quick smile. "You will be wakened early, so do not linger now. You may sleep the day out, if you wish. So long as you are not restless and do not talk in your sleep."

Jalal-im-al made a sign to protect himself from evil. "Those who speak in their sleep are the tools of demons and Allah will turn his face from them."

"Quite possibly," Saint-Germain said affably. "But for the moment, to bed with you. Rogerio, watch over him," he added, once more in Greek.

"And you?"

"I've got to find the access to the place above the ceiling without rousing suspicion. An hour before dawn, come to me." He was already walking about, looking up, making note of the structure of the room, checking the length of the beams. "Oh, and Rogerio—if there should be any questions, I conjured up demons to aid me last night. Boast of it to the slaves. You may be as inventive as you like short of claiming I destroyed the house entirely." His tone was light but tense and Rogerio knew enough not to question his master at such times.

"At the hour before dawn," he said, and led Jalal-im-al from the room, promising the young man that he would not disturb him until it was necessary to do so.

When Rogerio returned to Saint-Germain's laboratory, he found his master standing on a stool that had been put on a table. He was making a last adjustment in a section of the ceiling. "Is that ready?"

"I think so. The space above is cramped, but not impossible. If the weather stays chilly he will want a blanket, and perhaps a layer of bedding against the boards. It will muffle sounds, as well." Saint-Germain climbed down off the table and dusted the front of his clothes. "I'm fairly sure that part of the ceiling will stand all but the closest scrutiny. I'm delighted that there was so much ornamentation painted between the beams."

"But what will you do with him?" Rogerio neither looked nor sounded distressed, but there was concern in his eyes.

"I will send word to Chol, and I think it will be fairly easily arranged. He is aware that he can demand a high price for such a service, and this will work to our advantage." He took the stool off the table and set it on the floor. "I think you'd better take a few of those sapphires I made last week and put them out. By now the slaves will have learned that I was engaged in large conjurings last night, and will expect me to have something to show for it. I'll give one to Padmiri, and that should satisfy the household."

"Very well, I'll get out the jewels. Anything more?" Rogerio's reserve was more telling than his opposition would have been.

"You disapprove, old friend. Why?"

"It's a great risk. There is danger enough without this. If he should be discovered, he will die, and Padmiri, and you and I. You don't like Jalal-im-al. You've said that before. Yet you do this for him." Rogerio went to the Roman chest and opened a concealed drawer.

"True enough. I don't like him much. But I understand how he must feel, having seen what he has seen." His grief was clear as still water: he no longer resisted or denied it. "The warriors of Jenghiz Khan, the men of Kali, they're the same madness."

Rogerio said nothing more. He came back to the table, his hand held out. In it rested three sapphires, two blue and one black, each beautifully starred. "Here. The largest has a tinge of purple in it. Padmiri would be complimented."

Saint-Germain touched the sapphires. "Yes. An excellent choice. Leave them near the copper pan. The slaves will be sure to see them, and they will gossip about them."

"And Loramidi Chol? When do you send word to him?" Rogerio arranged the sapphires beside the pan as he had been told.

"Not today, I think. It will be better tomorrow. Once word reaches here from the palace of the killing of the Delhi mission, there will be an uproar. It will be wisest if we do not intrude in this. However, since I have made such fine jewels, it will be unremarkable that I wish to obtain more supplies. Tomorrow I can request Chol visit me and it will be assumed that the sapphires have exhausted my resources. You might hint as much if you are asked questions," Saint-Germain added with an amused twist to his mouth.

"Of course." Rogerio started for the door. "I'll wake Jalal-im-al now, if you think it wise."

"Yes. And I will spend the day resting. After last night, no one will think it strange. I will have time to think, and to restore myself. Also, I will not have to answer too many questions." He indicated the place in the ceiling. "Make sure tnat it is properly closed once Jalal-im-al has concealed himself." He paused to look at the jewels, then spoke more briskly. "We should have him away in six days, eight at the most. Feeding him may be awkward, but it will be accomplished somehow. For the time being, we can find bread, and tonight there should be other edibles we can filch for him."

"I can say that you have asked for local food as part of your studies." Rogerio was still carefully neutral.

"No, I think not. It might rouse suspicions. Everyone can understand eating food, but experimenting with it? Better to steal a little of it than create needless puzzles." He had reached the door, but made one last comment before going through it. "Jalal-im-al is an impetuous, brave, foolhardy young man. Be certain that he understands that he will have my aid only so long as he does precisely as I tell him to do. If he disobeys me in any way, I will abandon him to whatever fate Tamasrajasi wishes to give him. I have heard that it took the eunuch who killed her father four days to die. Tell him that."

Rogerio nodded once. "I will do what I can."

Saint-Germain chuckled. "My old friend, disapprove of me if you must, but remember that I do not require that you stay with me. If you wish to leave, tell me, and it will be arranged." His eyes had grown somber and he gave his servant a long, steady look.

"I have been with you since that rainy day in Rome. I would need more than pique to leave you." His austere features creased into a fleeting smile, and he was no longer rigidly disapproving.

"You reassure me," Saint-Germain said easily, but with utter sincerity. Then he was through the door, and Rogerio was left alone in the laboratory in the predawn half-light.

---◄●►---

A memorandum from the reservoir builders to the cham-
ɔerlain of the Rani Tamasrajasi.

Most respectfully, we of the building supervisors at
work upon the reservoir begun on the order of the Rajah
Kare Dantinusha request that the chamberlain of the
god-favored Rani Tamasrajasi place our questions before
her.

The reservoir, as perhaps you are not aware, is more
than half completed, and there must be certain critical
work done now if the structure is to withstand the onslaught of the rains, which will begain in about ninety
days. As we must undertake these tasks almost at once,
we most respectfully beseech the Rani to make her decision known to us at once. If we delay in these precautions, then the structure will be unsound and will
doubtless be much damaged by the rains. It is not certain to us that the Rani wishes the reservoir to be built,
and if she determines that the work must be abandoned,
though it was the wish of her father that the work go
forward, then it is senseless to keep so many men labor-
ing at a grueling job that is not to be continued.

Let us assure the Rani that if she is determined to
have this reservoir made, then by this time next year it
will be almost complete and the gardens around it may
be planted. That is not so long a time to wait for a
beautiful and pleasure-giving place to emerge from what
has been little more than a marsh.

Already the waters have risen behind the dam, and a
good portion of the land that was bog is now under the
waters. It will not be long before the fringe plants die off
and the lake will begin to clear. There is sufficient rock
on the floor of the lake to allow for the building of kiosks and pavilions on the various islands that are to be
constructed. It is a matter of greatest importance and

honor to those who work on this construction that we have the approval of the Rani, as we do not wish to offer her or the memory of her father an insult by being desultory in carrying out her orders.

With the knowledge that the Rajah ordered a good and pious act when he ordered work begun on the reservoir, we ask that the Rani consider her answer in this light, for it would be most lamentable that we do not complete this. The gods will have their will accomplished, no matter what we do, but the will of the Rajah is in accord with that of the gods and it is most wise to be acquiescent to the demands of the lord as well as the gods. No one intends to instruct the Rani in piety, for it is manifest in every aspect of her life. Yet we know that one young, new to majesty and filled with the uncertainties of women may falter when it is best to proceed. We wish her to know that we are all wholly inclined to finish the work that has been begun, for her honor, the honor of her father and the honor of the gods.

With all duty and humility, we ask that you, her chamberlain, bring our plight to her attention soon. We will keep working until we have orders to desist. However, we must also have shelter and food for our workers, and that has not been furnished of late. There are requests, also, for timber and cut stone which have not been attended to, and so our industry flags. We ask that you mention this when you bring this to the Rani's attention.

May the bounty of the gods be yours, and may the Rani rule long and enjoy all the fruits of their favor.

> The Building Supervisors
> for the construction of the
> Rajah Kare Dantinusha's reservoir

9

NOT A single lamp burned in Padmiri's house: it loomed up against the darkened bulk of trees, anonymous and troubling. Beside its massive shadow the feeble glimmer from the lights of the slaves' quarters was pathetic, a swarm of fireflies teasing a sleeping elephant.

Saint-Germain drew in his horse some distance from the house. He had been in the saddle since midafternoon, when he had entrusted the heavily disguised Jalal-im-al Zakatim to Loramidi Choi. It had taken most of the morning to convince the little merchant that it would be possible to get Jalal-im-al out of Natha Suryarathas safely, but he had capitulated at last when Saint-Germain had offered him a handful of gold. He had been glad to conclude the meeting, and anticipated a diminishing of his anxiety. Instead of a lightening of mood, however, his thoughts had grown darker as the day faded. Now, as he waited, looking at the house, a cold fatalism possessed him. He dismounted and looped the bridle reins over a nearby branch. Next he adjusted the scabbard that hung at his right side—he fought equally well with either hand, and had learned that carrying his weapon on the right occasionally gave him an advantage. The katana's hilt was somewhat longer than he was used to, so he slung his belt a little lower on his hip. Satisfied, he gave the horse one firm pat on the flank, then started toward the enormous blackness of Padmiri's house.

Near the slaves' quarters he paused, silent and stealthy as a cloud passing the moon. He could hear the hushed voices from within, and the occasional louder admonition to be quiet. There was a section of wall near a window where the moonlight fell all dappled with forest leaves, and it was there Saint-Germain crept, then pressed close to the wall, an irregular darkness in the uneven shadows.

". . . against the Rani," one of the older slaves was saying in a tone of suppressed emotion. "If it were otherwise, the gods would have deserted us and the country."

"But they say that Kali is her goddess," a younger one put in, "and if that is so, her devotions will not allow that protection."

"Our mistress is the Rajah's sister. She would not be mistreated for such ends unless she herself desired it. The gods would not take her as an unwilling sacrifice," the older slave insisted.

"Do not speak so loudly," a tired voice interrupted.

"Then where is she?" demanded one of the others, wholly ignoring the request for lowered voices. "If the soldiers did not take her away, what has become of her? Where has she gone?"

This was a question none of them wanted to answer, and

Saint-Germain, knowing the uneasy hush for what it was, began to fear.

"The soldiers were here to aid her. It was the foreigners whom they sought, not our mistress." This was a new voice, with a superior inflection. Saint-Germain thought the man must be one of the higher-ranking household slaves and not one of the more menial ones. The ranking and authority among the slaves was as rigid and complex as the relationships of one caste to another. When a well-placed slave spoke, the others heard him out with respect.

"Then why did they take only one of the foreigners, and our mistress disappear from her own house?" This voice was angry.

"She is with the other foreigner. Bhatin said that he has been her lover, and practiced terrible barbarities on her." A greedy laugh followed this announcement.

"The soldiers have taken both the servant of the foreigner and our mistress," the angry voice insisted.

"And the other foreigner, the master, has fled." Saint-Germain recognized this voice—it belonged to a eunuch who guarded Padmiri's house. Saint-Germain had intended to ask one of these men what had happened while he was away, but now he knew that it would not be possible.

"The foreigner is a magician, and a man of the West." The pronouncement was the most complete condemnation, and although Saint-Germain had heard himself spoken of in similar and less complimentary terms many times in the past, the barb still struck home.

"And the soldiers said that he is a creature of Shiva." Now the slaves were truly shocked, awed by the terrible implications of that statement. Shiva, who danced in serenity on the unholy Burning Ground, who was lord of graveyards, dead, and undead things—his creatures all evoked dread in his worshipers.

"Our mistress did not think so," the man muttered, but the others hushed him; it was some time before any conversation began again, and this time the slaves spoke of inconsequent things.

Saint-Germain lingered near the window a fair time, but he gleaned nothing else of interest, and that alone served to increase his apprehension. What had happened here while he had been gone? The question had returned to plague him. The soldiers had come. Whose? Tamasrajasi's? Thuggi?

Troops sent by the Sultan to avenge the death of his mission? The soldiers had taken one of the foreigners, who Saint-Germain was certain was Rogerio. Where had he been taken? The soldiers had wanted the other foreigner, no doubt himself. Why? And Padmiri was missing, either also a prisoner, or perhaps something worse had befallen that admirable woman. His fingers moved as he recalled the texture of her hair. The day before, he remembered with an immediacy that made him have to stop the melody in his throat, he had taught her two Western songs, one in Greek, one in the corrupt language of the Franks. Between that time, when they had laughed together at her lilting mispronunciation of the words, and this time, she had left her house, for soldiers had come there. Saint-Germain would have liked to be able to demand the truth from the slaves huddled in the chamber on the other side of the wall, but it was useless. None of them would admit to knowing what had become of their mistress, least of all to him. Whatever had happened to his servant and Padmiri, Saint-Germain would have to find out on his own.

When the rushlights in the slaves' quarters were extinguished, Saint-Germain slipped away from the wall. He went with caution now, yet with amazing swiftness. His hand closed on the katana's hilt. His heeled boots made less sound than the padding of a housecat. With feral grace he vaulted onto the lowest terrace of the house—the one outside the room where he had first loved Padmiri. Here he paused, taking stock of the dark around him. There was no sound, no hint that the house was not empty; nevertheless he sensed that someone waited for him on the inside. He moved toward the door, his dark eyes catching, for an instant, the shine of moonlight.

He eased the nearest door open, no more loudly than the breath of wind that shivered through the trees. Now he stepped into the room, going across the floor quickly. His eyes, unhampered by dark, searched out the corners of the place, and he realized that whoever awaited him, he, or they, were not in this wing of the house. He entered the hall and stood, undecided. Doubtless he would be expected to return to his own quarters, to his laboratory. A man might lie in wait there, confident that his prey would return. How to turn the trap, if there was a trap, Saint-Germain wondered, and looked toward the ceiling. His smile was vulpine.

A little distance along the corridor, Saint-Germain made

out a few loose planks in the ceiling, above the cornices, bowed beams and piering. It might be possible, he told himself. He pulled the lacing from his jacket, and with it he tied the katana close against his leg, just above the knee. He measured the distance, took a few quick steps and sprang upward lithely, grateful that only the walls had been plastered. He grabbed for the projections of an ornamental scroll of one of the beams where it met the elaborate cornice. There, bracing himself with shoulders and elbows, he dangled over the empty hall as he worked, one-handed, at the ceiling. When he felt the planks slide under his hand, he swung himself onto the beam, steadying himself on the short piering, before shoving the planks aside. He scrambled into the narrow, uneven space between the ceiling and roof, brushing cobwebs aside as he began to make his way toward the wing where his quarters were. Once he almost stepped on a large snake curled in a trough between beams; another time he startled a spider the size of his hand in its filmy web. He noted, with irony, that there were no rats here, and was not surprised. At last he found the bedding where Jalal-im-al had lain hidden, and he nodded somberly. He had made very little sound as he traversed the house, and now he was even more careful. A short distance farther on he came to the trapdoor he had made in the ceiling of his laboratory. His attention sharpened as he began to lift the boards. It was slow, agonizing work, done with great patience. A noise, a slip now, and the advantage he had sought would be lost. There was always the possibility that no one was in the laboratory below him, but he was convinced now that it would be here he found those who hunted for him. He pulled the boards through their hole and set them down with no more than a gentle tap, but it was loud enough to make him wait a few moments before he dropped through the hole to the floor.

"What?" a startled voice cried out as Saint-Germain landed, drawing the katana as he straightened up.

"There!" another said in a higher register.

So there were two of them, Saint-Germain told himself. At least two. He shoved the nearest table aside, taking delight in the crash it made as it struck the wall. There was space to fight now, without treacherous islands of furniture that were more dangerous than the swords of the two men who rushed toward him.

"Demon!" the higher voice shouted, and Saint Germain re-

alized that it was Bhatin, Padmiri's chief eunuch. The other
man was trying to slip around to Saint-Germain's flank.
Saint-Germain spared him one glance. It was Sudra Guristar,
Commander of the palace guard.

Bhatin made a sudden rush at Saint-Germain, a shimtare
held high over his head, ready to cleave downward. The katana, light and flexible in Saint-Germain's grasp, deflected the
blow, then turned with an easy turn of the wrists, and nicked
Bhatin's knuckles almost playfully. Bhatin shrieked and staggered back.

That was the moment when Guristar made his rush. Saint-
Germain pivoted to meet this attack, slicing a long, horizontal swath before him. Guristar dropped to the ground and
slid, cursing and calling Saint-Germain a variety of foul
names.

"Guristar!" Bhatin called, an edge of hysteria in the name.

"Quiet!"

Saint-Germain chuckled, and saw his opponents falter.

"Unnatural thing!" Bhatin muttered. "Drinker of blood."

"Ah." There was an abiding regret in the sound. Saint-Germain faced the eunuch. "You watched."

"Yes!" He took three stumbling steps forward, then retreated. "I watched. *Creature of Shiva!*"

"You think me that, and you dare fight me?" Saint-Germain asked, pursuing Bhatin, the katana resting in his hands.

When the eunuch screamed, it was from panic. He grabbed
his shimtare and threw it at Saint-Germain even as he turned
to flee. The shimtare clattered and rang on the floor. Bhatin
collided with one of the shelves and his hands closed around
the neck of a large glass vessel. He swung around and threw
this, too.

The vessel glanced off Saint-Germain's upper arm, then
shattered as it fell, strewing its shards over the room.

Guristar was on his feet again, but could not see well
enough to attack. He began to pick his way over the bits of
glass, wincing as they were crushed underfoot.

Bhatin had grabbed another vessel and was about to throw
it when he felt the flick of steel on his shoulder. It was impossible that so light a blow could be mortal, but as he dropped
the second vessel, he felt his own blood run over and through
his fingers, hot and pulsing. His life was gone before the katana finished slicing through his ribs.

The sound of Bhatin's body falling alerted Guristar. He

came toward Saint-Germain as fast as the glass-spattered floor would let him, with his shimtare thrust forward.

Saint-Germain met this onslaught deftly, swinging the katana up to let the inferior steel of Guristar's shimtare clash on the finer blade. He was determined to force the guard Commander to reveal where Rogerio and Padmiri had been taken, and for what purpose. Now he did not fight to kill, but to overwhelm and disarm. He drove Guristar back across the room with a series of rapid strikes and slashes, following relentlessly as Guristar retreated.

In all his years commanding the palace guard, Guristar had never fought an opponent like this. He had been against the Muslims once, and their maddened assault had filled him with a strangely invigorating terror. There was a giddiness in that combat that was entirely lacking in this ruthlessly controlled attack. His shimtare had never felt heavier or more unwieldly, or his arm more leaden. Surrender was unthinkable, but he longed to throw down his weapon and end the fight. Dimly, he was aware that had Saint-Germain truly pressed his stoccata he would have delivered a death-blow more than once. He shouted out his defiance, but could not stop retreating. Then, appallingly, glass powdered treacherously, his ankle twisted, and he fell. His shimtare spun out of his hands and the glass dug hundreds of little claws into him. He raised his arm in what he knew was a futile effort to slow the katana.

The Japanese blade hovered, then swung aside. Saint-Germain moved to Guristar's side. "Why were you waiting for me?" he asked conversationally. There was little sign of exertion about him; he was not sucking in air as Guristar was, and there was no odor of sweat on him. "Tell me."

"I will not." He had pride, he told himself, and it was necessary to conduct himself well with this alien being.

"But you will, you know," Saint-Germain corrected him pleasantly. The tip of the katana rested no more than a finger's length from Guristar's throat.

"Creature of Shiva!" Guristar tried to move back, but found that he was close to the wall, with nowhere to go.

"Where is my servant?" Saint-Germain inquired, as if he had not heard Guristar's outburst.

"Elsewhere!" Guristar attempted to laugh, then thought better of it. "Gone."

"Yes, I'm aware of that." It would be simple, Saint-Germain realized as he bent over Guristar, to batter this man to pieces. His own capacity for fury distressed him, and he held it back. He had too much remorse in him already, and breaking this man's bones would not help Padmiri or Rogerio. "And Padmiri, where is she?"

There was the slightest hesitation in Guristar's answer. "She's . . . gone as well."

"I see." Guristar did not know where Padmiri was, Saint-Germain inferred from this answer. "Why have they been taken?"

"Creature of Shiva!" Guristar pounded his hand on the floor and instantly regretted it. The side of his hand began to bleed and the glass lodged in the cuts.

"You may call me that as often as you like. But you will answer my questions." The katana flicked nearer. "Where is my servant?"

"May every god humiliate and excoriate you." The words were ragged, and, to Guristar's acute embarrassment, his voice cracked.

"Where is Padmiri?" Saint-Germain had decided to let Guristar think he believed the Commander knew where the Rajah's sister was.

"A diseased water buffalo fucked your ass." Why didn't the man kill him, if that was what he wanted?"

"You're becoming desperate," Saint-Germain said with a faint smile. "Eventually you'll say that my mother coupled with pariah dogs and drank the semen of leprous camels, but my questions will not change."

Guristar had no response as impotent rage welled within him. "Spawn of corpse-eaters. Debaucher of pigs. Turd of a pox demon."

"Where is my servant?" Saint-Germain's tone was the same as before; he wore a fixed, icy smile. "Where is Padmiri?"

"Bhatin said you lay with her, and tasted her blood. He said that you have nothing of a man about you." Guristar was howling now.

"Neither had Bhatin," Saint-Germain reminded Guristar. "Where is Rogerio? Where is Padmiri?"

With as much cunning as he could muster, Guristar answered, "If you kill me, you will never find them in time." He looked up into Saint-Germain's enigmatic dark eyes. The questions were not repeated.

"Will you lead me to them?"

"Perhaps," Guristar said, feeling suddenly quite powerful. "You will have to do just as I say."

"Oh, no, Commander," Saint-Germain said sardonically, all the while wondering what Guristar had meant—never find them in time?

Some of his fear returned. "You will have to come with me. As my prisoner."

"No, Commander." The katana touched his forehead, lightly, lightly, and blood ran into Guristar's eyes. "You will take me to them, and you will do it at once. If they have suffered any hurt, you will pay for it in full. Believe that."

"They are to be given to Kali," Guristar said in a rush, and saw Saint-Germain's face harden.

"When? Where? Tell me." The pleasant tone was gone. Saint-Germain spat the words out, taking a step backward so that he would not be tempted to inflict greater damage on Guristar.

Misreading this action, the Commander of the guard determined to return a portion of the torment Saint-Germain had given him. "She would rather have you, creature of Shiva. You're a better sacrifice." He said this sourly, recalling how Tamasrajasi had gloated when she told him how she wanted to use Saint-Germain. "She will take what the goddess gives her, and offer it with the greatest honor."

"To Kali?" He waited, then repeated in a low, precise, horrific tone, "To Kali?"

"Yes, yes. To Kali. Yes." His fear had returned so absolutely that his bones seemed to melt within him.

"Take me there," Saint-Germain said with quiet, indisputable authority.

"You cannot save then," Guristar protested as he began to struggle to his feet. "It's senseless to try." There was more to his objection than a warning: Tamasrajasi had told him that if she could not offer the foreigners to Kali, she would offer him. He was devoted to the Rani and her young, intoxicating body, but the thought of the knives of sacrifice and the long, degrading ritual sickened him.

"Guristar." The voice was calm, absolute. "You will take me there. Or I will kill you by slicing open your abdomen and letting you bleed to death."

"And you would drink my blood . . ." Guristar cried on a rising note as all his fears crowded in upon him.

"Your blood?" Saint-Germain regarded him with contempt.

"What would your blood give me?" With a sudden disgusted gesture he sheathed his katana. "You will take me where my servant and Padmiri are. You will not attempt to delay or mislead me. If I have reason to believe you are doing so, I will kill you."

Guristar did not doubt this: he resisted the urge to abase himself. Creatures of Shiva, he said inwardly, were governed by death and so might contaminate him without intending to do so. This foreigner was filled with menace. As Guristar paused to pick the bits of glass out of his hand, he stared at his blood, spreading like a shadow down his arm, and for a moment he felt profoundly insulted. That a creature of Shiva should refuse his blood! He wiped his hand against his loose trousers.

"Where is your horse?" Saint-Germain asked, standing aside to let Guristar precede him through the door.

"Behind the garden wall." His hand was throbbing now, and his legs ached. His eyes felt like cinders in his head.

"We will get it as soon as I have mounted. My horse is not far from the slaves' quarters." His crisp diction and outward assurance covered his great turmoil. Where had Padmiri gone? Had she been captured, or had she escaped? How could he free Rogerio? Where was he? What would be done to him? Had already been done to him? To silence these useless, desperate questions, he said to Guristar, "Tamasrajasi attends this sacrifice, you say?"

"Attends? She is the priestess," Guristar answered with pride. "It is she herself who will take the knife to you, creature of Shiva. You are not to be given to anyone but her." He came to a forking in the corridor and looked back toward Saint-Germain.

"Toward the north, Commander. And out through the reception room." He began to walk faster, as if seeking to outstrip the anxiety that filled him. He reached out to prod Guistar, ignoring the protest that greeted this.

"Execrable creature of Shiva!" Guristar shouted, though he hurried.

The echo of this imprecation rang in Saint-Germain's mind. Creature of Shiva, creature of Shiva. He moved more quickly, recalling that Shiva was the god who danced on the Burning Ground, accompanying himself on a drum that was the implacable beat of time itself.

Text of a formal document from the Rani Tamasrajasi of Natha Suryarathas to the Sultan Shams-ud-din Iletmish in Delhi.

Conquering Lord of the lowlands and self-proclaimed Sultan at Delhi, the Rani Tamasrajasi, daughter of Rajah Kare Dantinusha, honors you with this message which she had deigned to write with her own hand.

It is her obligation to inform the Sultan that those men he caused to be sent here have become victims of misplaced zeal and have paid the price of the Sultan's arrogance.

Not long ago a band of Thuggi, good holy men who are devotees of the Black Goddess, happened to encounter the Sultan's men as they disported themselves in a manner both depraved and shocking to the Thuggi. Not able to endure the depth of the insult which had been offered them, the Thuggi rose in righteous indignation and belabored the Sultan's men after the methods of their sect. Lamentably, the men of the Sultan were not prepared to deal with the demands of the Thuggi, and so all have perished.

The Sultan will understand that this affront to his dignity was only recently brought to the Rani's attention. There are matters of this kingdom which must take precedence in her work over matters that are more properly the concern of other rulers. Indeed, were it not that the Sultan is nearly her equal in rank, the Rani would assign the task of sending this missive to her chamberlain. Only her respect for a fellow-ruler moves her to take the responsibility upon herself to inform him of this unfortunate event.

Because of the unrest the presence of the Sultan's mission brought to this country, the Rani proposes that the Sultan not trouble himself to send others to take the

401

place of those who died. The disruption has not vanished and it would not be wise to attempt to bring others to this country when it is likely they would be similarly received. Caution and wisdom should temper the Sultan's impetuosity. There is no immediate need in Natha Suryarathas for the Sultan's representatives, and the lack of welcome must be regarded as indicative of the attitude of the country. At the periyanadu, held while the Rajah Kare Dantinusha was still alive, it was made plain that the Sultan would do well not to honor us too much with his presence and the presence of his representatives.

Naturally, if the Sultan does not send men to us and there is little communication between the countries, it is not likely that the need for tribute to Delhi will be as strong as before. The Rani has heard the various arguments put forth on the question of tribute and has decided that as the Sultan has stolen lands that were rightly the territory of her kingdom, tribute is an insult to the majesty of the Rani and all of her nobles, and to continue in this degrading arrangement would offer the gods an intolerable insult as well as humiliating the kingdom of Natha Suryarathas itself.

The Rani wishes to remind the Sultan that she can, at an order, put a thousand elephants and two thousand pikemen and four thousand horsemen into the field against the men of the Sultan. The Rani's elephants are enormous and of fierce temper. Her fighters are ready for battle and their lances and shimtares shine bright as the sun at midday. The Rani's horses dance at the call to arms and her cavalrymen ride faster than the wind behind the rainstorms. Nothing in the Sultan's experience can match the strength and might of the Rani's forces. The Rani cautions that Sultan that any provocation will bring all the might of her army down upon his men, and the valor of her troops will awe the Sultan's warriors.

It will be most satisfactory if this constitutes the entire communication between the Rani and the Sultan. There is little to be gained in messages of any nature. If the Sultan is desirous of war, let him send his heralds with proper challenges and addresses, otherwise the Rani will not look for any word from Shams-ud-din Iletmish or his representatives.

As the Sultan does not admit to the sanctity of the

Rani's gods, she will not trouble to address them upon his behalf. And yet, the Black Goddess may find the Sultan worthy of her attention, and should that come to pass, the Rani will make sacrifice for his acceptability.

> Tamasrajasi
> daughter of the Rajah Kare Dantinusha
> Rani of Natha Suryarathas
> in the first year of her reign

10

NOT FAR from where the trail branched away from the road there were guards. They waited at the rough timber bridge that spanned the narrow, swift river that coursed through the defile and fell in three spectacular cascades to join the Chenab.

"Who comes?" one of the guards demanded. He was a large man in a light-colored garment armed with a wickedly curved knife.

"It is Sudra Guristar, Commander of the palace guard," was the answer he gave with a nervous glance at Saint-Germain.

"Who is with you?" The guard did not approach the two mounted men, but neither did he give ground.

"The creature of Shiva. The foreigner." He had been warned not to let these men know that he was, in fact, Saint-Germain's captive, and now he was pleased he had given his word.

"The Rani is at the temple," the guard said, and motioned to his fellows to stand aside so that the two horses could pick their way over the flimsy bridge.

The trail wound back into the water-carved defile. The trees crowded in, occasionally so densely that it was not possible to see the moon-brightened sky overhead. Guristar led the way, conscious always of the long katana that still hung from Saint-Germain's belt. The blood on his face had caked and dried, but his head was hammered with pain. Every step his horse took, each beat of his heart made Guristar grind his teeth. As the path grew steeper, Guristar began to exult. In very little time he would give this creature over to his mistress, and her gratitude would bestow power upon him, and all the satisfactions of her young flesh. For the first time that night, the wounds he had suffered seemed to be worthwhile.

"What river is this?" Saint-Germain asked as the trail led along the riverbank for a short way.

"It is the Kudri," Guristar said, resenting this intrusion on his thoughts. The temple was not much farther and he wanted to spend the last of the ride contemplating the rewards that awaited him.

"The Kudri," Saint-Germain repeated, wondering why he should know the name. Then he drew in his horse as another guard approached and the river ceased to hold his attention.

This guard recognized Guristar as soon as the Commander spoke, and instructed the two riders to take their horses to a narrow meadow to the side of the trail, and to walk the rest of the way.

As Saint-Germain pulled at the reins, he called out to Guristar, "You will speak only when I can hear you, guard Commander, and you will make no gestures or signals of any kind. If you attempt it, I will spit you on this blade."

Guristar was tempted to dispute this, but held his peace. It would not be too long now, and the full pleasure of revenge would be his. "I will not make gestures or signals," he said as he drew in his horse.

"Dismount," Saint-Germain ordered him, bringing his horse close to Guristar's.

"As you say," Guristar muttered, getting out of the saddle quickly. He secured the reins to one of a number of posts. Not far away, other horses were similarly tied; one of the horses whinnied and was answered by Saint-Germain's mount.

"Stand clear of the horses," Saint-Germain said, and got out of the saddle. He twisted the reins around the post once, not liking to take the time to tie them. "The temple is through those shrubs, isn't it?" With his vampiric eyes he could see the squat, serrated pillars that fronted the building, and could almost make out its color.

"Yes," Guristar said, and started toward it.

"Slowly, guard Commander. I do not need you to announce me. We will enter together." He kept his place slightly behind Guristar, and one hand was on the katana's hilt.

"We won't be challenged again," Guirstar said as he parted the lush vegetation and stepped onto the rough stones in the space before the temple.

"You will forgive me if I do not entirely believe you," Saint-Germain responded. They trod up the low steps and passed between two of the columns. There the murmured sound of chanting reached them, and an overpowering incense of rank and flowery odor hung on the air. "Which way?"

Guristar pointed through one set of pillars to the side of massive doors. "Through there. She is waiting."

Saint-Germain indicated that Guristar should go before him. "I think that your mistress will want to see you first." He fell into step behind Guristar, moving so quietly that his heeled boots made the faintest gentle tappings on the stone floor. Where in this place, he asked himself as he looked around, where was Rogerio being held? Was Padmiri somewhere within these walls, or had she truly escaped? In the narrow corridor beyond the pillars there were a number of lamps hung, casting flickering pools of light over the statues and low-relief carvings that lined the walls. They were not good to see.

At the end of the corridor a door stood ajar, and Guristar hesitated on the threshold. He gave Saint-Germain a swift, infuriated look, then called out, "Tamasrajasi? Rani? Great Mistress?"

"My Commander," came the Rani's voice. "You've returned to me. What have you brought?"

"The thing you sought, Great Mistress." It was demeaning to have to address Tamasrajasi in this way while Saint-Germain watched him, but Guristar did not want to antagonize the Rani, not now when his own power was so tantalizingly close.

"Enter at once, my Commander, and bring the thing I want with you." She laughed as she gave her permission.

The room was made of dark stone and the profusion of lamps that hung from the ceiling were shaded with red cloth. There was an altar, quite small, at the far end of the chamber, and on it the torn bodies of dogs lay at the feet of the black stone representation of Kali.

"Ah. My creature of Shiva." Tamasrajasi stepped into the light. Except for two massive necklaces of ivory balls carved into the likeness of skulls, she was naked. Her body had been stained with the juice of certain berries and appeared almost as black as the stone goddess she so clearly had chosen to represent. There was a glistering shine to her eyes. "Saint-Germain, my father's sister's lover." She walked toward him, her hips swaying and the necklaces sliding on her breasts.

"Tamasrajasi," he said without emotion. He had recognized at once that any show of weakness on his part now would please the Rani.

"You slept beside Padmiri, so my spies tell me, and you sucked her veins." She smiled widely, horrible and splendid.

"I would not describe it that way," Saint-Germain demurred.

"That is the way of Shiva's creatures." She came up to him and put her hand on his shoulder. "Guristar brought you to me."

"Not precisely," Saint-Germain said, taking her hand from him. "I forced him to lead me here."

She laughed again, this time with incredulous delight. "What would bring you here?"

"My servant. Padmiri." The coldness of his eyes struck her, and she became petulant.

"Your servant was brought here at my order. Padmiri is another matter. It will not be long until I see her again." There was such quiet malice in this promise that Guristar felt he must hasten to explain himself to the Rani.

"Padmiri was not at her house, Tamasrajasi. You know that our search was most thorough, and we did not find her. There are guardsmen who seek her even now, and doubtless they will bring her to you before the night is over. For the moment, you have this creature of—"

"He said that he forced you to lead him here," Tamasrajasi cut in sharply. "Is that the truth?"

Guristar faltered. "In part. There was a battle—"

"As I see from your face," she interrupted again. "Do you tell me he did that to you?"

"The glass on the floor did part of it," Guristar said, not looking into the Rani's face. "I slipped on the glass, you see. He attacked me while my hands were bleeding and I could not hold a shimtare."

"And you let it happen? You did not throw yourself on his blade?" She waited for him to answer, then walked toward him, hands on her hips. "Good Commander, I have asked you a thing. I want to hear your answer. Do not delay."

The reddened light touched her shoulders, her breasts, the rise of her flank. Guristar devoured her with his eyes, thinking of the times he had plundered her body. His groin was hot, tight, and he felt enormous. To take her now, with the trappings of the goddess on her . . .

"Sudra Guristar!" she snapped. "Tell me if what this Saint-Germain has said is true."

"True?" he repeated, dazed by the intensity of his lust. "It is partly true. He would not let me die. He cut me with the sword he carries, but he would not let me die." Impulsively he reached out and touched her breats.

Tamasrajasi gave him an appraising, lascivious look. "You wish to possess me, my Commander? For the Black Goddess?"

Without stopping to consider the implications of her taunts, Guristar deepened his hold on her. "Yes, my Rani, my Great Mistress."

"Then you shall. Soon, my commander." She stepped back from him; then, without looking at him, she asked Saint-Germain, "What do you think you will gain by coming to me?"

"The life of my servant and Padmiri," he answered her, very composed. "I assumed, from what Guristar has said to me, that you would rather have me than either of them."

"Better all of you," she said at once. "You are here, and your servant."

"I also have my sword, Tamasrajasi." He put his hand on the hilt of the katana. "If you betray me, I will—"

"Kill me?" She did not quite smile, but there was a cruel mirth in her averted face.

"No, Tamasrajasi: myself." It would be an easy thing to do, he realized. The katana was more finely sharp than any blade he had ever handled. One quick upward swipe and his head would be cut from his body. He had had more than three thousand years: he could not convince himself that they were enough.

Her eyes opened a little wider at his pronouncement. "You would deprive me of my sacrifice, should you do that."

"My servant goes free, and Padmiri. Otherwise it will take every worshiper in this place to get this weapon from me. And you still will not have a sacrifice." He folded his arms and watched Tamasrajasi as she walked the length of the black stone room to stand before the statue of Kali. He kept his negligent stance, but all his senses were keenly stretched, for he knew, from the unique perceptions of his kind, that they were not alone in this dark room.

Tamasrajasi stared at the statue on the altar. It was old, much older than the temple, and crudely done. The features were a mocking grimace on a head far too large for the clumsily dancing body. Her weapons and her necklaces of skulls were shapeless with wear and time, but there was force in the statue yet. The stonecutter had brought a power to his creation, the power of complete belief. Tamasrajasi put her fingers into the coagulating blood of the dogs, and touched her fingers to the flat stone tongue of the goddess. She breathed deeply and began a swift, high chant in a disturbingly sweet voice.

Watching her, Guristar reveled and suffered in his hunger for her. She had promised him her body, but he did not wish to wait for it. Had they been alone, he would have embraced her now. He looked about, and saw Saint-Germain regarding him sardonically. "Unclean thing!" he whispered, but would not look at the Rani again, hating what the foreigner would say to him.

Finally Tamasrajasi ceased her chanting and came away from the alter. "Very well, creature of Shiva. You have come to me. I have a use for you, which you must accept. If you will, then your servant will be released. If you do not accept, then we will kill him in our own ways, our own time, and be sure that you watch. Padmiri is another matter. If she is brought here during the time of the rites, she will be given the chance to die on the altar. If she refuses, and you are still alive, then she will participate in your death, but at the end of it, she will be free. That is most solemnly promised to you."

"I will see my servant depart, and you will have no word with Padmiri alone," Saint-Germain said quickly.

Tamasrajasi took umbrage at this. "I will not demean a sacrifice with lies and deceit." Her eyes narrowed. "Your servant will have proper escort so that he may not disturb the ritual once it has begun. When he leaves, he will not be allowed to return."

"Very well." Now that the actuality of his own death was near, Saint-Germain had one anguished moment of absolute recusancy, of soul-wrought denial. What lunacy had brought him here? Why had he thought he had to protect Rogerio and

Padmiri at so dire a cost? Then the abnegation passed from him as quickly and as inexplicably as it had come to him.

"He will be expected to leave my kingdom at once, and take nothing with him." She was enjoying making conditions and watching this creature of Shiva bow to her will.

"And Padmiri will be left alone, if she chooses not to come to your altar?" His strength was back now; he faced Tamas-rajasi coolly.

"For as long as she lives," Tamasrajasi vowed with a wicked grin.

"Will you make an oath before your goddess that no one, not you, not your agents, not their servants, *no one* will attempt to harm her in any way?" He stood in silence, his hand on the hilt of the katana. His penetrating gaze was on her face, and when she could no longer bear it, she made a gesture of acquiescence.

"Yes. Yes, before Kali, and in her name, I give full protection to Padmiri, sister to my father. No one of mine will harm her." For the first time that night, Tamasrajasi was nervous, and venomously she determined to punish Saint-Germain for his temerity. "Now, will you listen while I tell you how you will die?"

"I will listen." He heard Guristar give a sigh of satisfaction, but gave no sign of noticing.

Tamasrajasi paced along the room, and as she talked, her qualms faded. "Shiva is the consort of Kali. Therefore it is appropriate that you, a creature of Shiva, should do the act upon the altar with me. . . ."

"That is not possible," Saint-Germain told her in a voice that was almost kind.

"How do you mean?" She turned on him, her face rigid with anger.

"It isn't possible. When I became . . . a creature of Shiva, there were a number of capabilities I ceased to have. I cannot weep. I do not eat or drink, as you know it. And although I am whole, so far as possessing testicles and penis go, still I do not function as men do. I cannot do the act, upon the altar or anywhere else." He had long ago ceased to be distressed with this lack in himself, but rarely did he feel relief because of it. Now he had a rare sense of jest, and justice.

"You must!" Tamasrajasi came toward him, one of her hands raised and clenched. Then she stopped. "It is said that Shiva's creatures, when glutted on blood, are insatiable."

Saint-Germain was still—there was too much coldness in him.

"Tell me! If there were enough blood . . ."

"I do not know, Tamasrajasi," he said clearly, quietly.

"Yes: enough blood, and yours would be the lusts of ten men. When Shiva joined with Parvati, all the world shook from their passion and the land became fertile in imitation of them. There will be those who will be honored to offer their veins to you so that the work may be done. They will extinguish themselves in your excitation. "Yes." Her expression changed. "Yes, that will be best. You will take lives into yourself, many lives, so that you will be a man for me, for as long as it is necessary. As the blood fills you, so you will fill me, and we will couple in praise of the fecundity of Kali and Shiva, and when you release your seed into me, then will be the time to sever your head." She gave him a coquettish glance. "Does it trouble you, to hear me tell you how you will die? Your death as you spurt your semen forth will be like Shiva's death, and I will dance, I will exalt your dying."

Vainly Saint-Germain tried to convince himself that death was death and one way was no worse than another. He had been close to death many times, had known its touch once. But he was repelled by the Rani's terrible glee. It would be a simple matter to draw the katana, and as he drew it, to slice upward, cutting his spine and ending this dreadful night.

"If you would rather have it otherwise, let me tell you what I shall have done to your servant." Her step became bouncy, girlish, and she tangled the fingers of one hand in the skull-shaped beads of her necklace. "Your servant will be brought to the altar. That much you must allow us if you will not give yourself for sacrifice. We will have to bind him, because otherwise too many would have to hold him."

"No," Saint-Germain said softly.

"We will burn off his skin, bit by bit, and each little section will be offered to the Black Goddess. We will start with the fingers and toes." She turned at the end of the room and came back toward him. She seemed unaware of Guristar now. "You would have to watch. That would be required. And then Padmiri. If you deprive us of you, we must use her. That, also, you will have to watch." She stopped before Saint-Germain. "After seeing what we do, creature of Shiva, you may wish to be sacrificed. It might be more pleasant, the death I offer you, than living. Don't you think?"

"Let me see my servant depart and hear the vows of those who escort him that he will be taken safely to the border of this abattoir." His tone had thickened with revulsion.

Tamasrajasi bowed her head respectfully. "That will be done, Lord Shiva."

"I am not Lord Shiva," Saint-Germain said vehemently.

"You stand in his place, and you will be honored as he is," Tamasrajasi replied with the assumption of humility. "You will be taken to a place of state and wreathed in flowers and praised. You will be given sacrifice, too, so that you are the more holy."

The hideous absurdity of her proposal nearly drove Saint-Germain to laughter, but he stifled it in his throat, as he supposed it presaged madness. But what else was there, if not madness. Padmiri, he thought, Padmiri, flee this place. Go far away, as far as you can. And he hoped fervently that she would never learn how he died. He did not know if this hope was born of shame or love, and he wasted no time in questioning it. "Tamasrajasi," he said as reasonably as he was able, "I am not Lord Shiva. I am not, in any way I understand it, one of his creatures. Yes, I am a vampire, but I am not what you think me. I don't know what you seek to gain from my death, but I warn you, it will not happen."

Her smile was seraphic. "Those who worship Kali seek nothing. Nothing. We wish to be free of the Wheel forever, to be burned out of this life and all lives to come. You know that Kali promises us destruction, creature of Shiva, and an end to all things."

Saint-Germain had no answer for her. He watched her, seeing her youth and her voluptuous body, seeing the bloom of life in her, and could not imagine what it was that made her long for oblivion. Those who were wretched might desire to trade their youth for an end to their torments, but Tamasrajasi was powerful, in excellent health, wealthy and all but adored by most of her people. Her father had cherished her and made her his heir. And she yearned for the ultimate dissolution.

"Come," she called out happily, holding her hand out to him as she walked away from him. "You must be robed. When you have been made ready, you will see your servant ride away with men vowed to deliver him unharmed to my border."

"Great Mistress!" Guristar burst out. "What of me? I have brought this sacrifice to you. You have said that I may take you. Tonight." He had meant it for a demand but it came out a question.

"Yes, Guristar, my Commander, tonight you shall have me. I have said it." There was that illusory quality of play about her, as if she were still a child. Saint-Germain started after her, asking himself if it might be that riancy which made him unable to think of her as a woman grown, though her body was richly mature.

As Tamasrajasi reached the door to the chamber, two robed men stepped out of the deepest shadows and stood on either side of Saint-Germain. "These are the men," she announced without turning to look at them, "who will guide your servant. They will do everything I ask of them, and they will not fail." She went down the corridor with lithe steps, and listened to the steps behind her. The two men had a soft tread as their sandals scuffed the stone floor. Saint-Germain's boots made a sharp report. Tamasrajasi decided that it was an excellent omen.

The room she led them to was on the far side of the sanctuary. It was ornate, filled with murals in bright gold and reds, and redolent with that peculiarly unappetizing incense. The floor was made of vari-colored alabaster, and at the far end there was a pearl-encrusted throne within the arch of hammered brass almost wholly covered with gold leaf.

"See?" Tamasrajasi said merrily. "Here you will be elevated and revered. You will be dressed as a god, your face will be painted so that it will shine."

"I want to see my servant first," Saint-Germain said. While he walked to this chamber, he had resigned himself to what lay ahead of him. "I wish to see him now."

Tamasrajasi frowned, pouting, then cocked her head to the side. "Why not? I will allow him to aid you in preparation. He *is* your servant, and he should be pleased to help invest you for worship." She spoke to the men beside Saint-Germain. "Go and bring the other foreigner here. Do it at once. It is my will that he be here."

Neither man spoke, but both turned and left the room. Saint-Germain heard their steps retreating. "How long will this take?"

"The dressing? A fair time. There is a ritual to it." She was teasing him again, for she knew he was not asking her about the matter of dressing. "After you are dressed, there are invocations to be said and a number of chants to sing. You will be anointed and wreathed in flowers. Then the real ceremony will begin. Most of those who will come here to worship will not enter the temple until the darknest part of the night, in honor of Kali. Then they will see what I will do with Guristar"—here she giggled with the unfeigned mirth of a child—"and then they will give themselves for worship and sacrifice, and when that is done, then you will be brought to the altar. It will depend on how quick you are to spend your seed in me as to how long that will be. I hope that you will not be too quick."

"It may not happen at all," Saint-Germain warned her. "What then?"

"By dawn," Tamasrajasi went on as if she had not heard him, but there was an irritated line between her brows, "it will have ended and those who have been here will depart. Pyres will be made for the dead, and the men who keep the altars here will throw the ashes into the cold waters of the Kudri."

"And you?" He was more puzzled by her than before. "What will you do, Tamasrajasi?"

"I will return to my palace and prepare for war," she said serenely. "My army will rise and we will take back the lands that the Sultan at Delhi has stolen from us."

"But your army . . ." He had seen the palace guard and knew from his conversations with Padmiri that Dantinusha had reduced the number of his soliders to a minimal level as a token of good faith to Shams-ud-din Iletmish.

"I have six thousand war elephants. And they will be ridden by archers and spearmen. There are nine thousand horsemen in my cavalry, and they will trample the invaders beneath them. Ten thousand warriors will follow on foot, and everywhere they go, they will destroy all that they find in their path." She was radiant. "I will ride on the foremost elephant. I will be in armor of black stone and my spears will be of darkest iron."

Over the centuries, Saint-Germain had seen many sorts of madness, and he had learned both fear of and compassion for those so afflicted. Yet her visionary rapture filled him with bitterness and pity.

"Great Mistress," said one of the men in the door as he abashed himself. "The foreigner." And he thrust Rogerio into the room.

Saint-Germain went down on one knee to aid his servant, and whispered to him in Frankish, "Do nothing to interfere."

Rogerio looked up, mildly dazed. "They came to the house in the afternoon," he said in Greek.

"Speak Frankish!" Saint-Germain rose and held out his arm to Rogerio.

Tamasrajasi was scowling. "I do not know what you are saying to him," she complained.

"If you had troubled to ask the slaves at Padmiri's house, you would have learned that my servant has a poor command of your language. He needs to know that he is in no danger from your men, who will escort him to the border." He added in Frankish, in almost identical inflections, "Do not let them know you understand more than one word in ten. You are in gravest danger."

Rogerio scrambled to his feet and gave Tamasrajasi a bemused smile. "I will do as you wish, my master," he said in Frankish.

"I will tell him that the men who brought him to this room will be his guides and that he is to trust them," Saint-Germain said to Tamasrajasi, then went on to Rogerio, "You are to get away from them as soon as you may."

"And you?" Rogerio's blue eyes were apprehensive. "When will you leave here?"

"When I can," Saint-Germain said gently.

"No." Rogerio's voice rose slightly. "Give me your sword and we will fight them until death."

Saint-Germain held up one hand. "Rogerio, old friend, do as I tell you." He turned toward Tamasrajasi and explained, "My servant does not know where he is to go, and it frightens him. He will obey me now." This time he did not meet Rogerio's eyes. He pulled the scabbard-and-katana from his belt and held it out to Rogerio. "For all the forgotten gods, Rogerio, do as I tell you."

"Yes, my master," Rogerio said, bowing slightly, taking the proffered Japanese sword. "Is there anything else, my master?"

Saint-Germain looked at the pearl-covered throne but in his mind he saw Rome on a rainy day. The Flavian Circus was not complete and the beggars who lived under its half-finished arches were amusing themselves by tormenting a dying man. There were other images that came swiftly: enormous triangular sails flapping in a hot wind, and below them, Saint-Germain, miserably ill, Rogerio waiting patiently beside him; two horses racing out of the ruins of Milan, men clinging to their backs, pursued by shouting mailed knights on lathered mounts; a garden in Tunis on a spring night, torches burning, and two companions lost in talk for most of the night as neither of them required sleep; the wild cliffs near Ranegonde's castle, where, under a pall of clouds, two men stood off the attack of a famine-crazed rabble; an afternoon in Lo-Yang amid the chaos of packing, chests open and waiting for garments, vials, bedding, treasures, and the moment of departure. He imagined a sandy-haired man with the appearance of early middle age tied to a stone altar, screaming as his flesh was slowly burned away. Saint-Germain put his small, beautiful hands to eyes that had not wept in more than three thousand years. "No," he said. "Nothing else."

◄●►

A notice from Sudra Guristar to all the guardsmen under his command.

> To those who have the honor to serve and guard the person and possessions of the most glorious Rani Tamasrajasi, be vigilant, for there are enemies who seek to endanger the well-being of this Great Mistress and disrupt the propriety of the country. It is your duty and privilege to prevent any such happening.
>
> The sister of the late Rajah Kare Dantinusha, who recently died at the hands of a slave he had brought into his household, has been revealed as a dangerous and insidious spy. For many years her various eccentricities have been regarded as the diversions of a woman without husband or children to fill her hours, and for that reason much was tolerated that ought not to have been, for it has been learned that she is deep in the toils of de-

monic influences. It is quite possible that she is allied to
the agents of the Sultan at Delhi for the purpose of
bringing the entire country of Natha Suryarathas under
the Muslim rule. Doubtless an attractive marriage has
been offered her by the men of the Sultan. Not an instant too soon were those perfidious men struck down by
the courageous, pious men who battled with them not so
many days ago. So lost to all respect, devotion and
honor is the woman Padmiri that she has given housing
and hospitality to a creature of Shiva whose influence
the Rani Tamasrajasi has but recently discovered.

Padmiri is to be found. Our Great Mistress orders it
be done. Padmiri is to be brought before her for judgment and punishment. There have been men searching
for this sister of our fallen Rajah but their efforts have
not been sufficient. The woman, crafty in her wiles,
eluded us when the first attempt was made to apprehend
her. Doubtless she was guarded by the spirits given her
by the creature of Shiva she has taken as her lover. Yes,
she did not hesitate to do this, in spite of all her praised
learning, and her supposed love of the truth. She surrendered herself to the embraces of one who uses her
foully, who perverts her, respecting neither her woman's
nature nor her age. Who among you would be so lost to
his sense of propriety that he would presume to make
love to a woman of fifty-two who had never borne him a
child? Think of the enormity of this and let it inspire
you to be persistent in your search for Padmiri so that
her contamination shall not touch us all.

It was noted that there were three horses gone from
Padmiri's stables. It is known that Padmiri herself, most
properly, knows nothing of riding horses, but there are
those around her who would doubtless be blind enough
to follow any order she might give, for slaves are known
to have only the will of their masters to rule them, and
therefore think nothing of performing reprehensible acts.

When Padmiri is found, she must be brought at once
to Rani Tamasrajasi, either at the palace or at the
temple on the Kudri where she performs sacrificial rites.
It is appropriate that Padmiri, so lost to religion, should
be made to realize the extent of her failings in the
temple, and those who succeed in bringing her to the
temple will be doubly rewarded. There is great merit in

apprehending this woman, and greater merit in making sacrifice at the time Padmiri becomes a captive.

It is the will of Rani Tamasrajasi that this be done.

> Sudra Guristar
> Commander of the palace guard
> for the Rani Tamasrajasi
> in the first year of her reign

11

TWICE SHE was nearly thrown from the saddle, and had clung to the mare's mane with terror-tightened hands; once the mare, startled by a sudden noise in the forest, had almost bolted. Riding was exhausting and her muscles, unused to such rigorous exercise, tugged and ached. She dared not ride on the roads, for she had seen the guardsmen at her house and feared that they searched for her as well as for the foreigners she had welcomed. The paths and tracks which she was forced to use were narrow, winding, ill-kept and steep. Several times she lost her way and had to retrace her course, and often it was more by accident than design that she stayed on the right way.

Padmiri was more than halfway to her brother's palace—she could think of it in no other way—when she came upon a band of villagers trudging along the rutted, dusty path. She pulled in the mare, inexpertly guiding the animal to the side of the road so that the small procession could pass. She saw that everyone of the group was wearing wreaths and necklaces of dark flowers, and all carried woven baskets containing live things.

"Wait!" Padmiri called out, her hand extended to the elder at the front of the band.

"We dare not, Reverend Lady," the elder answered back over his shoulder. "It is near sunset already, and there is a great way to go."

"But where are you going?" She had only seen the strange flower wreaths twice before in her life, but recognized them with foreboding.

"To the temple on the Kudri," the answer came back faintly. "For sacrifice."

Padmiri dragged the mare back onto the trail and pushed through the throng. When she was abreast of the elder, she said, "Tell me what will happen at the temple. What is the nature of your sacrifice?"

"The Rani has proclaimed that everyone must offer," the elder said rather wearily. He held up the basket he carried, and small, bright eyes peered out through the slats. There was a snuffling whimper.

"And the Rani herself?" Padmiri demanded, irritation and worry building in her.

"She officiates," the elder said, adding, "I do not wish to offend the Reverend Lady, but we must not linger."

"Of course." Padmiri stopped the mare and let the people file past her as consternation grew in her. Tamasrajasi had ordered sacrifice and would officiate at the ritual. The villagers wore dark flowers and carried live animals to the temple on the Kudri. She remembered the rumors she had heard of Thuggi and at the time had thought nothing of them. Now her mind was crowded with suspicions, all of them increasing her anxiety. She tried to still her apprehension. Tamasrajasi was a young, beautiful and powerful woman. What would worship of the Black Goddess give to her? Tamasrajasi might bow to one of Kali's other faces, the loving Parvati, but to Kali herself? She could not convince herself it was impossible. Disheartened, she started back along the track toward her own house. There was no reason to go to the palace now, not today. She would have to present herself to her brother's daughter the next morning. The prospect of spending the night in the forest terrified her, yet she did not know whether it would be wise to return to her house, for if there were guardsmen there still . . .

The mare shied, whinnying loudly, and Padmiri was rudely jerked out of her reverie. It was almost dark now and Padmiri had no idea where she was. The trees seemed gigantic, threatening. She had no way of telling what had made the mare frightened, but whatever it was had not departed, for the horse skittered, sidling on the trail, unwilling to go forward and too afraid to run. Her eyes rolled and her coat was flecked with foam. Padmiri, who was almost as frightened as the mare, patted her neck uneasily and wished she could recall the phrases her brother had used to quite his horses.

There was a sound of something on the path, something fairly large that scraped and slithered. The mare danced on her front legs, attempting to rear, but was not able to because of the way Padmiri clutched her neck. The sound came nearer, and Padmiri thought she was able to discern a slightly lighter patch of wavering movement on the darkened path.

A low, agonized wail came from the shape and it was only then that Padmiri realized it was a man. She dared not dismount, for she did not think she could get back on the mare again: her body was too sore and in this wild place, anything might prevent her from climbing into the saddle again.

"Help . . . me . . ." the shape groaned mindlessly. His words, more than his accent, revealed him as a foreigner, for no Hindu would ask for or expect to receive aid.

"Who are you?" Padmiri asked harshly.

"A traveler . . . Oh, Lord of Fire . . ." He dragged himself nearer Padmiri's mare. "I didn't know . . . I didn't know . . ."

"What?" She was repelled and fascinated at once by this half-seen stranger. If only she were able to ride expertly so that she could guide the mare well, or could remount with confidence!

"Help me!" He tried to reach a hand out to her, but the arm fluttered weakly and it was only then that Padmiri realized that the tendons in his knees and elbows had been cut. It was too dark for Padmiri to see him clearly but she felt his torment. "Reverend Lady! *Help me!*"

"How?" she asked helplessly.

The man sobbed roughly, deeply, and then lay still. At first Padmiri thought he had died, but then she heard him murmuring, "I didn't know. For Kali, they said." The words grew more jumbled. "Kali sacrifice. No. No. Another one. Skulls. Arms, Lord of Fire! All foreigners. Two others."

"What others?" Padmiri asked sharply.

It was with considerable difficulty that the maimed man was able to speak now. "Others. Two. One first. Then another. It was the second one . . ." His voice became much softer but the words were clear. "The second one was the one they wanted. Once they had him, they took me away from the temple. They got out their knives. Lord of Fire, the knives! They would not kill me here on the road." The voice trailed off and the man moaned. Then he made one last effort. "Reverend Lady, help me. The others are lost. They are given to Kali. Help me. Help me."

"How did you get here?" Padmiri was trying to decide whether or not the two foreigners were Saint-Germain and his servant. Rogerio had been taken by guardsmen, but not his master. She did not want to believe that Saint-Germain had been caught. She reminded herself that there were other foreigners in Natha Suryarathas. The man lying on the road was a foreigner. It must be someone else who had been taken for sacrifice.

"They took me away from the temple." He seemed to doze a moment. "They didn't kill me. They cut me. They left me. There was a . . . a shrine. Shiva. They said . . . his creature . . ." The voice faltered again. "I'm . . . cold."

The mare snorted, whickered and then sprang forward. One of her hooves struck the figure in the road as she began a headlong plunge down the narrow dark pathway.

Branches lashed at Padmiri's arms and face, and no matter how she tugged on the reins, the mare did not respond. Had she been less terrified, she would have screamed, but fear robbed her of her voice, and she would do nothing more than hang on until the mare stopped from exhaustion.

When that finally happened, Padmiri knew she had come a considerable distance from where the maimed Parsee lay, but she had no sense of where she was. The foreigner had mentioned a shrine to Shiva or one of Shiva's creatures. She drooped in the saddle, not wanting to think anymore, the aftermath of her ordeal flooding her with shivering weakness. It was full night now, and the moon had not yet risen. She let the mare pick her way down the track as she regained her wind. Padmiri did not want to wander in the forest all night—she knew too well the fate of many of those who became lost—nor did she want to encounter the Rani's guards. Fatigue was rapidly draining both fear and judgment out of her. She longed for sleep.

"Ah!"

The startled cry brought Padmiri fully awake and until that moment she had not realized she had been dozing. There was someone on the path ahead of her. Her first inclination was to demand of the speaker who he was, but she mastered that. She brought the mare to a halt.

"Who is here, brother?" asked a voice out of the gloom.

"Another worshiper? You are late, brother," said a second voice.

"Where are you bound, brother?" The third voice was distinctly malign. "Answer us."

Padmiri did not know what to do. She must answer the men or come to harm, but if they learned she was a woman, she might risk greater hurt. Almost before she actually realized she had done it, she responded in the fluting accents of her own eunuchs, "I am not worthy to attend the sacrifice. My master, however, is there."

The men on the trail chuckled. "And you wanted to see done what you cannot do," the third voice suggested.

"I have seen that," Padmiri answered with the petulant quality she had heard Bhatin use when speaking of the men she had taken as lovers.

"Not this way, you have not. Tonight," the voice grew boastful, "a creature of Shiva will—"

"Quiet!"

"Impious one!" The two voices hissed at once, and the third one said in an undertone, "The eunuch might find the Pars—"

"Don't!" the second insisted.

There was a slight pause, and then the third voice said with overelaborate casualness, "How far have you come along this road, brother?"

"Some distance," Padmiri said truthfully, and her mouth was dry.

"Was there anyone else on the road?" the first voice inquired.

"Men from the village bringing sacrifice. It grew dark soon after that." She was finding it more and more difficult to speak in imitation of a eunuch.

"Brother," said the third voice, "dismount and walk a way with us."

"It would please me," she said, and was shocked to hear a tremor in her words, "but my master would . . . beat me if he learned of it." She hoped that they might assume her fear was not of them, but the fictitious master. Eunuchs as a group, she knew, had the reputation of being cowards.

"Not tonight. Your master will have more than enough of beating if he is at the sacrifice." It was the first voice again, pride making the man speak more loudly.

"Who is your master?" the third voice demanded suddenly, and the three unseen men waited for her answer.

Padmiri paused an instant too long. "Bisla Ajagupta," she

said, disasterously uncertain, selecting a wealthy upper-caste scholar as her abusive master in the hope that he would not be known to these men.

"He is not among those at the temple," the second voice said in an undervoice that Padmiri was not intended to hear.

"My master left at a late hour. He bade me follow him as soon as I finished my assigned duties." No, that was not the way a slave would speak, not even a high-ranking household slave.

There were a few muttered words, and then the third voice spoke again. "Is it that you wish to see the temple, brother? Do you wish to make sacrifice? We will assist you."

Padmiri felt rather than saw the two other men move toward her in the darkness. She wanted to flee.

"Tamasrajasi herself will offer a creature of Shiva on the altar to Kali," the third voice went on insinuatingly. "There will be other sacrifices before that."

With an abrupt, angry scream, Padmiri clapped her heels to the mare's sides and slapped her with the ends of the reins. The mare lurched once, then broke into a gallop.

There were shouts and oaths and the third voice yelled, "A woman! It was a woman!" before the forest around them erupted in sounds from the animals disturbed by this sudden outbreak of noise. Padmiri did not stop to listen. She urged the mare to a run, and only when the way grew suddenly steeper did she let her mount trot, and then walk. The mare was panting, and though Padmiri was inexperienced with horses, she knew that the mare was near the limit of her strength. As they crested a rise, Padmiri brought the mare to a stop as she listened for any pursuit. The three men had been on foot and she knew she had long since outdistanced them. But there had been others on the road and she did not want to meet with them. The silence reassured her and she allowed herself to relax in the saddle for the first time since she got onto the mare's back, which now seemed to be days ago. She was growing stiff and the ache in her legs and back fatigued her. How did the guardsmen do it, day after day? How did they grow accustomed to saddles and horses? She chided herself for triviality, and admitted that she did not want to think about what the three men had said. Yet she must. There was no one else to do it. If what the dying man—he must have been the Parsi the three men mentioned surreptitiously—had told her was correct, there were two foreigners who would be sacrificed. The three men as well as the Parsi had spoken of a creature of Shiva. She did not think of Saint-Germain as such a being, but there was reason to designate him that way.

All her life Padmiri had been taught that the world followed the course made for it by the gods and the Wheel. Nothing she or anyone could do would change that. She had learned at an early age that interference was always disastrous. And she had been taught that as a member of the ruling military caste, she had certain absolute rights that could not be denied. She had seen sacrifices offered to Kali when she was eleven years old, and the recollection made her wince. Nothing she could do would change what the gods had ordained. She looked up sharply. Anything she did must be the will of the gods. Her face lightened to a half-smile, and she began to feel strength return to her. The sacrifices would be offered at the temple on the Kudri. Somehow she would have to discover where she was, and quickly, for she had much to do before the middle of the night.

It was by accident that she came upon a clearing some little time later. Untouchables lived there, in huts that were little more than earthen dens. Two old men tended a fire. One was a leper and most of his face was gone; the rags around his hands covered the stumps of missing fingers. The other was skeletally thin. Both abased themselves profoundly as Padmiri approached.

"Exalted One, forgive us for speaking, but you must not come here. We are Untouchables." The emaciated old man had a voice as thin as his body.

"I have lost my way," Padmiri said, shocked at herself for telling anything so degrading to an Untouchable. "Tell me where I am."

The Untouchables were still; then the leper said, "There is a river nearby. You call it the Chenab."

"How far is it to where the Kudri joins with it?" It was most inappropriate for her to ask directions of these people, but now that she had begun, Padmiri was filled with an odd exhilaration.

"Not far," the leper said after another considerable silence. "It is a distance walked from dawn until the sun stands at the crown of the trees. The Exalted One, having a horse, will get there more quickly." Never in his life had the old leper said so much to one of such high caste. Perhaps this was not an

Exalted One at all, but a demon come to bring more misfortune.

"What track shall I follow?" Padmiri asked.

The leper wanted to lie to her, but the vengeance of demons was worse than their pranks. "The path is there." He pointed with the rag-wrapped stump of his hand. "It leads to a wide road. Go up the road and there will be another path on the unclean side. That is where the Kudri is." He knew, as did most of the Untouchables living near the temple, that there were ceremonies and rituals being performed there this night, and that it was wisest to stay away from them. It was not for those of the Untouchables to question what those of higher castes did.

Padmiri pressed her mare onward, relieved to be away from the presence of the Untouchables. She began to hope that she might arrive in time.

By the time she reached the road, new doubts had assailed her. How could she simply enter the temple and end the ceremony? Not only would the act be sacrilege, she no longer thought it would be successful. There were guards around the temple, men such as the three she had found on the road, who would be pleased to serve the goddess with her suffering. The mare plodded up the road, as tired as the woman on her back. It was near the middle of the night and chill. One woman, alone, unarmed, what could she do against those gathered in the temple of Kali? She was near the turning at the Kudri; she heard the rush of the water plainly now. Padmiri no longer knew what the gods required of her. It was tempting to listen to the water and let what had been destined from the birth of the gods and the first turning of the Wheel come to pass. The splash of the Kudri was now a muted roar. It would run red in the morning, she thought. When the rites of Kali's temple were over, the river would still be tainted by the refuse of the sacrifice. . . . The Kudri. Padmiri brought her head up. Surely elephant-headed Ghanesh, intelligent and wise, had touched her! The Kudri, which her brother had ordered be dammed so that a pleasure lake could be built. Oh, most certainly the Kudri would run red in the morning!

By the time she reached the camp of the builders, her mare had foundered and was panting as she limped up the trail. Had Padmiri been less exhausted herself, she would have dismounted and left the mare behind, but she was afraid that once out of the saddle she would be unable to move. Her one fear remaining now was that the builders themselves had gone to the temple and there would be no one to put her plan into effect.

The huts of the builders were hide-covered wooden frames and many of them were empty. There were six fire pits in the camp but only four of them held smoldering embers, and Padmiri directed the mare toward them.

"Arise!" she shouted, remembering how her father had ordered his men. She did not question her actions anymore. Ghanesh had shown her what the gods had intended her to do.

At first no one responded to this summons, and she felt her apprehension flicker a last time. Then an arm came around one of the hide flaps of the nearest hut and a surly voice demanded to know who had come there.

"I am Padmiri, sister to him who was your Rajah, Kare Dantinusha, and father to the Rani Tamasrajasi!" It was impossible that she would not be believed. There was no one in this country who would be so foolish, so presumptuous, as to claim that rank unless it was genuine.

One of the men emerged at once and abased himself. "Reverend Lady," he said as he rubbed his face in an attempt to waken.

"I am here with orders for you," Padmiri informed him. "Have two of your men lift me out of the saddle." There was nothing odd in this request, where those of high caste often had slaves whose sole function was to sleep at the foot of their beds in case they should happen to cough in the night and need someone to wipe their lips afterward.

"At once, at once," the builder said as he gathered his thoughts. He raised his voice and bawled, "The sister of the Rani's father is in our camp! Acknowledge her!" If he thought it odd that a high-caste woman should come unaccompanied to a builders' camp, and on horseback, he said nothing. Padmiri was glad now that she had long had a reputation for eccentricity.

Slowly men came from the huts. They were dressed roughly and most of them were filthy. All of them abased themselves to her, and then the first man she had spoken to pointed out two of the others. "The Reverend Lady wishes to dismount. Assist her."

As the two men came to aid her, Padmiri wished that they were slaves of her own household, not artisan-caste workers unknown to her. She bit back a yelp as one of the men took her foot from the stirrup and swung it over the mare's back. When she finally stood on solid ground again, Padmiri was seized by a kind of vertigo. Her legs no longer seemed the right length and when she started to walk she almost lost her balance. That would not do. She had much to accomplish before she returned to her house.

"Why have you honored us, Reverend Lady?" asked the camp leader.

Padmiri had invented an answer to that question as she had ridden up the twisting path to the builders' camp, and she said with authority, "My father's child and heir is known to you. Doubtless you are aware that she makes sacrifice this night, this hour, in the temple to Kali below the first falls."

"Yes, Reverend Lady, we know of that." The builders had decided that the rituals boded ill for their work. When they had petitioned the Rani, they had hoped for other results, but it seemed now that the pleasure lake would not be made.

"I have the honor to bring you word of her wishes in this regard," she announced, pleased when the builders gave her their utmost attention.

"What does the Rani require of us?" the camp leader asked.

"It is the nature of Kali," Padmiri said grandly, "to take pleasure in destruction and fecundity. Those who worship her and offer her sacrifice do it in the hope that there will be great fertility and complete oblivion. Therefore, it is suitable that those who sacrifice their bodies with lust should also do so with destruction." Several years before, one of the great scholars who had visited Padmiri had spent much time discussing the merits of the worship of Kali. At the time Padmiri had listened and questioned, but now she dredged up all that she had been told. "It is therefore most appropriate that as the sacrifice proceeds and the rituals are enacted, that the worship itself should be extinguished."

"You tell us that?" The leader of the camp wondered what the Rani wanted of him and his stoneworkers. Surely even she would know that they could not destroy a temple in a few hours.

"It is the wish of my father's daughter that the dam you have made here be destroyed at once, so that the water it holds back innundate the temple and thereby consume all within it while it cleanses the stones of the blood which Kali desires, so that nothing remains. There is no better sacrifice than this." Padmiri knew enough of the devotions given Kali to be convincing now. "It will earn you much merit to do this thing, for you will offer the greatest sacrifice and enable those in the temple to reach the full consummation of their rituals."

The men heard her out patiently, and then the leader held out his hands. "But, Reverend Lady, we cannot do it."

"Cannot?" Padmiri repeated in her most imperious manner. "You will tell your Rani that this cannot be done when she has already said that it must be?" The builders were her last hope! She had no other. "In the morning, must I inform her that her will was denied by builders?"

Tamasrajasi had not ruled long, but already it was known that she would not be thwarted in anything she desired. The builders exchanged uneasy glances.

"At the least you will finish on the elephant's foot," Padmiri said coldly while her thoughts raced. She did not know how she would get back to her house if the men here refused to carry out her orders. And what would become of her afterward, she dared not consider at all.

One of the men who had assisted Padmiri off her mare spoke up. "At the base of the dam, Mihir, there are blocking stones. They are not mortared. If we take sledges and braces, we can knock them away, and then the water will do the rest."

"Yes," the camp leader agreed unhappily: though it was the will of the Rani, he hated to see the dam destroyed. "That is one way, of course. It is dangerous."

The man who had spoken lowered his head respectfully. "There are those of us who will undertake this work for the merit it earns us in the next life."

Mihir glowered a moment, and then resigned himself to the orders he had received. "Yes, it will be done that way." He saw the smile on Padmiri's face and misinterpreted it. "I suppose you wish to have sufficient time to return to the temple?"

Padmiri was startled. "No . . ." She was astounded to hear her voice continue in regretful accents, "I have not been allowed this honor. The Rani wishes the temple to be cleansed before dawn, and if the work is as arduous as you say, you must not hesitate any longer. I will abide here"—the thought of walking any distance at all made her feel slightly sick—

"and when it is over, I must call a periyanadu, for such is the will of the Rani." How far had the celebration advanced? she wondered. What had Tamasrajasi done?

The camp leader abased himself again. "It is the Will of the Rani," he said formally. "The dam will be destroyed so that the temple of Kali may be cleansed before dawn." He turned to his men and gave the sign that they should gather their tools.

When the men left, Padmiri went and sat near the largest of the fire pits. It did not provide much warmth, but now that the heat of her activities had deserted her, Padmiri was grateful for every spark in the embers. Ghanesh she decided, had taken his hand from her forehead once the builders departed, for she felt drained of all emotion. Neither terror nor desire nor vengeance moved her now. She waited in stillness to hear the first rush of the unleashed waters.

◄●►

Text of a letter from the Brahmin Rachura to the Sultan Shams-ud-din Iletmish.

To the Sultan at Delhi in the ninth year of his reign, the Brahmin Rachura, who has sat at the side of the Rajah Kare Dantinusha and the Rani Tamasrajasi, sends his greetings.

Doubtless this missive must alarm you, good Muslim, as the circumstances which require it be sent alarm me. Under most conditions it would be unthinkable for this communication to occurr, but I have learned of a few matters that cause me to approach you, for I made specific assurances to the Rajah Kare Dantinusha, and it has come to pass that I must act upon the instructions he left me.

Not very many seasons ago, there was civil war in Natha Suryarathas, when brothers and cousins rose against the Rajah to their own ends. War exacted its price from us, on those who chose to challenge the will of the gods and bring much karma upon themselves. Also, there has been the matter of the tribute sent to you, O Sultan, and although I am not a worldly man, yet I assume that one of the purposes of this tribute is to prevent any of the Rajahs from acquiring enough wealth to make it possible to raise an army large enough to defeat the ones that you command. You are abhorrent to me, but I have heard things of you that lead me to think of you with respect. It has been said of you that you have made and caused to be kept a treaty with the demon known to the world as Jenghiz Khan. If this is true, and there are many who aver that it is, then it says much for you. I am subject to the Wheel, as you are, and if it is the will of the gods that one such as you must deal with this great destruction which has come upon the world, it is not for me to question what the gods have caused.

I have been told that you recently were sent a document by the Great Mistress, Rani Tamasrajasi, and that much of what it contained was rash. She is very young—old enough for motherhood, most truly, but still more a girl than a woman. It is most unfortunate that she should so address you. I believe that the Commander of the palace guard has not yet had the opportunity to explain to her how matters stand between Natha Suryarathas and Delhi. She is a girl born to rule, of commanding nature and great honor. Were you to see her, you would know this as you know the bodies of your wives. You would know that the dreams she has come from the greatness of her family and the nobility of her caste. It is, however, essential that you do not confuse this great majesty of mind with a daily truth. Tamasrajasi does not possess an army at this time. Her forces are limited to the palace guard and a few men who tour the borders in the dry months, and place the standard of the kingdom where it may be seen and respected by all. I cannot doubt that if her ambitions were realized she would take a great many warriors into battle and would most certainly triumph, but it is not possible at this time. The will of the Rani is the essence of truth, and what she has told you reflects the broadness of her vision and the strength of her karma, but there is as yet no force to do her will. It is not known when there will be. Most surely she desires to take on all the trappings and glory of battle, and it is not to her discredit that this is her wish. That she has not yet found the means to achieve her ambitions in no way diminished her.

Before you send your men to pillage this land and vent the whole scope of your anger upon Natha Suryarathas for the insult you believe our Rani has given you, be cautious, O Sultan. To attack one who is inspired by the gods will gain you many debts to pay in lives to come. Your reputation now is enviable for one in so unsettled a land. If you wage war with us, there will be others who will join with us, and you yourself will decrease the strength that has made you successful with the demon Jenghiz Khan. Allow our Rani her visions, but march only when you hear the tread of elephants and see the standards.

In that I have betrayed the trust of my Rani but kept my faith with my Rajah, I have now shown myself unworthy to serve the Great Mistress Tamasrajasi. I have given my word that my things are to be burned and I will myself leave the palace to live in humble circumstances where the rest of my life may be spent in meditation and contemplation. It is the custom among those of us who know the turning of the Wheel to do this at the end of life, particularly where debts have been incurred. Do not seek to have any discussion with me, for that will not be tolerated by me or by the great Rani herself, whose service I have abused with this disloyalty.

Purva Rachura Jarut
Brahmin

12

EARLIER THE smaller animals had been bled and burned, and while this was done, they had robed him in golden silk and placed a crown on his head. Incense made blue wraiths in the air that did not entirely mask the stench of burning flesh and fur. Later there had been larger animals—goats, rams, asses and a horse. While the knives had done their work, the worshipers wreathed him in flowers and chanted the traditional words of praise as they bent forward to touch his feet with bloody hands.

Saint-Germain told himself that he would become inured to it, that he need not participate in this butchery. He was unmoving, distant, but he heard the shrieks and howls and bellows of the animals and the hungry cries of those gathered to make sacrifice. Stoically he thought of Rogerio arriving at the border, traveling to Delhi and then to . . . where? He had many homes and Rogerio was known at all but the most ancient of them. But would his old friend go there? He wished to believe that it did not matter, that once he died the true death, none of it would matter.

One of the priests approached his pearl-covered throne and prostrated himself, reciting words in a high, nasal singsong. Saint-Germain chose quite deliberately not to listen. He turned his thoughts to Padmiri. No word had come of her. If that meant she had not been taken prisoner or had been used more cruelly still, then he was . . . content. He kept his dark eyes turned slightly away from the enormous statue of Kali, and remembered other times and other gods.

Tamasrajasi slit the throat of a large ram, standing so that the blood fountained over her. She screamed ecstatically, her face delirious with an emotion that was the dark side of rapture.

At her signal, a huruk began to give out a steady, tense beat. As soon as the worshipers were caught by its pulse, it was joined by the high, wailing dhakevi, which was sacred to Kali, as it was made of horn and bone. The music was repetitious, insidious. It twisted and writhed in on itself, growing tighter, then looser, like the coils of a vast serpent. As the ram toppled at last, the instruments played more loudly, insisting, pleading, cajoling.

Tamasrajasi began to dance. Her movements were slow and sinuous, at first hardly more than a series of gradually changing postures, made with great precision and formality. Then she began to extend her motions, making broader, more emphatic gestures. The instruments kept up the same spiraling melody, which now began to gain speed. Tamasrajasi danced with it, letting the sound run through her so that every variation of pitch, each intricacy of rhythm was picked up in a turn and angle of her head, the placement of a foot, the direction of her eyes, the arch of her hips, the curve of her arm, the position of her fingers. Her dyed skin was spattered with blood and she glistened in the torchlight as she turned, posed, turned, posed, turned, and turned, and turned.

Those who had come to sacrifice watched her with devotion that bordered on adoration. Theirs was more than idolatry, for the woman they fastened on with their eyes was their priestess and ruler, the absolute mistress of their lives. It was this woman, supple as a child, whose will was the law of their homeland. She had chosen to array herself in the symbols of destruction, and therefore they sought it eagerly for the opportunity to be like her.

The dance grew increasingly more frenetic. Much of her discipline was lost, but Tamasrajasi was not aware of it. There was only the glory of her power and the excitement of the music. She felt the worship and lust and envy of those who watched her, and it goaded her on.

Sudra Guristar stood near the altar, swaying with the movement of the crowd and the music. His state of mind was elevated and he thought himself inaccessible, a cloud hovering over the place rather than a man in a crowded corner of a stone room. As entranced as he was by Tamasrajasi, he was also growing quite impatient with her. He had wanted her to show the worshipers that she had given herself to him, that she was, in fact, secondary to him, though her rank was greater. Now she lured them all with a promise that she could not fulfill, not to all of them. He could not unbraid her here with so many watching her, but he vowed that as soon as the sacrifices were finished and they left the temple, he would tell her how far she had transgressed. Next time he visited her quarters, he would leave bruises behind, and not all from lovemaking.

She was very near him and when her eyes met his, they taunted him. Guristar started to reach out for her, but she escaped him and with distorted movements which were no longer graceful she approached the altar and made the three ritual abasements to the huge black statue. Behind her the crowd moaned and the music stopped. The temple fell silent as Tamasrajasi stepped onto the altar.

The quiet intruded on Saint-Germain's thoughts more than the noise and music had done. He saw the worshipers were looking toward the altar, and his eyes followed theirs. The despair that he had kept at bay surged over him as he stared at Tamasrajasi. She was elated, filled with the submissive concupiscence of her audience and her own sublime theodicy.

Her laughter was abandoned to the point of madness. She displayed herself lubriciously, her hands sliding over her body, leaving smears of blood on the breasts and thighs.

Sighs, murmurs, groans of longing and frustration ran through the assembly. A few of those watching began to touch themselves as Tamasrajasi had touched herself. The huruk started to beat again, this time in jumping, erratic, feverish pulses. The worshipers were no longer swaying, and where they had been passive in their yearning, now cupidity asserted itself. Languor disappeared, and in its place there was a mercurial excitement that moved like a physical presence from one of the worshipers to another.

Tamasrajasi dropped to her knees on the altar. Her tongue flicked over her lips. "Sudra Guristar," she called gently, as she might call a frightened child. "Come, my Commander."

This was what Guristar had wanted since the ritual began, yet he hesitated an instant before stepping forward. He knew what was required of him, and his body was ready. There was one quiver of doubt in his mind, which he stifled at once. Tamasrajasi was at last acknowledging him before her people. For a dizzying moment he felt the full glory of his power, ebullience coming perilously close to shock. He walked to the altar, aware of those who watched him, reveling in their passions as much as his own.

"My Commander. It is as you wished it to be." She reached down and pulled off the jacket he wore, then threw it aside. "Put your hands on me, my Commander. Do all that your desires demand of you." She had his shirt now and was starting to unwind his sash.

Guristar seized her buttocks with both hands, pressing his face to her red-streaked abdomen. His sash was gone and his pleated trousers dropped around his ankles. He felt Tamasrajasi take him by the shoulders and turn him to face the gathered worshipers. His distended organ blushed more hotly than his face; his pride made him want to dance as Tamasrajasi had done, but he did not do this.

"This is my Commander," Tamasrajasi said, her voice loud and husky at once. She turned him back to face her. "Now, my Commander, make your sacrifice for Kali." Her fingers reached down his chest and she made room for him on the altar. "Lie under me, my Commander," she instructed as he tried to pull her down. "Tonight I am the goddess."

It was little enough to indulge her that far, Guristar

thought. What mattered was that she had granted his request and chosen him before all those who had come to the temple. He leaned back and moaned with pleasure as Tamasrajasi straddled him. Nothing had ever excited him so much. Never had he felt himself so massive. The huruk was beating to his breathing. As Tamasrajasi enveloped him he feared that his erection would harm her, perhaps even kill her. He lunged into her, once, twice, three times, when he heard the avid shout from those pressing nearer the altar. Before he could look about or ask what had happened, the pain hit him and he roared.

Tamasrajasi stood up and held her hands out with Guristar's sacrifice for the crowd to see. Blood ran through her fingers to the other puddles on the floor. "The first offering!" Tamasrajasi cried out, then stood between Guristar's legs where the blood gushed out.

The reaction was immediate. The frenzy which had been a current building in the crowd burst forth at full fury. Men, women, old, young, attractive, brutish, fell on one another without regard. The sounds were unbelievable.

On the altar, Tamasrajasi stared down at Guristar, holding in one hand his severed organ, in the other a short, thin knife. She smiled at his revulsion and agony. "My Commander. Think of your aspirations. What an offering to Kali." And she slit his throat, watching with a detached, slightly critical smile before signaling for one of the officiating priests to drag the body off the altar so that she would have room. Tamasrajasi handed her prize to the priest and indicated that it should be burned in the brazier before Kali's statue. As she stood again, she looked across the stone room and her eyes met Saint-Germain's. She grinned and waved the knife at him before scanning the worshipers for another likely sacrifice.

Saint-Germain had seen a great deal of depravity in his long years, and was largely unaffected by it. This was different. It was as if all the worshipers were in the throes of a seizure, suffering the paroxysms of a terrible contagious disease. He could not hold himself entirely aloof from what was happening around him, and he experienced a resurgence of the pity he had felt earlier, but with more poignance and disgust. He was being defiled, just as all those in the temple were, and for the amusement of a voluptuous child. This wild coupling, the excess of it, the blood, all of it was empty. At his feet three men labored over the flesh of one woman, sating themselves without satisfaction. Saint-Germain closed his eyes a moment, but could not recapture the separation he had found for a time. Now he understood the full insanity he saw, the maniacal fury of it, and the hatred.

At her place on the altar, Tamasrajasi had another man with her, and as she rode his loins, she reached down casually and castrated him as she had Guristar. This time she allowed the priests to slit his throat while she singled out another man. When she had tired of this and there were more than a dozen mutilated corpses at the side of the altar, Tamasrajasi came across the stone floor to Saint-Germain. "Soon I will bring your offerings. Would you prefer men or women to fill your veins?"

It was useless and he knew it, but Saint-Germain made a last attempt. "Tamasrajasi, I am not precisely what you think, and I doubt that all the blood in this temple would have the results you wish. It isn't the blood, Tamasrajasi, it's another matter entirely."

"If you will not tell me," she said as if she had heard nothing of what he said to her, "I will select as I see fit. It will be a good death for those who give you drink. Shiva is a worthy god." The dark juice which had stained her body was streaking now, and in places it had rubbed away entirely. She had the look of someone monstrously bruised, beaten to the point of death.

"Tamasrajasi . . ." He stopped: it was futile.

"When I lead you to the altar," she said thoughtfully, "I want you to embrace me as you have my father's sister. Bhatin told me that it was not like anything he had seen before, that even she was fulfilled."

He did not tell her that it was impossible. There was not time enough left to him, or left to the world, he added sadly, for Tamasrajasi to learn this. His feet were cold on the stones but the temple shimmered with a heat that did not come entirely from the braziers and torches around the huge room. Nor was the cold entirely from the stones.

The musician who had been playing the huruk threw the drum aside and flung himself at a knot of entangled bodies. Only Saint-Germain was aware that the drumming had stopped. As Shiva, he told himself ironically, he ought to be the one with the drum. It pained him to think of the passing time, the beat of Shiva's drum.

Suddenly a young woman came up to him. Her eyes were febrile and she moved as if mounted on sticks. There were scratches and welts on her and she carried a knife in one hand. "Exalted Shiva," she said to him as she bent low before him. "Take my life from me."

Saint-Germain reached out to the woman and lifted her up. His compelling eyes were compassionate and grieving. "I am not Shiva. Keep your life, use it for something better than this." He reached for the knife, but before he touched her, the woman wrenched away from him and in a series of short, gouging strokes of the blade almost eviscerated herself before she fell. Not since his own death had Saint-Germain known such inner darkness as possessed him now. He started to rise, to walk toward the altar where Tamasrajasi lay in flowers and blood. If destruction was so precious to her, that much he would give her.

So great was the noise within the temple that the thunder of the crashing wall of water as it bore down the narrow defile was inaudible until the first of the flood struck the stone pillars.

Tamasrajasi saw Saint-Germain come toward her, and assumed the momentary faltering of the worshipers in their demented activities was in anticipation of what he would do to her when he reached the altar. She held out her arms to him and scowled when he looked away from her toward the wall. The angry scream she was ready to give became a horrified sigh as the roar grew louder and one of the pillars buckled.

Where there had been confusion before there was now chaos. Bodies, linked together in a variety of ways, now struggled to break free in order to run.

The water now struck with all its fury, its speed and weight. The stones cracked, sounding like bones breaking, and the Kudri, dammed for three months, smashed through.

Saint-Germain was flung upward as the wall began to collapse. He dropped back into the water before he could ready himself for it, and he feared that he would be broken against the temple stones.

There were many bodies in the water around him, and he could hear the thrashings and shouting over the gigantic voice of the river. The last of the torches was extinguished and the temple was completely dark. Water dragged at the walls, at the people, impartially. The flood had been moving rapidly when it hit. Forced into the confines of the temple, it exploded, sending the pillars outward and casting bodies about as leaves were tossed on a swollen stream.

A falling piece of masonry caught Saint-Germain's side and abraded it badly. He fought free of this trap and let the current carry him away from the ruin of Kali's temple. His mind was dazed, and there was a rushing in his ears that did not come from the water. Suddenly a man's arm wrapped around him, clinging, squeezing, the body dangling from what had appeared as the only safety. Determined, and reluctant, Saint-Germain roused himself enough to fight free of the drowning man holding him. The current caught him again and thrust him farther away from the temple, toward the gorge where tall cascades brought the Kudri to the Chenab.

At last his alarm woke him to action. To fall with the water, to be broken by it, this frightened him, but more terrifying still was the prospect of taking such a fall and being only injured. He had an instant's vision of himself on the bottom of the river, mangled but alive, alive and *conscious* until the water itself wore his flesh away. He struck out with his arms and was amazed when he broke the surface of the flood in two or three strokes.

His first attempt to catch himself was a failure. The rock he had reached for was left quickly behind, and there were long abrasions on his arms and hands. The others caught in the flood were around him, a few of them making feeble attempts to resist the water, but most of them still now. Saint-Germain pushed a corpse away from him and as he did realized that it was one of the men who had died on the altar, not one caught in the flood.

A rock outcropping loomed ahead, and this time Saint-Germain used the last of his quickly ebbing strength to grab it. His arms caught the stone, slamming him into it with such force as would have broken bones in many men. He willed himself to hang on though the impact jarred him to faintness. His face was against the rock and the water battered him. There was one bright thread of thought, of memory alive in his mind: the rest was as dark as the river raging, unfettered, toward the cataracts that were less than ten steps from the rock where Saint-Germain clung.

About the time the night faded into dawn the waters receded, leaving behind a devastation that was appalling. The flood had scoured away much of the vegetation, but where it had taken plants, corpses had been left behind. From the ruin of the temple to the cataracts there were shattered, bloated bodies.

The sun woke Saint-Germain, searing him, unprotected as he was. Light burned like acid on his back, but his arms refused to release the rock. Finally, when a dim realization that he was dry, whole, and naked broke through the blackness, he gathered himself for one last effort. He had no strength left. His arms were ragged with scrapes and cuts, his back was torn, and the sun basted him with pain. It took him half of the morning to crawl twelve paces to the shelter of the forest, where he gratefully let himself sink into temporary oblivion.

When he wakened at nightfall, he was no longer in the forest, but lying on cushions in a spacious, old-fashioned room he had never seen before. He was too exhausted to be surprised. Gingerly he tried to move his arms and was oddly pleased that although there was pain, he encountered no stiffness. His wounds had been dressed but not bandaged: two of the cuts were fairly severe but Saint-Germain knew from long experience that in a few days they would heal completely, leaving no scars. Since he had risen from his first death, nothing had left a lasting mark on his skin. He started to roll to the side and realized then that he had been wrapped in a long, loose robe of very fine silk. He touched it wonderingly. Where was he? How had he come here?

A slave seated near the door looked up as he moved and gave a little shriek before bolting from the room.

Saint-Germain looked around the room more carefully. It could be no accident that he was here, not if he had been dressed in silk and his hurts treated. A feeling, too leaden to be euphoria, yet still light-headed, stole over him. He was in that dangerous lassitude which hid genuine enervation. The cushions on which he lay offered him no comfort, for none of them contained his native earth. Did any of the bags of it remain now? he wondered with curious detachment. How absurd, how ironic to survive that debauched rite and devastating flood only to succumb for lack of earth or blood. It would not be long before he would lie quiescent, hoarding what small spark of strength was left to him. His unknown benefactor, he thought, might assume he was dead and build a funeral pyre for him. The fire would be the end of him. He tried to chuckle but stopped as he heard the echo of his own voice.

A deep blue gown brushed against his shoulder and Saint-Germain opened his eyes with a start. Had he been dozing? As he looked up, his vision swam. Before he realized he had spoken at all, he said, "Padmiri?" not expecting an answer, convinced that this was an illusion of her.

"Saint-Germain," she said, and sank down beside him. There was a faint smile on her lips that had nothing of joy in it.

"You?" He touched her face fleetingly with his bruised hands. "I was afraid they had taken you prisoner."

"I was afraid they had killed you." She caught one of his hands in hers and held it. She did not quite sigh—she was too private for that.

"They nearly did." He could see the strain in her face. Dark patches underscored her haunted eyes and the lines of her face had deepened. She was majestic in her mourning; Saint-Germain could not share her sorrow, and would not add to it by telling her what he had seen in Kali's temple before the water came through.

She was content to sit beside him in silence for a time, and then she said, as if resuming a conversation, "The river was not as kind to Tamasrajasi as it was to you. We found her only this afternoon, washed up on one of the sand spits in the Chenab. I have ordered that her pyre be built there and the ashes be allowed to wash away." She got up and crossed the room. It was night but the room was well-lit by torches and lamps. She stopped beside a cluster of crudely made candles with sizzling wicks. "I didn't think they'd find you. I believed you were dead. When they told me . . . I did ask them to look for you, so that you could be given proper rites." There was a nightingale singing over the garden; its plaintive notes brought tears to Padmiri's eyes.

"Is that why you had your men search for me—so that I would not be left for the carrion eaters?" He had not intended to speak so harshly, but before he could modify his words, Padmiri answered him.

"That was part of it, yes. I gave orders that all the bodies that could be found should be collected into one place for the proper rituals. Tamasrajasi . . . that was another matter." She brought her hands up almost to her face as if wishing to hide behind them.

Saint-Germain braced himself on his elbow so that he could look at Padmiri, but after a moment his arm began to tremble and he sank back on the cushions. "Padmiri, I didn't intend to say that to you. I'm not thinking very well. The sun, the water, they rob me of . . . life." He turned his head and regarded her evenly. "I am grateful, Padmiri."

She drew her hands into fists. "There are more than one hundred dead on the Kudri and the Chenab. And I wanted them dead." When he did not speak to her, she lashed out at him. "But you survived. You."

"Does that disappoint you?" Nothing in his tone accused her or offered her apology. He was not inclined to argue with her and did not know how to comfort her.

"No, it angers me." She took a few steps toward him. The nightingale sang on, unheeded. "You are badly hurt. I should not be speaking of this now."

"Because of my hurt?" He was growing weary again and that infuriated him. His will could not sustain him now.

"I'm too . . . confused," she said and Saint-Germain wondered what it was that she had wanted to say instead. "Tamasrajasi is dead. She left no one behind her. There is no heir. So for a little time, Natha Suryarathas is mine. The palace guard, what is left of it, has brought me word that they will defend me."

"Then you are Rani." Saint-Germain closed his eyes briefly, and in that little time he accepted the loss of her. "You are Rani and I am a foreigner. And I am . . . what I am." So there it was. The candles sputtered, then grew brighter, touching the side of her face with golden light.

"I may not ask you to stay." She came the rest of the distance to his side but did not kneel at once.

Why did this hurt him so much when the horrors of the night before had numbed him? He could not speak of this to her, so he asked another question that had been waiting at the back of his mind. "And Rogerio?"

"He crossed the border shortly after dawn. I . . . I sent a messenger after him at sunset." She touched his hand, and it seemed to her that she reached across an enormous gulf.

"I thank you for that," he said after a moment. "He and I are . . . old friends." If only he were not so listless! He tried to speak more animatedly. "Where are we?"

"Where? Do you mean this house?" She saw the irritation he had stifled cross his features. She went on quickly, soothingly. "This is the house of one of my uncles. He was executed in the time of the rebellion. My brother gave orders that his slaves were to be installed here and the building kept in readiness for his use. He never came here, but the slaves remained. No one said that they should be moved, and so this house was never closed. I'd forgotten about it. One of the guardsmen reminded me of it."

"And what of your house?"

"I have not yet returned to it. My slaves will take care of it until I do." She moved closer to him and pushed his tangled, matted dark hair back from his face. "Your things, all your things, are there."

He nodded. "Thank you." He would be able to rest on his native earth. His weakness no longer seemed as dangerous to him but he resisted its pull on him. "May I go there before morning?"

Padmiri drew back from him. "Before morning?"

Gently he touched her arm. "Padmiri, I told you once that I did not want to use you. It was not lightly said." He was tempted to pull her down beside him, to use every sort of persuasion he knew to coerce her into loving him again. It would be an honorless, reprehensible act, and he loathed himself for the need growing in him. With an effort he was able to continue. "Without your help, I might have died the true death more than once in the last two days. I will not abuse so fine a gift, Padmiri," he said with vehemence. "I wish to leave so that I can have a day to rest on my native earth. It is necessary for me. It will restore me."

She understood him. "Blood would be better."

He flinched at the acuity of her perceptions and his own inward hunger. "Blood alone, no, it would not. You know what is needed. But you have Natha Suryarathas, Padmiri, and it would not be wise for you to lie with any foreigner, particularly anyone as foreign as I am." He had hoped that this would amuse her and saw instead that she was weeping. He reached up, taking her face in his hands. His penetrating eyes met hers and he made no attempt to deny his passion. "Padmiri, Padmiri, what now?"

"I want you to love me, man of Shiva. You will use me, and I will use you, openly, without hypocrisy. Let me be only myself this once. And then, man of Shiva, you must go."

"Very well," he said, drawing her down to him. His caresses, his kisses, were lingering, lonely for her even as he

shared the culmination of her desire. As Padmiri answered
his increasing ardor with renewed passion, she wished for one
wild instant that he would use her utterly, that he would take
all the life in her rather than give her such great pleasure,
such unquenchable love as a gesture of farewell. Nothing he
had done before had roused her as he did now. Every touch
of his hands, his body, his mouth, brought their special frui-
tion until there was no nuance of her sensuality he had not
explored, save one.

She did not weep when he left, for tears, she had learned,
were an indulgence, and one that a Rani could not afford.
From the terrace she watched him ride away, four guardsmen
for escort, until the morning sun dazzled her eyes.

———◆———

A letter from Saint-Germain to Jalal-im-al Zakatim.

May Allah reward you with sons and prosperity in
this life, and with all the delights of Paradise after it,
Jala-im-al.

I am sending with this note a small gift to acknowledge
my gratitude for the hospitality you have shown my servant Rogerio in the sixteen days he has been with you. It
was most cordial of you to be his host so short a time
after your own return to the Sultanate.

Your slave brought the various supplies I requested
some time ago. I am most particularly pleased with the
various European earths which you have supplied. Be
sure that I will put them to excellent use. As you know,
my own supply was seriously depleted, so these are a
welcome addition.

After all the kindness you have done me, I am sorry
to have to refuse your inquiries regarding the death of
the Rani Tamasrajasi. It is most important to you, I realize, but I do not feel it is wise to discuss what occurred. There are a great many rumors, as we are both
aware, and it is well not to fuel those particular flames.

I have just spoken with the young woman who accompanied Rogerio here. You wished me to tell you what I could learn of her, and that I am more than willing to do. This young woman comes from China. Her two traveling companions, one of whom was her brother, are no longer with her. The brother died and the other deserted her. In Puna she tried to find an appropriate companion for her continued travels and fell victim to a rogue. She was offered passage on a ship bound for the west, and when she persisted in refusing to give her body to the captain's use, he put her into restraints and sold her as a slave at his next port. That is where your uncle bought her, and what you have said and what she tells me now are very much the same.

This woman is a Christian, of the sort called Nestorian in the West, but there are many good churchmen who would find her customs of worship disturbing. Her congregation wished to send her to the West with the purpose of finding other Christians. As I am to leave soon, I offer to pay you whatever price your uncle gave for her so that she may continue the journey she began about three years ago.

Your trader has visited me and we have agreed on a route and a departure day. He has assured me that it will not be difficult to get passage into Egypt, and so I have authorized him to secure a proper vessel and crew for the voyage. As I have told you before, I am a very bad sailor, lamentably.

Let me say that I believe the Sultan will find the new Rani of Natha Suryarathas a most excellent woman. She is intelligent, educated and responsible. You have met Padmiri, and you know for yourself the quality of the woman. In her life she has seen many changes of fortune and will not make hasty decisions or unwise promises.

Your message to me asks if I long for my home—yes, I do, intensely. I have seen much of the beauty and horror of the world and have traveled far, very far. Yet there is a special joy I feel when I stand on my native earth that is like no other in this world.

I beg you will excuse the brevity of this note. There is much I have to do before sunrise. I think you again for what you have done. If an Infidel's gratitude has any worth to a follower of the Prophet, then you have mine, Jala'-im-al.

May Allah watch over you and reward you.

Saint-Germain
in the eighth year of the reign of
the Sultan Shams-ud-din Iletmish

Epilogue

A letter from the Rani Padmiri of Natha Suryarathas to Saint-Germain.

To the foreign alchemist called Saint-Germain from the Rani Padmiri, greetings.

I have given this to my messengers with instructions that it be given to Jalal-im-al Zakatim in Delhi, who will know what trader can find you. Doubtless this will not reach you quickly, but that is of little importance.

When you left me, I feared to think of you at all, and did not want to know what had become of you. But that was more than six years ago. Now that I have a little time to myself, I think often of you, and I have wished to tell you that all you gave me was not lost.

When I consider my life, it appears to be a shadow, nothing more than a crude outline on a wall, until I knew you. For all those years I was hidden, and glad to hide, paying myself with a few pleasures, so circumspectly. My scholarship protected me as much as my isolated house did. To be sure, there are other protections. I now sleep with a guard at the foot of my bed and another outside the door, and no matter where I go, or when, slaves come with me so that there will be no doubt as to my importance. This protection is a ritual, but the other was more pernicious, for I was ill with it, and never knew it. You intruded on that. When we spoke together, I believed that only my curiosity was being satisfied. When we lay together, I thought that you awakened only my senses. When you were gone, I began to see what my life had been and what it had become.

That does not mean I wished at first to become Rani. When my brother's daughter died, I thought that it was wrong for me to rule, that I should find one of my male relatives to govern here. But all of them were dead, a few from old age but most of them from the rebellion

445

against my brother. There were five boys, none of them older than seven, who are fairly distant cousins and might one day succeed me, but there was no one then, and will not be anyone for several years, who might have assumed the throne. For the first year, I wanted most fervently to retire to my house again and content myself with studies. The second year I found my tasks difficult but I was not as eager to leave them. Now I have come to appreciate my position. I cannot say whether or not I like it, only that it is appropriate. They call me the Just Mistress, Saint-Germain. When they speak of my brother Dantinusha, they call him the Wary. Of Tamasrajasi they do not speak at all.

Two years ago I took a lover—my sixth. He is ardent and obliging, but I have come to realize that all we do together is ultimately intended to please him. He is more satisfied when I am aroused, and so he rouses me. It has been so with all but you. Only now have I come to understand that all you did to give me pleasure was for my pleasure, not for yours. You told me, I recall, that your pleasure was in my pleasure. At the time I had no comprehension of what you meant. Now I know I have been most fortunate and have had a very rare gift from you.

Now I am near the end of my life. There is a winter in my bones that the sun cannot thaw. The Wheel turns for me as it does for everyone—even you. When my funeral pyre is lit and my body consumed by the flames, my soul will be at ease. When you left, I called you a man of Shiva, because of your nature and your needs. I have thought of late that this is not so. Shiva would dance on the Burning Ground where my pyre will be, and he would smile, as would all his creatures. But I think that you would not dance, or smile. You are too much bound to life to be any part of Shiva, and for that you doom yourself to the pain of loss: does having the moment pay for its loss, Saint-Germain? For if it does, then I will not mind that you are not with me now, and that you may never answer this question.

How long you have been alone! When you had been gone a fortnight I thought I could not bear it, and even now your loss is not easy to endure. You have had eons of loss and loneliness: What is mine by comparison?

My love for you did not cease when you left Natha Suryarathas, and it may not end when my life is done. The opinions of the Brahmins are divided on that. There is little merit in it either way, but I find that I do not love for merit.

Where this will find you, and when, I do not know. If the gods will that you read this, nothing will prevent you from receiving it, and if they will that these reflections are mine alone, then there is nothing in the world mighty enough to overreach them to bring this to you. It pleases me to think that you will see this and remember the time we spent together.

We have said farewell once, but let me say farewell again, beloved.

> the Rani Padmiri
> sister to the Rajah Kare Dantinusha
> Natha Suryarathas
> in the sixth year of her reign